BROOKLYN NOIR

BROOKLYN NOIR

EDITED BY TIM MCLOUGHLIN

AKASHIC BOOKS
BROOKLYN, NEW YORK

This collection is a work of fiction. All names, characters, places, and incidents are the product of the authors' imaginations. Any resemblance to real events or persons, living or dead, is entirely coincidental.

Published by Akashic Books
©2004 Tim McLoughlin
Layout and Brooklyn map by Sohrab Habibion

ISBN: 1-888451-58-0
Library of Congress Control Number: 2003116590
Second printing
Printed in Canada

Akashic Books
PO Box 1456
New York, NY 10009
Akashic7@aol.com
www.akashicbooks.com

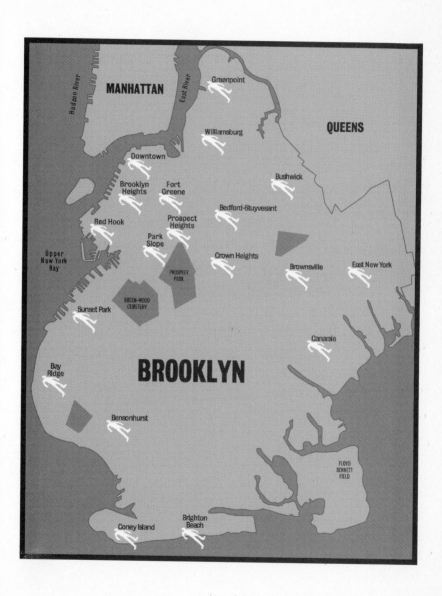

"Dere's no guy livin' dat knows Brooklyn t'roo an' t'roo, because it'd take a guy a lifetime just to find his way aroun' duh f---- town."
—from "Only the Dead Know Brooklyn" by Thomas Wolfe

TABLE OF CONTENTS

PART IV: BACKWATER BROOKLYN

INTRODUCTION
LOVE & CRIME

I recently received a phone call from one of my father's old friends. He's an interesting man who has led a dangerous life, and since my father's death I only hear from him every year or two. He was calling to tell me that his kid brother's daughter, fourteen years old, had gone missing. Thankfully, he called again the next day to say she'd been found safe at a friend's house. It had merely been a case of teenage angst acted out by briefly running away. I expressed my relief, and told him I'd take down the homemade flyers I'd posted. We talked for another few minutes, then signed off.

"Take care, you know I love you," he said as he hung up.

He is six-feet four-inches tall, and is a pretty formidable guy still, at age sixty-three, with a face full of scar tissue and a triple bypass behind him. *You know I love you.* I thought about the fact that the only men I've known, other than my father, who are comfortable telling me that they love me, are also men capable of extreme violence. Is it a personality trait? Are these men just so much more emotional that they are capable of greater feeling? Love and hate, compassion and violence.

No. It's a code; an example of the language of inclusion. It has been used to the point of tedium in novels and films depicting organized crime families, but in the real world, membership in social alliances forged in the street can be between two people or twenty. And can stand for generations or dissolve the same evening. But the first thing that will emerge in such associations is a commonality of language, or pattern of speech, that suggests acceptance and loyalty, even if the individuals are from vastly different backgrounds.

The communities across Brooklyn depicted in this book are for the most part not representative of the popular image of the borough today. Most stories from Brooklyn don't focus on places like Canarsie, as Ellen Miller's moody, disturbing tale does, or East New York, as in Maggie Estep's clever, evocative story. And when the places are familiar, the enclave within often isn't. The Park Slope of Pete Hamill's "The Book Signing" is not a latte-drenched smoke-free zone celebrating its latest grassroots civic victory over some perceived evil, but the neighborhood of those left behind—the handful of old-timers living over the stores on Seventh Avenue and in the few remaining rent-controlled apartments, having to walk further every day to find a real bar or grocery store. The Williamsburg of Pearl Abraham isn't the hipster hang, but the Hasidic stronghold. What these underground communities share, though, and these writers capture brilliantly, is the language.

With the exception of a few characters, like Arthur Nersesian's predatory protagonist, all of the actors in these pieces belong to some sort of community, and it is their membership that defines, and saves or dooms them.

Some of these neighborhoods overlap and some are from opposite ends of the borough, and it doesn't mean a thing in terms of language. Two or three of these stories could take place within a half-dozen blocks of each other, and the players would barely know where they were if their places were shifted. Ken Bruen's "Fade to . . . Brooklyn" is actually set in

Ireland, and though I know a number of people who consider Ireland just another part of the neighborhood, I like to think of it as our virtual Brooklyn story.

The tales presented here are as diverse as the borough itself, from the over-the-top violent world of gangster rap, to a Damon Runyonesque crew of hardboiled old men. There are sexual predators, dirty cops, killers, and a horse thief. So the stories are different, but as I read them again, preparing to let this book go—reluctantly, because I don't want it to end—I'm also struck by the way that they are similar. And that is in the most important way; because as any scholar sitting at the bar in a Flatbush gin mill knows, it's about telling a good story. It is my privilege to share ours with you.

Tim McLoughlin
Brooklyn, June 2004

PART I

OLD SCHOOL BROOKLYN

THE BOOK SIGNING

BY PETE HAMILL

Park Slope

Carmody came up from the subway before dusk, and his eyeglasses fogged in the sudden cold. He lifted them off his nose, holding them while they cooled, and saw his own face smiling from a pale green leaflet taped to the wall. There he was, in a six-year-old photograph, and the words *Reading* and *Book Signing* and the date and place, and he paused for a moment, shivering in the hard wind. The subway was his idea. The publisher could have sent him to Brooklyn in a limousine, but he wanted to go to the old neighborhood the way he always did, long ago. He might, after all, never come this way again.

The subway stairs seemed steeper than he remembered and he felt twinges in his knees that he never felt in California. Sharp little needles of pain, like rumors of mortality. He didn't feel these pains after tennis, or even after speed-walking along the Malibu roads. But the pain was there now, and was not eased by the weather. The wind was blowing fiercely from the harbor, which lay off in the darkness to his right, and he donned his glasses again and used both gloved hands to pull his brown fedora more securely to his brow. His watch told him that he had more than a half hour to get to the bookstore. Just as he had hoped. He'd have some time for a visit, but not too much time. He crossed the street with his back to the place where the bookstore awaited him, and passed along the avenue where he once was young.

His own aging face peered at him from the leaflets as he passed, some pasted on walls, others taped inside the windows of shops. In a way, he thought, they looked like Wanted posters. He felt a sudden . . . what was the word? Not fear. Certainly not panic. *Unease.* That was the word. An uneasiness in the stomach. A flexing and then relaxing of muscles, an unwilled release of liquids or acids, all those secret wordless messages that in California were cured by the beach and the surf or a quick hit of Maalox. He told himself to stop. This was no drama. It was just a trip through a few streets where once he had lived but had not seen for decades. After seventeen novels, this would be his first signing in the borough that had formed him. But the leaflets made clear that here, in this neighborhood, his appearance might be some kind of big deal. It might draw many people. And Carmody felt apprehensive, nervous, wormy with unease.

"How does it feel, going back to Brooklyn?" Charlie Rose had asked him the night before, in a small dark television studio on Park Avenue.

"I don't know," Carmody said, and chuckled. "I just hope they don't throw books at me. Particularly my own books."

And wanted to add: *I've never really left.* Or to be more exact: *Those streets have never left me.*

The buildings themselves were as Carmody remembered them. They were old-law tenements, with fire escapes on the facades, but they seemed oddly comforting to Carmody. This was not one of those New York neighborhoods desolated by time and arson and decay. On the coast of California, he had seen photographs of the enrubbled lots of Brownsville and East New York. There were no lots here in the old neighborhood. If anything, the buildings looked better now, with fresh paint and clear glass on the street level doors instead of hammered tin painted gray. He knew from reading the *New York Times* that the neighborhood had been gentrified, that most of the old families had moved away, to be replaced by younger people who paid higher rents. There was some unhappiness to all of that, the paper said, but still, the place looked better. As a boy he had walked these streets many times on nights like this, when most people retreated swiftly from the bitter cold to the uncertain warmth of the flats. Nights of piled snow and stranded streetcars. Now he noticed lights coming on in many of those old apartments, and shadows moving like ghosts behind drawn shades and curtains. He peered down a street toward the harbor, noticed some stubborn scabs of old snow, black between parked cars, and in the distance saw a thin scarlet band where the sun was setting in New Jersey. On this high slope, the harbor wind turned old snow into iron. But the sliver of sun was the same too. The day was dying. It would soon be night.

If the buildings were the same, the shops along the avenue were all different. Fitzgerald's bar was gone, where his father did most of his drinking, and so was Sussman's Hardware and Fischetti's Fruit and Vegetable and the Freedom Meats store and the pharmacy. What was the name of that drugstore? Right there. On that corner. An art supply store now. An art supply store! *Moloff's*. The drugstore was called Moloff's, and next door was a bakery. "Our Own" they called it. And now there was a computer store where a TV repair shop once stood. And a dry cleaners where men once stood at the bar of Rattigan's, singing the old songs. All gone. Even the old clock factory had been converted into a condominium.

None of this surprised Carmody. He knew they'd all be gone. Nothing lasts. Marriages don't last. Ball clubs don't last. Why should shops last? Wasn't that the point of each one of his seventeen books? The critics never saw that point, but he didn't care. Those novels were not literature, even to Carmody. He would say in interviews that he wrote for readers, not for critics. And said to himself: I'm not Stendhal, or Hemingway, or Faulkner. He knew that from the beginning. Those novels were the work he did after turning forty, when he reached the age limit for screenwriting. He worked at the top of his talent, to be sure, and used his knowledge of movies to create plots that kept readers turning the pages. But he knew they were commercial products, novels about industries and how they worked, his characters woven from gossip and profiles in *Fortune* or *Business Week*. He had started with the automobile industry, and then moved to the television industry, and the sugar industry, and the weapons industry. In each of them the old was destroyed by the new, the old ruling families decayed and collapsed and newer, more ruthless men and women took their places. The new one was about the food industry, from the farms of California to the dinner plates of New York and Los Angeles. Like the others, it had no aspirations to be seen as art. That would be pretentious. But they were good examples of craft, as honest as well-made chairs. In each of them, he knew, research served as a substitute for imagination and art and memory. Three different researchers had filed memos on this last one, the new one, the novel he would sign here tonight, in the Barnes & Noble store five blocks behind him. He hoped nobody in the audience would ask why he had never once written about Brooklyn.

To be sure, he had never denied his origins. There was a

profile in *People* magazine in 1984, when his novel about the gambling industry went to number one on the *New York Times* bestseller list, and stayed there for seventeen weeks. He was photographed on the terrace of the house in Malibu with the Pacific stretched out beyond him, and they used an old high school newspaper photograph showing him in pegged pants and a t-shirt, looking like an apprentice gangster or some variation on the persona of James Dean. The article mentioned his two ex-wives (there was now a third woman receiving his alimony checks), but the reporter was also from Brooklyn and was more intrigued by the Brooklyn mug who had become a bestselling author.

"You went west in 1957," the reporter said. "Just like the Dodgers."

"When they left, I left too, because that was the end of Brooklyn as I knew it," Carmody said. "I figured I'd have my revenge on Los Angeles by forcing it to pay me a decent living."

That was a lie, of course. One among many. He didn't leave Brooklyn because of the Dodgers. He left because of Molly Mulrane.

Now he was standing across the street from the building where both of them had lived. The entrance then was between a meat market and a fruit store, converted now into a toy store and a cellphone shop. Molly lived on the first floor left. Carmody on the top floor right. She was three years younger than Carmody and he didn't pay her much attention until he returned from the Army in 1954. An old story: She had blossomed. And one thing had led to another.

He remembered her father's rough, unhappy, threatening face when he first came calling to take her to the movies.

Patty Mulrane, the cop. And the way he looked when he went out in his police uniform for a 4-to-12 shift, his gun on his hip, his usual slouch shifting as he walked taller and assumed a kind of swagger. And how appalled Patty Mulrane was when Carmody told him he was using the GI Bill to become a writer. "A writer? What the hell is that? I'm a writer too. I write tickets. Ha ha. A writer . . . How do you make a living with that? What about being a lawyer? A doctor? What about, what do they call it now, *criminology?* At least you'd have a shot at becoming a lieutenant . . ." The father liked his Fleischman's and beer and used the Dodgers as a substitute for conversation. The mother was a dim, shadowy woman, who did very little talking. That summer, Molly was the youngest of the three children, and the only one still at home. Her brother, Frankie, was a fireman and lived with his wife in Bay Ridge. There was another brother: What was his name? Sean. Seanie. Flat face, hooded eyes, a hard tank-like body. Carmody didn't remember much about him. There had been some kind of trouble, something about a robbery, which meant he could never follow his father into the police depart-ment, and Seanie had moved to Florida where he was said to be a fisherman in the Keys. Every Sunday morning, father, mother, and daughter went to mass together.

Now, on this frozen night, decades later, Carmody's unease rushed back. Ah, Molly, my Molly-O . . . The fire escapes still climbed three stories to the top floor where the Carmodys lived. But the building looked better, like all the others on the avenue. On the top floor right on this frozen night, the shades were up and Carmody could see ochre-col-ored walls, and a warm light cast by table lamps. This startled him. In memory, the Carmody flat was always cold, the win-dows rimmed with frost in winter, he and his sisters making drawings with their fingernails in the cold bluish light cast from a fluorescent ceiling lamp. His father was cold too, a withdrawn bitter man who resented the world, and the youth of his children. His mother was a drinker, and her own chilly remorse was relieved only by occasional bursts of rage. They nodded or grunted when Carmody told them about his ambitions, and his mother once said, in a slurred voice, "Who do you think you are, anyway?"

One Saturday afternoon in the Mulrane flat, he and Molly were alone, her parents gone off to see Frankie and his small child. Molly proudly showed him her father's winter uniform, encased in plastic from Kent's dry cleaners, and the medals he had won, and the extra gun, a nickel-plated .38 caliber Smith and Wesson, oiled and ready in a felt box. She talked to him about a book she was reading by A.J. Cronin and he told her she should read F. Scott Fitzgerald. She made him a ham-and-swiss-cheese sandwich for lunch. They sipped tea with milk, thick with sugar. And then, for the first time, they went to bed together in her tiny room with its window leading to the fire escape. She was in an agony, murmuring prayers, her hands and arms moving in a jittery way to cover breasts and hair, trembling with fear and desire. *"Hold me tight,"* she whispered. *"Don't ever leave me."*

He had never written any of that, or how at the end of his first year of college, at the same time that she graduated from St. Joseph's, he rented the room near New York University, to get away from his parents and hers, and how she would come to him after work as a file clerk at Metropolitan Life and they would vanish into each other. He still went back to Brooklyn. He still visited the ice house of his parents. He still called formally in the Mulrane apartment to take Molly to the Sanders or the RKO Prospect. He was learning how to perform. But the tiny room had become their place, their gangster's hideout, the secret place to which they went for sin.

Now on this frozen night he stared at the dark windows of the first floor left, wondering who lived there now, and whether Molly's bones were lying in some frozen piece of the Brooklyn earth. He could still hear her voice, trembling and tentative: "We're sinners, aren't we?" He could hear her saying: "What's to become of us?" He could hear the common sense in her words and the curl of Brooklyn in her accent. "Where are we going?" she said. "Please don't ever leave me." He could see the mole inside her left thigh. He could see the fine hair at the top of her neck.

"Well, will ya lookit this," a hoarse male voice said from behind him. "If it ain't Buddy Carmody."

Carmody turned and saw a burly man smoking a cigarette in the doorway of a tenement. He was wearing a thick ski jacket and jeans, but his head was bare. The face was not clear in the obscure light but the voice told Carmody it was definitely someone from back then. Nobody had called him Buddy in forty-six years.

"How are ya?" Carmody said, peering at the man as he stepped out of the doorway. The man's face was puffy and seamed, and Carmody tried to peel away the flesh to see who had lived in it when they both were young.

"Couldn't stay away from the old neighborhood, could ya, Buddy?"

The unease was seething, but now Carmody felt a small stream of fear make its move in his stomach.

"It's been a long time," Carmody said. "Remind me, what's your name?"

"You shittin' me, Buddy? How could you figget my name?"

"I told you, man, it's been a long time."

"Yeah. It's easy to figget, for some people."

"Advanced age, and all that," Carmody said, performing a grin, glancing to his left, to the darkening shop windows, the empty street. Imagining himself running.

"But not everybody figgets," the man said.

He flipped his cigarette under a parked car.

"My sister didn't figget."

Oh.

Oh God.

"You must be Seanie," Carmody said quietly. "Am I right? Seanie Mulrane?"

"Ah, you remembered."

"How are you, Seanie?"

He could see Seanie's hooded eyes now, so like the eyes of his policeman father: still, unimpressed. He moved close enough so that Carmody could smell the whiskey on his breath.

"How am I? Huh. How am I . . . Not as good as you, Buddy boy. We keep up, ya know. The books, that mini-series, or whatever it was on NBC. Pretty good, you're doing."

Carmody stepped back a foot, as subtly as possible, trying to decide how to leave. He wished a police car would turn the corner. He trembled, feeling a black wind of negation pushing at him, backing him up, a small focused wind that seemed to come from the furled brow of Seanie Mulrane. He tried to look casual, turned and glanced at the building where he was young, at the dark first floor left, the warm top floor right.

"She never got over you, you prick."

Carmody shrugged. "It's a long time ago, Seanie," he said, trying to avoid being dismissive.

"I remember that first month after you split," Seanie said. "She cried all the time. She cried all day. She cried all night. She quit her job, 'cause she couldn't do it and cry at the same time. She'd start to eat, then, *oof,* she'd break up again. A million fuckin' tears, Buddy. I seen it. I was there, just back from the Keys, and my father wanted to find you and put a bullet in your head. And Molly, poor Molly . . . You broke her fuckin' heart, Buddy."

Carmody said nothing. Other emotions were flowing now. Little rivers of regret. Remorse. Unforgivable mistakes. His stomach rose and fell and rose again.

"And that first month? Hey, that was just the start. The end of the second month after you cut out, she tells my mother she's knocked up."

"No . . ."

"Yes."

"I didn't know that, Seanie. I swear—"

"Don't *lie,* Buddy. My old man told your old man. He pulled a gun on him, for Chrissakes, tryin' to find out where you was."

"I never heard any of this."

"Don't lie, Buddy. You lie for a livin', right? All those books, they're lies, ain't they? Don't lie to me."

"I didn't know, Seanie."

"Tell the truth: You ran because she was pregnant."

No: That wasn't why. He truly didn't know. He glanced at his watch. Ten minutes until the book signing. He felt an ache rising in his back.

"She had the baby, some place in New Jersey," Seanie said. "Catholic nuns or something. And gave it up. A boy it was. A son. Then she came home and went in her room. She went to mass every morning, I guess prayin' to God to forgive her. But she never went to another movie with a guy, never went on a date. She stood in her room, like another god-damned nun. She saw my mother die, and buried her, and saw my father die, and buried him, and saw me get married and move here wit' my Mary, right across the street, to live upstairs. I'd come see her every day, and try talkin' to her, but it was like, 'You want tea, Seanie, or coffee?'"

Seanie moved slightly, placing his bulk between Carmody and the path to Barnes & Noble.

"Once I said to her, I said, 'How about you come with me an' Mary to Florida? You like it, we could all move there. It's beautiful,' I said to her. 'Palm trees and the ocean. You'd love it.' Figuring I had to get her out of that fuckin' room. She looked at me like I said, 'Hey, let's move to Mars.'" Seanie paused, trembling with anger and memory, and lit another cigarette. "Just once, she talked a blue streak, drinkin' gin, I guess it was. And said to me, real mad, 'I don't want to see anyone, you understand me, Seanie? I don't want to see people holdin' hands. I don't want to see little boys playin' ball. You understand me?'" He took a deep drag on the Camel. "'I want to be here,' she says to me, 'when Buddy comes back.'"

Carmody stared at the sidewalk, at Seanie's scuffed black shoes, and heard her voice: *When Buddy comes back.* Saw the fine hair at the top of her neck. Thinking: Here I am, I'm back.

"So she waited for you, Buddy. Year after year in that dark goddamned flat. Everything was like it was when you split. My mother's room, my father's room, her room. All the same clothes. It wasn't right what you done to her, Buddy. She was a beautiful girl."

"That she was."

"And a sweet girl."

"Yes."

"It wasn't right. You had the sweet life and she shoulda had it with you."

Carmody turned. "And how did she . . . When did she . . ."

"Die? She didn't die, Buddy. She's still there. Right across the street. Waitin' for you, you prick."

Carmody turned then, lurching toward the corner, heading to the bookstore. He did not run, but his legs carried him in flight. Thinking: She's alive. Molly Mulrane is alive. He was certain she had gone off, married someone, a cop or a fireman or car salesman, had settled in the safety of Bay Ridge or some far-off green suburb. A place without memory. Without ghosts. He was certain that she had lived a long while, married, had children, and then died. The way everybody did. And now he knew the only child she ever had was his, a son, and he was in flight, afraid to look back.

He could sense the feral pack behind him, filling the silent streets with howls. He had heard them often in the past few years, on beaches at dusk, in too many dreams. The voices of women, wordless but full of accusation: wives, and girlfriends, and one-night stands in college towns; women his own age and women not yet women; women discarded, women used, women injured, coming after him on a foggy moor, from groves of leafless trees, their eyes yellow, their clothing mere patchy rags. If they could speak, the words would be about lies, treacheries, theft, broken vows. He could see many of their faces as he moved, remembering some of their names, and knew that in front, leading the pack, was Molly Mulrane.

Crossing a street, he slipped on a ridge of black ice and banged against the hood of a parked car. Then he looked back. Nobody was there.

He paused, breathing hard and deep.

Not even Seanie had come after him.

And now the book signing filled him with another kind of fear. Who else might come there tonight, knowing the truth? Hauling up the ashes of the past? What other sin would someone dredge up? Who else might come for an accounting?

He hurried on, the feral visions erased. He was breathing heavily, as he always did when waking from bad dreams. A taxi cruised along the avenue, its rooftop light on, as if pleading for a fare to Manhattan. Carmody thought: I could just go. Just jump in this cab. Call the store. Plead sudden illness. Just go. But someone was sure to call Rush & Malloy at the *Daily News* or Page Six at the *Post* and report the no-show. *Brooklyn Boy Calls It In.* All that shit. No.

And then a rosy-cheeked woman was smiling at him. The manager of the bookstore.

"Oh, Mister Carmody, we thought you got lost."

"Not in this neighborhood," he said. And smiled, as required by the performance.

"You've got a great crowd waiting."

"Let's do it."

"We have water on the lectern, and lots of pens, everything you need."

As they climbed to the second floor, Carmody took off his hat and gloves and overcoat and the manager passed them to an assistant. He glanced at himself in a mirror, at his tweed jacket and black crew-collared sweater. He looked like a writer all right. Not a cop or a fireman or even a professor. A writer. He saw an area with about a hundred people sitting on folding chairs, penned in by walls of books, and more people in the aisles beyond the shelves, and another large group standing at the rear. Yes: a great crowd.

He stood modestly beside the lectern as he was introduced by the manager. He heard the words, "one of Brooklyn's own . . ." and they sounded strange. He didn't often think of himself that way, and in signings all over the country that fact was seldom mentioned. This store itself was a sign of a different Brooklyn. *Nothing stays the same. Everything changes.* There were no bookstores in his Brooklyn. He found his first books in the public library branch near where he lived, or in the great main branch at Grand Army Plaza. On rainy summer days he spent hours among their stacks. But the bookstores— where you could buy and own a book—they were down on Pearl Street under the El, or across the river on Fourth Avenue. His mind flashed on *Bomba the Jungle Boy at the Giant Cataract.* The first book he'd ever finished. How old was I? Eleven. Yes. Eleven. It cost a nickel on Pearl Street. That year, I had no bad dreams.

During the introduction, he peered out at the faces, examining them for hostility. But the faces were different too. Most were in their thirties, lean and intense, or prepared to be critical, or wearing the competitive masks of apprentice writers. He had seen such faces in a thousand other bookstores, out in America. About a dozen African-Americans were scattered through the seats, with a few standing on the sides. He saw a few paunchy men with six or seven copies of his books: collectors, looking for autographs to sell on eBay or some fan website. He didn't see any of the older faces. Those faces still marked by Galway or Sicily or the Ukraine.

He didn't see the pouchy, hooded masks that were worn by men like Seanie Mulrane.

His new novel and five of the older paperbacks were stacked on a table to the left of the lectern, ready for signing, and Carmody began to relax. Thinking: It's another signing. Thinking: I could be in Denver or Houston or Berkeley.

Finally, he began to read, removing his glasses because he was near-sighted, focusing on words printed on pages. His words. His pages. He read from the first chapter, which was always fashioned as a hook. He described his hero being drawn into the mysteries of a grand Manhattan restaurant by an old college pal, who was one of the owners, all the while glancing up at the crowd, so that he didn't sound like Professor Carmody. The manager was right: It was a great crowd. They listened. They laughed at the hero's wisecracks. Carmody enjoyed the feedback. He enjoyed the applause too, when he had finished. And then he was done, the hook cast. The manager explained that Carmody would take some questions, and then sign books.

He felt himself tense again. And thought: Why did I run, all those years ago? Why did I do what I did to Molly Mulrane?

I ran to escape, he thought.

That's why everybody runs. That's why women run from men. Women have run from me too. To escape.

People moved in the folding chairs, but Carmody was still. I ran because I felt a rope tightening on my life. Because Molly Mulrane was too nice. Too ordinary. Too safe. I ran because she gave me no choice. She had a script and I didn't. They would get engaged and he'd get his B.A. and maybe a teaching job and they'd get married and have kids and maybe move out to Long Island or over to Jersey and then—*I ran*

because I wanted something else. I wanted to be Hemingway in
Pamplona or in a café on the Left Bank. I wanted to make a lot
of money in the movies, the way Faulkner did or Irwin Shaw, and
then retreat to Italy or the south of France. I wanted risk. I didn't
want safety. So I ran. Like a heartless frightened prick.

The first question came from a bearded man in his forties, the
type who wrote nasty book reviews that guaranteed him
tenure.

"Do you think if you'd stayed in Brooklyn," the bearded
man asked, "you'd have been a better writer?"

Carmody smiled at the implied insult, the patronizing
tone.

"Probably," he answered. "But you never know these
things with any certainty. I might never have become a writer
at all. There's nothing in the Brooklyn air or the Brooklyn
water that makes writers, or we'd have a couple of million
writers here . . ."

A woman in her twenties stood up. "Do you write on a
word processor, or longhand, or a typewriter?"

This was the way it was everywhere, and Carmody
relaxed into the familiar. Soon he'd be asked how to get an
agent or how he got his ideas and how do I protect my own
ideas when I send a manuscript around? Could you read the
manuscript of my novel and tell me what's wrong? The questions came and he answered as politely as possible. He drew
people like that, and he knew why: He was a success, and
there were thousands of would-be writers who thought there
were secret arrangements, private keys, special codes that
would open the doors to the alpine slopes of the bestseller
lists. He tried to tell them that, like life, it was all a lottery.
Most didn't believe him.

Then the manager stepped to the microphone and smiled and said that Mr. Carmody would now be signing books. "Because of the large turnout," the manager said, "Mr. Carmody will not be able to personalize each book. Otherwise many of you would have a long wait." Carmody thanked everybody for coming on such a frigid night and there was warm, loud applause. He sat down at the table, and sipped from a bottle of Poland Spring water.

He signed the first three books on the frontispiece, and then a woman named Peggy Williams smiled and said, "Could you make an exception? We didn't go to school together, but we went to the same school twenty years apart. Could you mention that?"

He did, and the line slowed. Someone wanted him to mention the Dodgers. Another, Coney Island. One man wanted a stickball reference, although he was too young to ever have played that summer game. "It's for my father," he explained. There was affection in these people, for this place, this neighborhood, which was now their neighborhood. But Carmody began to feel something else in the room, something he could not see.

"You must think you're hot shit," said a woman in her fifties. She had daubed rouge on her pale cheeks. "I've been in this line almost an hour."

"I'm sorry," he said, and tried to be light. "It's almost as bad as the Motor Vehicle Bureau."

She didn't laugh.

"You could just sign the books," she said. "Leave off the fancy stuff."

"That's what some people want," he said. "The fancy stuff."

"And you gotta give it to them? Come on."

He signed his name on the title page and handed it to her, still smiling.

"Wait a minute," she said, holding the book before him like a summons. "I waited a long time. Put in, 'For Gerry'—with a G—'who waited on line for more than an hour.'"

She laughed then too, and he did what she asked. The next three just wanted signatures, and two just wanted "Merry Christmas" and then a collector arrived and Carmody signed six first editions. He was weary now, his mind filling with images of Molly Mulrane and Seanie's face and injuries he had caused so long ago. All out there somewhere. And still the line trailed away from the table, into a crowd that, without his glasses, had become a multicolored smear, like a bookcase.

The woman came around from the side aisle, easing toward the front of the line in a distracted way. Carmody saw her whisper to someone on the line, a young man who made room for her with the deference reserved for the old. She was hatless, her white hair cut in girlish bangs across her furrowed brow. She was wearing a short down coat, black skirt, black stockings, mannish shoes. The coat was open, showing a dark rose sweater. Her eyes were pale.

Holy God.

She was six feet away from him, behind two young men and a collector. A worn leather bag hung from her shoulder. A bag so old that Carmody remembered buying it in a shop in the Village, next door to the Eighth Street Bookshop. He remembered it when it was new, and so was he.

He glanced past the others and saw that she was not looking at him. She stared at bookshelves, or the ceiling, or the floor. Her face had an indoor whiteness. The color of ghosts. He signed a book, then another. And the girl he once loved began to come to him, the sweet pretty girl who asked nothing of him except that he love her back. And he felt then a great rush of sorrow. For her. For himself. For their lost child. He felt as if tears would soon leak from every pore in his body. He heard a whisper of someone howling. The books in front of him were now as meaningless as bricks.

Then she was there. And Carmody rose slowly and leaned forward to embrace her across the table.

"*Oh, Molly,*" he whispered. "*Oh, Molly, I'm so, so sorry.*"

She smiled then, and the brackets that framed her mouth seemed to vanish, and for a moment Carmody imagined taking her away with him, repairing her in the sun of California, making it up, writing a new ending. Rewriting his own life. He started to come around the table.

"Molly," he said. "Molly, my love."

Then her hand reached into the leather bag and he knew what it now must hold. Passed down from her father. A souvenir of long ago.

Yes, he thought. Release me, Molly. Yes. Bring me your nickel-plated gift. Do it.

Her hand came out of the bag, holding what he expected.

HASIDIC NOIR

BY PEARL ABRAHAM

Williamsburg

It was a day no different from other days, a not unusual day in which I was doing not unusual things in my own slow way, what my wife who is quick in everything refers to, not always appreciatively, as my meditative manner. I've tried to explain that slowness is my method, the way I work, that this is how I solve my cases and earn a living.

Yes, she says, that's all right while you're working, but a meditative mind doesn't serve such tasks as feeding a child or stopping for a quart of milk on the way home.

She doesn't know that she's asking for the impossible. At the end of the day when I close and lock the door to my office, she wants me to turn the lock on my thinking mind, along with my desk and files, and arrive home free and clear, prepared to give her and the children my full attention. And probably she has a right to such a husband, but the habit of brooding can't be turned on and off at will.

On this not unusual day, doing my not unusual things, stopping before morning service at the *mikvah* for the immersion that all Hasidic men take once a day, twice on Fridays in honor of the Sabbath, the word my brooding mind picked out of the male rumble was MURDER.

Murdered in cold blood, I overheard a man say.

The delayed response—the speaker was probably under water—when it came, was a Talmudic citation, not unexpected in a world in which the Talmud makes up a large part of every young man's curriculum. More was said, there were details, some of which I'd previously heard and dismissed as talk, and names—the victim's, the victim's rival, and also for some reason the victim's brother-in-law—and I was all ears.

I waited my turn for immersion with murder on my mind. After all, such violence isn't a daily occurrence in our world. And the victim, a man belonging to Hasidic aristocracy—a nephew of the Grand Rabbi Joel Teitelbaum—known as the Dobrover rebbe, one of two relatives in line to inherit the Grand Rabbinic throne, wasn't just anyone. The rivalry between Dobrov and Szebed had been part of the Hasidic scene for as long as I could remember, dating back to the old rebbe's first stroke. For years there'd been volley after volley of insults and injuries between the two congregations, and the tales of these insults grew long beards. Along with others in the community, I'd grown a thick skin and generally remained unruffled by even the tallest of such tales. But murder! That was unheard of. And where did the Dobrover's brother-in-law, Reb Shloimele, administrator of Szebed's boys' school, enter into this story?

I spent the rest of the morning at my desk, closing the files of the usual, petty white-collar crimes, my regular paying cases, but my mind was preoccupied with this murder, which had arrived without a client, no one to pay for time or expenses. After so many years of hoping for the opportunity to stand the detective's real test, praying even, God protect us from evil, for a case replete with gun, body, widow, the complete grim pattern, here it appeared, a Hasidic murder, a rarity in this community, and I couldn't pass it up.

I'd had a modicum of experience working homicide, on the fringes really, assisting the New York Police Department

on several cases in the nearby Italian and Spanish neighborhoods. The police chief still calls occasionally with questions
about this part of the city that an insider could answer easily.
And now, after so many years, it was as an insider that I'd
come across this murder, and it was also as an insider that I
knew to judge it a politically motivated crime with perpetrators from the top brass. With the Dobrover rebbe out of the
way, Szebed could take the Grand Rabbinic throne without a
struggle. If I seem to be jumping to conclusions, note that I
grew up in this community and continue to live here; I am
one of them.

Anywhere else, murder, even when it occurs with some
frequency, is front-page news; in the Hasidic world, it's kept
out of the papers—another sign that this was an inside job.
Our insular world, may it long survive, transported from
Eastern Europe and rebuilt in Williamsburg, New York, an
American shtetl, has made a point of knowing and keeping
politicians, judges, and members of the press in our pockets.
I knew too well how this worked.

I also knew that asking questions was not an option. One
question in the wrong place, one word even, could alert those
who didn't want talk. When the highest value in a community is loyalty to the greater cause, meaning the continuity of
the status quo, all means to this end are imbued with religious significance, and are thereby justified. It was quickly
becoming clear to me that this murder had been handed me
for a reason, that it was for this case that I, a Hasidic detective, the first one in the history of Hasidism, had been
bestowed upon a community that usually eschewed new
things. I owed it to the higher powers that created me to pursue the murderers, but I would have to watch my step.

* * *

At noon, I walked the ten blocks to Landau's on Lee, my regular lunch counter, selected not necessarily for its excellence in food but for its distance from my office, because my wife insisted on some daily exercise, though I was partial to their sweet and sour pickles and their warm sauerkraut, having grown up on them, and would have walked twenty blocks for a Landau frankfurter with all the trimmings. On this day, I hoped to overhear something useful. It was late November, a cool stimulating day. I buttoned my black coat, pulled my black hat forward, and wrapped the ivory silk muffler twice around my neck, a gift from my wife when we were bride and groom.

The windows of Landau's were already steamy with cooking. I took the three steps down, entered, was greeted by the elderly Reb Motl Landau, who has known me, as he likes to say, ever since I was this high, indicating a place above his own head. I'm tall, 5'11", which is considered especially tall in these parts, populated as it is by mostly small-boned Jews of Hungarian descent, modyeros, the Romanian Jews like to call them, intending a bit of harmless deprecation since the word is also the name of a particular nut eaten there.

Without waiting for my order, Reb Motl set a loaded tray down in front of me, as if he'd seen me leave the office ten minutes earlier. My lunch: a frankfurter as starter, beefburger as entree, along with two sour pickles, a glass of water, and an ice-cream soda, nondairy of course.

I took my first bite, a third of the dog, noted the three-person huddle at the far end of the lunch counter, and raised an eyebrow in question.

Reb Motl nodded, drew five fingers of one hand together, meaning patience please, and went to serve another customer. He never played dumb and deaf with me. And we didn't waste words.

When Reb Motl returned, he picked up my crumpled wrappers as if this is what he had returned for, and grumbled, What don't you already know?

The word on the street? I asked.

You mean word at the *mikvah*, he corrected.

I nodded.

Guilty, he said.

I raised my eyebrows in question, meaning, Guilty of what?

Read the book, Reb Motl said.

What book? I asked, using only my shoulders and eyebrows.

Published to make the sins of Dobrov known, Reb Motl said, and moved on. This was a busy lunch counter and he couldn't afford to pause long enough to forfeit the momentum that kept him efficient.

I stopped at the bookstore on my way back to the office, wended my way past the leaning towers of yarmulkes at the entrance, the piles of ritual fringes, stacks of *aleph-bet* primers. As always, Reb Yidel was behind the counter, and when I asked for the book, which turned out to be a pamphlet, really, he pointed to a stack beside the register. I looked at the title page to see who had undersigned this bit of slander, and found no name, no individual taking responsibility for it. The printer, however, was a company known as the printing house for Szebed, and I said to myself, of course it would be Szebed, who else, but I was also disappointed. The motivation behind Szebed's publication of such a pamphlet was too obvious, too facile to be interesting, and I wished for a more complicated community with more difficult cases, more obscure motivations, a case that required mental agility, intricacies I could take pride in unraveling. It was use of the mind that had attracted me to detective work in the first place.

Reb Yidel rang up my copy but remained unusually silent.

Know what this is all about? I asked casually, as if my interest were entirely benign.

He shrugged, a careful man with a business and family to protect, and an example to me, who was also a business and family man, who could also benefit from caution. But it was precisely such caution that the perpetrators counted on to help them get away with their crime. They knew that few, if any, among us would risk antagonizing a powerful congregation with fat fingers that reached everywhere.

Any truths? I pressed on.

Who knows? he shrugged. I was pretty sure he knew, and waited.

There's a kernel of truth in every lie, he quoted.

And who is credited with writing the pamphlet? I asked as harmlessly as I could manage.

It is believed to be the work of Reb Shloimele, Szebed's school administrator, Reb Yidel answered neutrally.

The same Reb Shloimele who is also brother-in-law to the Dobrover? I asked, knowing the answer.

Reb Yidel nodded, but declined to say more. I slapped a five-dollar bill down on the counter and left without waiting for the change. Here finally was a detail to ponder, a motivation to unravel.

At my desk I thumbed through the cheaply printed pamphlet. There were accusations of corruption in the Dobrover kosher seal. Discrepancies were cited. A box of nonkosher gelatin, pure pig *treife*, was discovered in the kitchen at

Reismann's bakery. The egg powder used in Horowitz-Margareten matzohs came in unmarked industrial-size boxes. And the pizza-falafel stores in Borough Park, also known to be under the Dobrover seal, were inspected no more than once a month. How much could go wrong in the twenty-nine days between inspections? the writer asked rhetorically, then concluded that for a kosher seal, Dobrov's stamp stank of non-kosher.

I turned to the next chapter. So far, this was the kind of gossip you hear and dismiss regularly. What wouldn't Szebed do to annex Dobrov's lucrative kosher-seal business?

The next chapter attacked the Dobrover's intimate way with his disciples, their secretive, late-night gatherings and celebrations, accused him of messianic aspirations, and ended with the warning that the dangerous makings of the next false messiah were right here in our midst. This too I'd heard previously and considered hearsay. Besides, the days of messianic upheaval and dangers, dependent as they were on seventeenth-century superstitions and ignorance, were long past. We were living in a world in which every yekel and shmekel could read the news, had Internet access. The information super-highway, to use the words of a smart but foolish president, has arrived in our little community in Williamsburg too.

These allegations were followed by an interview with a former disciple in which a discerning reader would quickly recognize that the words had been placed in the mouth of the unwary young man. There were incriminating quotes from a Dobrover son and daughter, who, the pamphleteer pointed out as further evidence of criminality, had turned against their own father. The final chapter featured the court arguments that led to excommunication. From this, a facile argu-

ment for divorce followed, since the wife of an excommunicated man would suffer unnecessarily from her husband's
exclusion.

I closed the book in wonder. In the standard course, such
a series of events—going from initial suspicions to allegations
to accusations to excommunication by the court—would
span a lifetime. For all of it to have gone off in a couple of
years and without much of a hitch, a well-planned program
must have been in place. But who had planned so well, who
had known the ins and outs of Dobrov, and who had so much
private access to family members? I needed to find the children, talk to the sons, the eldest daughter too. Did they
understand that they'd been used—abused, rather?

At 5, when Hasidim gather in the synagogues for the afternoon service, I turned the lock on my office door and walked
to the Szebed synagogue, congregation of the murdered
man's cousin and rival for the Grand Rabbinic throne. Inside
I noted the recent interior renovations to the brownstone.
Exterior work was still in progress. And was it jubilation I
sensed in certain members of the congregation, jubilation at
the Dobrover's death?

I took a place at the back of the room, where I would
have a good view of all who came and went. During the service, I noticed an earnest young man dressed in the style of a
Litvak, an outsider, his face thin and pale, an unhappy face.
What was he doing here mid-week? It happened now and
then that someone's Litvak relative visited for a Sabbath and
attended services in a Hasidic *shtibel*, but this was mid-week,
when young men were at yeshiva; furthermore, this wasn't
any *shtibel*, it was Szebed.

After the service, a birth was announced, the name proclaimed: Udel, daughter of Sarah. Wine, plum brandy, egg kichel, and herring were brought in, and I watched as the cup of wine was passed from relative to relative. The young man appeared to be one of them, because he too received the cup. I eyed him as he went through the motion of sipping and passed it on. Not an outsider. Definitely related. Probably a brother to the young wife, though why would a Szebeder marry into a Litvak family? I wondered.

I went up to the table, poured myself a thimble of brandy in friendly gesture, and casually asked another family man beside me, And who is the young man?

Why, Dobrov's youngest son, brother-in-law of the new father, the man said.

Oh, I said, I didn't recognize him now that he's grown up—the usual nonsense adults speak, mere filler. Beneath the filler, I was beside myself. A Dobrov son dressed in the short coat and hat of a Litvak, *peyos* tucked behind his ears. His father and grandfathers must be churning in their graves. And where were the signs of mourning, the ripped lapel on the jacket, the loose flap on the shirt under it? There was none of that. And during the service no prayer for the soul of the deceased had been recited either. Clearly, the son wasn't mourning the father, not openly anyway.

I mingled among the men, made my way up to the young man as smoothly as I could manage, put my hand out to wish him a *mazel tov*. He extended a limp, unwilling hand, responded with the merest nod. His eyes, however, scanned my face, didn't seem to find what they wanted, and moved on. An unhappy soul, I thought, a very disturbed young man. I attempted to squeeze some reassurance into the pale thin hand, clapped it with my other hand before letting go, then taking a roundabout path made my way to the door, slipped out unnoticed, I hoped, and walked up and down the block, with an eye on the comings and goings at this house, a brownstone whose upper floors served as the Szebeder residence. The new mother, I guessed, was staying here with her newborn, and I wanted to see and know what might be going on among the women.

It was over half an hour before my stakeout was rewarded. The door opened, the Dobrover widow came to the door buttoned up in her long black fur and carrying her purse. Attending the widow to the door was her daughter, the young mother, and behind her, the Szebeder rebbetzin. Without warning, the daughter threw her arms around her mother and sobbed noisily. I'm quite certain there were wet trails on the mother's cheeks too. They remained this way, the daughter clinging to her mother, for some moments, then the mother disentangled herself and walked down the wide brownstone stairs.

Here finally were signs of mourning. I was quite certain this is what the tears were for, since giving birth is not normally, that is if the child emerges healthy, an occasion for tears.

Not knowing what else to do, I followed the older woman at a distance. As widow of the Dobrover, she should be mourning, sitting out the seven days of *shiva*. Instead, here she was, walking in the streets, leading me to an address I didn't know, not the residence of Dobrov, and it was then I remembered the divorce. Having divorced the Dobrover she couldn't mourn him. Imagine her feelings. I wondered at the torment every member of this family must be experiencing. The death of a husband and father one had disowned in life on what were surely false accusations; this was a tragedy.

* * *

It was a deep blue evening with a moon and stars brighter than the street lights, and the shadows of men on their way home grew long and lean. I wrapped my silk muffler tight against the wind. At home it would be past the children's dinner hour, they would be in bed by now, and I turned in that direction, up Ross toward Marcy Avenue, to tuck them in for the night, reflecting on the vulnerability of a wife and children, the ease with which an entire family can be destroyed.

I was in time to read several pages about the current favorite, the miracle-performing BeSHT and his disciples, and remained bedside long enough to see willpower lose out to fatigue. One by one, from the youngest to my eldest, who to prove her superiority to her younger siblings made a valiant effort every night to be the last one to fall asleep, their eyes closed.

In the kitchen my wife was washing up, putting things away. I joined her at the sink with a dishtowel, and told her about following the rebbetzin to a strange address.

Don't you know anything? my fine rebbetzin asked rhetorically. The poor woman remarried about a year ago, to a widower about fifteen years older than her. People say she was led by the nose for a long walk, to the end of the block and back again. By a scheming brother-in-law who convinced the world, the wife, and the children of the Dobrover's sins.

And what happened to the younger children? I asked.

Taken in by the brother-in-law, Reb Shloimele. The younger daughter, barely seventeen, was palmed off to her first cousin, Reb Shloimele's son, a bum, rumor has it, who would have had difficulty finding a father willing to hand over his daughter. The younger son, still a *cheder* boy at the time, was raised in Reb Shloimele's home, and at the age of thirteen, sent off to a Litvak yeshiva, with the intention, it was said, to further hurt the father.

That explained the strangeness of a Dobrov son in Litvak garb. And again Reb Shloimele made himself felt in this sordid story. I shook my head. So much evil under the noses of the most pious men, and in their names. I felt an obligation to bring this murder to light, to clear the innocent and accuse the guilty, but how to go about it? And whom to name? This brother-in-law was a mover and shaker, a *makher* in Yiddish, but he couldn't have acted alone. There were powerful men behind him but I couldn't accuse all of Szebed. And who would risk the congregation's ire, help point the finger, and haul the shameless sinners into Jewish court? None of the rabbis appointed to our house of judgment would risk political suicide. Since I couldn't expect assistance on the inside, I would have to go outside.

I attended my evening study session, then started walking toward home, but found myself instead on Keap Street again, in front of the Szebed residence, looking for something, I wasn't sure what. The door opened, I stepped into a nearby doorway and watched the young Dobrover son in his short coat and hat emerge alone, hurry down the stairs, and turn right on Lee. I followed at a distance, curious, wondering where he would go. He led me to 446 Ross, to the Dobrover home, dark and shuttered, and stood at the foot of the stairs looking up. Would he go up the stairs and enter his old home, which the angel of death had invaded? He didn't. After long minutes, he turned away and walked back. What struck me as exceptionally cruel was his inability to mourn publicly, a ritual intended as an aid to grief and recovery. Standing in the way of mourning were the laws of excommunication. An excommunicated man, considered dead, was denied living mourners; there would be no one to say *kaddish* for the Dobrover's soul. His enemies had succeeded in cutting him off both in life and in death.

It was my turn to walk the streets and think.

The perpetrators had used public opinion to help make their case to the judges. I too would have to take my case to the public. And since I couldn't afford print—even the cheapest pamphlet costs a goodly sum—I would have to use the poor man's version: the Internet.

At my desk the next morning I found a chat room with organized religion as its topic, soon steered the conversation to religious politics, and posted my story as an example of corruption, proclaiming the Dobrover's innocence. I didn't have to wait long for the important questions to come up, the who and why of every whodunit, and I pointed my finger to the brother-in-law as prime perp, offered as explanation the oldest motivation, envy, the reason Cain raised his hand against his brother Abel. I was convinced and was able to convince others that without the green worm of jealousy, the Dobrover rebbe and his family would have remained untouched.

Consider this brother-in-law: a promising yeshiva boy who in maturity proved to be a minor scholar with an impatient mind incapable of complex argument. Marrying the sister of the Dobrover rebbetzin, herself a woman of fine rabbinical stock, was his undoing. He would have sat at the table, listened to the deeply scholarly talk, and squirmed in ignorance. The first years of his marriage, he sat pressing the yeshiva bench unwillingly, because the husband of the Dobrover's rebbetzin's sister had to be a scholar, then seized the first opportunity that came his way and became the director of the newly founded Szebeder boys' school. The position fulfilled his need to move about and accomplish things, but at the Sabbath table the sense of his own inferiority would have deepened. And without scholarship to occupy his mind, he became a plotting busybody. The rivalry between the two congregations presented him with an opportunity. Knowing he would never be a significant player in Dobrov, he determined to curry favor at Szebed. Indeed, his reward for interfering in the life and marriage of Dobrov was proof enough of his motivation: He had recently been appointed administrative overseer of the entire Szebed congregation, not a scholarly position, but respectable enough to protect him from his detractors. In taking him on, in other words, I was taking on the whole of Szebed. The anonymity of the Internet, I hoped—I hadn't used my name—would protect me.

And that's where I miscalculated. I didn't count on the Internet's long and wide reach, nor its speed. Religious corruption, whether among priests or rabbis, has a captive audience in America. Well-meaning, sympathy-riddled letters came pouring in, as if I was the one who had suffered the heavy hand of the court. The chat room conversations went on for hours and days, and when I was too exhausted, continued without me, spilled over into new chat rooms. I spent hours online, returned to my office after services and dinner, and remained until midnight typing.

Who were the people chatting? A mixed group—the word *crowd* would be more correct—it turned out. There were both knowing and unknowing participants, meaning Hasidic and not. Also a good number who asked questions that revealed they knew nothing at all about Judaism. Within days, a reporter from the *Village Voice* asked for an interview, then a staff writer writing for the *New Yorker's* "Talk of the

Town." I agreed to give the interviews as long as I remained anonymous. I didn't meet them in person.

Is it necessary to say that I wasn't making my wife happy? She argued that I would remain anonymous only to outsiders. Anyone on the inside who wanted to know who was behind this would soon figure it out. Once known, my name would be mud, and our lives would be shattered. And of course she had a point. Good women are often prescient.

First an anonymous threat to cease and desist or suffer consequences was posted in what I was by now thinking of as my chat room, named *Hasidic Noir* by a participant, a wiseguy. I was accused of lying. Where were the mourners? this faceless voice asked. No one had performed *keria* (the ripping of the lapels), no one was sitting *shiva* (seven days of mourning), and no one had recited the *mourner's kaddish* (the prayer for the soul of the dead). He concluded with a declaration that there was no Dobrover rebbe or Dobrover congregation, that I was a careerist who had fabricated a murder for the sake of publicity.

Clearly this was coming from an insider with knowledge of the vocabulary and customs, someone who knew that excommunication rendered a man nonexistent to the community, hence his argument that there was no Dobrover rebbe.

The chat room became a divisive hive, with people taking sides, demanding to know what the words meant, who was the liar in this story, how to find out. One cynical participant raised the irrelevant question of my, not the murderer's, motivation. If the brother-in-law is jealous Cain, he asked, who is this snitch, and what's he going for? The next morning the *Village Voice* published the interview, and late that evening, when my wife and I were already in bed, there was a knock at the door.

I drew on my flannel dressing gown, removed the Glock I keep in the locked drawer of our night table, and instructed my wife to remain in bed. I opened the door, loaded gun in hand, pointing. These men should know what there is to know. Three Szebeder bums stood red-faced, mouths open, breathing hard. They must have used the stairs. If you didn't know better, you'd think they'd been imbibing. But I knew that if there'd been any excess, it had been verbal not alcoholic. To achieve a tough's appearance they'd had to talk themselves into a frenzy.

The barrel end of the gun quickly quieted them, as it often does those who want to live. The middle one in the group produced a letter. I opened it in front of them, keeping the gun aimed, keeping them fearful and rooted in place. At a glance, the letter appeared to be a court summons. The Jewish court, made up of the same rabbis who'd helped bury the Dobrover, was now calling me in.

I congratulated myself on achieving something of a goal. Two weeks ago these men wouldn't have given me the time of day. Now they were all ears. But if I didn't want to lose all that was precious to me—my wife, my children, and my livelihood—I would have to plan well. I would tell my story, but I would tell it publicly.

I looked at the quivering men at my door and felt sorry for them, mere messengers. We were told to bring you in, one mumbled.

Tell the court I'll see them tomorrow, at 9 a.m. sharp, in the revealing light of day. There will be no nighttime shenanigans. Good evening.

I shut the door and waited for the sounds of their steps, first shuffling, then sprinting to get away. I bolted the door, inserted the police lock, looked in on the children who had slept through it all, assured my wife that everything was under control, and got to work on the small laptop I keep at home.

When I finally returned to bed at 3 in the morning, my wife hugged me silently and did her best to remind me that I am only a man, of flesh and blood, not iron. I knew that even though she was against what I was doing—for reasons of safety rather than principle—she couldn't help but be proud of the way I was handling it.

I slept well, and in the morning dressed as usual, in my charcoal gray suit, white shirt, black overcoat, and silk muffler. I pocketed the Glock as protection against the court's manhandling, their method of intimidation. This was a non-jurisdictional court, therefore without metal detectors, and without the routine of body searches, both unnecessary. A handful of appointed rabbis, intrinsically honest, would act as judges, but they owed their livelihoods to their patrons, the men who nominated, appointed, and paid for their services. There would be some younger scholars available to act as mediators. Also present would be the man who was bringing the case against me. Who would it be? I expected to see the man I'd fingered, the jealous brother-in-law, or if he didn't want to show his face, a representative.

I followed my regular routine, stopped first at the *mikvah*, which was buzzing. It was a perfect setting for murder, an underground hell, where locker room odors envelop you on entrance through the unassuming side door. Hurrying down the stone stairs and long tiled hallways, the curl and drip of the waterlogged vapors take over and then the low rumble of bass and tenor voices. At the entrance to the lockers, the bath attendant hands you your towel, one per person, and you move along toward your designated locker and the bench in front of it. You undo your shoes, remove your socks, left foot first, then the left leg of your pants, and so on, in the order in which you were taught to undress. Dressing, you reversed it, right foot first, insuring against the possibility of getting the day off on the wrong foot. And still the act of undressing provokes other indiscretions. While your hands are at work, your ears don't remain idle. They tune into the nearest conversation in the aisle, then onto the next nearest, and so on, staying with each one long enough to hear whether it's of interest. And of course there always is something of interest , a bit of information, gossip someone heard at home the night before, husbands picking up at the *mikvah* where their house-bound, child-bound, telephone-addicted wives left off the night before.

I didn't have to wait long to hear my own name, and then the name of the man I'd fingered, Reb Shloimele, the chief administrator of Szebed, though to hear the talk, not for much longer. A well-respected man of the community the day before, today his name was mud. With the generous helping of hyperbole typical of *mikvah* gossip, someone equated Reb Shloimele's crime with that of the biblical Amelek's, Israel's oldest enemy. In other words, Reb Shloimele was a sentenced man.

This time I expected the crowds, and the journalists with cameras. And I knew how much Szebed would hate it. The rabbis wouldn't approve. No one would like it, but the publicity would serve to protect me. I pulled the brim of my hat down to conceal my face and made my way through the throng. Questions, microphones, and cameras were pressed on me. I walked straight through, succumbing to none. The

Internet had done the work, the chat rooms had been devil-
ishly successful; it was enough. I had no reason to add fuel to
the fire and further enrage the sitting judges.

Inside, without much of a greeting and none of the usual
friendly handshakes, two men attempted to lead me, strong-
arm style, to my place at the table, completely unnecessary
since on my own I'd shown up at the courtroom. I shook
them off and walked alone, pulled out the chair, sat. The
judges frowned, but said nothing. They were pretending at
busyness, each taking a turn at thumbing through a pile of
continuous-feed paper in front of them, the tabs and holes
that fit a dot matrix printer's sprockets still attached.
Someone had provided them with a complete printout of the
chat room conversations, a fat manuscript titled "Hasidic
Noir." I suppressed a smile.

Throat-clearing and short grunts indicated the start of
proceedings. One judge asked whether the defendant knew
what he was accused of.

No, I said. As everyone here knows, I am a God-fearing,
law-abiding Hasid whose livelihood is detective work. I solve
petty crimes, attempt to bring to justice those who break the
law, my small effort at world repair.

There was a long pause. Read this then, the judge said,
and handed me a sheet of paper.

The complaint against me: libel, for attempting to
besmirch a man's name, to ruin a reputation.

The rabbi sitting directly across the table waited for me to
finish reading, then said, You know as well as we do that a
man guilty of libel must be judged, according to Jewish law, as
a murderer. Destroying a man's reputation is a serious crime.

I nodded and said, I'm well aware of that law because it
is precisely what I believe Reb Shloimele guilty of.

I made a long show of extracting the cheap pamphlet from my briefcase, pushed it across the table, and announced, as if this were a courtroom complete with stenographers, Let the record show that this slanderous pamphlet was submitted by the defendant as evidence of Reb Shloimele's guilt. Murder via slander, false slander, moreover, since not one of the accusations have been proven true without doubt.

I paused, looked from face to face, then continued slowly: And this court is guilty of acting as an accomplice to this murder. Even if Reb Shloimele managed to gather enough signatures to support the excommunication, and all the signatories were surely his Szebeder friends, by what right, I ask on behalf of Dobrov, did it grant the Dobrover rebbetzin a divorce and break up an entire family. Since you're citing Jewish law, you also know that breaking up a marriage unnecessarily is equal to taking life.

The rabbi's fist came down on the table with a thump. Enough, he said. Neither Reb Shloimele nor this court are on trial. Our sins are beside the point right now. You, however, have a lot to answer for. If you thought or knew that someone had been wronged, you ought to have come directly to us, and quietly. Instead, you took the story to the public, and not just the Jewish public. You are guilty of besmirching not only the name of a respectable man among us, but also the name of God, and worse, in front of the eyes of other nations. Retribution for befouling the name of God, as you well know, arrives directly from heaven, but this court will also do its part. You will be as a limb cut away from a body. Your wife and children will share your fate.

I took stock of the situation, decided that I was willing to take my chances with God, and since in the eyes of these men I was already judged guilty, I couldn't make my case worse. I took a deep breath and went all the way.

Which of you here would have been willing to listen to my story? Which of you here isn't paid, one way or another, by the Szebeder congregation. According to the law of this nation in which we live, you qualify as collaborators, and therefore ought to recuse yourself from this case. I exhaled and stood. And if, as further proof of your guilt, you require a body, here it is.

I took long strides to the door, opened it. As planned, an EMS technician wheeled into the room the Dobrover rebbe himself, frail and wraithlike, a man of fifty-three years with an early heart condition, attended by his young son in the Litvak frock.

The Dobrover appeared before us all as the Job-like figure that sooner or later every mortal becomes, but in his case the suffering had come at the hand of man rather than God, and that made all the difference.

The room remained silent for long minutes. An excommunicated man shows himself in the courtroom for only one purpose: to have the excommunication nullified, to be reborn to the community. This court had difficult days, weeks, probably, of work ahead.

I'd done my part for Dobrov. Now it remained to be seen what Dobrov would do for me. In the meantime, no one took notice when I snapped my briefcase closed loudly, adjusted the brim of my hat, and left. I had become a dead man, unseen and unheard.

©2004 Pearl Abraham

NO TIME FOR SENIOR'S

BY SIDNEY OFFIT

Downtown Brooklyn

I'm talking murder. Murder!" she says.

It's past noon. I'm sitting in my office near DeKalb and Flatbush, knocking off a corned-beef-lean bathed in cole slaw on seeded rye from Junior's. And there stands Sylvia Berkowitz O'Neil, not looking her age, in high heels, short skirt, and enough makeup to drown Esther Williams and Mark Spitz on a bad day.

Before I can crack wise, Sylvia takes her first shot. "Yer eating at Junior's? I'm working day and night, night and day, with an economy deli for the neighborhood, and you're supporting the competition? And don't tell me you never heard of Senior's!"

Senior's? She's got to be pulling *one* of my legs. But not Sylvia. A kid with an old baseball cap on backwards is standing by her side, the spitting image of Seamus "Scoop" O'Neil, my former pal, who run off to City Hall with Sylvia back when we were an item.

"So what's up? Why me? Why today after—has it been thirty, forty years?"

Sylvia doesn't miss a beat. "I need you, Pistol Pete," she says. "The cops have got Scoop in for murder. Murder. They say he done in Front Page Shamburger and Sherlock Iconoflip." Then, "Don't you ask a lady to sit down? What's happened to your manners? And this gentleman, about whom you don't seem to have the presence to ask, is our nephew I.F., named, of course, after the famous Izzy Stone, who you know was Scoop's hero all these many years."

So, I pull up two old bridges that I haven't unfolded in—gotta stop counting the years. Sylvia keeps yammering, reminding me I'm the only private eye she's ever really known, recalling the days when I was feeding Scoop leads, checking out scumbags for him, so he could blow the lid off the hustlers at Borough Hall—who made the deals with sewer, highway, and bridge contractors. I unwrap a White Owl, pull out the old Zippo, and am ready to light up.

"You are not going to smoke," Sylvia tells me. "I don't believe it. You still haven't caught on."

That's Sylvia. Hasn't skipped a beat, still telling me what to do. I bury the Zippo and start chewing the stogie.

"It happened at their weekly poker game," Sylvia says.

"What useta be their gang of six, what with the smoking and the drinking, what it done to their lungs and livers and kidneys, not to say their marriages and longevity. Well, now it's down to the three of them. Was three until Front Page and Sherlock—may their souls rest in a City Room—got knocked off."

Sylvia is not keen on interruptions, but I cut in. "Gotta play it straight with you for old time's sake, Sylv," I say. "Haven't hustled a case in must be five years. Been sittin' up here in the office on a long-term lease just passin' the time. Doin' a little this and that."

She knows I never been hitched, and I can tell by the way she kinda half smiles at me she suspects I'm still carrying the torch for her.

"Sanchez over at the precinct says it was poison—arsenic mixed with mustard—that done them in," Sylvia goes on.

"The cops found splotches of mustard on Scoop's cuff, his shirt, the zipper of his fly. Would you believe it?"

I'm studying the kid's cap. The mellow blue has me wondering if it's an old Brooklyn Dodger lid. "Hey, kid, you ever hear of Carl Furillo, Sandy Amoros? Duke Snider? I know you heard of Jackie Robinson. Everybody heard of Jackie Robinson."

"What's that got to do with anything?" Sylvia says in a huff. "I'm talking about my husband, held for murder. I'm giving you the facts, nothing but the facts, and you come up with a walk down Memory Lane. Who you think you are—Joe Franklin?"

But the kid is hooked. "Carl Anthony Furillo hit .296 for the 1955 World Champions. Edwin Donald 'Duke' Snider hit four home runs, batted in seven, BA .320 in the Series. 'Sandy' Edmund Isasi Amoros led the team with .333 . . ."

"Enough," Sylvia says, like she's letting the dentist know one more drill and she's outa there. "We didn't come here to talk baseball."

But the kid has cleared the fences. When Scoop and I seen the last of each other, we had this pact, at least I thought we had a deal, only talk, talk only, about *our* Dodgers, once O'Malley had packed up the gang including the great Sandy Koufax himself and hauled kit and caboodle off to L.A. I'm touched that the kid—did Sylvia say he was her nephew?—has got it all down pat. The memories, *my* memories of our church that was Ebbets Field.

"Everything isn't picture perfect between Scoop and me," Sylvia goes on. "I'm not gonna tell you it is. Like Senior's. Me opening the restaurant, a deli. I'm ordering my pastramis from Langers. You never taste a smokier, saltier, peppery flavor in your life. 'Yer ordering pastramis from L.A.,' Scoop says. 'I won't hear of it. First they steal our Dodgers. Now you're goin' head to head with Junior's with an L.A. pastrami.' That's what he says. No head for business."

"Say, kid," I say. "They call you I.F.? What you know about Izzy Stone?"

"He published an independent newsletter, received a Special George Polk Journalism Award in 1970, the same award the *Brooklyn Eagle* won for Community Service in 1948 and 1949. Stone thanked the Brooklyn Center of L.I.U. for what he called a great honor."

The kid gets no further than that when Sylv is back again.

"What is this? First down Memory Lane, now it's Old Home Week. The *Brooklyn Eagle* is dead and so are Front Page and Sherlock. Scoop is facing the hot seat and you're cutting up about Brooklyn bygones. You taking the case or I gotta fly a shammes in from L.A.?"

"Sanchez, you say?" I say. "Pablo Sanchez. He still around? Must be a sergeant since I seen him last. I'll give him a call." Sylvia is pumping her heels, the kid is flipping his lid, brim forward now. I can see the fading white monogrammed B. The number comes to me easy, 84th Precinct, 718-875-6811. I'm still chomping the stogie when I'm on the line with Pablo. "*Socorro! Socorro!*" I say by way of openers. "I gotta talk to you, *amigo*. I hear you got Scoop O'Neil in for *asesinato*. His wife Sylvia put me on the case. I gotta talk to him. *No puedo esperar.*"

"Come on over," Pablo says, "*Esperaré aquí.*"

"I'm on," I tell Sylvia and the kid. "You might as well come along for the ride."

"Sure I know my way around Brooklyn," the kid tells me as

we're ambling toward Gold Street. "I got a map." Then he says, "You ever hear of *Only the Dead Know Brooklyn?*"

"Not now," says Sylvia, wobbling on her high heels. "I'm in the dumps without more bad news."

I say, "Yeah. A story by Thomas Wolfe, the elder. I never knew kids your age even knew who he was."

"Izzy knows all about books and batting averages," Sylvia squawks. "But ask him to slice a corned beef and it comes out like he's working the Blarney Stone."

When we reach the old brown brick precinct house where they're holding Scoop, Pablo greets Sylv, "*Mucho gusto en conocerla, señorita.*" Then, he makes it clear, only one visitor at a time in the detective's office. He's arranged for me to have a confab with Scoop.

I'm sittin' on one of those hard-back chairs that must've been designed by a chiropractor to increase business when Scoop comes in looking like it's ten seconds after Bobby Thomson's home run that done us in in '51.

"Pete. Pistol Pete," he says, shaking his head from side to side, the flaps of his graying mustache twitching in the breeze. "It's been so long, so long ago and far away." For a second there I think Scoop is gonna break into a song. Scoop useta be like that, a walkin', talkin' Broadway musical with subtitles. I understand why Sylv scratched me for him. All that freebee entertainment. Scoop plunks in the chair across the desk from me. "Can you get me outa here? I done nothing wrong. We're playing deuces wild and I'm drawing to an ace and two twos when they cave in—Sherlock and Front Page, two of the greatest beat reporters who never won a Polk Award."

"Hey, you win a Polk Award?" I'm checking out Scoop's memory.

"Nominated twice," Scoop says with a long sigh. "I had Al Landa and David Medina pitching for me, but couldn't get past that flack Hershey they brought in from *Newsday.*"

The marbles are there, so I ask him for the story. "No song and dance, Scoop," I say. "We only got so long. Sanchez is doing us a favor. Just a run through, not twice around."

Scoop confirms pretty much what Sylvia has told me—the history of the poker game, the poisoned mustard, the clues on his cuff, pants, fly. I'm taking notes, scratching times, names, the menu. Seems the scene of the crime is a small office off the main drag of Senior's, the deli Sylvia has opened less than a month ago.

"I never wanted her to do it," Scoop says. "What we need a business for at our age? We should be rolling in the clover or at least the sands of Miami Beach. But you know Sylvia, once she got it in her head to make pastrami on rye with a slice of cheesecake for McDonald's prices, there was no stopping her. She's talking franchises coast to coast, going public on the big board, and we're lucky if we can pay the bills even with my kid—" Scoop breaks off, shrugs, collects himself. "I mean our nephew I.F. Izzy. Ain't he an egg cream with a dash of cinnamon if you ever seen one?"

Egg creams with cinnamon? That's a new one on me, but I let it pass. I'm hearing "my kid" before "our nephew." I say, "Tell me something, Scoop. This nephew of yourn, he's your sister's kid? Molly who I remember lived in Sea Gate before she run off with a retired cutter from the garment district and moved to South Fallsburg?"

"Naw. Naw," Scoop says. "The cutter—may his creases rest in peace—is long since gone. Molly married again, an artist. She's got a place in Brooklyn Heights, right there looking over the southern tip of Manhattan."

I know Scoop has no other sisters or brothers and this "nephew" definitely does not run in Sylvia's family. I put it to him: "This kid, I.F. Izzy. He is or is *not* Molly's son?"

Scoop shrugs, comes as close as I've ever seen him to blushing, starts fumbling for a butt. I'd stake him to a White Owl, but it is definitely not a good idea to light up a fat stogie in a precinct house when you're being held for murder.

"He's no nephew," Scoop says like he's breaking the Lindbergh case. "The kid is my son. Not by Sylvia. Sylvia and I couldn't have kids—not in the cards for us."

I'm sitting cool as a cucumber, no *how do you do*, no *it's all news to me*. It's a confession, right out of Bernard Macfadden's *True Story, Truer Romance, Truest Experience*. A marriage gone lightly sour, a career diving for cover, not much happening except for poker with the boys and a chippy who likes to sing duets. Scoop tells me he picked up I.F.'s mother in a journalism class he was teaching part-time at L.I.U. twenty years ago.

"A good kid. I really liked her, had a lot of respect for that babe. Would have broken up with Sylvia for her, but she— Martha Gellhorn Washington—would you believe it, named for one of the great foreign correspondents of her time, who also never won a Polk Award. Anyway, Martha said it was just a fling. I was too old for her, not really her type. But she wanted to have the kid. When Martha's number was up, got hit by an external fuel tank jettisoned from a F14 Tomcat, something like that, there was our kid hanging in there, out in L.A. He thinks I done her wrong, set his mamalochen up for disaster. He drops the line to Sylvia. The rest of the story you can write for yourself."

Pablo is flashing a signal. I lip read: *Son las dos en punto.* I got to wrap it up now that it's 2 o'clock.

I say, "So your kid, I.F., winds up living with you and Sylvia. And the day of the poker game—was I.F. there for the Last Lunch?"

Scoop raises his hands and slaps them on the desk. "Turns out Sylvia is crazy about the kid. Moves I.F. right in with us, signs him on for Senior's full time. He's with her, day and night. Night and day. *You are the one. Only you beneath the moon and under the sun. Whether near to me or far . . .*" Scoop cuts out for the solo, but I got no time for musical interludes.

"Answer the question, Scoop," I say. "Where was I.F. when the mustard hit the fan?"

Scoop tells me I.F. was right there. "Matter of fact . . ." Scoop lowers his voice. I got no idea who he thinks is listening to us, but I register that this is prime cut information. "I'm not sure I.F. picked up those sandwiches from Junior's for us. Sylvia would hit the ceiling if she knew my guys and me were not even considering Senior's mini-stuffed. We are strictly Junior's disciples until—pardon the expression—until the day we die. We always order the same," Scoop says. "Sherlock and Front Page go halves on a pastrami and corned beef. For me it's white meat turkey, lettuce and tomato, with Russian on the side. The first week of each month we split a hunk of cheesecake."

"And the mustard?"

"I noticed a little blob on my jacket when James L., the old man who works part-time for Sylv, handed it back to me as I was coming out of the crapper after lunch. I may have took a swipe at it and smeared it on my cuff and fly. Who knows? I was deep into the game. I don't even remember unwrapping my sandwich. Once we upped the stakes to one and five and I'm down big bucks, what do I know from mustard? I'm thinking about losing C notes and lots of 'em. Last

I remember before the guys caved in was pouring the tea for Front Page, the decaf for Sherlock, the straight java for me," says Scoop, and breaks into song. *"I like java. I like tea. I like the java jive. It likes me . . ."*

He's into the soft shoe as Pablo Sanchez escorts him back to the holding cell.

As soon as we check out of the precinct house, Sylvia is all over me. "I knew you could solve it, Pistol Pete. So tell us, who done it?"

I say, "Slow and easy, sweetheart. Like I told you, I'm a little out of shape, been sitting on the bench too many years." Then I tell her I got to get a look at the scene of the crime.

We're in the neighborhood. A hop, skip, and jump and I'm sitting at a big table loaded with bowls of sauerkraut, pickles, jars of ketchup—mustard! There's not a customer in the joint. But the walls are plastered with pictures—all shots of the great Dodgers of our past—Hodges, Reese, Stanky, Roy Campanella, and a blowup the size of a billboard on Times Square of Scoop interviewing the immortal Jackie Robinson.

Sylvia ducks back into the kitchen to get us some eats. Never mind that I just come off half a late lunch. That's her cover. She wants me to cut it up with I.F., so he can tell me what an Auntie-Mame-stepmother she's turned out to be.

Only it doesn't break according to Sylvia's script.

I'm asking the questions and I.F., true to his name, talks straight. He's known his father was a Brooklyn newspaper hack since he was five years old.

"My mother told me his name, left me a number to call if anything happened to her when she ran off on foreign

assignments. The Balkans, Middle East, Afghanistan, anywhere someone was taking a shot, dropping a bomb, throwing a stone, was Mama's beat. I lived mostly in L.A. with
grandparents and eventually foster homes. No complaints.
When I heard my mother died, I checked in with the number she gave me. Sylvia answered the phone. She asked me
who I was. I told her. I didn't know Scoop never told her
about me. I guess I blew it. Less than a day later Scoop calls.
He's wiring me money to come to Brooklyn. He and Sylvia
have talked it over, he said. They want to meet me, get to
know me, make up for all the lost years."

The kid is telling me all this without a blink, a snicker, or
a tear.

"So you come to Brooklyn," I say, going for the extra
base. "What happens next?"

"I did a little preparation, beefing up." For the first time
I.F. half smiles. "When I want to know about a place I read
the poets and study the baseball teams. Are you familiar with
Marianne Moore's 'Keeping Their World Large'?"

Before I can apologize or fake it, the kid is into a verse:
"They fought the enemy,/we fight fat living and self-pity/ Shine, O
shine/unfalsifying sun on this sick scene."

I say, "I'm gonna think about that."

The kid is on a run. "Marianne Moore was born in
Kirkwood, Missouri, grew up in Carlisle, Pennsylvania, but
lived for a long time on Cumberland Street in Brooklyn."

"Hey, that's real interesting," I say. "Marianne Moore.
Soon as I reread *Boys of Summer* I'm gonna look into
Marianne Moore." Then, I send my fastball down the middle.
"So tell me, you know any reason Scoop would have to do in
Front Page and Sherlock?"

I.F. shrugs, gives his Dodger cap a twist and twirl. "How

many reasons you want?" he says. "Would about ten thousand dollars in debt from the poker games be a reason? Or the fact that he discovered soon as Sylvia heard about me she had a romp in the hay with each of them?" As he's circling the bases, I.F. goes on with a dose of Walt Whitman. *"I do not press my fingers across my mouth,/ I keep as delicate around the bowels as around the head and heart,/ Copulation is no more rank to me than death is."*

I'm getting that same uneasy feeling I get when his old man breaks into song. Songs, poetry, batting averages. Maybe I'm on to something. Call it the prayer gene.

I'm thinking over my next pitch when Sylvia's voice comes from the kitchen. "You boys ready for a little snack? This corned beef is right out of the brine. You never tasted nothing like it in your life." I hear the slicer and then Sylvia comes to the door with this kitchen saw. I never seen a chef in high heels and an apron color coordinated with her hair dye.

"So?" she says, pointing the slicer at me. "I can't wait any longer, Pistol Pete. Who done it?"

"Well, Sylv," I say. "We got five possibilities here."

"Solving a murder is that logical, an exercise in Kant's pure reason?" I.F. pulls the cap around so the Dodger logo is facing me.

"Starting back to front there is always the possibility of suicide, but a double suicide over a pastrami and corned beef?" I get an immediate waiver on number one. "So we have two, three, and four. Number two is Scoop with the mustard stains, who has motive and clues."

"I didn't hire you for that," Sylvia reminds me. "Not Scoop. My Scoop may be a good-for-nothing—but he'd never spoil perfectly good corned beef and pastrami sandwiches with poisoned mustard."

"Scoop is the patsy," I go on. "He's set up. Try it this way—someone with a motive to knock him off frames him for a double murder."

Sylvia calls into the kitchen, "James Lamar, we need coffee. Black with those sandwiches."

"That could be you, Sylvia," I say quietly. "You're number three on our suspect list."

"Me?" Sylvia stamps her foot and switches on the slicer.

Her eyes are shifting fast as Koufax's curveball. "You got to be out of your mind. I put up with that son of a bitch lying, cheating all these years, and you can't see I love him?"

"The motives are there for you, Sylv," I say again. "And you had the opportunity. How tough would it be for you to smear the mustard and plant the clues on Scoop's shirt, cuff, fly? Knock 'em all off with one big splash of doctored Gold's Own, or was it French's?"

I.F. has been sitting cool and easy but now he stands up, starts smacking a fist into a palm. "We don't use Gold's mustard," he says. "That's Junior's special blend. But when Junior's delivers, it's packets—no pre-smeared."

"You've obviously given this a lot of thought, sonny boy," I say to I.F. "So, you're telling me the sandwiches were made at Senior's? You got your old man and his two cronies squatting right there in your step-mamalochen's deli and it's your call on what to do about them ordering out."

"This is too much. You're insulting me." Sylvia switches off the slicer and plunks into a chair. She's sitting under a shot of Sandy Amoros's spectacular running catch of Berra's fly ball in the seventh game of the '55 Series.

"Let's assume the sandwiches were made here that fatal day. Nothing to do with Junior's. That suggests our killer is a home team spoiler."

"James Lamar, where are you when I need you?" Sylvia says again. "I want that coffee black."

"You're saying my father has been framed, and the killer, the person who smeared the mustard, works right here at Senior's?" The kid breaks off and, with a wry smile right out of the L.A. handbook, *We Own the Dodgers Now*, says, "Why not me? Abandoned son. Oedipus knocks off King Laius, also known as Seamus 'Scoop' O'Neil, and in the next act, according to your script, I marry Iocasta, also known as Mama Sylvia, and I inherit the Kingdom of Senior's."

"Marries his mother?" Sylvia repeats. "That is the most disgusting story I ever heard. I've had enough of you, Pistol Pete. I shoulda known better . . ."

"Let him talk," I.F. says, as the door from the kitchen swings open and a guy must be my age comes limping in carrying a tray of mini-deli sandwiches and a decanter of java.

"Tea time," I say, trying to change the mood. "Don't mind if I do." I move to the tray like Robinson feinting off third base. Then I sit back and say, "I'm not saying it is, just could be."

"So?" I.F. says. The Dodger cap is rotated so the logo no longer faces me. "Sylvia or me—who's your pleasure?"

"Youse want skimmed or regular with the coffee?" James Lamar is wearing a baseball cap, too, with the logo facing the wall. "Wese outa half an' half."

"Excuse me, James Lamar," I say. "Anybody ever call you Dusty?"

The smile is big as Willie Mays's glove making the basket catch. "For shure. For shure. And how'd you know dat?"

"Ladies and gentlemen," I say like Walter Alston calling Clem Labine in from the bullpen, "we got our *deus ex machina*."

James Lamar—Dusty!—plunks the tray down and makes a move for the mustard jar.

I'm on my feet, pull out the ole Smith and Wesson for which I plunked down 250 smackeroos for the permit just last year without any thought of ever using it again. "Not so fast, Dusty," I say. "And if you don't mind, would you be so kind as to pull the visor of that cap around?"

Sylvia is still not convinced. "What's that got to do with anything? What is going on here? And that Day Ox you was talking about . . ."

"*Deus ex machina*," I.F. corrects her. "God from the machine. Introduced at the last minute often by a crane in ancient Greek and Roman drama to resolve an insoluble dilemma."

"On the button," I say to I.F. "And if you will be so kind as to take a gander at Dusty's cap, you can appreciate the motive for murder."

"I don't see nothing," Sylvia says, "only a crummy old baseball cap with an SF logo."

"The logo of the San Francisco, formerly New York, Giants," says I.F. as the light is beginning to dawn. "We have here a former New York Giants fan who has never forgiven the Dodgers."

"You got it right, kid," Dusty snarls. "And I'm up to my keester with all this Dodger talk, all them pictures and not one shot of Master Melvin Ott, King Carl Hubbell, Sal Maglie, the Greatest Willie Mays . . ."

Before he can run down all the rosters from '35 through '57, I throw him the spitter: "And we might add James Lamar 'Dusty' Rhodes, who come from nowhere to run off with the 1954 World Series."

"You better believe it," Dusty says. ".667, two home runs, seben, I said seben runs batted in and dat was a four-game series. So where is Dusty on dis wall? Do I hear a woid, one stinkin' woid from any of them wiseguys pitchin' cards, talkin' Dodgers, Dodgers, Dodgers. Dem Bums. And youse. Youse got the noive to talk *Deus? Deus.* Latin prayers in this joint?"

Dusty goes quietly after that.

We spring Scoop the next afternoon. Sylvia wants to celebrate with a steak at Gage and Tollner's. She's had enough of the deli business—"Bad memories"—and declares this her farewell party.

I.F. invites us to join him for a stroll through the Brooklyn Museum. "I'd like to take a look at Bierstadt's *Storm in the Rockies, Mt. Rosalie.* A guy I met on the plane, flying in from L.A. last week, told me he's a friend of Robert Levinson who was the chairman of the board and could recommend me for a job there. Then we can amble over to the lobby of the former Paramount Theater. It's the Eugene & Beverly Luntey Commons of the Brooklyn Center, L.I.U. now. We could sit and read poems by Robert Donald Spector and maybe be lucky enough to run into JoAnn Allen or Mike Bush, all stars of their faculty."

Scoop breaks into a chorus of "Thanks for the Memories" and Sylvia takes his hand like two kids on their way to the boardwalk at Coney Island.

Out of the blue, I.F. says to me, "Harold Patrick Reiser, 1941 through 1948, a Dodgers' Dodger until he ran into a fence." Then he gently nudges my holster. "It's been a pleasure doing business with you, Pistol Pete."

WHEN ALL THIS WAS BAY RIDGE

BY TIM MCLOUGHLIN

Sunset Park

Standing in church at my father's funeral, I thought about being arrested on the night of my seventeenth birthday. It had occurred in the trainyard at Avenue X, in Coney Island. Me and Pancho and a kid named Freddie were working a three-car piece, the most ambitious I'd tried to that point, and more time-consuming than was judicious to spend trespassing on city property. Two Transit cops with German shepherds caught us in the middle of the second car. I dropped my aerosol can and took off, and was perhaps two hundred feet along the beginning of the trench that becomes the IRT line to the Bronx, when I saw the hand. It was human, adult, and severed neatly, seemingly surgically, at the wrist. My first thought was that it looked bare without a watch. Then I made a whooping sound, trying to take in air, and turned and ran back toward the cops and their dogs.

At the 60th Precinct, we three were ushered into a small cell. We sat for several hours, then the door opened and I was led out. My father was waiting in the main room, in front of the counter.

The desk sergeant, middle-aged, black, and noticeably bored, looked up briefly. "Him?"

"Him," my father echoed, sounding defeated.

"Goodnight," the sergeant said.

My father took my arm and led me out of the precinct.

As we cleared the door and stepped into the humid night he turned to me and said, "This was it. Your one free ride. It doesn't happen again."

"What did it cost?" I asked. My father had retired from the Police Department years earlier, and I knew this had been expensive.

He shook his head. "This once, that's all."

I followed him to his car. "I have two friends in there."

"Fuck'em. Spics. That's half your problem."

"What's the other half?"

"You have no common sense," he said, his voice rising in scale as it did in volume. By the time he reached a scream he sounded like a boy going through puberty. "What do you think you're doing out here? Crawling 'round in the dark with the niggers and the spics. Writing on trains like a hoodlum. Is this all you'll do?"

"It's not writing. It's drawing. Pictures."

"Same shit, defacing property, behaving like a punk. Where do you suppose it will lead?"

"I don't know. I haven't thought about it. You had your aimless time, when you got out of the service. You told me so. You bummed around for two years."

"I always worked."

"Part-time. Beer money. You were a roofer."

"Beer money was all I needed."

"Maybe it's all I need."

He shook his head slowly, and squinted, as though peering through the dirty windshield for an answer. "It was different. That was a long time ago. Back when all this was Bay Ridge. You could live like that then."

When all this was Bay Ridge. He was masterful, my father. He didn't say *when it was white*, or *when it was Irish*, or even the relatively tame *when it was safer.* No. When all this was Bay Ridge. As though it were an issue of geography. As though, somehow, the tectonic plate beneath Sunset Park had shifted, moving it physically to some other place.

I told him about seeing the hand.

"Did you tell the officers?"

"No."

"The people you were with?"

"No."

"Then don't worry about it. There's body parts all over this town. Saw enough in my day to put together a baseball team." He drove in silence for a few minutes, then nodded his head a couple of times, as though agreeing with a point made by some voice I could not hear. "You're going to college, you know," he said.

That was what I remembered at the funeral. Returning from the altar rail after receiving communion, Pancho walked passed me. He'd lost a great deal of weight since I'd last seen him, and I couldn't tell if he was sick or if it was just the drugs. His black suit hung on him in a way that emphasized his gaunt frame. He winked at me as he came around the casket in front of my pew, and flashed the mischievous smile that—when we were sixteen—got all the girls in his bed and all the guys agreeing to the stupidest and most dangerous stunts.

In my shirt pocket was a photograph of my father with a woman who was not my mother. The date on the back was five years ago. Their arms were around each other's waists and they smiled for the photographer. When we arrived at the cemetery I took the picture out of my pocket, and looked at it for perhaps the fiftieth time since I'd first discovered it.

There were no clues. The woman was young to be with my father, but not a girl. Forty, give or take a few years. I looked for any evidence in his expression that I was misreading their embrace, but even I couldn't summon the required naïveté. My father's countenance was not what would commonly be regarded as a poker face. He wasn't holding her as a friend, a friend's girl, or the prize at some retirement or bachelor party; he held her like a possession. Like he held his tools. Like he held my mother. The photo had been taken before my mother's death. I put it back.

I'd always found his plodding predictability and meticulous planning of insignificant events maddening. For the first time that I could recall, I was experiencing curiosity about some part of my father's life.

I walked from Greenwood Cemetery directly to Olsen's bar, my father's watering hole, feeling that I needed to talk to the men that nearly lived there, but not looking forward to it. Aside from my father's wake the previous night, I hadn't seen them in years. They were all Irish. The Irish among them were perhaps the most Irish, but the Norwegians and the Danes were Irish too, as were the older Puerto Ricans. They had developed, over time, the stereotypical hooded gaze, the squared jaws set in grim defiance of whatever waited in the sobering daylight. To a man they had that odd trait of the Gaelic heavy-hitter, that—as they attained middle age— their faces increasingly began to resemble a woman's nipple.

The door to the bar was propped open, and the cool damp odor of stale beer washed over me before I entered. That smell has always reminded me of the Boy Scouts. Meetings were Thursday nights in the basement of Bethany Lutheran Church. When they were over, I would have to pass Olsen's on my way home, and I usually stopped in to see my father. He would buy me a couple of glasses of beer—about all I could handle at thirteen—and leave with me after about an hour so we could walk home together.

From the inside looking out: Picture an embassy in a foreign country. A truly foreign country. Not a Western European ally, but a fundamentalist state perennially on the precipice of war. A fill-the-sandbags-and-wait-for-the-airstrike enclave. That was Olsen's, home to the last of the donkeys, the white dinosaurs of Sunset Park. A jukebox filled with Kristy McColl and the Clancy Brothers, and flyers tacked to the flaking walls advertising step-dancing classes, Gaelic lessons, and the memorial run to raise money for a scholarship in the name of a recently slain cop. Within three blocks of the front door you could attend a cockfight, buy crack, or pick up a streetwalker, but in Olsen's, it was always 1965.

Upon entering the bar for the first time in several years, I found its pinched dimensions and dim lighting more oppressive, and less mysterious, than I had remembered. The row of ascetic faces, and the way all conversation trailed off at my entrance, put me in mind of the legendary blue wall of silence in the police department. It is no coincidence that the force has historically been predominantly Irish. The men in Olsen's would be pained to reveal their zip code to a stranger, and I wasn't sure if even they knew why.

The bar surface itself was more warped than I'd recalled. The mirrors had oxidized and the white tile floor had been torn up in spots and replaced with odd-shaped pieces of green linoleum. It was a neighborhood bar in a neighborhood where such establishments are not yet celebrated. If it had been located in my part of the East Village, it would have long since achieved cultural-landmark status. I'd been living in Manhattan for five years and still had not adjusted to the large number of people who moved here from other parts of the country, and overlooked the spectacle of the city only to revere the mundane. One of my coworkers, herself a transplant, remarked that the coffee shop on my corner was *authentic*. In that they served coffee, I suppose she was correct.

I sat on an empty stool in the middle of the wavy bar and ordered a beer. I felt strangely nervous there without my father, like a child about to be caught doing something bad. Everyone knew me. Marty, the round-shouldered bartender, approached first, breaking the ice. He spoke around an enormous, soggy stub of a cigar, as he always did. And, as always, he seemed constantly annoyed by its presence in his mouth; as though he'd never smoked one before, and was surprised to discover himself chewing on it.

"Daniel. It's good to see you. I'm sorry for your loss."

He extended one hand, and when I did the same, he grasped mine in both of his and held it for a moment. It had to have been some sort of signal, because the rest of the relics in the place lurched toward me then, like some nursing-home theater guild performing *Night of the Living Dead*. They shook hands, engaged in awkward stiff hugs, and offered unintelligible condolences. Frank Sanchez, one of my father's closest friends, squeezed the back of my neck absently until I winced. I thanked them as best I could, and accepted the offers of free drinks.

Someone—I don't know who—thought it would be a good idea for me to have Jameson's Irish whiskey, that having been my father's drink. I'd never considered myself much of a drinker. I liked a couple of beers on a Friday night, and perhaps twice a year I would get drunk. I almost never drank hard liquor, but this crew was insistent, they were matching me shot for shot, and they were paying. It was the sort of thing my father would have been adamant about.

I began to reach for the photograph in my pocket several times and stopped. Finally I fished it out and showed it to the bartender. "Who is she, Marty?" I asked. "Any idea?"

The manner in which he pretended to scrutinize it told me that he recognized the woman immediately. He looked at the picture with a studied perplexity, as though he would have had trouble identifying my father.

"Wherever did you get such a thing?" he asked.

"I found it in the basement, by my father's shop."

"Ah. Just come across it by accident then."

The contempt in his voice seared through my whiskey glow, and left me as sober as when I'd entered. He knew, and if he knew they all knew. And a decision had been reached to tell me nothing.

"Not by accident," I lied. "My father told me where it was and asked me to get it."

Our eyes met for a moment. "And did he say anything about it?" Marty asked. "Were there no instructions or suggestions?"

"He asked me to take care of it," I said evenly. "To make everything all right."

He nodded. "Makes good sense," he said. "That would be best served by letting the dead sleep, don't you think? Forget it, son, let it lie." He poured me another drink, sloppily, like the others, and resumed moving his towel over the bar, as though he could obliterate the mildewed stench of a thousand spilled drinks with a few swipes of the rag.

I drank the shot down quickly and my buzz returned in a rush. I hadn't been keeping track, but I realized that I'd had much more than what I was used to, and I was starting to feel dizzy. The rest of the men in the room looked the same as when I walked in, the same as when I was twelve. In the smoke-stained bar mirror I saw Frank Sanchez staring at me from a few stools away. He caught me looking and gestured for me to come down.

"Sit, Danny," he said when I got there. He was drinking boilermakers. Without asking, he ordered each of us another round. "What were you talking to Marty about?"

I handed Frank the picture. "I was asking who the woman is."

He looked at it and placed it on the bar. "Yeah? What'd he say?"

"He said to let it lie."

Frank snorted. "Typical donkey," he said. "Won't answer a straight question, but has all kinds of advice on what you should do."

From a distance in the dark bar I would have said that Frank Sanchez hadn't changed much over the years, but I was close to him now, and I'd seen him only last night in the unforgiving fluorescent lighting of the funeral home. He'd been thin and handsome when I was a kid, with blue-black hair combed straight back, and the features and complexion of a Hollywood Indian in a John Wayne picture. He'd thickened in the middle over the years, though he still wasn't fat. His reddish brown cheeks were illuminated by the roadmap of broken capillaries that seemed an entrance requirement for "regular" status at Olsen's. His hair was still shockingly dark, but now with a fake Jerry Lewis sheen and plenty of scalp showing through in the back. He was a retired homicide detective. His had been one of the first Hispanic families in this neighborhood. I knew he'd moved to Fort Lee, New Jersey long ago, though my father said that he was still in Olsen's every day.

Frank picked up the picture and looked at it again, then

looked over it at the two sloppy rows of bottles along the back bar. The gaps for the speed rack looked like missing teeth.

"We're the same," he said. "Me and you."

"The same, how?"

"We're on the outside, and we're always looking to be let in."

"I never gave a damn about being on the inside here, Frank."

He handed me the photo. "You do now."

He stood then, and walked stiffly back to the men's room. A couple of minutes later Marty appeared at my elbow, topped off my shot, and replaced Frank's.

"It's a funny thing about Francis," Marty said. "He's a spic who's always hated the spics. So he moves from a spic neighborhood to an all-white one, then has to watch as it turns spic. So now he's got to get in his car every day and drive back to his old all-spic neighborhood, just so he can drink with white men. It's made the man bitter. And," he nodded toward the glasses, "he's in his cups tonight. Don't take the man too seriously."

Marty stopped talking and moved down the bar when Frank returned.

"What'd Darby O'Gill say to you?" he asked.

"He told me you were drunk," I said, "and that you didn't like spics."

Frank widened his eyes. "Coming out with revelations like that, is he? Hey, Martin," he yelled, "next time I piss tell him JFK's been shot!" He drained his whiskey, took a sip of beer, and turned his attention back to me. "Listen. Early on, when I first started on the job—years back, I'm talking— there was almost no spades in the department; even less spics. I was the only spic in my precinct, only one I knew of in Brooklyn. I worked in the seven-one, Crown Heights. Did five years there, but this must've been my first year or so.

"I was sitting upstairs in the squad room typing attendance reports. Manual typewriters back then. I was good too, fifty or sixty words a minute—don't forget, English ain't my first language. See, I learned the forms. The key is knowin' the forms, where to plug in the fucking numbers. You could type two hundred words a minute, but you don't know the forms, all them goddamn boxes, you're sitting there all day.

"So I'm typing these reports—only uniform in a room full of bulls, only spic in a room full of harps—when they bring in the drunk."

Frank paused to order another shot, and Marty brought one for me too. I was hungry and really needed to step outside for some air, but I wanted to hear Frank's story. I did want to know how he thought we were similar, and I hoped he would talk about the photo. He turned his face to the ceiling and opened his mouth like a child catching rain, and he poured the booze smoothly down his throat.

"You gotta remember," he continued, "Crown Heights was still mostly white back then, white civilians, white skells. The drunk is just another mick with a skinfull. But what an obnoxious cocksucker. And loud.

"Man who brought him in is another uniform, almost new as me. He throws him in the cage and takes the desk next to mine to type his report. Only this guy can't type, you can see he's gonna be there all day. Takes him ten minutes to get the paper straight in the damn machine. And all this time the goddamn drunk is yelling at the top of his lungs down the length of the squad room. You can see the bulls are gettin' annoyed. Everybody tells him to shut up, but he keeps on, mostly just abusing the poor fuck that brought him in, who's still struggling with the report, his fingers all smudged with ink from the ribbons.

"On and on he goes: 'Your mother blows sailors . . . Your wife fucks dogs . . . You're all queers, every one of you.' Like that. But I mean, really, it don't end, it's like he never gets tired.

"So the guy who locked him up gets him outa the cage and walks him across the room. Over in the corner they got one of these steam pipes, just a vertical pipe, no radiator or nothing. Hot as a motherfucker. So he cuffs the drunk's hands around the pipe, so now the drunk's gotta stand like this"—Frank formed a huge circle with his arms, as if he were hugging an invisible fat woman—"or else he gets burned. And just bein' that close to the heat, I mean, it's fuckin' awful. So the uniform walks away, figuring that'll shut the scumbag up, but it gets worse.

"Now, the bulls are all pissed at the uniform for not beatin' the drunk senseless before he brought him in, like any guy with a year on the street would know to do. The poor fuck is still typing the paperwork at about a word an hour, and the asshole is still at it, 'Your daughter fucks niggers. When I get out I'll look your wife up—again.' Then he looks straight at the uniform, and the uniform looks up. Their eyes lock for a minute. And the drunk says this: 'What's it feel like to know that every man in this room thinks you're an asshole?' Then the drunk is quiet and he smiles."

Marty returned then, and though I felt I was barely hanging on, I didn't dare speak to refuse the drink. Frank sat silently while Marty poured, and when he was done Frank stared at him until he walked away.

"After that," he continued in a low voice, "it was like slow motion. Like everything was happening underwater. The uniform stands up, takes his gun out, and points it at the drunk. The drunk never stops smiling. And then the uniform pulls the trigger, shoots him right in the face. The drunk's head like explodes, and he spins around the steam pipe—all the way— once, before he drops.

"For a second everything stops. It's just the echo and the smoke and blood on the wall and back window. Then, time speeds up again. The sergeant of detectives, a little leprechaun from the other side—must've bribed his way past the height requirement—jumps over his desk and grabs up a billy club. He lands next to the uniform, who's still holding the gun straight out, and he clubs him five or six times on the forearm, hard and fast, *whap-whap-whap*. The gun drops with the first hit but the leprechaun don't stop till the bone breaks. We all hear it snap.

"The uniform pulls his arm in and howls, and the sergeant throws the billy club down and screams at him: 'The next time . . . the next time, it'll be your head that he breaks before you were able to shoot him. Now get him off the pipe before there's burns on his body.' And he storms out of the room."

Frank drank the shot in front of him and finished his beer. I didn't move. He looked at me and smiled. "The whole squad room," he said, "jumped into action. Some guys uncuffed the drunk; I helped the uniform out. Got him to a hospital. Coupla guys got rags and a pail and started cleaning up.

"Now, think about that," Frank said, leaning in toward me and lowering his voice yet again. "I'm the only spic there. The only other uniform. There had to be ten bulls. But the sergeant, he didn't have to tell anybody what the plan was, or to keep their mouth shut, or any fucking thing. And there was no moment where anybody worried about me seeing it, being a spic. We all knew that coulda been any one of us.

That's the most on-the-inside I ever felt. Department now, it's a fucking joke. Affirmative action, cultural-diversity training. And what've you got? Nobody trusts anybody. Guys afraid to trust their own partners." He was whispering, and starting to slur his words.

I began to feel nauseated. It's a joke, I thought. A cop's made-up war story. "Frank, did the guy die?"

"Who?"

"The drunk. The man that got shot."

Frank looked confused, and a bit annoyed. "Of course he died."

"Did he die right away?"

"How the fuck should I know? They dragged him outa the room in like a minute."

"To a hospital?"

"Was a better world's all I'm saying. A better world. And you always gotta stay on the inside, don't drift, Danny. If you drift, nobody'll stick up for you."

Jesus, did he have a brogue? He certainly had picked up that lilt to his voice that my father's generation possessed. That half-accent that the children of immigrants acquire in a ghetto. I had to get out of there. A few more minutes and I feared I'd start sounding like one of these tura-lura-lura motherfuckers myself.

I stood, probably too quickly, and took hold of the bar to steady myself. "What about the picture, Frank?"

He handed it to me. "Martin is right," he said slowly, "let it lie. Why do you care who she was?"

"Who she *was*? I asked who she *is*. Is she dead, Frank? Is that what Marty meant by letting the dead rest?"

"Martin . . . Marty meant . . ."

"I'm right here, Francis," Marty said, "and I can speak for

myself." He turned to me. "Francis has overindulged in a few jars," he said. "He'll nap in the back booth for a while and be right as rain for the ride home."

"Is that the way it happened, Frank? Exactly that way?"

Frank was smiling at his drink, looking dreamily at his better world. "Who owns memory?" he said.

"Goodnight, Daniel," Marty said. "It was good of you to stop in."

I didn't respond, just turned and slowly walked out. One or two guys gestured at me as I left, the rest seemed not to notice or care.

I removed the picture from my pocket again when I was outside, an action that had taken on a ritualistic feel, like making the sign of the cross. I did not look at it this time, but began tearing it in strips, lengthwise. Then I walked, and bent down at street corners, depositing each strip in a separate sewer along Fourth Avenue.

He'd told me that he'd broken his arm in a car accident, pursuing two black kids who had robbed a jewelry store.

As I released the strips of paper through the sewer gratings, I thought of the hand in the subway tunnel, and my father's assertion that there were many body parts undoubtedly littering the less frequently traveled parts of the city. Arms, legs, heads, torsos; and perhaps all these bits of photo would find their way into disembodied hands. A dozen or more hands, each gripping a strip of photograph down in the wet slime under the street. Regaining a history, a past, that they lost when they were dismembered, making a connection that I never would.

PRACTICING

BY ELLEN MILLER

Canarsie

When my father started to bench-press me, I figured he meant business. For real. Finally.

By the time he started bench-pressing me, I'd already wisely given up hope that he'd ever make good on his promise. But the bench-pressing seemed an encouraging sign, enough of a reason to believe my father, so I suspended my doubt.

I didn't simply hope. I *believed*.

He'd been promising for two years—twenty-five percent of the time I'd spent being alive, being his daughter. Being alive and being his daughter were the same single thing. The only thing and everything. All I wanted from the world.

The first time was supposed to be my sixth birthday present. I bugged him. I nagged him, like a wife. I irritated myself when my talking-out-loud voice would whine—like a child, which I insisted I wasn't—*But you promised*, even though my thinking-inside-myself voice had long ago admitted defeat, told me the truth, convincingly and correctly maintaining, *Nothing doing. Pretend he never said a word. Forget it.* Then, out of the blue, he'd say, "Later, I promise," and he'd give me a wink. Dad was the only man I'd ever meet who didn't, upon winking, instantly become a calamitous schmuck. "We have plenty of time."

The promise itself was a present, a gift he offered not only to me, but also to time, to the future, stored in a box filled with mystery, tension, delay, buildup, all to be revealed later. If his promise had been packaged and wrapped, the gift-card's envelope, taped seamlessly to the top, would have read, *Do Not Open Me Until . . .* but the calligraphy would have stopped short of naming the holiday. He kept me guessing and waiting, waiting, but since I couldn't tell time, I couldn't know for how long. Exactly what, at eight years old, did *later* mean? His words, spoken to the future, "We'll go later, next month," didn't sound a helluva lot different from, "We'll go later, in fifteen years." *One month. Fifteen years.* What was *later*? When did *later* bleed into *too late*? How much time was *plenty of time*? What sensations could be expected when *plenty of time* elapsed and disappeared? When did *too late* become *never*? Time, always warped and subjective, was especially so when I hadn't been around long enough to develop and practice the rote, unoriginal, possibility-canceling, chance-choking, constricting—that is, *adult*—habits of experiencing time, living in time, doing time, apprehending in a felt way, without having to concentrate so hard my eye sockets pounded, how long fragments of time were supposed to last until they stopped being fragmentary and became durable, lasting. *How long? Long enough. To last. Until. Lasting.*

Instead of bringing me up, the day I turned six he brought home a squat glow-in-the-dark clock. An alarm clock. I couldn't read it; I couldn't set it. I'd look at its various meaningless appendages—arms, hands, digits—then quickly turn from the pale, sickish, muffled green glow. When I couldn't sleep, the tick contributed its two cents to my considerable, familiar insomnia and anxiety.

Soon I appreciated the stunning appropriateness of the term *alarm clock*.

Perhaps he intended to teach me early on—to route my thoughts along an acceptable, suitable course immediately, starting my expectations off right at age six—that clocks were meant to be punched.

His promise, so handsomely packaged in that gift-box, contained nothing, so I'd done good to halt hope in its tracks. To stop hoping for Dad to make good on his word, or for much of anything else, seemed a wise idea, a useful policy to adopt more generally, to apply more globally, as an apotropaic. A prophylactic against disappointment. Disappointment was dangerous.

But he started again just before I turned eight. "We'll have so much fun. Just you wait." Repetition, and the slippage of much too much time—even I knew by then how long was *too long*, how much was *much too much*—between the initial promise and its most recent nonfulfillment, emptied the promise-box of all the substance it probably had never had, so I gave him a piece of my mind. "You're full of bull. You're just all phony baloney."

"I'm what?" Mock horror. Mock indignation. Mock mockery.

"I said, Dad, that you are all yak and no shack." I didn't know what I meant, but I liked how tough it sounded.

"The things that come out of your mouth." He snorted. "Where do you get them?" In mock fury, he commanded, "Get your tush over here. Right now, you little . . . you little . . . you little *you*."

He shook his head gravely, freighting the final pronoun, *you*, with extra volume and vocal emphasis, so that the *you*, by whom he meant *me*, almost sounded like it referred to something special. Like some languages had one *you* for politely addressing outside-people and another *you* for informally addressing inside-people; other languages had one *you* for speaking to superiors and another *you* for speaking to subordinates; English—rather, my Dad's peculiar delivery of English—conferred upon me a separate, specific second-person pronoun. It sounded and was spelled the same as other *you*'s, but Dad's *you*, as in, "you little . . . *you*," referred just to *me*. My very own second-person pronoun! Now *that* was one tremendous gift if there ever was one.

But even having my very own personal pronoun was risky, because it's pretty tough to keep stopped-hope stopped up when *you* are getting all *you*ed up, when someone you really like keeps promising you scary, fun, exciting stuff—and even tougher for the *me* of that moment to remain securely devoid of hope, to make smart, self-denying decisions with Dad *you*ing me—the long ooo of it broad and extended, like a hand.

"Now," he announced, rubbing his hands together—like a man who's busted his ass all week, eaten crow at a job he hates, but it's Friday, and his dinner at Abbracciamento on the Pier, a thick steak pizzaiolo, fatty, bloody meat sizzling, cheese bubbling, is being served by a hot-to-trot miniskirt, he's salivating, thinking, *this is gonna be yummy*—"we start practicing." Before I noticed his swift crouch and downward reach, he'd grabbed my ankles and flipped me, along with the rest of the visible world, upside down. Queasy with suddenness, I tried focusing hard, to keep everything from whirling too wildly, on the paint-splatters everywhere covering his stumble-proof, good-luck work boots. Together, we slid to the floor. I righted myself to sitting too fast; my subadequately upholstered tush—a bony *butt* without cushioning *ocks*—banged to the linoleum. "We gotta be prepared," he declared. "I'm gonna need some big muscles if we're gonna do this."

I was a weedy child at sixty pounds. My father was a bridgeman. A workingman. To work, in the true, original sense, meant to move heavy objects, to transfer energy from one system to another, causing an object, against its own resistance and stationary inertia, to move. Work called for muscle, math, multiplication. Work was the product of the force used to move something stubbornly heavy and the distance the object had successfully moved in the direction of that force. Dad had been working for a long time.

His biceps were strip steaks, marbled not with fat, but lined with web-works of veins materializing from under his skin. "Put them back! Put them back inside!" I'd cry, when I was little—which, by the time I turned eight, I adamantly decreed I wasn't, not anymore—while futilely pushing and pressing individual bulging veins back underneath his skin to keep him intact, to return his veins to their proper place inside, where all matters blood-related belonged. And Dad's thighs and calves were sometimes hard to look at without contemplating mint jelly.

The man had muscle. Nonetheless, he was determined to bench-press me, sans bench, every night. For strength. For practice. A delaying tactic, I understood later, but then, like a fool, I'd already reversed my own prior, better judgment. Stupidly, I again hoped, and I believed that his teasing promise had finally and for real tipped away from the tease toward its promise: the bridge—although I would have gone with him anywhere. I would have had to have gone with him anywhere. Lucky, lucky me: As it happened, I'd been hungering to go up on a bridge with him for years, but if he'd have wanted to go somewhere else, or if he'd have wanted to do something else, there wouldn't have been much else for me, other than to go, and to do.

After dinner we'd meet in the living room for practicing. He'd go horizontal on the floor, stretching his arms to their widest span. Like a career waiter, deftly steadying a sterling tray, piled nearly to toppling with fragile tableware, he'd broaden and flatten his right hand's fingers, balancing me delicately, without a flinch, at the bony hollows of my throat and chest. I'd soften my scrawny structure, make myself pliant. When he'd stabilized my torso, he'd wrap his flung left palm around my ankles for lift-off. Muscles and veins popping out all over him, our bodies perpendicular, his arms pumped my body—first up and aloft, far from his, then down, low and close—up and down, up and down until I was flying and falling, flying and falling, breathless, giddy, shrieking, stoned with giggles. He grunted with pretend exertion, like it was so laborious. When he decided we were finished—always, always, he made this determination unilaterally, so I could never anticipate when the end was approaching and temper my wishes accordingly—he lowered me, I rolled off him, and he moaned, exhaling gigantically, like he was so winded.

Bedtime followed. He'd toss me like a gunny sack over one shoulder and carry me firefighter-style to the living room couch, which was my bed, right there in the room where we practiced. Not far to get to my bed. No transitional cooling-off time. After the wild velocity and proximity of practicing, the end's abruptness, the severance accompanying his "Good-night, *you*"—separations always hitting the one who stays behind harder than they hit the one who goes on ahead—I'd marinate in a living room redolent with breath, heat, his man-smell, my flannelly kid-having-fun smell, while he went away to his own bedroom. I'd have trouble falling asleep in that still-buzzing living room. Overstimulated, alone, all jagged up, for hours I'd twist myself into pretzels of indecision.

Should I or shouldn't I? I shouldn't. I shouldn't. I knew that I shouldn't.

Much later on, comfortable without the burden and benefit of empirical evidence to negate or support my hypothesis, I'd maintain that sexual acts per se were meager foreplay for the truer pleasure, the deeper intimacy, of shared sleep. Whoever has access to a helpless, sleeping body owns it, controls it, can do anything to it, so it was natural that I'd only ever slept with Dad. Sleeping with him was bad. I knew that. I also knew that bad things weren't necessarily wrong things, but interrupting his sleep was criminal; if we'd had religion, it would have been sinful. Hours before completely confessing to my sorry self that I'd already decided to go ahead and do it, I'd cringe with the afterward-shame, the dirty regret that should have sunk in later—or the next morning, his eyes still bloodshot, his features absent of all signs of being rested—and which should have deterred me. I hated myself for interfering with his sleep, even more so for loving to do it. For exploiting the wakeful one's God-like power of ultimate say-so over a defenseless body. He worked very hard at a dangerous job to keep me housed, schooled, fed, clothed. He needed rest. Badly. Too often, always knowing better, I couldn't defeat the urge to do wrong, especially once the light appeared, and I'd re-remember that not having closed my eyes during the night would neither retard nor prevent the arrival of the too-bright morning, of another next day with unbounded possibilities to be survived or not.

The dark was a mild worry. What kept me awake and afraid was me. Something about me. I scared myself. Lots. *Grow up.* My thinking-inside-myself voice told me off. *Stop being a baby.* I'd abandon the couch, slip into his grown-man's bed, straddling his chest, gently, gently alighting my fingers along his lash-lines. Softly, softly, and firmly, too, I'd press his lids up and open, until I saw his red-webbed eyes' whites, and I asked, I begged, "Dad? Are you in there?"

"Of course, Bee," he'd mumble sleepily. As if the answer was a certainty beyond all doubt, that his still being in there, inside himself, whole within his own intact body, as planned, as promised, would always be the case.

*

NEW YORK CRIMINAL LAW STATUTES: PENAL LAW, PART 3.

Title O. Offenses against Marriage, the Family, and the Welfare of Children and Incompetents.
Article 260. Offenses Relating to Children, Disabled Persons, and Vulnerable Elderly Persons.

§ 260.10. Endangering the welfare of a child
A person is guilty of endangering the welfare of a child when:
1. He knowingly acts in a manner likely to be injurious to the physical, mental or moral welfare of a child less than seventeen years old or directs or authorizes such child to engage in an occupation involving a substantial risk of danger to his life; or
2. Being a parent, guardian or other person legally charged with the care or custody of a child less than eighteen years old, he fails or refuses to exercise reasonable diligence in the control of such child to prevent him from becoming an "abused child," a "neglected child," a "juvenile delinquent," or a "person in need of supervision," as those terms

are defined in articles ten, three and seven of the family court act.

Endangering the welfare of a child is a class A misdemeanor.

If caught, that's a year or less in jail. No one with even half a brain in his head gets caught.

⚜

Canarsie Pier's stink of briny rot rendered plausible what otherwise seemed unlikely: that Canarsie had once been a sleepy fishing village. Ninety years before Dad and I stood at our jump-off point for more sophisticated practicing—"a whole new level," he'd said—most of the neighborhood's few thousand residents, mainly Italian immigrants, made their living fishing, crabbing, clamming, or oystering Jamaica Bay's rich waters and beds. By the 1920s pollution and the Great Depression had destroyed Canarsie's shell-fishing industry. Shellfish, aquatic homebodies, were loath to travel far from home, and they generally remained inside the calcareous houses they built for themselves. Food was delivered to their bodies by built-in siphons that drew water into their shells for filter-feeding: first capturing food, then spitting out water. I'd guiltily consider the attachment of shellfish to their houses whenever Dad and I collected shells at Brighton Beach: Every shell in our dry, deadly hands was once someone else's house! How selfish to bring back to our home, for frivolous ornamentation, the self-made homes of other beings who'd have preferred to stay put, soft bodies encased under solid cover, however temporary and illusory the protection might be.

If sedentary living made clams and other shellfish suscep-
tible to accumulations of high concentrations of human-made
poisons—bacterial coliforms from sewage, polychlorinated
biphenyls from industry—the Bay's fish traveled for food, in
mobile homes of skin and scale, to mixed and open Atlantic
waters, so fish weren't as vulnerable to dire accumulations of
pollutants. In warm weather, crag-faced, gravel-voiced old-
timers would cast long for eel and fluke or snag butterfish or
samplings of Jamaica Bay's increasing population of Canarsie
White Fish—floating used condoms—right off the Pier's
decaying edges. Word on the Pier, from above, state and federal environmental officials, and from below, locals, people
like us, was: "You can fish, but you can't clam."

Canarsie Beach Park was part of Gateway National
Recreation Area—not a *National Park,* as if a park was too
much to wish for; we needed to maintain realistically low
greenery expectations—but a *Recreation Area.* Still, the place
was Federal enough to have behatted, uniformed rangers.
And rules. The Department of Health had officially and con-
sistently declared Jamaica Bay unswimmable for fifty years:
No primary-contact recreation—activities in which bodies
made direct contact with raw water, especially total bodily
submersion—allowed. Secondary contact recreation, like
fishing or boating, where skin contact with water was mini-
mal and ingestion improbable, was permitted. Clamming, I
guessed, was ultra-forbidden because it required getting the
whole body into the water to dig.

Practicing here, jumping off Canarsie Pier into Jamaica
Bay, to simulate the worst potential payout of our gamble
with gravity—falling together off a bridge into deep water,
which he risked every day, just not while toting me along—
required forbidden primary contact recreation. Immersion in

Jamaica Bay "violated Federal rules," Dad warned, voice somber, conspiratorially soft, "As in, *the Feds*. You get it?"

"I got it."

"Good."

Bench-pressing hadn't been practicing; it was pre-training, basic conditioning, a barely callisthenic, chicken-feed beginner's warm-up leading us to this. To Canarsie Pier. For the *for-real practicing*—if those particular words, strung together and placed next to each other, made sense. Which they didn't.

Dad started when he was fourteen. Until his death at forty-five, every workday of his life, he was scared. Two kinds of work were obtainable in the world: the safe and the dangerous. Experience and practice never made Dad unafraid. Silently, without fanfare, he tolerated extreme fear-states and accepted the probability of grave injury or death as standard workaday inevitabilities, like lunch with the gang or alone up on a scaffold, like fatigue, like fumes. His morning routine: get into whites, shave, shower, shit, like a military man, brush teeth, drink pot of coffee, slap on boots and cap, drive to site, start working, get crushingly, heart-stoppingly, *fittingly* panicked about dying in the coming hours. Dad did frightening things that other people didn't want to do; other people didn't have to do them, because people like Dad did. Blood poisoning did him in after twenty-four years of exposure to industrial chemicals, mostly paints containing an odorless, oily, poisonous benzene derivative, absorbed through skin: *aniline blue*. *Aniline blue* sounded like a song title or poem, the name of a daughter or lover. Lyrical, sing-song *aniline blue* killed him, but before that happened, I'd planned on his dying in a bridge fall.

* * *

There were laws against it.

Child protection laws with tucked-in bylaws that defined bringing children to dangerous workplaces as criminal offenses. Take Our Daughters to Work Day wasn't designed for the daughters of pile driver, jack hammer, or forklift operators. Taking kids to perilous worksites violated child endangerment laws, laws ratified and upheld—lackadaisically, since the continuance of selected human genera wasn't a big deal, even when specimens were found in bulk—for protection I didn't want.

The laws against it didn't stop us. Did laws ever stop anyone who wanted to do something really bad from doing something really bad? A failure of nerve stopped us. *His.* All his. He, the adroit, well-built, well-practiced man, who did it daily, for real, chickened out. I, who hadn't yet mastered long division or my dread surrounding it, was ready to jump right in.

Upon starting work at a new job, Dad would half-promise and half-threaten to cart me along to the worksite, fix me in place around his tough neck, my legs parted, one leg dangling off each of his shoulders, and lug me around the job all day, up and down the tiers of the bridge, everywhere work required him to be while he painted. A regular workday, but with a Beth on his back. He'd try not to let me fall. He'd do the best he could. His six feet and three inches—a tall Jew!—guaranteed me an even better view than his of water, sky, skyline, land, of the whole place that Mark LaPlace, a mixed-blood Mohawk, who, along with many Indian ironworkers, drove in every week from the Caughnawaga reservation near Montreal, called the City of Man-Made Mountains.

Earthbound, at home or school, the world was scary and too big as it was. High on a partially completed bridge, higher yet on Dad's shoulders, the world would swell to unmanageable dimensions, awesome frights, sickening beauties. The anticipation of visual sublimity wasn't what thrilled me at every promise-threat. I thrilled to Dad's singular power to scare me, to his correspondingly exclusive power to soothe me. Dad could reassure me; I'd *believe* his reassurances, trust in them, because he knew, the cells that made him *him* understood how bad fear could get. Climbing together, he'd have his rope, hook, muscle-meat, and deeply treaded, break-a-leg boots, acting on behalf of his physical integrity and safety. All I'd have was a perfunctory pat on the head, a *knock 'em dead, kiddo,* and his body. I'd be terrified and love it, love him for terrifying me, for his unique capacity to assuage terror he'd authored himself. If some evening, he'd casually, passingly mention taking me up—*maybe tomorrow . . . you never know, do you?*—the next morning, suited up in my dungaree overalls, prepared for action, I'd park my tush on his lunch pail, so he couldn't leave without first reckoning with me, as a housecat might tuck her body within the lining of a suitcase her owner was packing for a journey, not-so-subtly notifying her master, *You're not going anywhere unless you take me, too.* As if the cat, no matter how well-loved, had any say at all in the matter.

Every day he left without taking me, until I was twelve and *God damn it to Hell* he died and stopped *not* taking me.

Before he pulled that stunt, he kept on pledging and daring me to go. I'd dare him back with a fiercely incautious, *You'd better believe it!* As if I, no matter how well-loved, had any say at all in the matter.

* * *

Every one of New York City's children grew up in the shadows of bridges. A smaller subset grew up or died in the penumbrae of bridge deaths. Child endangerment was a Class A misdemeanor, as naughty as a misdemeanor could be before it graduated up a grade to felony. So it was one crime, child endangerment, if I hung around bridge bases when school was out so Dad could half-look after me—babysitters and summer camp didn't exist in our economic cosmology, the unfeasibility of camp accounting for my never learning how to swim—and it was another crime, child neglect—which was often a felony, not to mention a big fat bore—if he left me alone at home.

An outlaw either way.

Even when school was in session, most of the guys in all the gangs brought their sons to work, where they received their real education. Bridge-building was existence itself, what their fathers before them had done, what their sons after them would probably do. Ironworkers formed multi-generational lines of risk-takers, cold-nerved men bonded together like the high steel it was a life's assignment to connect. Those burly, balletic men—who took chances only circus acrobats, suicidal souls, Wallendas, or bridgemen would take, who pronounced me *cuter than a button,* who bear-hugged me *till the guacamole would come outa them ears,* who gave me quarters just because I was Lefty Tedesky's girl—were criminals? Plain as day, it couldn't have been a crime when Chicky Testaverde, who spun cable, brought his fourteen-year-old, Danny, to a job, and it couldn't have been a crime when a tall ladder caught Danny's curious eye, and the boy asked, "Can I climb that?"

Chicky replied, in a resigned, benumbed, *oh-no-here's-where-it-all-begins* voice, "Awright, but don't fall." Could

Chicky authoritatively have refused, without Danny laughing in his face as father and son stood right there on a bridge-construction site, where Chicky was now working iron, where both might have been remembering that Chicky's father, Danny's grandfather, had worked the Williamsburg Bridge, lifting steel beams with derricks pulled by horses?

Danny climbed that ladder higher and higher, until he stood alone on a slippery top beam—a beam much higher than Chicky had bargained for or would have allowed if Danny had asked—and looked around, taking in the world's magnitude, and marveled at how extraordinarily far he could see from that height, and instantly decided that ironwork was what he'd someday do. Down at the base, Chicky went all-out ape. "Get down, Danny, you crazy fuck, damn you! You'll kill yourself up there. And if you die, Danny boy? You know what'll happen if you die?" Danny smiled down at everyone, smiled what the men called a *shit-eating grin*. I couldn't see how eating shit was anything to grin about, but I figured adults knew things I was too young to understand. "If you die," Chicky screamed at the sky, "I. Will. Fucking. Kill. You."

Wearing an *aw-shucks-I'm-caught-but-I'm-cute* mug, Danny climbed down. Everyone, high and low—physically, up on the bridge and down at the base, and professionally, at every station within high steel's complex system of ranking its men—applauded and cheered. One after another, ironworkers thumped his back hard; sometimes truly to hurt him, because he'd done wrong, he'd gone against his father, and sometimes to congratulate him, as a display of respect, because he'd proven himself bridge-worthy. Danny had demonstrated his passion for and merit within his family's legacy precisely by defying it in its current incarnation: Chicky. Mostly the men's back-clapping extended both—

contempt and admiration—through the infliction of pain. Just a little pain.

Or a lot. But a lot usually happened at home. Like what they did in public was practice for what they'd do at home. Like they saved *a lot* up during the day. For later.

Chicky played at grumbling and grousing but couldn't persuasively beat down his smile—crooked-lipped, prominently lacking some teeth, but jam-packed with filial pride—when he submitted that Danny's ascent had earned Danny his first beer. Chicky kept a cooler with sodas and beers in his Buick's trunk on days when the walking bosses weren't around. He called, "Little Tedesky!" I jumped to attention. "Couldja make yourself useful? Shake a leg? Get my boy here a beer?"

Chicky tossed me his car keys and threw me an approving nod when I caught them no problem. Keds crunching gravel, I ran toward the parking lot, delighted to have a task to fulfill for the men. Danny, overjoyed with his big day's second distinct launch into masculine adulthood—his illicit, under-age drink, perhaps not his first, as Chicky chose to think—jogged close behind me.

"Today's your day," I said, palming the clutch of keys off to him. "You get to do the whole thing." He unlocked and opened the Buick's trunk, pried off the cooler's squeaky Styrofoam lid, retrieved a Rheingold, took a long pull. He offered me a sip.

"Just don't tell." Immediately following the initial sip, my arms and legs felt heavy and achy, but they ached good. Another sip, and they ached real good. Another, and I became unsteady. I grabbed Danny's arm so I wouldn't skin my knees stumbling to the gravel.

I'd never seen so hairy an arm on someone so young. Up

close. With my free hand, I touched the hair on the arm I held hostage, mussing the hair against the whorls of its natural growth configuration, then smoothing it back, as I'd done at home with the wall-to-wall shag. Back and forth, up and down his arm. I was simultaneously lost in and intensely concentrated on the beat, the rhythm of cyclically creating swirling arm-hair chaos and then returning it to tidy normalcy. He didn't stop me. His breath was raggedy. I continued stroking, ruining a pattern, restoring a pattern.

Distantly, Chicky hollered, "I said one beer, not the whole six-pack." Danny neither responded nor registered hearing his father. Now he had gooseflesh, his soft, young, black arm-hairs standing straight up, a phenomenon I'd later learn was scientifically called *piloerection*. Chicky shouted, "You writin' a book or somethin'?" Danny, who got to see his arms and their hair every day, was as transfixed as I was. His breathing steadied, slowed, deepened. Nearly but not quite rupturing my reverie, from afar Chicky yelled, angrily, "Danny? You deaf or just not listening to me today? If I have to come over there . . ." Wordlessly, Danny stared at my hand gliding along his arm's shaft. Touching his arm-hair, and the arm-skin underneath, was awfully pleasant and vaguely disturbing, a brand new, unnamable inner commotion that started to spook me. I didn't want to stop petting him, but I thought I should mention what I'd half-heard. "You're dad's mad. You're in trouble." Danny didn't hear me. Chicky bellowed, "Hey, Lefty. People's gonna think your girl's the type who hangs around parking lots. See what's doing over there, will ya?"

My father approached us, boots grinding gravel. Once the beer can came within his eyeshot, his face became a blade of disapproval, features finely sharpened and narrowed. And it cut. I'd done bad. I scrambled for a strategy to fix it.

Perhaps for the first and only blessed time, being a child spared me something. Still young enough to play innocuous tickle-wrestle games, without pulling my hand from Danny's arm, I wiggled my fingers, ten desperate, panicked worms, deep into Danny's belly, like I was tickling him, "Cootchie-cootchie-cooo." Quick-footed, quick-witted Danny followed my lead, doubling over and laughing maniacally, then cootchie-cootchie-cooo-ing my armpits. I shrieked, too, with crazy-person laughter. Although Dad seemed relieved that all Danny was doing was tickling me—the man had no idea that *I* was doing all the doing, or thought as much—I knew right then that it was officially and indelibly safe to say that I really had a problem, that I was disgusting, that there was poison in my putrefied blood, that I'd been born bad.

A bad seed. A bad egg. Three hundred million bad seeds in a grand hurry toward a head-on collision with one bigger bad egg. The blood-script of a messy but astonishingly idiot-proof recipe for bringing into being a being *born bad*. An accident—a statistically improbable accident—waiting to happen. That would be me.

For decades I'd awaken with a start, sweatily, those two words in my mind, on my tongue. *Born bad.*

When Dad first warned me that taking kids up on bridges was against the law, he'd explained, in his serious-man voice, "Here's the tricky thing, Beetle. The laws weren't made for People Like Us. Mostly, People Like Us have to *obey* the law, but we don't have to *respect* it. And we sure as hell don't have to like it. Ain't one law says you have to respect the law." I was proud. We were tough. We meant business. Me and my bad Dad. A tough team. Once pledged to the team, there's no getting off. Ever.

Even after death, there's no quitting the team. Danny loyally stuck by the Testaverde team, as the team did by him, long beyond his death—his premature payment of the ultimate union dues—two years after his transcendent ladder-climb. Violating child labor laws, and working illegally, without papers, Danny had quit high school to work iron. The walking bosses had looked the other way at his age, because Danny was a crackerjack cabler, skilled beyond his years, until the day he'd slipped and fallen off a too-slippery beam.

The men, as Dad recounted the story, struggled to catch him, nearly falling off themselves, but they only managed to grab hold of his shirt. His Alexander's-boys'-department polyester shirt. In a wakeful nightmare, a day-mare, the men watched impotently as Danny plummeted, and his shirt flew off, and his naked back looked so startlingly white against the black water. Water as hard as concrete, water harder than steel, water that murdered bodies falling from such heights by breaking them into many pieces, even if the lungs managed miraculously to carry on functioning during the descent.

No one could bear to look at Chicky.

Finally, the men watched as, from deep within him, Danny's intestines sprung pyrotechnically out of his insides and into the open air, unfurling like some kid's birthday-party streamers, launching skyward, as if powered by a spring-loaded catapult. The remnants of his body sunk heavily into the water, piece by broken piece. His guts were the last part of him anyone saw. His guts—up, up, up—as they soared.

All the men removed their hard hats, tacitly arriving at a collective mandate that the workday was over—and not just for Danny. Most of them immediately headed down off the bridge, but some were immobilized, stunned still, including several who required hours of humiliating, never-to-be-mentioned-again coaching and hand-holding from other men. Three guys were physically incapable—it wasn't emotional or anything, they swore, but sheerly, physiologically impossible—to unbolt their locked-shut eyes. The three had to be embraced and carried down the whole way.

Criminals. All of us.

"If we're gonna climb a bridge together, I have to teach you the right way to fall off. Into water. When you know how to fall right, we can go up and know what to do if God forbid something goes wrong. But remember: None of these things are allowed. There's rules against it, so you can't tell anyone what we're doing. Afterwards, you can't tell anyone what we did."

"If it's not allowed on Canarsie Pier, let's skip it. It's rinky-dink anyway. We could jump off a real bridge in Jamaica."

He grinned amusedly. "You think it's legal across the county line? In Queens County, but not Kings County?"

I stood awhile, crossed and uncrossed my legs, which locked at my stiffened, knobby knees. I lost my balance a little during one crossover, caught myself, and swallowed hard. I hadn't meant Queens. I'd meant the island. From the commercials. Ocean waves. Palm trees. Sunsets. And that music. I folded my arms across my chest. "I meant the beach."

"Forget Bergen Beach. We're good enough right here. Anyway, how's stepping from flat sand into the ocean like jumping off a bridge? 'Slike taking a walk, not a fall." I hadn't thought through the spatial aspects that far—although secretly, anticipating our trip to the bay in for-real Jamaica, I'd packed my knapsack with my bathing suit and two towels and placed toothpaste, toothbrushes, shampoo, suntan oil, soap, and snacks in my Fonzie lunchbox. Peering down into this Jamaica's bay, I saw that these logistics weren't analogous to a work situation either. Canarsie Pier's setup didn't provide the slightest simulation of the long-distance free-fall from those heights to those depths, and *that* was what I'd wanted him to show me. The distance between Canarsie Pier's cement banks and Jamaica Bay's foul water was a matter of sad little inches—nothing compared to the vast expanses of absolute nothing between a bridge's tensile steel and the suck of rushing, fluctuating open water. My stomach sat low, depressed with the first signs of *starting-to-be-sad* stomach syndrome.

"First off, when you're falling more than twenty feet, you don't know diddley-squat about what's floating around you. You could hit Jimmy Hoffa for all you know. You don't know how deep the water's gonna be. Make like you're blind. A leap of faith."

I got quiet. I got cold, even though the night was hot, and when I shivered, poking through my Danskin, my nipples mortified me. He wore only pale, unpatterned blue boxers. No shirt. No one was around, so it was okay, he said. He figured cops wouldn't hassle us at 1 a.m., so we went then, in the small hours. It was to be our secret.

The distinction between secrecy and privacy. A tough one.

The sky was yellowish and bearing down, pressing the low roofs of the attached houses with green awnings beyond Seaview Avenue, closing in on the Pier's hot concrete. He asked, all sympathetic and paternal, "Getting cold feet?"

"What are you? High as a kite on drugs?" The question had been popping out of Canarsie's parental mouths.

"Then pay attention. I'll explain it as many times as you need, but I'll only demonstrate once."

"Why?"

His features clustered to a pinch of nose and lips—a disgusted look, I thought, standing with my squinched-raisin nipples and ignorance. "I'm not allowed to jump in even once. I can't go twice. They'd cart me to jail if they knew you were doing it, too." I was dry ice, frozen and burnt. "Learning how to fall is the most important thing you'll ever learn, and they won't teach you that in school. The trick is to do exactly what doesn't come naturally. When you're falling, you won't be able to see or even think, but if somehow you can, try to fall wherever the water's deepest."

"But then I'll drown."

"Drowning's always a risk, but that's a swimming problem, not a falling problem. And if drowning is your main concern, you lucked out big time, because you can only drown if there's a miracle and you survive the fall and the hit. The deepest water is furthest from shoreline. Assume the water isn't deep enough to stop you bashing yourself against the shore bottom. Hit bottom with your head, you break your skull. Hit bottom with your legs, they snap like Pick-Up Sticks. Go for the deepest part. Stay away from all objects, especially anything that supports the bridge."

"Then there's nothing to hold onto. To help me. Float."

"This is true. Nothing to help you out, but also nothing to smash yourself into. All kinds of garbage collects near bridge supports. Sure, a little raft would be nice to find, but you're more liable to find something a lot bigger and a lot harder than you are. Then you'll pay." He turned around, looked behind himself. "Checking for John Law. Coast's clear. Okay now. Jump feet first. Stay straight. If you aren't perfectly straight, you'll break your back when you hit." I was trembling, and not because of the extreme temperatures my skin had touched. He said, "I thought you wanted this. What's with the Gloomy Gus *punim?*"

"I'm just listening."

"Totally vertical. Feet first. Squeeze your feet together tight. And your butt cheeks."

"Butt cheeks?"

"If you don't squeeze your cheeks, water's gonna rush in. Screw up your insides. Internal damage and such like."

"Rush in where?" What fun, to watch a big strong man squirm. I knew where he was talking about, that it embarrassed him to talk about it. I knew that things could go inside that place just as things could come out of that place. "Rush in where?"

"Into your insides. Your tummy. And you'll get one helluva stomachache. Always make sure to cover your privacy real tight." Outside his boxers, he cupped his hands around his parts, like I was some guy at a row of urinals.

"Why? Why should I? Why should I cover my privacy?"

"You just have to." I wanted to watch him wriggle out of this one. I remembered how one winter, when we'd gone to see the human polar bears go swimming at Brighton Beach, I'd asked him why men had nipples. He'd blushed and changed the subject to his favorite: ironwork. And a few years earlier, I'd asked him where babies came from. Flustered, pink-faced, without a trace of levity or irony, he said, in a voice possessed of an untainted, artless sincerity never heard out of grown-ups' mouths, "Ummmmm, you should ask your mother." My question was sufficiently stress-provoking to make him forget that I didn't have much of a mother to ask, and that if I did ask the mother I came from, he and I wouldn't have been having this conversation. This situation.

"Just do what I tell you and remember to protect your privacy."

The thick yellow sky pushed down on my skull and brain. "First you said I couldn't think or see straight. Then you said to remember to cover my privacy. How'm I gonna remember if I can't think?"

"Trust me." To trust someone who kept checking behind his back did not come easy.

"Explain why you did that." I pointed, accusing his shorts of something. The idea of his parts poked out; the idea of his sheltering hands obscured the idea of the bulge. "Izzat fair? You said you'd explain it however many times, then you don't explain it, not even a tiny bit?" He looked around frantically. "Dad, we're alone, but it doesn't matter anyway, 'cause everything's all wrong."

"Wrong? What's wrong? I'm steering you wrong?"

My talking-out-loud voice said, "No," but my thinking-inside-myself voice bawled, *You already did. This was supposed to be something else. You're pulling a change-up on me and you don't even say you're sorry.* I started crying, then I stopped myself.

"I know it's scary, Butterfly," he cooed, all kissy-face-buddy-buddy. "I'll demonstrate. Better to learn by example." He plopped onto the concrete and lay flat, flat everywhere except for the forcefully un-flat, trace afterimage of the ghost in his shorts. "Another thing to know. Remember how we make snow-angels?"

"That's winter. In the snow. It's summer now. Everything's different."

"Pretend with me. As practice." He spread his arms and legs apart, wide. His pectorals and deltoids emerged, tautening, hardening, and his boxers gapped, puffed, and puckered in places I thought would've worried him if he hadn't been busy trying to get in good with me—after he'd rooked me, no less. His arms and legs described arcs on the concrete. "While you're falling, making snow-angels in the air generates resistance and slows down your plunge." He flapped his limbs like a dying bug, too stunned to flip from his back onto twitchy, kicky legs.

I was done. No more pretending. No more practicing. I wasn't lying down on hot concrete, no way no how, to make fake snow-angels in the summer. I was done bench-pressing, too, because falling lessons, and all the practicing building up to it, had always held zero promise. For me. I said, "This is C-R-A-P crappola."

"I don't like that word."

"Well, tough titties. I don't like this. I don't even think I like you. I'm going home." As if it would work this time, I said it again—*I'm going home*—as if I had any say at all in the matter. He appeared embarrassingly eager to scuttle like a caught cockroach off the Pier, but if he hadn't been ready to leave, if he'd wanted something else, somewhere else, or something more, I would've been stuck. I had no keys. I wondered whether it was accurate to call it *our house* if only one of us had keys.

Chicky Testaverde came by a couple of times that summer to have grief-drinks with Dad after he'd already been at the bar, talking ironwork, having several after-work drinks with the guys. He never confessed to suffering days so stricken it took five after-work drinks to calm his once-nervy nerves. He never confessed to icing over with bone-seizing fear while on bridges now, unable to move in any direction, sometimes hugging a girder or a beam, eyes crushed closed for five minutes. But he spoke like a man indicting himself for murder, which implicated us as coconspirators, when he wept, "I shoulda known to keep my kid off the bridge."

Later during the summer of the Pier business, the three of us—Dad, awkwardness, and I—got in the car, tooled around, listened to AM radio and the wind roaring through the open windows. The drives were probably his uncomplicated method of getting through the hours. His directions and destinations were always questionable and unquestioned. One night he'd gotten lost, maybe missed an exit if he'd had one in mind, near the Belt Parkway's labyrinthine, accident-prone Ocean Parkway intersection, a snaky Mobius-mess of ramps, exits, merges, under- and overpasses. Traffic was slow.

He drove the Olds below an overpass on whose brick someone had spray-painted in darkest black, *Hi Scummy.*

We noticed it, read it, and looked at each other. *Hi Scummy* jetted us into laughter so belly-felt it was unbearable, like being too-tickled. Our hysterics were a relief, too, the discharging of something that needed letting out. Laughter was going to kill us, because Dad was losing control of the wheel, swerving like an alkie. He pulled off at the nearest exit and parked. We genuinely could not stop laughing. We were having An Episode. I was scared I might wet my pants, but I also didn't care if I did.

When he could talk again, Dad asked, "You think the guy who wrote *Hi Scummy* was pissed off at somebody who drives under that overpass-thing every day? To make sure the other guy really gets the message?"

"How would Scummy know the guy's handwriting? And would Scummy know to look up there for a message?"

"Hmm. Smart one. Good point. Also, how would

Scummy know that *he* was the exact *Scummy* that the *Hi* was meant for? 'Cause for sure there's more than one person who takes this route and fits that description." He paused, changed tone, adding a grim voice to his voice. "That's if we used words like that, Beth. And we don't. Those words aren't allowed, so we don't use them."

"Oh," I said, earnestly. "What about words like *Dummy-fuck-o?*"

"Beth! Brat! Enough! You know the rules about words."

"Rules schmules!" I waved away his admonition. Laughter was lots better. "What about this? Maybe the person who wrote . . . that thing . . . that *Hi* . . . is mad at the drivers."

"All of 'em? In every single car?"

"Well, not mad, exactly, he just thinks they're, you know, that they're scummy!"

"What did you just say?"

"Scummy!" I hooted. I hollered. I spat a few spit-bubbles out my mouth, not on purpose, but a couple hit him, which was nice. "I can say that! You can't stop me! I'm Scummy! You're Scummy! Everybody's so Scummy, Scummy, Scummy!"

He tried to paste his *I-am-stern-and-strict* face onto his face. "Cut out the crap, Beth! What did I just—?" Mid-scold, he gulped, gagged, as he tried to swallow back laughter, quacking glottally at the precise moment he was trying to play the part of an *I-know-what's-best-for-you* type Dad— "What did I just tell you?"

"You told me not to say *scummy*. But you also said *crap*, and before that you said *scummy* a million-zillion times, so you can't be mad. Nuh-uh. The rule is phony baloney. Like you." He gunned the engine again, and we went quiet, listening to the Olds' hum, meandering on small streets toward wherever he and I were headed, that night, that summer.

Then, I *Eureka!*-ed. Out my mouth, before I knew it was coming, I shouted, "But maybe it might be a nice thing! Think about it. Maybe the person who wrote *Hi* to Scummy isn't a mean Dummy-fuck-o. Like it's the opposite. Maybe he and Scummy are bestest best friends, and Scummy doesn't mind. It's only a bad name if it hurts Scummy's feelings, but Scummy likes him, so he likes it, he likes his name, so it's nice to be Scummy."

Dad shook his head hopelessly. "I've been around a lot longer than you, kiddo, and I've heard all sortsa nicknames, but I never heard anyone call a good buddy Scummy. Nice try. Close, but no cigar."

My hands fluttered up dismissively, then flopped in my lap as I kept myself from sighing, "Some people just don't ever get it." I twisted, faced him head-on. "Dad, will ya use the noodle God gave you? This guy went to a helluva lotta trouble. He walked on those highways, with the cars and trucks zooming by. Look! There's no road shoulder. He must of been scared."

"You got that right. He was shit-scared."

"But we don't use words like that, do we?" I inquired, all innocent. He reddened. I let him sweat that one out a minute, then continued, "This guy climbed up the walls, and he had to tiptoe around those No Pedestrian Traffic signs just to hang upside down, like bats do, off that overpass. It's high up there, especially to be upside down, and the bricks are crumbling. That's scary."

"Well taken," he said. "Go on. Argue your point." His gaze burned a dimple into the side of my face.

"I'm tellin' you. All that *tsuris?* Why bother with it? To

say hi to some scummy stranger-type of person who wasn't his friend? It doesn't make sense. Not unless he likes Scummy."

He added, in his dropped-register, *this-is-cautionary-so-pay-attention* tone, "But Beth-Bug, a lotta times people like things that aren't so good for them. Especially small people like you."

"You call me *Boll Weevil* all the time. A lot of people think boll weevils are icky and gross, and they would say you're being a big Dummy-fuck-o by calling me by a bug-name, but we know you mean it nice. Same with Scummy. Personally, I think Scummy and his best friend have these private names. Scummy likes being Scummy."

Leaning in toward the windshield, my father peered at the sky through the streaky, dirty glass. Refusing to look at me, he smiled. Then he tried to quash the smile by contorting his face, cranking his jaw around to set his lips in their *man-who-means-business-no-kidding-for-real* arrangement. Then his whole face relaxed, forfeited its struggle against its own mouth, and he smiled like he was the man who'd invented the light bulb. He touched my cheek. "And you, Boll Weevil. In my book, I'd have to say that *you* are one terrific allrightnik."

You.

We stayed stopped at the Stop sign for longer than a Stop sign mandated legally. He was staring ahead of himself, into the middle distance. Then his face changed, dropped, and he stared at his lap. His smile faded, his eyed looked darker and more heavily lidded than they had moments before, and the car's temperature seemed to fall fifteen degrees. He was thinking, I could tell, and it wasn't about anything good. "What now?" I asked. "Am I in trouble?"

After an empty pause, he spoke absently. "Nah. It's just . . . I just still think it's not a very nice thing to call a friend."

"Uh-duh-uh," I muttered. "Guess what? Just because something's not very nice doesn't make it wrong."

Some thirty years later, I was still alone and without plans to forgive myself for something I'd said in a conversation we'd had when I was six. After work and school, first grade—we both "knocked off," as he put it, at 3 p.m.—I hung around him in the living room while he read the paper. Then he made dinner, such as it was. That unforgivable evening, he cooked up a vat of "Jewish Spaghetti." I never knew what inherently Jewish characteristic was discernable in these pale, overcooked noodles—People Like Us called them *noodles*, not *pasta*—that he boiled and smeared with a sugary, gummy, aggressively orange sauce—as orange as laboratory signs indicating the presence of radioactive biohazards—spicelessly dotted with sticky, translucent tiles of onion.

Jewish Spaghetti was disgusting. Jewish Spaghetti was nearly inedible. I loved Jewish Spaghetti. I loved how one small bowl of Jewish Spaghetti became seventeen oil drums of Jewish Spaghetti in my gut. A gift that kept on giving.

As we chewed and chewed and chewed, I ruminated on my teacher's introductory lesson—hurled at us first thing that morning, right after she took attendance—about the dizzying, fearsome procedures involved in telling time. The devices: sun dials, hourglasses, wristwatches, atomic clocks, mechanical clocks. The standards: Greenwich mean, Tidal, Atomic, Geologic, Standard, Coordinated universal, Ephemeris. The calendars: solar, lunar, Babylonian, Egyptian, Hebrew, Muslim, Julian, Gregorian, Worldsday, Buddhist, Persian, Coptic, Chinese. The Maya Great Circle.

Not even to mention the Laboratory of Tree-Ring Research headquartered in Tucson, Arizona.

Topping it horrifically off, the Metric System and New Math were hurtling respectively across the Atlantic and through deep space toward Public School 276. I wasn't smart or good enough to keep up with it or figure it out. Dad, who was unquestionably not *new* when I got him, couldn't help me. I could only try to tattoo facts on my memory, to remember without understanding.

Suspiciously, I asked him, "Are you old?"

"I'm a little old, but not too old. Like you're a little young, but not too young."

A suction grabbed at whatever lived between my ribs and started draining it out. "If you're a little old now, then soon you'll be a lot old. When you're a lot old, you die, right? Isn't that what happens?"

"Yeah, that's how it goes. I won't be a lot old too soon. That's much later. I'm not planning on dying any time soon." I coughed. With my fork and fingers, I shaped and reshaped orange spaghetti spirals, not piles of the pasta, but plain, wormy lines of it, flat on my plate. Then I worked on spirals within spirals, still two-dimensional. I gulped. I gulped hard.

"Lookit. C'mon now," he cooed. From the spirals on my plate, I made and unmade a maze. He slapped his big hands on the table. "Look at me, Beth." I couldn't look at him. I concentrated. I complicated my noodle-maze. It looked maze-like. It was crap. Its twirls nauseated me. If I, who'd created this, couldn't find a way—not one workable entry or exit point—to get myself into and out of the maze, then no one else could lead. Just going in circles and more circles. Round and round forever. Like clock-hands. Like fears. "I said, look at me. Listen good. We got Jewish Spaghetti to eat. Food to mess with. Bridges to climb. We got a lotta living to do before

I do something stupid like that." I ditched my fork, busied my orange fingers making braids, then helices.

"But Daddy, when you die will you be died forever?" *Aniline blue. Dyed forever.*

"That's what dying is, kiddo. But I'm not planning on doing that. Not for many years. Not for the foreseeable future." *Later. A little old. Soon. A little young. A lot old. Too soon. Not too young. Much later. Any time soon. Forever. Many years.* How many years made *many years?* And *foreseeable future?* A foreseeable future wasn't possible. Unforeseeable was the future's crux. Unforeseeability made the future *the future.*

All this shape-shifting, fake-out doubletalk. Time couldn't be told. There was no reason even to bother trying to tell time. Time did not listen.

"Aw, Baby Beth, don't cry. You're killing me. Seeing you miserable? That's what'll be the death of me." I wiped my face with the quicker-picker-upper I'd used as a napkin, did the usual little-kid shit, whimpered, sniffled.

I really didn't want him ever to die. And I didn't mean to kill him.

"Not for nothing, don't'cha think it's kind of hard to be so serious and sad when you got stripes of tomato sauce going down your *schnozz?*" I slid my index finger down my already sizable nose, and it came back greasily orange. Still inconsolable, I reached my index finger across the table, and striped his nose with my sauce. He stuck three of his fingers into my maze and war-painted my cheeks, which my face's controlled ache told me were *dimping*—the gerund form of a verb he invented just for me, its infinitive form, *to dimp,* referring to the sudden appearances of my dimples while eating or suppressing a smile. I poked a finger into my plate, stirred until my finger was slick with sauce, traced creepy-smiley-clown lipstick around his mouth's perimeter. He stood, opened the fridge, handed me a can of orange soda. "This'll make you feel better." I drank some, cheered up a little, then a lot. Then all better.

I was so saturated with relief and unruly joy that my lips and tongue could almost taste the blood connecting me and my father. I was a balloon-skin about to burst into bits with the force of detonating affection and hope, hope, hope. I barreled toward him, bounded up into his arms, beaming, bobbing my cocksure head, shouting with unadulterated confidence: "You're right! You're not going to die any time soon. I just know it!" I spilled out of his arms. I wanted him to see how happy I was, now that I'd figured it out. "Nope!" I jigged a hippy-hoppy succession of leap and skips that he'd called, since I'd been a baby, Beth's Dance of Sudden Elation. "I was being crazy, all wrong, before. Now for sure I know that you're going to live at least another two weeks!"

Guilty as charged.

The good news, when we buried him, was that for the first time in twenty-four years, as his dead body dropped lower and lower, groundward, down, down, down, he had no fear at all. Burying him was the opposite of going up to work. Supine in his coffin, the cheapest my mother's boyfriend's money could buy, he descended, disappearing toward the world's bottom, groundward, instead of climbing to its top, rising up and above, skyward. Sharper, closer to the surface of feeling even than grief, were the bones of my rib cage, truly a cage now, except the heart it was constructed to incarcerate, mine, had turned to nothing. The cage's new inmate was Zero, the nothing that most definitely was something, an absence more present than my hands in front of me.

After the burial I packed my knapsack with my few things and moved into my mother's house. I wasn't going anywhere. Even while primed in a permanent state of cat-like readiness, I was solidly *placed*. I was keeping vigil. I was staying; I was staying vigilant. I assumed the position, like a long-distance runner poised to bolt at the sound of a gunshot that wouldn't fire a second too soon. Fast and forward. No promises would be made, fulfilled or not, at 617 Flatlands Avenue, where I'd live with the mother who'd let me go. Where I'd live with the simplest fact—*no one was ever going to help me ever*—and where I'd live with the impenetrable tangle, the un-unravellable knowledge-knot that my mother had never wanted me around, but there I was, living with her as she resigned herself to living with me in a house attached on both sides and jam-packed with no-Dad and no-cry and plastic-covered furniture, exponentially accelerating my develop-ment into the little waste of sperm that I was.

And am.

PART II

New School Brooklyn

CROWN HEIST

BY ADAM MANSBACH

Crown Heights

Tap tap BOOM. Birds ain't even got their warble on, and my shit's shaking off the hinges. I didn't even bother with the peephole. It had to be Abraham Lazarus, the Jewish Rasta, playing that dub bassline on my door.

BOOM. I swung it open and Laz barged in like he was expecting to find the answer to life itself inside. A gust of Egyptian Musk oil and Nature's Blessing dread-balm hit me two seconds after he flew by: Laz stayed haloed in that shit like it was some kind of armor. He did a U-turn around my couch, ran his palm across his forehead, wiped the sweat onto his jeans, and came back to the hall.

"I just got fuckin' robbed, bro."

Funny how a dude can cruise the road from neighbor to acquaintance to homeboy without ever coming to a full stop at any of the intersections. Me and Laz, our relationship was like one of those late-night cab rides where the driver hits his rhythm and the green lights stretch forever. He came upstairs and introduced himself the day I moved into his building two years ago: got to know who you live with when you're moving four, five pounds of Jamaican brown a week. He sized me up, decided I was cool, and told me his door was always open. I didn't really have too much going on then—just a half-time shit job in an office mailroom and a baby daughter Uptown who I never got to see—so before long I was coming by on the regular to smoke. If Laz wasn't already puffing one of those big-ass Bob Marley cone spliffs when I walked in, my entrance was always reason enough for him to sweep his locks over his shoulder, hunch down over his coffee table, and commence to building one.

I used to call his crib Little Kingston. All the old dreads from the block would be up in there every afternoon: watching soccer games on cable, chanting down Babylon, talkin' 'bout how horse fat an' cow dead, whatever the fuck those bobo yardie motherfuckers do. I never said much to any of them, just passed the dutchie on the left hand side. Jafakin-ass Lazarus got much love from the bredren, but a domestically grown, unaffiliated nigga like me stayed on the outskirts. Whatever. Later for all that I-n-I bullshit anyway.

I flipped the top lock quick. "What happened?"

"Motherfucker walked straight into my crib, bro, ski-masked up. Put a fuckin' Glock 9 to my head while I was lying in bed. Ran me for all my herb." His hand shook as he lifted a thumb-and-finger pistol to his temple. Fear or rage; I couldn't tell.

"How many?" I asked. "Who?" In Laz's business, you don't get jacked by strangers. Strictly friends and well-wishers.

"Just one, and he knew where my shit was."

"Even the secret shit?"

"Not the secret shit. I still got that. But the other ten are gone—I just re-upped yesterday. Son of a bitch filled a trash-bag, duct-taped me up, and bounced."

"Didn't do a very good job with the tape, did he?"

Laz shook his head. "He was too petro. That was the scariest part, T. He was shitting his pants more than I was. And that's when you get shot: when a cat doesn't know what the fuck he's doing."

"You want a drink?" I didn't know what else to say.

"You got a joint?"

"Yeah. Yeah. Hold on." I went to the bedroom and grabbed my sack. Laz was sitting on the edge of the couch when I got back, flipping an orange pack of Zig-Zags through his knuckles.

"This might be kinda beside the point right now," I said carefully, falling into the chair across from him, "but it's probably time to dead all that cosmic-karmic open-door no-gun shit, huh?"

The bottom line was that Lazarus was practically asking to be robbed. He never locked his door, and the only weapon in his crib was the chef's knife he used to chop up ganja for his customers. He had some kind of who-Jah-bless-let-no-man-curse theory about the whole thing, like somehow the diffusion of his positive vibrations into the universe would prevent anyone from schiesting him. That and the fact that all the small-timers who copped off him knew that Laz was tight with the old Jamaicans who really ran the neighborhood. Plus, Laz was convinced that he looked crazy ill strutting around his apartment with that big blade gleaming in his hand: a wild-minded, six-two, skin-and-bones whiteboy with a spliff dangling from his mouth and hair ropes trailing down his back. Half Lee "Scratch" Perry, half Frank White.

It was an equation that left plenty out—the growling stomachs of damn near every young thug in the area, for starters. A year ago, all Laz's customers were dime-bag-and-bike-peddling yardmen, and everything was peace. Then the hip hop kids found out about him. I told Laz he shouldn't even fuck with them. *I know these niggas like I know myself,* I said. *They're outa control. They trying to be who Jay-Z says he is on records, dude. You don't need that in your life.*

He shrugged me off. *They're babies. I man nah fear no likkle pickney.* Any time Laz started speaking yard, I just left his ass alone. But he should have listened. You could practically see these kids narrowing their eyes at my man every time he turned his back. It had gotten to the point where I'd started locking the door myself whenever I came over.

"It was Jumpshot," Laz said, as a calligraph of smoke twirled up from the three-paper cone he'd rolled. "It had to be."

I leaned forward. "Why Jumpshot?" So-called because he liked to tell folks he was only in the game because genetics had failed to provide him with NBA height. Or WNBA height, for that matter.

"Two reasons." Laz offered me the weed. I shook my head. He blew a white pillow at the ceiling. "Three, actually. One, he sells the most. He's got the most ambition. Two, that shit last month, when he complained and I sonned him."

"Hold up, hold up. You did what? You ain' tell me this."

Laz cocked his head at me. "Yes I did, bro. Didn't I? He came by at night, picked up a QP. I was mad tired, plus mad zooted, and I gave him a shitty shake-bag by mistake. So the next morning he shows up with two of his boys, dudes I don't even know, bitching. Little Ja Rule-lookin' cocksucker. I was like, 'Okay, cool.' Sat him down, gave him a new bag, took the one he didn't want, and threw it on the table. Then I brought out the chalice, like, 'Now we're gonna see if y'all can really smoke.' Part challenge, part apology, you know. My bag and his bag, bowl for bowl. And you know I can smoke, bro."

He had told me this story. It was funny at the time, hearing how Laz had smoked Jump and his boys into oblivion, burned up half Jump's new herb sack before the kid even got out of the room. The way Laz told it, Jumpshot's crew had passed out, but Jump himself refused to go down; he'd sat there all glassy-eyed, slumped back, barely able to bring the chalice-pipe to his lips, while Laz talked at him for hours like he was the dude's uncle or something—regaled him with old smuggling stories from the island days, gave him advice on females, told him how to eat right, all types of shit. After a while, Laz said, he'd put this one song on repeat for hours, just to see if Jump would notice. "Herbman Trafficking" by Welton Irie, Laz's theme music: *Some a use heroin, some a snort up cocaine/but all I want for Christmas dat a two ganja plane/as one take off the other one land/we load the crop of sensimilla one by one/they tell me that it value is a quarter million/me sell it in the sun and a me sell it in the rain/ca' when me get the money me go buy gold chain/me eat caviar and me a drink champagne . . .*

"So what's the third reason?" I asked.

"I recognized that motherfucker's kicks. He got the new Jordans last week." Lazarus stood up. "I gotta send a message. Right?"

I threw up my hands. "I'd say so. Yeah. I mean, you gotta do something."

"Come see Cornelius with me."

"Man, Cornelius doesn't know me."

"You're in there all the time."

"So? I'm just another dude who likes his vegi-fish and cornbread. Whatchu want me there for, anyway?"

"'Cause I'ma go see Jumpshot after that. And I'd like some company, you know what I'm saying?"

"I know what you're saying, Laz, but I'm not tryna just run up on a armed motherfucker. What, you just gonna knock on his door? Say you're the Girl Scouts? Why would he even be home?"

"If he's not home, he's not home. If he is, I'll play it like I'm coming for help, like, 'You're the man on the street, find out who jacked me, I'll make it worth your while.'"

Laz looked sharper, more angular, than I'd ever seen him. Like he was coming into focus. "I guess if he wanted to shoot you, he woulda done it half an hour ago," I said.

"Exactly. Now he's gotta play business-as-usual. Besides, I'm known to be unarmed. Now you understand why: so when I do pick up a strap, it's some real out-of-character shit."

"I don't wanna be involved in no craziness, Laz." I said it mostly just to get it on the record. Once you put in a certain number of hours with a cat like Lazarus, you become affiliated. Obligated. It starts off easy-going: You come over, you chill, you smoke. *Ay T, you hungry? I'm 'bout to order up some food. Put away your money, dog. I got you.* Then it becomes, *Yo T, I gotta go out for a hot second. Do me a solid and mind the store, bro. Or, Man, I'm mad tired. Can you bring Jamal this package for me? I'll break you off. Good lookin' out, T.*

I stood up and walked out of the room.

"Fuck you going?" Laz called after me. I could tell from his tone that he was standing with his arms spread wide, like Isaac Hayes as Black Moses.

I came back and shook my duffel bag at him. "Unless you wanna carry those ten bricks back home in your drawers."

"Good call."

We drove to the spot, and I waited in the car while Laz talked to Cornelius. Most innocent-looking store in Crown Heights: Healthy Living Vegetarian Café and Juice Bar. X-amount of fake-bodega herb-gates with, like, one dusty-ass can of soda in the window, but Healthy Living was a high-post operation.

They sold major weight, and only to maybe two or three cats, total. You had to come highly recommended, had to be Jamaican or be Abraham Lazarus.

The funny thing was that Cornelius could cook his ass off. You'd never know his spare ribs were made of gluten—that's my word. Tastier than a motherfucker, and I ain't even vegetarian. All Cornelius's daughters worked in there, too, and every one of them was fine as hell. Different mothers, different shades of lovely. I stopped flirting after Lazarus told me where he copped his shit. Started noticing all the scars Cornelius had on his neck and forearms, too. He was from Trenchtown, Laz said. Marley's neighborhood. You didn't get out of there without a fight.

The metal gate was still down when we got there, but Cornelius was inside sweeping up. He raised it just enough to let Laz limbo underneath. I watched them exchange a few words: watched the face of the barrel-chested, teak-skinned man in the white chef's apron darken as the pale, lanky dread bent to whisper in his ear. Then Cornelius laid his broom against a chair and beckoned Laz into the back room.

It wasn't even a minute later when Laz ducked back outside and jumped into the ride. He didn't say anything, just fisted the wheel and swung the car around. His face was blank, like an actor getting into character inside his head. I'd always thought his eyes were blue, but now they looked gray, the color of sidewalk cement.

"So what he say?" I figured he'd probably ignore the question, but I had to ask.

"He said, 'Abraham, there are those that hang and those who do the cutting.' And he gave me what I asked for." Laz opened the left side of his jacket and I saw the handle of a pistol. Looked like a .38. Used to have one of those myself.

"I was hoping Cornelius would tell you he'd take care of it," I said.

Laz shook his head about a millimeter. "Not how it works, T." He made a right onto Jumpshot's block, found a space, and backed in—cut the wheel too early and fucked it up and had to start over. "Bumbaclot," he mumbled. There was another car-length of space behind him, but Laz missed on the second try, too. I guess his mind was elsewhere. He nailed it on the third, flicked the key, and turned to me. Surprising how still it suddenly felt in there, with the engine off. How close.

"It's cool if you want to wait in the car, T." Laz said it staring straight ahead.

I ground my teeth together, felt my jaw flare. Mostly just so Laz would feel the weight of the favor. "I'm good."

"You good?"

"I'm good."

"Let's do this."

It was a pretty street. Row houses on either side, and an elementary school with a playground in the middle of the block. I used to live on a school block back Uptown. It'd be crazy loud every day from about noon to 3—different classes going to recess, fifty or sixty juiced-up kids zooming all over the place. Basketball, tag, double-dutch. Couldn't be too mad at it, though. It was nice noise.

A thought occurred to me and I turned to Laz, who was trudging along with his hands pocketed and his head buried in his shoulders like a bloodshot, dreadlocked James Dean. "It's too early for a tournament, right?"

That was Jumpshot's other hustle. Dude had eight or ten TVs set up in his two-room basement crib, each one equipped with a PlayStation. For five or ten bills, shorties from the neighborhood could sign up and play NBALive or Madden Football or whatever, winner take all. Even the older kids, the young thug set, would be up in Jump's crib, balling and smoking and betting. Jumpshot handled all the bookie action, in addition to selling the players beer and weed—at a mark-up, no less, like the place was a bar or some shit. It was kind of brilliant, really.

"Way too early," said Laz.

We stopped in front of Jumpshot's door. "Play it cool," I reminded him.

"We'll see," said Laz, and a little bit of that Brooklyn-Jew accent, that soft, self-assured intonation, surfaced for a second. It occurred to me that maybe this wasn't the first time he'd done something like this. Maybe he didn't own a gun because he didn't trust himself with one. I don't know if the thought made me feel better or worse.

"He's got a loose ceiling tile in the bathroom," said Laz. "Right above the toilet." And he pressed the buzzer, hard, for about three seconds.

Static crackled from the intercom and then a grainy voice demanded, *Who dat?* A bad connection to ten feet away.

Laz bent to the speaker, hands on his knees, and over-pronounced his words: "Jumpshot, it's Abraham. I've got to talk to you. It's very important."

A pause, two heatbeats long, and then, "A'ight, man, hold on."

I tried to catch Laz's eye, wanting to read his thoughts from his face. But his stare was frozen on the door. This much I was sure of: The longer Jumpshot took to open up, the worse for him.

But Jump's face appeared in the crack between door and

jamb a second later, bisected by the chain-lock. He flicked his eyes at both of us, then closed the door, slid off the chain, and opened up. He was rocking black basketball shorts, a white wife-beater, and some dirty-ass sweatsocks. If he hadn't been asleep, he sure looked it.

"Fuck time is it?" He rubbed a palm up and down the right side of his face as he followed us inside.

"Early." Next to Jumpshot, Laz looked like a gaunt, ancient giant. "But I been up for hours."

"Yeah?" Jump said, sitting heavily on his unmade bed and bending to pull a pair of sneakers from underneath the frame. "Why's that?"

Lazarus reached into his jacket and pulled out the .38, held it at waist height so that the barrel was pointing right at Jumpshot's grill. "I think you know the answer to that," he said calmly.

Jump looked up and froze. Just froze. Didn't move, didn't say shit. I gathered he'd never stared into that little black hole before.

Lazarus smiled. "Where's my shit, Jumpshot?" he asked conversationally. I gulped it back fast, but for a sec I thought I might puke. It wasn't the piece, or the fact that Jump suddenly looked like the seventeen-year-old kid he was. It wasn't even the weird fucking sensation of another dude's life passing before my eyes the way Jump's did just then. What turned my stomach was that Lazarus looked more content than I had ever seen him. Like he would do this shit every day if he could.

Jump opened his mouth, made a noise like *nhh*, and shook his head. I was beginning to feel sorry for him. I'd expected more of the dude. Some stupid Tony Montana bravado, at least: *Fuck you, Lazarus. You gonna hafta kill me, nigga.*

"T."

"Yeah, man."

"Go take a look around, huh? I'ma have a little chat with my man here."

"Sure." I headed for the bathroom.

"What are you looking at him for?" I heard behind me. That rabbi voice again. "Look at me. That's better. Now listen carefully, Jumpshot. You listening? Okay. Here's the deal. You give me everything back, right now, no bullshit, and you get a pass. You get to pack your shit up and roll out of Dodge." There was a pause, and I could almost see Laz shrugging. "Who knows, maybe a broken leg for good measure. To remind you that stealing is wrong."

Finally, Jumpshot found his voice. It was raspy, clogged, but it cut through the stale air like a dart. "I didn't steal nothing." Like if he spoke deliberately enough there was no way Lazarus could not believe him. "I . . . have . . . no . . . idea . . . what you're talking about."

I walked back into the room right on cue, and threw two bricks onto the bed. Jump started like I'd tossed a snake at him. "That was all I could find," I said. Jumpshot's face was a death mask now, so twisted that any lingering trace of sympathy I might have had for him straight vanished.

"Oh, and this." I handed Laz the gun. Jump raised up so fast I thought he might salute.

"I never seen that shit before in my life!" The veins in his neck strained; I could see the blood pumping.

"What, that?" Lazarus pointed at the bricks and raised his eyebrows. "That's weed, Jumpshot. Collie. Ishen. Ganja. Sensi. Goat shit. People smoke it. Gets them high. Or did you mean this?" Lazarus held up the Glock, and as soon as Jumpshot looked at it, *bam:* Lazarus swung the gun at him and hit Jump square in the face, the orbit of the eye. Knocked him back onto the bed, bloody. Jump let out a clipped yelp and grabbed his face, and Lazarus leaned over him, gun in the air, ready to pistol-whip the kid again.

"At least this shit is loaded," Laz said, eyes flashing. "At least you robbed me with a loaded gun, Jump. Next time, change your fuckin' shoes." *Bam.* Lazarus slammed the gun down again—hit Jump on the hand shielding his face. Probably shattered a finger, at least. Jump screamed and twitched, curled like a millipede, this way and that. Nowhere to go, really.

Lazarus straightened, a gun in each hand, and swiped a forearm across his brow. "Ten minus two leaves eight," he said. "So where's the rest, Jump?"

"Fuck you." Jump said it loud and strong, as if the words came from deep inside him.

"No, Jump," Lazarus said. "Fuck *you*." He turned and pulled the biggest television off its stand, whirled and heaved it toward Jumpshot. Missed. Thing must have been heavy; Lazarus barely threw it two feet. It landed upright. The screen didn't even break.

Lazarus glanced over at me, a little embarrassed. "Fuck this," he said. "Sit up, nigger. I'm through fucking with you. Sit up!"

Jumpshot did as he was told. Blood was smeared across his face, clotting over one eye. "Laz—"

"Shut up. Believe me, Jumpshot, I could fuck around and torture you for hours. Trust me, I know how. I even brought my knife. But I don't have time for all that. So I'm going to wait five seconds, and if you don't tell me where the rest of my shit is, I'm going to shoot you in the fucking chest, you understand? Go."

"I don't fucking know, man. You gotta believe me, Abraham, I swear to God I never seen that shit be—"

"Four."

"Please, man, I swear on my mother's—"

Lazarus snatched a pillow off the floor and fired through it. Didn't muffle shit. Whole building probably heard the sound. Jump fell back flat. Lazarus wiped off the Glock and tossed it on the bed. Crossed his arms over his chest and stared down at Jumphot. The blood was spreading beneath him, saturating the blankets. "What could this fool have done with eight pounds of weed in two hours?"

"Maybe we should talk about it someplace else," I suggested.

"Mmm," said Lazarus. "That's probably a good idea." But we stood rooted to our spots, like we were observing a moment of silence. I watched Laz's eyes bounce from spot to spot and knew he was wondering if there was anything in the apartment worth taking. Watching him was easier than watching Jumpshot.

"All right." The moment ended and Laz spun on his heel. We stepped outside. After the dimness of the apartment, the block seemed almost unbearably bright.

We drove back to the crib and ordered breakfast from the Dominican place. Laz had steak and eggs. "Aren't you supposed to be a vegetarian?" I asked.

"Usually," he said with his mouth full, swiping a piece of toast through his yolk. He shook his head. "Eight fuckin' pounds."

"Only thing I can come up with is that he took it straight to one of the herb gates on Bedford," I said. "On some pump-and-dump shit."

Lazarus nodded. "That's the only thing that makes sense.

Anybody else would ask questions." He slid his knife and fork together neatly, as if a waiter was going to come and clear our plates. "I'll never see that weight again, basically."

"At least it was paid for, right?"

"Half up front, half on the re-up. That's how Cornelius does business." He steepled his hands and tapped his fingertips against his chin. "I'm gonna have to leave town, T. Take what I've got left, go down south, and bubble it." He lowered his head, toyed with a lock. "I swore I'd never do the Greyhound thing again. But it's still the safest way to travel."

"How long you talking about?" I asked.

Laz shrugged. "A month or so. I'll go see my bredren in North Kack, bubble what I need to bubble, let shit blow over. You can mind the shop, right? Keep the business up and running so the Rastas don't start looking for a new connect?"

"If Cornelius will fuck with me, I can."

"He will. I'll set that up before I go."

"When you gonna bounce?"

Lazarus reached over and grabbed the duffel with the bricks in it. He walked over to his closet and dumped an armload of clothes inside, then bent down and pulled a floorboard loose. Inside the hollow was a roll of dough and one more brick. He tossed those in, too. I neglected to mention that it was my bag he was packing.

"I'm ready now," he said.

Laz took a shower, made a few phone calls. I went up to my crib and did the same, then came back down and rolled us one last spliff. We smoked in silence. Always the best way. When it was over Laz stubbed the roach, pushed off palms-to-knees, and stood. "Everything is set," he said, and tossed me his car keys. "You might as well get used to driving it."

We were quiet all the way to Times Square. I kept waiting

for Laz to start peppering me with instructions, but he just leaned back in the passenger seat, rubbing his eyes. Occasionally, he'd sing a little snippet of a Marley song to himself: *Don't let them fool ya/or even try to school ya.* Maybe it was stuck in his head and he just had to let it out, or maybe the song made him feel better. He had a good voice, actually.

I parked the car, walked him up to the ticketing desk, and then down to the terminal. The bus was already boarding. I offered Laz my hand; he clasped it, then pulled me into a shoulder-bang embrace. "Hey, listen," he said. "That shit with Jumpshot. I'm sorry. I didn't mean to call him a nigger. I was heated. You know I didn't mean anything by it, right?"

"I know," I said.

He leaned in for another soulshake. "Hold it down for me, bro."

"No doubt," I said.

"I'll see you in a month. And I'll call before then."

"Do that."

"All right, bro. One love."

"Be safe," I said.

"No doubt."

"Peace."

"Peace." He glanced over his shoulder, hefted the duffel bag, and disappeared up the steps.

I walked to the far side of the terminal and checked my watch. Laz's bus was due to depart at 1:15. It was 1:13 when the two DTs I'd tipped off cut the line, flashed their badges at the driver, and boarded. I didn't wait to see them haul Laz off, just got on the escalator, made my way back to the car, and rolled back to Brooklyn. Climbed the stairs to my apartment, triple-locked the door, and rolled myself another joint. Slipped on my brand new Jordans, stacked my eight bricks into a pyramid, and just stared out the window, taking in my new domain. *So long, Lazarus,* I thought. *I never liked your fake ass anyway. Just another punk whiteboy beneath it all. Damn near shit yourself when I put that nine to your dome. Probably serve your whole sentence and never figure out what happened. Probably call me every week from the joint, talking about, "What's going on, bro?" Probably expect cats to remember who you are when you get out.*

HUNTER/TRAPPER

BY ARTHUR NERSESIAN

Brooklyn Heights

```
CATCHMEFUCAN, late 30s, divorced,
graduate school type, nipple and foot
bottom, descriptive tinkle torture,
only literary straps, no working class
ropes or common place marks. Looking
for a little pen pal punishment.
```

This enticed me for solely one reason: This would be the notice I'd post were I hunting for me. Circular logic to most, but to me this entry was bait for a sting. Still, I figured, I have the willpower to finger the flames without getting burned. To CATCHMEFUCAN, I wrote back, I'd love to try to be more than a pen pal—GOTCHU.

Well, GOTCHU, you can always try. Just be prepared to join the graveyard of so many others that failed, cause you won't succeed.

Thus we started our little cat-and-mouse relationship. I figured maybe I'd get some pud-pulling tidbits. *Cinch the ropes around my wrists, pour hot wax on my breasts, clamp me if I'm naughty, smack me if I'm nice . . .* Blah blah blah, the usual stuff you'd expect from an S&M shatroom. But with her it was different.

She'd have none of that. Whenever I mentioned that I'd love to give her a tweak, she'd write something dismissive like, **That's not necessary.**

It was as though some ponytailed Dorothy from Kansas had accidentally ventured into this Oz of Bondage and Domination. I could see why she didn't get much action. No one else would have put up with her.

Do you realize that you advertized in an S&M chat room? I finally asked after weeks without so much as a slap or tickle in the endless exchanges.

Course I do, you randy lad.

And yet whenever I make any advances along that line, you seem surprised.

I have to get to know you better before I can fully reveal that side of myself to you.

This is the Internet! We're never going to meet.

I pass a million people every day. You're my only love-bug. A meeting of minds is far more intimate than a meeting of bodies.

So how long do you have to know someone for before we can get intimate?

The longer you can wait, the better it'll be, she replied with all the smugness of a red-hot poker cauterizing my wounded heart.

Her e-mail exchanges always took something out of me. Afterwards, I'd have to nurse myself back to my indestructible self developing the innermost buds of fantasies that one day would blossom. On that fateful day when I finally had her, I could act out all my dreams. But even my dreams were hindered, until I found out what her dreams were. Without her realizing it, I had to learn what scared her more than anything else, to extract the sweetest nectar of her fear.

Occasionally I'd test her borders, nothing gross or icky, just little things, like **Why'd you divorce?** or, **What are your** measurements? Wondering if she was actually still married, or if she was in a wheelchair.

She'd invariably turn the questions into sarcastic come-backs.

I divorced cause I knew I'd meet you, or, You see me every night on cable, I'm Anna Nicole Smith.

So soon, in order to keep it earnest, our e-missives became little more than a line or so. One long banal conversation that lasted for weeks and then months. Whenever I turned on my computer, she was always right there. Like warm little homemade muffins just waiting for me, but they always had a little needle inside, some funny little dig. Slowly, like a voice in my head or a low-level addiction, I came to thoughtlessly expect it. I learned to eat around what used to get caught in my throat. At the end of a long, empty day, a day of resisting the urge to follow a thousand lonely ladies home and bring them to my ecstatic world, I knew I could read CATCHME's little comments du jour. It became something to look forward to. I couldn't go to sleep without an exchange.

One night about three months into our little chat, she must've had a little too much too drink, because she let out a slip: It's three in the morning and I just made a big boo boo.

What kind of a boo boo?

A naughty one.

How naughty?

Very very naughty.

Naughty girls need to be disciplined, I pushed.

But who will take time to do that?

Just type in where you are, lost little girl, and I'll

come get you. When I hit *send*, I knew I shouldn't have. I knew I was pushing too hard.

She didn't write me back for a month after that—punishment by deprivation—and I thought I had lost her until one day I got a new message: Boy, it was a beautiful day today, wasn't it?

I wanted to write back that she could eat my stinking shit and if I ever saw her I'd strangle her with her own intestines as I fucked her death wounds. Instead I wrote, Sure was!

With sudden regularity, the e-mails resumed. Though they took on a bit more depth, they still remained along the surface. She'd talk about her little garden, and soon she mentioned other potted plants of domesticity: the old oak trees on her block; the aggravating honks of trucks that double-parked in front of the supermarket around the corner, causing constant traffic bottlenecks. She mentioned that every morning while watering her rooftop plants, she could see the Williamsburg Savings Bank clock from the back of the building and the Jehovah's Witness digital clock toward the front, and the two-minute discrepancy between them. She talked about how she liked going on strolls near the waterfront over the cobblestoned streets in her neighborhood.

I get dehydrated quickly when I go on walks, I replied, and hoping that she'd slip up and tell me the area she lived, I asked, You don't get out much either do you?

I'm not agoraphobic, but I am a bit of a homebody.

One day, when I casually mentioned that I had a birthday coming up, she wrote back, Let's do something for your birthday.

Like what?

A visual date, she proposed. At 6 p.m. tonight, I'm going to be on my rooftop holding a wine glass, toasting the western tower of the Bridge. You do the same.

Which bridge?

The Brooklyn.

It's a date, I replied.

That afternoon I dropped a hundred dollars on a high-powered pair of field glasses. Because she said the western tower I thought that perhaps she was in one of the new high-rises around the South Street Seaport in Manhattan. I arrived a half an hour early and when I walked across the bridge toward the western tower, I spotted a middle-aged woman also holding binoculars. She was in her forties, small, dehydrated, in drab clothes. Nothing to look at, easy to kill. All I could think was, she had the same idea as me. When I approached to make small talk, she suddenly lifted her spy glasses and yelled, "Holy shit!"

When I turned to see what she was looking at, I saw a gentle cascade of grayish feathers.

"What happened?"

"The falcon just grabbed a pigeon."

"What falcon?" I asked.

"A peregrine falcon nest up there with a fledgling." She was pointing to a small stone doorway high above the second pillar. By her general demeanor, I knew this Audubon member wasn't *her*.

I still had fifteen minutes before her toast. I spent the time scanning both sides of the river for any glint of a wine glass. After an hour, feeling empty and pissed, I headed back to Brooklyn and walked to the F train stop at York.

A teenage girl was waiting all alone at the farthest end of the platform. I seriously considered dragging her a few extra feet into the darkness of the tunnel. But before I took a step, I realized the token clerk got a good look at me. If she screamed, there would only be one escape route. I was actually relieved when someone else finally showed up.

Upon arriving home, an e-mail was waiting for me: Happy birthday to you.

I wrote back that I was in agony for her.

Agony?

I know this sounds odd, but I think I've fallen in love with you.

That's funny. Tell me another.

I'm serious. I can't get you out of my head. I'm always thinking about you. Can't we just put all the bullshit aside and meet somewhere like two adults? We'll just have coffee and if you like what you see, we can go on a proper date.

To be quite honest, I'm nothing special to look at. Right now, you claim to be in love with me and we didn't even meet. I've gone on dates with guys who've used me in the most degrading ways and then decided never to call me again. Frankly, I don't even like sex. (I only like what it symbolizes.)

Me neither! We don't have to have a sexual relationship. I can love you as a friend.

We can be friends on the Internet.

In order to assuage my obsession, and allay my fears of rejection, I need to meet you face to face.

And by meeting you, I stand to lose everything, she replied, as though we were corresponding in some god-damned nineteenth-century epistolary novel like two star-crossed lovers.

I promise, even if you're old, fat and limbless, if you got bad skin or an overbite, if you smell awful or can't dress, or your eyes are too close together, or your ears stick out, whatever irregularity or infirmity you got, I will forever maintain our friendship.

I'm sorry but no.

Are you a man? Is that it, because if that is the case, even that I will not mind, but I need to see you.

Please try to understand—I just can't.

I feel that this is cruel and manipulative on your part and I resent it.

I've only adhered to the stated rules of our friendship.

You led me to believe that this relationship would eventually lead somewhere.

And so it has. I feel I know you, and here we are arguing with all the intimacy of old lovers.

Are you married? Or in a relationship?

Not that it matters, but no. Please try to understand that anonymity is for both our sakes.

That is so fucking patronizing! And I resent this mock legal formality as if you have some bullshit authority!

You're right, I'm sorry, but frankly you're scaring me.

I don't mean to, but if I can't find some resolution to this, you'll leave me with no recourse other than to cease this relationship as it presently exists.

When did you become such a needy person! The thing I always found most attractive about you was that you always sounded so firm and strong. I took you to be a lone wolf but here you are a braying little lamb.

I didn't respond.

Perhaps we can work something else out.

I didn't respond.

Perhaps I can speak to you on the phone. Would that be acceptable? You can give me your number and I'll call you at some specified time.

I didn't respond.

What exactly is it you hope to gain from our meeting? If anything, I believe it will kill the love—a word I don't use lightly—that does exist.

I didn't respond.

Do you want me to be more vulnerable, is that it?

Though I wanted to respond, I didn't. I really was half hoping she'd just go away—for her own sake.

Suppose I send you a nude photo of myself—deleting my face of course—my nudity will be fully vulnerable for you to see. If you respond to this, I will e-mail the photo. I will also trust that you won't simply laugh at my less than perfect body and then never return my messages. This is my last and best offer, and let me assure you that even if we were to meet (which we won't) you'd never get such a candid view of me. If you don't reply to this final offer, I will be compelled to bid you farewell and give up this e-mail address.

I finally responded: **I am inclined to accept this offer, but I suppose I must do so with a word of caution. In matters of the heart, there are no lies, nor is there right and wrong. Despite all the cliches to the contrary, the heart is a shark. It consumes what it must, and turns its back on what it cannot use. This photo might very well do the trick, and satiate the hunger of obsession, but there is a chance that I will still find myself pining for you. If so, then I'm truly sorry.**

Spare me the bad Tennessee Williams prose. If I am going to stand naked before a mirror, and snap a goddamn polaroid of myself, then scan it into my computer and e-mail it to you—some whiny clown whose name I don't even know—I damn well insist that I get some assurances for it.

Specifically promise me that you will continue our correspondence without any more bullshit. Otherwise, goodbye forever.

It wasn't exactly like I had a lot to lose. Still, in an effort to drive a hard bargain, to get the very most I could, I said, All right, but let me begin by saying, I can spot a phony picture right off. If you do take a self-portrait, I expect it to be well lit, well focused, and in color. In addition to your body, I will require your hair—not just pubic, but head hair. And if you dye your hair or put on a wig, and I sense that too, the deal is off. I understand you don't want to show your face, fine. But a woman's hair is very important to me, it allows me to grasp some sense of her character and identity.

Although I'm beginning to fear that I seriously miscalculated you, she replied, an offer made is an offer kept. I suppose I can reveal my hair, but first I plan to wash and brush it, so if you find that "phony" say so now. Let me also specify that the photo will not be some raunchy piece of pornography. I will stand nude, in a lit room at a distance of several feet, and snap the photo using my polaroid camera, but I'm not some hussy, so if that is what you're expecting, say so now as I do not want to degrade myself any more than I have to. If you send me a follow-up e-mail saying you were expecting to see "pink" or some crap like that—just forget it, buster. It'll be a straightforward shot, minus my face.

I replied: I know you well enough to know that you wouldn't pose in some pornographic fashion, and you should know me well enough to know that I wouldn't expect such a tawdry thing. Though you probably don't believe me, this is not for erotic purposes.

* * *

Three days passed without a word. Then on the night of the fourth day, checking my e-mail account, I saw it: her e-mail with an attachment had arrived. The re: said, `Why not take all of me.`

When I hit the attachment, I slowly watched a naked form loading onto my screen. As she was revealed, I could barely catch my breath. I didn't remember seeing anyone quite as erotic. The entire time I knew it was her, simply because she really was quite ordinary. Her brushed-out shag of red hair, then an oval whited-out face, strong shoulders, a firm, lean torso. Beautiful breasts, a flat unscarred abdomen. Below that was an untrimmed tangle of reddish brown pubic hair, so rich I could smell her. All unscrolling into a typical, intelligent, early-middle-aged woman, who clearly watched her diet and occasionally exercised.

The one detail that particularly caught my eye was just above her ankle. It was a small green sea horse.

The correspondence had quickly devolved into a game of stud poker. After seeing the photo, I had this instinct to fold. The little voice in my head said, *this is as much as you can ever hope to hurt her.* So, if only to do that, it made sense not to reply.

Therefore I made no response. Of course, she grew indignant sending her own unrequited e-mails. But I never opened them and I only read the re: line—`Where are you?` and, `Am I that Ugly?` and, `I thought you were a man of your word.` Finally, after the second week, I got a re: from her that read, `I forgive you, I only hope this the worst thing you ever did.`

When I opened the message, it said, `If vanishing after seeing me nude is the worst thing you've ever done, I'm` glad I could sacrifice myself for you—if only to give you a taste of the darkness.

No, I've done a lot worse, I replied.

Thank god, and I was beginning to think you a boy scout.

That's funny coming from such a girl scout.

Oh, I do a million little, awful things every day.

Like what?

Like ignoring the elderly lady who sits outside my building and greets me every morning. Or yelling at mothers whose children scream too loud in the playground across the street. Or just contributing to the mediocrity of the routine world by filling up space, taking resources and only leaving a trail of excrement behind.

None of those are even illegal.

Perhaps, but how many awful legal acts equate to one small illegal thing? For that matter, are certain illegal acts really even that awful?

Murder is illegal, but is it always awful? Do most people even earn their right to exist? I think the worst things in life are actually quite legal.

That's true in theory. In a world of six billion people in which most contribute nothing, I'd rather live among fewer people of a high quality. However, I am not a murderer.

What does that mean? To be a murderer, you simply commit murder.

Actually there are common traits that go into the composition of many homicidal minds. For starters, psychologists found that babies who aren't held and shown affection during a crucial period of their infancy lose a basic human empathy that flowers into compassion and understanding.

How do they test for compassion among infants?

They found that babies who were held and hugged and kissed and loved will cry when other babies are crying, demonstrating empathy (not to be confused with sympathy), while infants that were not loved remain silent while other babies wept.

I didn't remember other babies crying when I was growing up, but if they did, I probably just found it annoying. I wrote back, asking about other ingredients that go into the murderous cookie dough.

They found an inordinate amount of killers suffered from some kind of head trauma.

I did remember hitting my head as a kid, but I also remembered other kids of my age group suffering from head injuries. In my old neighborhood, kids fell out of trees, off bicycles, down stairs all the time.

What else? I persisted.

Many violent personalities were victims of violence themselves during their childhood.

You sound like you've read your stuff, I fired back, pissed at her simplistic, Martha Stewart recipe for how to shake and bake a murderer.

Only because I live in constant fear of crime. Is that so wrong? Don't you have any fears?

Sure.

What are they?

It was the perfect opportunity, so I wrote back: I'll tell you mine, but only if you tell me yours.

Fine, you first.

Attempting to be truly macabre, I wrote: Having my penis slowly dissected with my own scalpel. What about you?

Being cut off. Just floating in a bottomless pit of blackness, still alive, with only your own worthless existence to contemplate. That's the most harrowing thing I can think of. Apparently she had given the question some thought.

That engendered my newest fantasy. When I finally found her that's what I'd do. After blinding and paralyzing her, I'd submerge her in a sensory-deprivation tank with water matching her skin temperature so that she'd feel nothing. Then I'd slip a tube down her throat for oxygen, and an IV drip in her arm for nutrients. I'd just leave her alive for a month or two until she slowly starved to death.

Some weeks later, two events occurred within days of each other. The first was a simple warning from my e-mail server, stating that I was running out of space for my account. Always a pack rat, reluctant to delete anything, I was forced to download all the e-mails she had sent to me. Upon doing this, I reread all her little messages—they had all the tedium of a drawing-room romance. Aside from that, though, I became aware for the first time exactly how many little geographic references she had made over the weeks and months.

While walking home the next day, I noticed that the decennial census had just commenced. Young folks with shoulder bags that read *U.S. Census* were tramping around my neighborhood. Immediately, it struck me that this would be an ideal cover for someone who wanted to inconspicuously canvas an area. I let out an accidental squeal as I realized that an excellent opportunity existed for me to find her.

I had planned to simply join up and work for the census, but the very next afternoon I stopped at a local Burger King. That's when I saw a group of them. Four census enumerators were going over their forms with what looked to be a supervisor. I bought a burger and coffee, and taking off my jacket, I headed to a small table at one end where they were sitting. Slowly sipping my coffee and eating my burger, I waited.

When one census enumerator was up getting food and another was in the bathroom, only two remained at the table. I approached discreetly and draped my jacket over the nearest *U.S. Census* bag, which was sitting on the floor. Then, pulling it under my arm, I dashed out.

Now it was a question of which neighborhood. All the clues were there. It was simply a matter of triangulating the various details she had mentioned in her e-mails. I extracted and isolated every single geographical reference into a list. The three most significant details were that she lived a few blocks from the river, and that there was a view of both the Brooklyn Bridge and the Statue of Liberty. In Dumbo you couldn't make out the statue. From Cobble Hill you couldn't see the Bridge. Only Brooklyn Heights allowed views of both—it was just that easy. In fact, those two simple variables only allowed about a three-block stretch of real estate. She had to either be on Montague Terrace, Pierrepont Place, or Columbia Terrace. Montague Terrace had a playground across the street that she had mentioned. Behind the Breukelen, a door-manned apartment building, was a row of three small brownstones. She had to be in one of them. Two of the brownstones were single-family occupancies. The last one had apartments.

I came early the next day, ready to wait her out. Try to see if I could spot a curly-red-haired middle-aged woman with a dark green sea horse tattoo on her ankle. Red is a minority hair color, so the fact that I had insisted she show it was further proof of my superior intellect.

Her sea horse would be the confirming mark, yet she would have to be wearing a dress or shorts in order to spot the tattoo. As this was unlikely, I realized I might have to subtly interrogate any possible suspects. After four hours, a half-dozen women had come and gone from the buildings, but no big red.

Finally, around 4, before everyone came home from work—and the risk of her sharp screams could get me caught—I pulled on the census bag, put on a hat, a pair of tortoiseshell glasses, and decided to knock on a few doors.

In the first brownstone was an old lady that loved to talk. In the second building was a shy kid whose parents weren't home. Each of them was a perfectly useful victim, and though I couldn't help but think that the police would eventually interview these two, I was hopeful that the disguise might work. After all, most people aren't very observant.

When I finally came to the old outdoor intercom of the last building, I felt my heart beat in my ears, and I knew she was here. Ringing the first-floor and then the second-floor apartments, I got no response. Upon pressing the loose top-floor button, I wondered if the buzzer was even connected to anything.

"Who is it?" a woman's timid voice peeped out.

"Census."

A buzz sounded and the downstairs door popped open, allowing access to a musty, dark stairwell. There were no bikes, shopping carts, or baby carriages in the hallway. If there were other tenants in the building, I saw no immediate signs of them. By the time I got up the stairs to her door, it was slightly ajar. I opened it and called out, "Hello, U.S. Government, anyone home?"

"Hi there," a middle-aged woman muttered.

"Hi, we didn't get your census form," I began, looking her up and down. Her hair was a brownish red bundle, so she could've been the one, but it wasn't decisive. She was wearing loose shapeless pants, so it wasn't evident if she had the tattoo on her calf. As I took a form out of my bag and started slowly going through the questions, she spotted the fact that the sides of my shirt were wet with perspiration—the result of hours in the sun waiting for her. I kept wiping off my forehead to keep the sweat from dripping on the form.

"Would you like a Coke?" she graciously asked, taking a can from her fridge.

"No thanks," I replied. "Are you married, single, divorced?"

She opened a water faucet and just let it run until it was cold. The slight spray of cool water splattering on my hot neck finally compelled me to say, "Actually, a cup of water would be perfect."

She grabbed a glass from a high shelf, filled and put it down before me. While I pressed it to my forehead, she said, "If you don't mind, I'll fill this out myself."

As she marked in the various boxes, I sipped the water and surveyed the room. Floral wallpaper, evenly spaced reproductions, various pictures and knickknacks—all the trappings of middle class housekeeping. I was desperately trying to ascertain whether her spouse or lover was in the other room. If she had a dog or cat, I would've seen it by then. But was a kid or parent sleeping in the back? All was quiet as she checked through the income boxes and then onto the questions of ethnicity.

"All done," she replied a moment later, folding the form in half and handing it back to me.

"Can I get another glass of water?" I asked. When I

offered her my empty, holding it up to the light, I could see traces of some powder sliding down along the sides. She drugged me! "Holy shit!"

She bolted into the bedroom. I jumped to my feet and raced behind. Inside was a queen-size bed with four metal posts—perfect.

"What the fuck did you slip me?"

"Nothing! I swear!"

With my right hand I yanked her wrist up tightly behind her back, painfully. With my left hand, I reached around front, ripping open her shirt so that her breast tumbled out.

"What did you slip me!"

"Nothing, I swear! It must have been soap from the dishwasher."

I shoved her face forward and yanked up the right leg of her pants. There it was—the dark green sea horse.

Suddenly I felt myself growing weak.

"You drugged me, you bitch!" I grabbed some ties dangling from her doorknob and had to work quickly, securing her before I passed out. Then when I came to, I could finish the job.

"I can't believe I found you," I said, circling the silk tie around her right wrist firmly, pulling it tightly around the post, knotting it again and again.

"Please leave me alone!" she begged as I began with the second wrist. Tying the knot, twisting, cinching, retying, until all she could do was wiggle.

"You know who I am, don't you?"

"No!" she groaned. "Who?"

"It's me! I reached right up the ass of the Internet and pulled you out," I explained, as I secured her right ankle to the right post of the bed. I felt her head shaking violently.

She was weeping as I collapsed on top of her. "You must have known I was coming for you," I added, feeling so little keeping me conscious. "You had something ready for me. Didn't you?"

That's when I saw that she wasn't crying at all, she was giggling, but I had her arms and one leg tied tight. I hit her hard across the face. My lids and limbs were so heavy, and her free leg was kicking—I couldn't lasso it to the post. Sluggishly, I raced up and fit the tie into her laughing mouth. I tied it again and again. *She'll be ready for me when I* . . .

Smacks across my face, whack upon whack, till I start blinking. I'm handcuffed and she's looking down on me.

"Men are such half-wits," she says.

"What are you talking . . . ?" I'm barely able to speak.

"What's your handle?"

"My what . . . ?"

She smacks me some more. As I awaken, I see I am in a stone room, probably her cellar. I'm spread out on the frame of an old metal army cot without a mattress. My wrists and ankles are cuffed to the four corners. In the bright light, crusted splotches of blood are visible on the floor. She keeps hitting me hard across the face.

"What the fuck!" I yell out.

She empties the contents of my wallet on my chest. She is holding my knife. I can see that she has clipped a square of my pants away so that my genitals are exposed.

"Listen carefully, because I don't want to lose my temper. I've been e-mailing with five of you little piggies. I got the first one immediately, and the second one three months ago, so that leaves three. What name do you use when you e-mail me?"

"I'm GOTCHU." I can barely open my mouth.

"Oh, you're the idiot that I sent the faceless photo to," she explained. "The others all insisted on seeing my face."

"But . . . but I caught *you*," I say groggily.

"You caught me?" she asks. "I sent enough geographical references for a retard to figure out where I live, and it took you what, six months? The other guy figured it out in six weeks."

"Witnesses saw me come into your house!"

"Who's going to find you missing?" she asks. "You don't work for the census. You don't live around here."

"What are you going to do?" I'm slurring, barely able to keep my eyes open. "Are you going to kill me?"

"On the contrary, I'm going to do everything I can to keep you alive as long as possible," she says. "Oh, but don't worry, your scalpel is going to get used, after all."

NEW LOTS AVENUE

BY NELSON GEORGE
Brownsville

On a recent late-fall Saturday afternoon Cynthia Green was walking down New Lots Avenue in East New York with her seven-year-old daughter Essence and an armful of groceries from the local bodega. The slender, pale-skinned young woman was thinking of how to convince her mother to babysit Essence that night so she could go out, when a black sedan pulled up beside her. The black man inside called out, "Act like you don't know me!" Being that this was the kind of car only a cop would be seen in and she wasn't carrying anything more criminal than two forties, she decided to stop.

When she looked at the driver, Cynthia said, "What you doin' around here?"

Cousin Johnny replied, "Workin'." He was a thick-shouldered, brown-skinned man with the makings of a soon-to-be-large natural do. He was wearing a green road Donavan McNabb jersey. There was small Sony video camera on the seat next to him.

"Workin' in this car?"

"Nice, huh?"

Cynthia knew cousin Johnny as a cop. And he still was, only more so.

"Now I'm with DEA."

"Since when?"

"Since the last two years. You don't keep up with your relatives, do you? Anyway, how's my favorite cousin doing?"

They exchanged family updates—what this and that cousin or aunt was doing. Then Cynthia said, "You better be chill around here."

"Don't worry," he replied, "all I'm doing is taking pictures right now. You know the Puerto Rican dude who lives over there? They call him Victorious?"

"The Victorious that lives over there?" She pointed toward a brown two-story row house. Johnny nodded affirmatively. "Yeah," she added, "I know him well."

"Well," her cousin said, holding up the video camera, "this is for him."

Victorious was a highly entrepreneurial member of the Five Percent religion. Had a job in the cafeteria of a municipal office building downtown, sold jewelry that his wife made, and, according to cousin Johnny, was extremely close to some Latino brothers from Colombia about to make a major move into East New York and Brownsville. Victorious had gone to junior high school with Cynthia, had hung out with her on the block many nights and shared his dope cheeba over the years. He was a homie.

"So," she asked, "he's in deep trouble?"

"No more than any of the other people I take pictures of. I'm all over the five boroughs. It pays good." Johnny was from a rock-solid middle class family in St. Albans, Queens. Both his parents had worked for the city, and he'd gone to John Jay, majoring, of course, in criminal justice. Now he lived in Jersey in a cozy little suburban home just like his white colleagues. Except that Johnny was black, which made him perfect for the kind of work he was doing now—spying on other people of color working in the underground economy.

As Johnny sat, camera in lap, he teased little Essence, who welcomed the friendly male attention. Cynthia, who was feeling all sorts of conflicting feelings, said, "I know it's good money and benefits, but niggas is buck out here." Johnny seemed unconcerned. He'd made his decision about the kind of life he was living a long time ago. There was nothing Cynthia could say that her aunt Lucille hadn't said many times before. Johnny just picked up his video camera, flipped the switch, and took a nice shot of Cynthia and Essence.

"Tell your mother I send my love," he said, as his cousin walked away and Essence waved at him.

That evening, when Johnny's car was gone (perhaps replaced by another, but who could tell?), Cynthia stopped by Victorious's place. His parents lived downstairs and Victorious and his wife upstairs. Cynthia wondered if they could take a walk together. He was a lanky, slightly handsome yellow-skinned man with a goatee and a baldy. There was the tip of a tattoo visible on his neck just above the turned-up lapels of his beige Rocawear jacket.

She could see his breath in the cold and how the patterns of his breathing changed as she spoke. It surprised him that she had a DEA agent for a cousin, but nothing else she said did. Victorious told her the DEA had busted his apartment just the month before, confiscating "a lot of money," but didn't find any drugs. His wife had been there alone when it happened and the DEA had given her a receipt on the way out. She hadn't been sleeping too well since that visit. In fact, he finally admitted to Cynthia, she'd moved back to her mother's house in Bushwick just last week. Victorious told Cynthia what he told his wife—the money had come from the city job and from selling her jewelry, the drug stuff was just some mess. Cynthia didn't speak on it: That part wasn't her business. But he was a long-time friend. That's why they were standing under the bare branches of a tree on New Lots Avenue on this night in thirty-degree weather.

"Just be chill," Cynthia told him finally. "Maybe you better try and get your money back, you know, and start a video store or a laundry. People always have to get their clothes washed."

"Good looking out," he said, and then gave her a hug. She could feel his body shaking slightly, though his face was impassive. After Cynthia left, Victorious stood in the doorway of the two-story building, his head turning left and right as he peered into cars parked along the street and listened to the roar from the elevated IRT train a few blocks away. He'd lived on New Lots Avenue his whole life and almost every day thought about when he'd be ready to move.

The next afternoon, when Johnny rolled by the house, video camera on the seat, he noticed that the curtains on Victorious's windows were gone. It wouldn't be until the day after that he discovered Victorious had moved.

SCAVENGER HUNT

BY NEAL POLLACK

Coney Island

The nighttime air at Coney smells like corn dogs and fried clams and a little bit like garbage. It's a good smell, once you get used to it, and a good place. There are lights and activity and you never know who's going to walk past. For an old man who's kind of curious, but also kind of not interested in talking to anyone, it's perfect. I can watch the people and still concentrate on my world, a swirl of wooden horses and songs from the thirties that no one remembers anymore. I oil the poles when they get squeaky, track real horses in the *Post,* and count the quarters at the end of the shift. There's not much conversation. I'm basically an ugly bastard with a thick accent, and I don't want to scare anyone. Why should I play to type? I wasn't born to be the creepy guy who runs the carousel.

In the summers I keep the ride open late. You never know when a bunch of teenagers from Montclair might show up. The Puerto Rican families stay out until midnight on the weekends. More and more, too, I get the kids—I call them kids, but they're in their twenties—out on a date, trying to impress each other on the bumper cars and Whack-A-Mole. Big night for them, I guess, to look at the freaks, or to pretend like they're freaks themselves. When they make it over to me, which they almost always do, I slow the carousel down so they can enjoy each other. The young have certain needs. I was young once, too, and once there was romance in my life.

Sometimes special circumstances arise. It was after 11 p.m. I yawned into the newspaper; no one had been by for a ride in at least forty-five minutes. I decided it was time to shut down.

Two girls came along the boardwalk. They weren't beautiful in the way that you see on TV, or naturally beautiful, either, but they had style. In fact, they had a style that I hadn't really seen before, hair done a certain way, t-shirts of a certain design, their skirts real short, cut at a certain angle. They had a look about them that just seemed, well, contemporary. I'm not a contemporary guy, but I could still tell.

They stopped in front of me. I felt my breath sting my chest, which happens when I get excited. One of them said, "*Please* don't tell me you're closed."

I gulped. Sixty-four years old, and still a sucker. "Just about to," I said.

"Shit!" she said. "You've got to let us ride."

"What?"

"We really need to ride the carousel."

She reached into her purse and took out a twenty.

"For both of us," she said.

"It doesn't cost that much." Then—don't ask me why—I said, "You two ride for free."

The other girl, prettier than the first, touched my arm. I felt a jolt travel down my spine and into my brain. I've always been stupid around women.

"Aren't you sweet?" she said.

"We're gonna ride for three songs," said her friend.

"Okay," I replied.

I was going to lose a little money. I didn't care. It had been a profitable summer. So I started up the carousel.

The first few notes of the organ coming to life scare me. It sounds like someone being resurrected from the dead, against his will. Didn't seem to bother the girls, though. One of them got on top of a tall black horse in the front. The other took a digital camera out of her purse. While the first girl rode and waved, the other one took pictures. When the song ended, they switched places quickly.

While the second song was still playing, the girl who was taking pictures walked to my booth.

"I'm gonna get on the carousel with my friend," she said. "Will you take our picture together?"

"Okay."

"We're on a scavenger hunt," she said. "We need proof of being in different places and doing different things."

"Sounds fun."

"It's very fun. You should come with us next time."

"Oh, I don't think so," I said. "I have to . . ."

"I was kidding," she said.

"Oh."

She got on the carousel for the third song. They sat together on a bench. I stood in front of the ride, camera ready.

"Take our picture!" called out one of them. I couldn't tell which. The carousel had started moving and they were blurry. The first time around, I got them with their arms in the air, shouting. But it was a little out of focus.

"Again!" one of them said.

When they came around the next time, the photo took nice and clear. The girls were kissing. Not on the cheek, either. Really kissing. And they kept kissing until the ride was over. I'd never seen girls do that before.

"You get the pictures?" the first one asked.

"Oh yes."

"You got us kissing, right?"

"Yes."

She put the camera in her purse. The other girl patted my hand. I blushed.

"See you next time," she said.

No one was going to Coney a dozen years ago. It was really at its low point. So when I bought the carousel, I didn't expect to make any money. I'd retired from my city job with some savings. When you start at twenty-two, you can stop work pretty early. My wife and I didn't have any kids, and we didn't enjoy each other, either. She doesn't like traveling, and I don't like going out to dinner. I needed something to do. One day, I was walking down the boardwalk, trying to remember what it'd been like as a kid. There was a *For Sale* sign.

I talked to the Russian who was taking care of the ride. He obviously didn't give a shit. The paint on the horses was chipping off, the poles were rusted, and the room was decorated with a faded mural dating, at the latest, to 1965, but probably further back than that. It was dingy and depressing.

"Who wants to ride a fake horse, anyway?" the Russian said.

He was asking a little more than I had available, but what the hell? I went to the bank and pulled some financing together. A guy I knew from the city was able to grease the walk-through inspection. After I closed the deal, I went home for dinner.

"Where've you been?" asked my wife.

"I just bought the Coney Island carousel," I said.

She looked at me hard. I've never been able to figure out why she hates me so much.

"So?" she said. "You think you're special?"

I'd definitely made the right choice.

The heating system was old but still pretty efficient. I spent the winter—which was miserable, with winds like knives—chipping away the rust. I bought some industrial cleaner and gave the whole place a scrub, which took about ten days. Then I hired some mural painters, real cheap, students from Parsons. They did up the horses beautifully. I wasn't as happy with their work on the mural, but it was fresh paint, so it didn't really matter. I hammered together a comfortable little booth to sit in. Someone came out and worked on the organ. Before I knew it, April had arrived.

I went up to Martha's Vineyard for a few days, and didn't take my wife. Told her I was going to visit mother in the home. The carousel operator on the island couldn't have been nicer. I was a quick study. The day after tax day, 1992, I opened the ride.

The girls came back two weeks after their first visit. It was around the same time of night. They looked even cuter than before, if that was possible.

"Remember us?" asked one of them.

"Yes," I said.

"I'm Katie, and this is Diane."

I took Katie's hand. "Hello," I said.

"Can we ride the carousel tonight?" said Diane.

"Of course!"

She handed me a twenty.

They got on together this time. But they didn't ask me to take a picture. They just rode around. Katie pulled out a little flask, and they sipped from it. I didn't usually allow drinking on the ride, but it was late and no one was going to get in trouble.

They got off when the song ended.

"You want to ride with us?" Diane asked.

"I can't," I said. "I have to operate . . ."

"I can do it!" she said. "For one song! You can show me how."

For some reason, I said okay. It didn't take a genius, after all. She picked it up pretty quickly. Did a practice spin. Then Katie and I got on. We sat together on a bench.

The carousel started going round.

"This is so fun!" she said.

"Yes," I agreed.

When the ride stopped, Diane got up from the booth. Katie and I were sitting on the bench. Diane pointed the camera at us. And then Katie kissed me, hard, on the lips. I felt her tongue tickling my teeth, and I opened my mouth gratefully. My eyes were closed. Through the lids, I could see the flash going off. She kept kissing me. It felt wonderful! Another picture. And then it was over.

"Hey," she said, "you're a great kisser!"

"Thank you."

She got up. Diane was scrolling through the pictures. Katie went over to look.

"Holy shit!" she said. "Did I really do that?"

"You did!" Diane replied.

"We're gonna win this one!" said Katie.

They walked away, giggling.

"Wait!" I called out. "You've still got one more song!"

"Next time, handsome," said Diane. She whispered something in Katie's ear. Katie laughed like crazy. They turned around and looked at me and laughed even harder. I laughed back. I wanted them to know I understood.

I got home around midnight. My wife was still awake. She was always awake.

"What are you smiling about?" she asked.

"Nothing," I said.

Sometime in the last ten years, Coney got hot. The people attending the Mermaid Parade started getting younger. Lines got longer at the freak show. Riding the Cyclone became cool again. I saw a headline, *"Not Your Father's Coney Island,"* in that *Time Out* rag. I raised my prices by a dollar. Summers became extremely active. Then they opened the ballpark, and things really went nuts.

The new kids seem desperate to me. For fun, or for something. I spent the sixties behind a desk at the Water Department. My kid brother took me to a Springsteen show in 1975. It was okay, but I never really had a taste for rock-n-roll. Not like I want to deny other people their good time. Life just doesn't seem like a party to me, and it never has. Except with those girls.

I couldn't stop thinking about the girls and their scavenger hunt. First, I'd never had a kiss like that. Second, the whole idea of a scavenger hunt as an adult activity baffled me. I thought it was something for a child's birthday party. Just a dumb activity for dumb times, I supposed, like goldfish-swallowing, pole-sitting, or telephone-booth-stuffing. Maybe they're trying to forget that there's a war on. Or maybe they don't know.

Still, I couldn't wait for them to come back.

They showed up late on Sunday night of Labor Day weekend. There were still a few people riding the carousel, because it was a holiday. Katie winked at me. Diane waved. I smiled. They leaned against the entrance, smoking.

It took about half an hour for me to get everyone else out of there.

"Hello, ladies," I said, approaching them. "Good to see you."

"Good to be seen," Diane said.

"Another scavenger hunt?"

"Yeah," said Katie. "High-stakes. Winner gets ten grand."

"No kidding?" I said. "How can I help."

Diane looked around.

"Pull down the gate," she said.

"We don't close for a little while."

She sidled against me, and I felt something stick into my ribs. Her eyes glared.

"You're closed," she said.

I pulled down the gate.

"Shut off the lights," Katie demanded.

"What?"

"Shut down everything."

"Aren't you going to ride?" I asked.

Diane pulled the gun out of my ribs and waved it in front of my face.

"Do it!" she said.

I turned the lights off and shut the power down. The grate was closed. Diane nudged me into the booth. She pointed the .38 at my head. Katie stood behind her, with the camera.

"Open the cashbox," Diane said. She then took a picture. The flash went off.

"But . . ."

"Open the fucking cashbox!"

I did, and took out the money: $275.

"Throw it on the floor," Katie said.

I hesitated. Diane pressed the gun hard into my ear. I threw the money. Katie took a picture. Then she bent over and started picking the money up. There was enough light coming in from the boardwalk that she could find most of the bills. I looked at her face, back-lit by neon, and she didn't seem so beautiful anymore.

"Now get on the floor yourself," Katie said. "On your back."

I did what she asked. Diane bent over me. She put the gun in my mouth.

"Try anything, and I pull the trigger."

Katie took another picture.

With her spare hand, Diane undid my belt buckle, and the button and zipper of my jeans. She seemed to hover for a second.

"I can't do this," she said.

"What?" Katie replied.

"I'm not going to suck this guy's cock."

Oh, please do, I thought.

"Well, I'm not going to do it, either," Katie said.

They both stared at me. I stared back. Maybe one of them would change her mind.

"Get up and open the gate," Diane said.

I sighed and did what they said. Diane caressed my cheek.

"You're not going to tell anyone, are you?" she asked.

"No," I said. "Keep the money."

"Good boy," said Katie.

"But don't come back," I added.

"Don't worry," Katie said, "you'll never see us again."

And they were gone.

I stopped for a couple of drinks on the way home. On the television hanging over the bar was a news report. Some yuppie kids had been arrested trying to stick someone up in front of the *TKTS* booth in Times Square, and a similar incident had occurred at the Bronx Zoo. They said they'd been on a scavenger hunt. *The Scavenger Hunt Robberies,* the news called them.

By morning, the *Post* would have reports of a half-dozen. Mine wasn't among them. It never would be.

I got home around 3 a.m.

"Who do you think you are?" said my wife.

"No one," I answered.

Just the creepy guy who runs the carousel.

THE CODE

BY NORMAN KELLEY

[PRODUCED BY T-SOUND. 17:20; EP]

Prospect Heights

> *Free people are free to make mistakes and commit crimes
> and do bad things.*
> —**Donald Rumsfeld**

Code had always survived by the philosophy that he lived by; he recognized no other man's law but his own: Take whatever is needed and fuck all the rest. He was the real thing: a bona fide nigga-man who lived and survived the streets. Unlike an array of fake niggaz who recorded stories about the 'hood, he was the real deal. He had the scars to prove it, the wages of sin, and he made sure that bitchez paid special attention to them when they worshipped his battle-scared body. No bitch ever left his threatening grip without kissing his keloid medals of the street, wounds received from rival niggaz and Five-Os.

Upon arriving upstate he had shanked two motherfuckahs Day One who looked at him as if he were sweet meat. He wasn't gonna play that faggot shit. He got their minds right—as well as the whole cellblock. He had no time for that shit. His time was short and he wasn't going to be cornered into taking sides in simple-minded prison gangs. A tag quickly went down that Code wasn't somebody you wanted to fuck with. He sat alone and was given respect. OGs nodded and went their way; the younger ones just kept moving.

Code did his time: He worked in the prison shops, did his daily 300 push-ups, and worked on his rhymes. He was planning to make his own luck when he returned to the city and produce his masterstroke: *The Code*. It would be the story of one bold, bad, crazy nigga's life in the 'hood, back in Brooklyn, back in Prospect Heights. It would have everything that urban contemporary airplay craved: phat beats, flowing delivery, and the chronicle of a real nigga's life, not back in the day but here in the moment, meaning a nigga telling it like it is—gun-play, lurid depiction of urban scenes, and plenty of fucking. He was going to go even further and have the screams of snuffed-out bitchez mixed in. Of course, no one would know if the cries were true or not (except him), but he would let others know that when he spoke of contemporary urban reality, he was *beyond* keepin' it real. He was making it a fuckin' reality. He had no time for fake niggaz frontin' a reality he already knew about.

When Code's lurid tales of murderous mayhem coursed their way through the underground, neighborhoods that had been relatively quiet spiked in crime. It took awhile for the police to figure out what was going on in certain neighborhoods, but they eventually found a correlation between Code's underground tapes and an increase in robbery, spousal abuse, and urban cowboy antics. He "Ain't Fuckin' Around," as he relayed in one song:

> *There was nobody or*
> *No one to hold me down*
> *I've kicked every motherfuckah*
> *Even my mama around*
> *Niggaz knows me as a man about town*
> *Ain't no motherfuckah who doesn't know that*
> *I ain't fuckin' around*

Or:

> Yeah, baby, let me do it to you
> I knew you'd love it since you're just cooze
> I've never met a bitch that wouldn't do the do
> It's my God-given right to smack you & be cruel
>
> You know you like
> You know you like that
> You know you like it
> And if you don't you're still gonna be smacked

"You Know You Like It" was accompanied by the dick-hardening, ass-smacking sound of a woman screaming, *"Yeah, fuck me!"* That caught the ear of Dr. Rhyme, one of hip hop's most influential producers, the genius behind *Da Sick Niggaz Convention.* Rhyme put his trackers out to find that "crazy motherfuckah with the sick-ass lyrics and slick production."

Word went out on the street, and Code's hands went into his pocket when two unfamiliar niggaz unexpectedly approached him at his local hang spot, Club Prospect on Franklin Street.

"Who the FUCK sent you?" he screamed at one, who was down on his knees, mouth bleeding from the pistol whipping he had just received from Code. Code was nervous; rumors were circulating that two of the other chart-topping rappers, Wuz Dat and Killadelic, had ceased their war and were thinking about jacking his ass up: The new nigga on the block was a threat. And Code could always smell another nigga's evil ways blocks ahead.

The club went silent: The doors were locked and all the customers witnessed the legendary Bad One in action. Only a few were disgusted by Code's criminal-mindedness. Most of the patrons, young men and women from the neighborhood, had become inured to the random display of violence, which was increasingly the soundtrack to their reality. Watching Code was like watching a power fantasy in actual play. He was a brother in control and knew how to handle another nigga. Even the club's exotic dancers stopped moving and watched Code at work. Finally, one of the men was given permission to reach into his jacket pocket and retrieve a card with Dr. Rhyme's telephone number.

With his 9mm's barrel jacked up against the roof of one of the nigga's mouths, his foot on the neck of the other emissary from Rhyme & Crime Records, dialing his cellphone with his thumb, Code found that the doctor was in New York. The doctor wanted to know if he was ready to be a serious music playa. If so, would he join him for dinner in Manhattan?

Used to Mickey D's or curry goat with dirty rice and beans, Code and his thuggish trio of bodyguards rolled into an Upper East Side restaurant on 61st Street. Their presence caused some consternation (it was mainly the display of do-rags, sports jerseys, oversized trousers, and untied shoes) until Dr. Rhyme approached the maitre d' and interceded. A gray velvet jacket was placed on Code, and his boys were told to park their rumpled asses at a bar that kept him in their eyesight.

"I'm sorry about that misunderstanding with yo' niggaz," said Code as he sat down, referring to Rhyme's messengers.

Dr. Rhyme was gracious; as a former Cali gang-banger, he understood the dictates of security; it was the code of the streets. Obviously, his agents hadn't approached Code with respect, and respect was important. He would dispose of them accordingly.

Code was nodding to all that Rhyme said, but kept his eyes on the most magnificent-looking one-eyed bitch he had ever laid his own bloodshot eyes on. She was dark, and Code, like most niggaz, tended to go for the current J. Lo model of Boricua negritude. But T-Sound was *fine*, despite the one eye, and she displayed her finery with even more subtlety when she excused herself and went to the ladies' room. Code assumed that she sucked Rhyme's dick; that's what bitchez were good for. That, and giving a nigga a son. Rhyme recognized the trajectory of Code's male gaze.

"She's one of my producers," said Rhyme. "T-Sound discovered your tape and listened to it. Girl got ears."

"And one eye," Code retorted. Not bad for a one-eyed bitch—and with a wicked ass to boot, thought Code. If she didn't return, he'd have to start licking the chair she sat in.

She was Tanya Sonido, from *el barrio*, and Code was trying to calculate how he could get her away from his new contact, the man who was going to produce his way outta the ghetto. He may have to kill him to snatch her. He had done it before—but before business?

"Will she be my producer?" asked Code.

Rhyme looked at him. "You don't mind a woman producing your sound?" This was unheard of, and Rhyme recognized that this was one nigga who didn't give a fuck what other niggaz said or thought.

"Shit, she could suck my dick while doing it."

Rhyme nodded: "Yeah, she's a bad motherfuckah . . ."

"You Negroes talking about me?" asked a suave voice.

The two turned around and found T-Sound standing behind them. She returned to her seat and flashed the whitest pair of teeth that Code ever saw on a black woman. It was also her almond-shaped *eye* and wide, sensuous smile. She was an older woman, maybe about thirty. She probably knew how to really fuck a man. Not like these amateur bitchez who watched skeezer videos and acted like they could hump. This bitch could probably fuck as well as a dude; that is, putting her back into it as if she had a dick. Men knew how to fuck; bitchez just got laid.

Dinner proceeded with Rhyme and T-Sound finding their prospective new talent something to eat on the exotic menu. After coffee and cognac, they—Code, along with his boys—went to Rhyme's nearby hotel room and discussed his vision for his project, *The Code*.

While fixing drinks at the room's wet bar, Rhyme saw the effect that T-Sound's bod was having on Code. It was her pulchritudinous figure and that black eye patch. There was something mysterious, remotely kinky, about a fine-looking woman wearing an eye-patch that got some men's third leg thumping in their pants. There was heat between them, the bitch and the nigga. Rhyme watched them as they sat down and talked about his lyrics, life, and production ideas; who he listened to and what he wanted to incorporate. It would be a chronicle of gunz, bitchez, and bodacious niggatude. Code was surprised that T-Sound had produced many of the CDs that he liked and had been deejaying in clubs. Code mentioned that he enjoyed listening to women screaming and hollering, and told her that he watched a lot of porn.

"So do I," she said, "but I like to watch men getting their asses busted."

Code smoothed the waves on his head. "Shit, the only people who do that are faggots."

"Yep, and they be the only ones getting it up the ass, baby. I especially enjoy she-males busting a nigga's ass."

"Whut?" He looked at Rhyme and then back at her.

"Have you tried it?" asked T-Sound, an inquisitive arch rising over her good eye.

"Fuck *no*," laughed Code, slightly put off that a bitch he

was getting hard for would ask a 100-percent black man like himself that kind of question. "I'm the fucker; not the fucked!"

"Too bad." She looked him over as if she were imagining herself doing something very nasty to him.

"If you were a dude, I'd have killed you for . . ."

Tanya tossed her head back. A mane of rich black hair swept through the air as she sat invitingly across from him. Her legs were parted slightly, as if she was offering a taste of herself.

"Well, come on, nigguh," she challenged. "You want to slay me like you do those niggaz back in Brooklyn? Or you wanna fuck this *Boricua* bitch? This *black* bitch? This *disease-free* bitch? I got something for you."

She rocked her head as if she was good to go, kicking it to him in Spanish. "*Yo, popi* . . ."

Rhyme watched him. Tanya was taunting him before a room full of men, his niggaz. This would have been different if it were just him and the boys, but Tanya was playing with fire. A few seconds went by and Code gave her a hard nigga stare, an icy glance that he had perfected when deciding another man's fate.

Rhyme understood what was going on and walked over with a drink and handed it to Code, who took it down in one swallow and said to his boys, Bebop and Cisco, "Let's roll. I'll have my lawyer contact you about a contract. Bitch, I'll see your fine ass in the studio." He grabbed a fist full of crotch before he went out the door, then added, "You better not bend over while we're there, or you'll get this!"

With that, they left.

"Damn, that nigga was fine," moaned Tanya as she grabbed her own crotch, taking a drink from Rhyme. "I wanted to fuck his ass there on the spot!"

"Shit, that boy would have shot you, Tanya."

Tanya reached down and pulled up a Glock pistol from between the cushions of the couch. "Or he would have died trying. How much do you think we can get for him?"

"Well . . . if we do this CD, he'll be a premium," surmised Rhyme.

A few months later, a contract signed and time spent in the studio, Tanya walked into Club Prospect on Franklin Street and sat down beside Code, who was sticking dollar bills in a dancer's G-string with his teeth. He could feel himself thickening even when she sat an inch or so away. Lately he had been having dreams about her . . . pulling her clothes off, inching his way down to her crotch, getting her hot and nasty for his *coup de grâce*. But now she wanted to talk about some business, music business.

"Look, one of them sounds like someone is being choked to death," she said, flicking an ash of her clove cigarette into a tray on the bar.

It was homage to an original gangsta, the legendary Nate Ford, he told her. Ford excelled in the "asphixiation of love," a love/death grip. Ford had learned that by choking a bitch, his hands on her throat, he could involuntary cause her vaginal muscles to firmly grip his dick as he simultaneously exploded into and suffocated her.

Not even the Marquis de Sade had that one in his arsenal of techniques, Ford was reported to have told a Russian business associate as they sat around one evening laughing over coke and cognac. "Kinky technique," Code explained. Ford had even shown his Russian guest a video of himself snuffing a young Puerto Rican woman. On the tape, Ford leered into the camera and then, with the brio of ultimate contempt, pulled out and discharged over the dead woman's body. *"Good to the last drop,"* Ford then said. This was the sort of video that Code collected.

"That's what you want on your debut album?" asked T-Sound. "You want people to see you as a sick, demented fuck?"

"I don't care what people think," snarled Code, his eyes narrowed nearly to slits, mocking an African mask. "I am the last of a dying breed: the last of the bad-ass niggaz. True to form, true to the code: I just want niggaz to buy my music . . ."

"And shine your shoes . . ."

"Whut?"

"Skip it," said T-Sound. She wasn't going to engage in self-disgust just because of dealing with low-lifes like him. This was a business, and it sometimes became nasty when dealing with nasty people.

"T-Sound . . ." he rolled off his tongue.

"What?" She was looking at a dancer who could have made better money by keeping her clothes on.

"How'd you lose your eye?"

"Fighting a nigga who wanted to get some *free* pussy *the hard way,"* she coolly replied. "He didn't understand any part of the word *no."* She went into her hand purse and pulled out a matching onyx cigarette case and lighter.

"Did he get any?"

"No," she said, lighting the cigarette. Tanya turned and faced him fully. A shadow fell across her face, the dark patch growing into a partial shroud over one side of her head. "All he got was an eyeball, but his balls got some of this!" She pushed a little black switch upward on the lighter with her thumb, and a gleaming, sharp two-inch blade appeared.

What Code found menacing wasn't the blade, but that she was too cool; nothing frazzled her. She was just like him: a deadly nigga. Weeks ago he had walked into the recording studio with his boys, armed, stinking of liquor, and she had thrown out his bodyguards with her even bigger, badder, and bolder bodyguards, niggaz who worked day jobs with the city's most feared gang, NYPD. He tried to stare her down during a disagreement about one song in which he was going for the soap-soft. After dissing women for ten tracks, he wanted to include some lovey-dovey sop—asking a "girl" if she would love him even if he didn't have money—after having extolled the sociopathic virtues of getting it by any means necessary on the rest of the recording!

T-sound had told him: "Look, it is clear to me that even though you enjoy *fucking* us, you don't like or have any respect for women. So who are you trying to fool with this track, your mother? Niggaz like you don't have mothers. You're the classic son of a bitch, *tu sabes?*"

She told him this an inch from his face, like a Marine DI to a jarhead, and added: "You gonna be hard, be hard all the way. No half-steppin'. Save that pussy love shit for your second album—if you live that long."

Tanya Sonido. She looked like a woman, smelled like a woman, and even dressed like one. She wore the kind of clothes—dresses, suits, or blazers with jeans—that accented a woman's best features, and she had *rounds* of features like the military had rounds of ammunition in Iraq. A phat, firm ass that didn't bust out the seams like other nigga bitchez; voluptuous breasts that hung underneath her shirts in their own right, not assisted by silicone injections. She had nice calves and strong-looking muscles that ran along her thighs, evidence of gym work, and nice definition to her shoulders and biceps. The bitch was *built*. She was hard like him: ghetto—but she had style and grace, and wasn't nigga-down 24/7. That was all he could ever be, and he was beginning to suspect that this was limiting.

T-Sound exhaled some smoke from her nostrils: "Hear that, Code? Hear 50 Cent kickin' it on the jukebox? That's the nigga you ought to have a problem with, not me. I'm on your side." She set down her cigarette and looked at him, her full red lips slightly parted. "Or are you having trouble concentrating?"

Suddenly it was getting hot. OGs had talked about a special kind of woman that men found hard to beat, hard to resist. The French called them *femmes fatales*, mysterious women that could do a nigga in if he wasn't careful. Code realized that his dick was getting hard due to his overpowering lust and *fear* of her. She could do what no other man or woman had ever been able to do: read him. She knew what he wanted from her, needed from her, and what he could never allow anyone else to do: become close to him. His rules of engagement dictated that he possess no friends, only associates; that he have no real love, only pussy; no family—that had been destroyed years ago.

But Tanya was different; she took her time with him. She reminded him that despite being shot four times; despite never being convicted of killing two men and exterminating another man and his two children; despite raping or gangbanging a dozen women of various races and nationalities, as well as engaging in numerous hold-ups and burglaries; and despite selling vast quantities of controlled substances, he was just breaking twenty-two. She could be his mentor and get him out of a life that he didn't mind rapping about, but had worn thin since the last time he was shot. The code dictated that a nigga didn't last too long.

But he did have a problem with her, and she had scoped that out earlier.

"You want to fuck *me*, right?" prompted T-Sound. She reached over in his direction to get another napkin from a bar dispenser for her drink. "No can do. Someone else has fucking rights to my cunt."

"Rhyme?"

She shook her head. "No, we're partners. My wet-box is saved for someone else . . . but you can either fuck my ass or come in my mouth. Two out of three ain't bad, is it?"

T-Sound, looking at her watch and announcing an impending meeting, told him that if he wanted to do it, it had to be now, in the piss-smelling, HIV-potential men's room of Club Prospect. "And you better get that tongue of yours good and moist, because you're going to stick it up my ass before you stick your third leg in me. See you in a few minutes, chocolate." She slid off her seat and grabbed a handful of him at his below-the-belt area. "Hmmm, I'm gonna like this entering my back door. She slipped into the men's room, making sure the video camera would capture them at the right angle.

Code went to work on his tongue. Water, followed by orange and grapefruit juice, and then some club soda with a twist of lime. He purchased a few sample bottles of one of those new-fangled sweet-tasting cognacs that all the niggaz had been singing about and promoting over the airwaves and in intellectually deficient shop-and-fuck magazines. He was going to drink them out of her ass-crack. Armed with them in the side-pockets of his urban fatigues, Code pulled out his notebook and jotted down a few pre-coital lines:

Now what does a nigga
Have to think about
When a goddamn nasty bitch
Offers her ass or her mouth!

* * *

The Prospect Place Ladies' Auxiliary liked what they saw. They saw fine-looking black meat inching in and out of an even finer, perspiration-coated posterior—Tanya's. The audio portion was still better, with Tanya saying all kinds of nasty things *en Español,* and the preferred exclamations in Niggaese about *bitch this* and *bitch that.*

"Believe me, girls, this boy can barely read," confirmed Tanya, "but he knows how to work a woman's ass."

The women cackled and hooted when Tanya told them that she had emptied him three times, enjoying the feel of his warm spunk oozing down her legs as she left him nearly drained on the john at Club Prospect.

"Watch this, ladies," she said, directing their attention back to the TV/video monitor. The tape showed a limp but massive black snake slowly retreating from Tanya's rear.

"*Mon Dieu,* that boy is hung!" said Francesca, an Afro-Francophone from Paris. "But can he *eat?*"

"He can be trained," Tanya commented with an authoritative crack of her crop against her boots. "Any man can be trained under the proper regimen."

"What's the word on the bidding?" asked Janette.

"It's starting at a million," replied Tanya.

"What?" said another woman, Carmen. "Why so much?"

"Because *your* GOP friends in the Log Cabin Society and several of the Sons of the Confederacy want a raw nigga as much as some of you do," Tanya explained, "and when *The*

Code is released and he suddenly disappears, he'll be a collector's item."

"No wonder they call it the *Log* Cabin Society," quipped Dominique.

"I heard that even a few Saudi princes are taking a bid on him," commented Francesca. *"Non?"*

"Oui," affirmed Tanya. "Raw niggaz are the rage; hip hop has advertised that."

The women assembled at Tanya's Prospect Heights brownstone, the crème of nouveau black womanhood, were wealthy. Businesswomen, achievers, well-known role models, church-going hot moms—they had all acquired a taste for supine men, especially hard-co' raw niggaz. Over the years, certain people had tried to eradicate the scourge of what some called *gangsta rap*, but had been less than successful. While others had managed to assassinate some well-known acts and perpetuate the myth that their deaths had been the result of incessant male-ego feuding, Tanya had been developing the art of "slutting," turning street niggaz into cunt-lapping dawgz.

There was no better example of her handiwork than "Juliette," a corseted, black-fishnet-wearing, muscular servant whose pecs had been tagged with the emblems of his gang-banging days. Jam-Bone Jones had been lured to Tanya's basement months ago. She could always pick the sluts by their inordinate fear of "faggots." These young ghetto bucks were obsessed with homosexuals and treacherous black women—people who had to be either exterminated or kept down. She could always tell which ones could be flipped. In her mind, Code was no different. Soon after showing him that her ass-muscles could squeeze him into a climax, she knew she had him hooked. She had even encouraged him to include the piece he had written about their toilet

186 // BROOKLYN NOIR

tryst, "Slutz and Dawgz," on *The Code*. That way, she thought, his mind would always be on her and what she could do for him—and *to* him.

After a long day at the studio, where she had castigated him for lame delivery, she had him stay behind for some vocal-relaxation exercises: She blew him. But she wouldn't allow him to speak or come near her without a withering comment or a comparison to 50 or Nas or Jay-Z, or the ultimate insult, Eminem. ("That cracker makes niggaz like you look counterfeit!" she told him after a flaccid flow.)

Jam-Bone Jones had been the same. He excoriated faggots but wasn't beyond sucking off a vivacious she-male like Dominique, and he was definitely surprised that T-Sound had a little something extra.

"What's the plan?" asked Darlene, while testing Juliette's serving etiquette. As the newly minted slut poured tea, Darlene grabbed "her" dangling meat and Juliette didn't even flinch. How could she with her exacting cycloptric mistress watching her every move, ready to punish her with the severe sting of a silver-tipped riding crop. Tanya looked every bit the bitch goddess; she wore a white linen shirt, jodhpur breeches, and knee-high riding boots.

"Well," said Tanya measuredly, "I thought I would appeal to his masculine nature and tell him that a bunch of hot bitches—you all—wanted to meet him. This will be the night of the CD release party at Club Prospect. He'll be high and ready . . . and hot. ¡Muy caliente!"

* * *

You got it! You got it!
You know you got it

When you see me
Gunnin' for yo' ass!
Blocks of motherfuckahs be running my way
Niggaz be gone when they see my 47/AK
Taking my time, drinking my wine
Shot another nigga couldn't tell time
Back at da crib, laying back,
Had a bitch suck my dick
She drown when I didn't hold back
You got it! You got it!
You know you got it
When you see me
Gunnin' for yo' ass!
—"Gunnin' for Yo' Ass"

The Source, Vibe, XXL, Murder Dawg Review, Rolling Stone, SPIN, and even one commentator on National Public Radio proclaimed the era of *The Code.* "*The most vicious piece of misogynistic and anti-gay pornography ever produced by the team of Dr. Rhyme and T-Sound,*" wrote a reviewer—and she liked it.

"*What's not to like/I'm a powerful motherfuckah when I'm on the mike,*" rapped Code as he walked the length of the bar at Club Prospect. The joint was jammed and nigga deep; the 'hood had turned out to see one of their own, who had gone platinum before the CD was even released.

"*King Kong with a powerful ding-dong!!!*" he roared, thumping his chest, grabbing his meat. "*Give me cash! I'm a ho' too! You got it! You got it! I want it!*" And they gave it to him—small green piles of dollar bills formed at his feet. Code tore off his shirt, used it to mop his face and chest, and thew it to his fans. Half-naked, his ripped musculature was coated in a thin sweat; he had the aura of a champion boxer, a new jack Muhammad Ali. As a matter of fact, he was thinking about calling himself that, toying with naming his next album

Jihad or *Real Niggaz Die*. He took in the adulation and the sullen stares of the wanna-be players, confident that he could whack any one of them as he jumped off the bar with his hands on his heater. A real nigga, he thought, was always ready to die. That's why the likes of Eminem and the legion of other pallid wanna-bes were counterfeit; they weren't going to die like real niggaz.

Rhyme sat in a special VIP section of Club Prospect, a cushioned alcove that rose above the floor and allowed him to peer down at an elevated angle at the masses. Code was making his way through the crowd, toward the club's door. Code's executive producer made a phone call: All was ready. The place was stinkin' on a midsummer night and management hadn't fixed the air conditioner. Everything was set. Tanya had left and waited outside. It was 9 p.m. and a crowd was still waiting to get in to see "King" Code.

With a phone to her ear, Tanya leaned against a car and took in a sultry summer breeze, an amazing relief after experiencing the sweatbox that passed for a club.

"T-Sound!"

Tanya, flipping down the cover of her c-phone, turned and saw him. He looked magnificent; the moonlight made his dark skin glisten. He was manly beautiful, gorgeous, and she was going to break him.

"The party is in there," he said, pointing back to the club.

"Nigga, are you high?" she asked.

"I'm always high when I'm with yo' fine ass."

Before he could say another word, she embraced him and burned his lips with an infinite kiss, brushing a thumb against an exposed nipple on his chest.

"Goddamn . . ." he said, catching his breath. "You can bring a nigga down with that."

"I want you to meet some people, Code," she said softly. "I'm having a special celebration at my place . . ."

"Naw, I got my peeps, my crew back there, and . . ."

". . . and then you can fuck me, *really* fuck me . . ."

Code looked at her. "We're talkin' pussy, right?"

"All that you can eat, nigga . . ."

"I'm way down for that."

"What about your peeps?"

"Fuck 'em!"

They wouldn't even have to take a car. Her place was only a few blocks away and they walked over hand-in-hand, crossing Washington Avenue, passing the stores he had once robbed, the owners he had brutalized because they didn't move fast enough or didn't have enough cash on hand. Code was excited. Things were finally coming together, coming his way. He could now get off the streets and do new things, like take the time to *think* about what was going on. No nigga had the time to think in the 'hood; it was all about survivin'. He had crawled, inched, shot, knifed, and fucked his way to this moment with this incredible woman.

When they turned onto Prospect Place, their pace slowed. A swarm of emotions swelled up in him; Code was feeling something that he had never known existed.

"Yo, I got to tell you something," he said, stopping at the ground floor entrance that led to her playroom and dungeon. She had a series of reinforced restraints ready for him.

"What?" she replied, as she unlocked the door; she felt that he sensed what was about to transpire.

"I . . . I . . ." he grappled. "Shit . . ."

"What's wrong, baby?" solicited Tanya, caressing his face. He was so handsome, she thought. So beautiful, but deadly.

"I've never been in love before," he answered, looking at

her with open and inviting eyes, no longer, at least at this moment, suspicious slits of mayhem.

Warmly murmuring a response, Tanya thought that this was indeed a very nasty business, but peered at him intensely and pressed him against the door, then knelt down. All that could be heard was the un-zipping of his trousers; all that he felt was her warm and experienced mouth, and the joy of repetition that her tongue offered. After she voraciously milked him, Code was changed. He was left feeling woozy, as if he been spiked, Vanessa Del Rio'd. Slowly, he opened the door and entered the basement that was blasting his music, the sound of the hip hop generation. It was young men like him who had dethroned a previous generation and ushered in the reign of the new HNIC, a reign in which authentication meant death.

Half-dressed as he had been since leaving the club, Code, still dazed, walked into a room with scores of naked women who appeared glad to see him, kissing his keloid medals of the street. He was offered a palette of tastes: breasts, asses, thighs, legs, buttocks, vaginas, cunts, and pussies. While being told that they were making a home movie of his triumph with a bevy of hot bodies, he didn't notice that he was also being given the "Dawg of the Year Award," a choke collar. Dominique fastened it around his neck just as Darlene lowered his trousers and stripped him of the rest of his clothes and his 9mm. The women admired his flaccid malething that ran halfway down his thigh. They could tell that he was happy to be in their presence, even happier when a group of them began devouring him, attending to every part of his body with probing hands and tongues, rubbing their sticky, lubricated orifices against his street-toughened, muscular black body.

When Francesca slipped on the black metal handcuffs, Code was still woozy from the weed and booze and Tanya's mouth-fucking, and didn't think too much about it when he was made to kneel down to service Dominique, who waited with opened legs; her warm aroma greeted his quivering nostrils. This was fun: doing dawg duty amongst all the booty. But his enthusiasm waned when he discovered Dominique's ever-enlarging cock staring him in the face—and hers was just as large as Code's. Protesting, struggling against the handcuffs now holding his arms behind his back, Code was forced into service upon feeling the cold barrel of his own "nigga-stopper" behind his right ear and the grip of the choke chain around his neck. Knee-deep into deep-throating Dominique, Code could feel his own backdoor being prepared for a rear-entry maneuver.

Upstairs, Tanya was offered a cognac by Juliette and sighed as she began the bidding, watching Code's ravishing on the monitor. In a few days, the training would begin and she would bust his opened, dark ass with her own twelve inches—without lubrication. As a fully equipped hermaphrodite, she would teach him how to service her wet slit while he lay on his back in a supine position with his legs and arms beneath him. His transformation from man to bitch would begin. In a few more weeks, Code would disappear and be corseted, shaved, lipsticked, and turned into "Charlene," sold to the highest bidder. Code's disappearance would drive up *The Code's* sales and further the rumor that the system had taken down another black man. No one would believe that he had been turned into a woman-manufactured male slut, especially not the brothers on the street. But T-Sound knew differently. Music, like sex, was a nasty business, a very nasty business.

PART III

Cops & Robbers

CAN'T CATCH ME

BY THOMAS MORRISSEY

Bay Ridge

T
he *fuck* are you doing?" shouted the squat, muscular man from his van. "I was just gonna park there!"

Detective Sal Ippolito heaved his bulk from the car and felt his temper start to rise. *Control.* He took a calming breath through his nose, enjoying the aromas wafting from the open back window of Epstein's Bakery, and tapped his windshield. "See that red light on my dashboard? That little sign next to it? I'm a cop. I get to park here because I'm working. Find somewhere else."

"You see *this* sign?" The man slammed a stubby-fingered hand on his door, above the *Bay Ridge Bread and Bakers* lettering. "*I'm* working, too. I got to pick up bread for my route. 'The fuck am I supposed to do that if you're in my way?"

Ippolito took another breath. Another delicious noseful of cookie-bread-donut goodness warmed his freezing nostrils. "Look," he said, restraining his annoyance. "It's Christmastime. How about giving me a little present by not busting my balls? The longer I stand out here talking to you, the longer it's going to be until I take care of things inside, and the longer until you get to pick up your bread. Go have a cup of coffee. Go do some shopping. Go do anything else, because until further notice this bakery is a crime scene and no one goes in or out. *Capice?*"

"It's 4 o'clock in the morning. 'The fuck am I going to go

shopping?" The squat man slammed his van into gear. "Crime scene, my ass. Go commit grand theft donut, ya fat pig."

Ippolito unconsciously rubbed his basketball stomach, fighting the desire to chase him down for premeditated ass-holery. "Hell with it." Crystals of salt and half-melted slush crunched underfoot as he turned and walked to the rear door. "At least I can resist *some* temptations."

Entering the bakery was like walking into a brownie: warm, moist, and sweet. Steam and heat thickened the atmosphere in a delightful contrast to outside. Ippolito licked his lips, taste buds searching for some of the chocolate or almond that flavored the air.

"H—hello?" A tiny, wizened woman edged into the kitchen. She was so bundled up against the cold, Ippolito doubted she would have been able to swing the fire axe she grasped. "Who are you?"

"Police, ma'am." He slowly took out his badge. "Detective—"

"Sally! Little Sally Ippolito!" The woman relaxed and lowered the axe. Its weight made her lurch forward. "Not so little anymore, eh?"

Ippolito frowned before he recognized her. "What are *you* doing here, Mrs. Funerro?"

"I called you people." The old woman shuffled over to lean against a sink filled with batter-crusted trays and pans. "Eppy used to save the first loaf of bread of the day for me. I haven't been sleeping well lately, so I thought I'd surprise him coming by. I've done it before when my goddamn insomnia kept me awake. I think that snippy waitress at the Bridgeview gave me regular coffee when I asked for decaf, just to be mean—"

"Mrs. Funerro, what happened? The operator said you told her there was trouble."

"I didn't want to say too much over the phone because I wanted to get this," she shook the axe, "to protect myself."

"From what?"

"I came to the back door, because I know Eppy leaves it open sometimes to let the heat out—isn't that a silly thing in this cold?—and when I called out, he didn't answer. I found him in the front. Well, his body. I was going to call Father Mulhern, too, over at St. Patrick's, but then I remembered Eppy is—well, *was*—Jewish. I don't know what those people do about death. Maybe I should call a rabbi?"

"Mrs. Funerro—" Visions of being trapped in the old lady's apartment when he was a grocery delivery boy years ago, delayed by tales of sciatica and back spasms, made him cut her off. "Did you say Mr. Epstein is dead? You found his body?"

She exhaled. "I *thought* the police were observant. How will you find clues if you aren't even listening to what I say?"

Ippolito unholstered his gun. Mrs. Funerro gasped. Putting a finger to his lips, he crept to the doorway with the surprising grace of the obese.

"I told you, *I* found his body. There's no one else here now."

He scanned the shop. Formica cases sat packed with fresh racks of oversized chocolate chip cookies, perfectly frosted layer cakes, and pastries of every shape and filling. Glass and stainless steel reflected the holiday window lights while the *Now Serving* sign was reset to zero, a string of number tabs hanging below it like a tongue. A flat tray filled with some kind of cookie waited atop the serving counter to be put away. Everything looked as normal as any of the dozen bakeries and bagel shops around the neighborhood, except for the wide red puddle staining the black-and-white tile floor. A slight slope had allowed it to spread almost to the front door.

Ippolito sighed. "Oh boy."

Epstein's body lay facedown behind the serving counter. Ippolito crouched and rolled him partway over. The front of his baker's whites was now squishy scarlet from the nasty, raw gash at his throat, while dozens of tiny rips revealed more wounds on his body. Their edges looked as though something had been gnawing at him.

What the hell? "You were the only person here?" he asked without turning. "No one else? No animals, dogs, or some rats, maybe?"

"Rats? Eppy kept a *clean* shop."

He gently set the body back down. No sign of a struggle was in evidence, but a gingerbread figure lay near Epstein's outstretched hand in a grotesque parody of the dead man. The cookie wasn't a traditional shape; still humanoid, it looked like a man in a suit and hat, holding a gun. The white frosting gave it a pin-striped suit and mobster attitude, still evident even though half its head and one shoulder had been bitten off. It had apparently come from the sheet of similar cookies inside the case—all those rows were symmetrical except the top, which presumably was missing the half-eaten one. Ippolito picked up a sheet of wax paper.

"Hello, saliva traces and DNA."

He started to rise, when he noticed something on the glass inside the case. In front of all the mouth-watering treats (*Resist the temptation!* he scolded himself), words had been written in what looked like Epstein's blood:

> *Run, run, as fast as you can*
> *Can't catch me . . .*

Mrs. Funerro came up behind him. "Did you find something? Is that a clue?"

Quickly he stood, using his bulk to block her view of the body and, more importantly, the writing. "You must have watched police shows on TV. You know I can't say anything." *Especially if I don't want everyone from here to Astoria to know about it.* He held the half-eaten cookie behind his back. "Forensics will tell us what happened. For now, I need you to do something very important."

The old woman leaned forward conspiratorially. "You want me to canvass for witnesses? I could do that—I know everyone from Shore Road to Fort Hamilton Parkway. Maybe somebody saw something. That snippy waitress got her break at the diner a little while ago. Maybe she knows something—she's always talking to those boys who go in there, the little gossip."

"No, no, that could be dangerous." Ippolito put an arm around her skeletal shoulder and guided her through the kitchen to the rear door. "I need you to go back to your house and write down everything you saw and experienced here tonight."

"Write down . . . ?"

"You're our main witness right now. We need to protect you." He nodded solemnly. "I'll have a car sent to watch your door, too. Just in case."

Hope enlivened her voice. "Am I . . . in danger, you think?"

"Just in case." He touched one beefy finger to the side of his nose. "But do me a favor—no axes. We can't have our most valuable witness hurting herself."

Now she was positively glowing. "Of course. Of course, you're right. But the Bridgeview is on my way. If I stop there I can question—"

"Straight. Home." He closed the door before she could argue.

Epstein had kept a small office next to the kitchen. Ippolito used its phone to make his report before going back out to the front shop to wait for assistance. Through the front window he watched snow begin to fall on an empty Fourth Avenue. Memories of his grocery delivery days returned like ghosts of Christmases past. *Way too many years ago. Years and pounds.* He started to smile until a glare reflected off the floor and reminded him why he was there. The car, a Mercedes SUV with a Christmas tree's worth of headlights, had stopped at a red light outside. A shirtless young man wearing a thick gold rope around his neck hung out the passenger window.

"I love you, Angieeee! Merry Fucking Christmas!" the man screamed. *"Aaaaaaaaa! I love you, Aaaangieeee!"*

Across the street an apartment window slammed open. "She don't love you, 'cause she's up *here* sucking my *dick! Just shut the hell up!"*

Now the driver of the SUV joined in. "You can't talk to my boy like that! *Fuck* you!"

"Fuck *you!"*

The light turned green and the SUV sped off in a screech of tires and obscenities. "Home sweet home," Ippolito shook his head. "Where everybody's a tough guy and no one takes crap from no one, because their boys have got their backs."

He turned away from the window and his memories to study the scene. The tray atop the serving counter was also filled with those mobster gingerbread men, in eight neat rows of four. Gingerly he avoided the pool of blood as he stood over them. The cryptic message on the display case was backwards from this side, but the baked goods looked just as wonderful. From this position he couldn't see the body either, and any of the smells death brings were smothered by the overwhelming scent of delightful holiday treats.

"*Temptation,*" he reminded himself. He stared into the display case, feeling like a child, before something odd caught his eye: One of the gingerbread mobsters had red hands. And they all had white frosting eyes and pinstripes, but red mouths.

Ippolito frowned. The gingerbread mobsters on the countertop looked identical, but with white frosting mouths. He picked one up and circled the counter, stepped over Epstein's body, and crouched to take one from inside the case. His knees creaked. Holding the two side by side he noticed the one from inside the case, in addition to the varied coloring, also seemed . . . bigger.

Fatter.

"*Hmph.*"

Carefully he replaced the larger one, an involuntary grunt escaping his pursed lips as he reached. "*Jesus,* I've got to lose some weight. My New Year's resolution." Still in a crouch, he leaned against the counter for support. The hand on which he rested his weight clutched the gingerbread mobster from the countertop.

"What are you looking at?"

The gingerbread mobster had no reply. Its white frosting eyes remained unblinking, its white frosting mouth remained in a fixed sneer.

The temptation proved too much. He cocked his head at the cookie and adopted the tone of the SUV driver: "Fuck *me?* Fuck *you!*" He chuckled as he bit off its head and chewed. "Yeah, I can eat you. It isn't New Year's yet." He took another bite. The gingerbread was still faintly warm, and a hint of cinnamon tickled his palate. It dissolved in his mouth like butter on hot pancakes, leaving an aftertaste of gingery vanilla.

"Wow," he smacked his lips. "Mr. Epstein, the world will mourn the loss of so great a cookie master—"

Scuttling above him made Ippolito's head snap up. He dropped the half-eaten cookie and started to rise, reaching for his gun. As he came eye-level with the counter he saw the flat pan was now empty. Before he could process this, he saw why.

And he screamed.

"God, he just called this in," the patrolman said sadly. "Can't have been more than twenty minutes ago."

Detective Mike Schofield's jaw tightened. "Well, obviously the killer came back."

Ippolito's body lay atop the body of the bakery's proprietor. It took two blankets to cover the mass, and both were sponging up blood. It was everywhere. Schofield noted spray patterns from severed arteries as well as smears that showed the hefty detective hadn't gone down without a fight. Judging by the damage to Ippolito's body, there had been more than one assailant.

The patrolman was staring at the display case's glass window. "What's this supposed to mean?"

Schofield glanced at it. "Whatever it means, it's written here, too." He pointed at the countertop. "'*Run, run, as fast as you can. Can't catch me . . .*' We'll see about that, scumbag. You don't kill a cop and walk away. We watch out for our own."

Next to the writing sat a tray filled with gingerbread mobsters. Schofield frowned. They were big and fat, overlapping each other in a way that would have made them burn in the oven if that was how they'd been cooked.

"Let me ask you something," he said to the patrolman. "You bake gingerbread men, you give them faces with white frosting, right?"

"Yeah."

Schofield pointed at the cookies on the countertop. "So how come these ones have red mouths?"

CASE CLOSED

BY LOU MANFREDO

Bensonhurst

T he fear enveloped her, and yet despite it, or perhaps
because of it, she found herself oddly detached, being from
body, as she ran frantically from the stifling grip of the
subway station out into the rainy, darkened street.

Her physiology now took full control, independent of her conscious thought, and her pupils dilated and gathered in the dim light
to scan the streets, the storefronts, the randomly parked automobiles. Like a laser, her vision locked onto him, undiscernable in the
distance. Her brain computed: one hundred yards away. Her legs
received the computation and turned her body toward him, pro-
pelling her faster. How odd, she thought through the terror, as she
watched herself from above. It was almost the flight of an inani-
mate object. So unlike that of a terrified young woman.

When her scream came at last, it struck her deeply and pri-
mordially, and she ran even faster with the sound of it. A
microsecond later the scream reached his ears and she saw his
head snap around toward her. The silver object at the crest of his
hat glistened in the misty streetlight, and she felt her heart leap
wildly in her chest.

Oh my God, she thought, a police officer. Thank you, dear
God, a police officer!

As he stepped from the curb and started toward her, she
swooned, and her being suddenly came slamming back into her
body from above. Her knees weakened and she faltered, stumbled,

and as consciousness left her, she fell heavily down and slid into the grit and slime of the wet, cracked asphalt.

Mike McQueen sat behind the wheel of the dark gray Chevrolet Impala and listened to the hum of the motor idling. The intermittent *slap-slap* of the wipers and the soft sound of the rain falling on the sheet-metal body were the only other sounds. The Motorola two-way on the seat beside him was silent. The smell of stale cigarettes permeated the car's interior. It was a slow September night, and he shivered against the dampness.

The green digital on the dash told him it was almost 1 a.m. He glanced across the seat and through the passenger window. He saw his partner, Joe Rizzo, pocketing his change and about to leave the all-night grocer. He held a brown bag in his left hand. McQueen was a six-year veteran of the New York City Police Department, but on this night he felt like a first-day rookie. Six years as a uniformed officer first assigned to Manhattan's Greenwich Village, then, most recently, its Upper East Side. Sitting in the car, in the heart of the Italian-American ghetto that was Brooklyn's Bensonhurst neighborhood, he felt like an out-of-towner in a very alien environment.

He had been a detective, third grade, for all of three days, and this night was to be his first field exposure, a midnight-to-eight tour with a fourteen-year detective first grade, the coffee-buying Rizzo.

Six long years of a fine, solid career, active in felony arrests, not even one civilian complaint, medals, commendations, and a file full of glowing letters from grateful citizens, and it had gotten for him only a choice assignment to the East Side Precinct. And then one night, he swings his radio car to the curb to pee in an all-night diner, hears a commotion, takes a look down an alleyway, and just like that, third grade detective, the gold shield handed to him personally by the mayor himself just three weeks later.

If you've got to fall ass-backwards into an arrest, fall into the one where the lovely young college roommate of the lovely young daughter of the mayor of New York City is about to get raped by a nocturnal predator. Careerwise, it doesn't get any better than that.

McQueen was smiling at the memory when Rizzo dropped heavily into the passenger seat and slammed the door.

"Damn it," Rizzo said, shifting his large body in the seat. "Can they put some fucking springs in these seats, already?"

He fished a container of coffee from the bag and passed it to McQueen. They sat in silence as the B train roared by on the overhead elevated tracks running above this length of 86th Street. McQueen watched the sparks fly from the third rail contacts and then sparkle and twirl in the rainy night air before flickering and dying away. Through the parallel slots of the overhead tracks, he watched the twin red taillights of the last car vanish into the distance. The noise of the steel-on-steel wheels and a thousand rattling steel parts and I-beams reverberated in the train's wake. It made the deserted, rain-washed streets seem even more dismal. McQueen found himself missing Manhattan.

The grocery had been the scene of a robbery the week before, and Rizzo wanted to ask the night man a few questions. McQueen wasn't quite sure if it was the coffee or the questions that had come as an afterthought. Although he had only known Rizzo for two days, he suspected the older man to be a somewhat less than enthusiastic investigator.

"Let's head on back to the house," Rizzo said, referring to the 62nd Precinct station house, as he sipped his coffee and fished in his outer coat pocket for the Chesterfields he seemed to live on. "I'll write up this here interview I just did and show you where to file it."

McQueen eased the car out from the curb. Rizzo had insisted he drive, to get the lay of the neighborhood, and McQueen knew it made sense. But he felt disoriented and foolish: He wasn't even sure which way the precinct was.

Rizzo seemed to sense McQueen's discomfort. "Make a U-turn," he said, lighting the Chesterfield. "Head back up 86th and make a left on Seventeenth Avenue." He drew on the cigarette and looked sideways at McQueen. He smiled before he spoke again. "What's the matter, kid? Missing the bright lights across the river already?"

McQueen shrugged. "I guess. I just need time, that's all."

He drove slowly through the light rain. Once off 86th Street's commercial strip, they entered a residential area comprised of detached and semi-detached older, brick homes. Mostly two stories, the occasional three-story. Some had small, neat gardens or lawns in front. Many had ornate, well-kept statues, some illuminated by flood lamps, of the Virgin Mary or Saint Anthony or Joseph. McQueen scanned the home fronts as he drove. The occasional window shone dimly with night lights glowing from within. They looked peaceful and warm, and he imagined the families inside, tucked into their beds, alarm clocks set and ready for the coming work day. Everyone safe, everything secure, everyone happy and well.

And that's how it always seemed. But six years had taught him what was more likely going on in some of those houses. The drunken husbands coming home and beating their wives; the junkie sons and daughters, the sickly, lonely old, the forsaken parent found dead in an apartment after the stench of decomposition had reached a neighbor and someone had dialed 9-1-1.

The memories of an ex-patrol officer. As the radio crackled to life on the seat beside him and he listened with half an ear, he wondered what the memories of an ex-detective would someday be.

He heard Rizzo sigh. "All right, Mike. That call is ours. Straight up this way, turn left on Bay 8th Street. Straight down to the Belt Parkway. Take the Parkway east a few exits and get off at Ocean Parkway. Coney Island Hospital is a block up from the Belt. Looks like it might be a long night."

When they entered the hospital, it took them some minutes to sort through the half-dozen patrol officers milling around the emergency room. McQueen found the right cop, a tall, skinny kid of about twenty-three. He glanced down at the man's nametag. "How you doing, Marino? I'm McQueen, Mike McQueen. Me and Rizzo are catching tonight. What d'ya got?"

The man pulled a thick leather note binder from his rear pocket. He flipped through it and found his entry, turned it to face McQueen, and held out a Bic pen.

"Can you scratch it for me, detective? No sergeant here yet."

McQueen took the book and pen and scribbled the date, time, and CIHOSP E/R across the bottom of the page, then put his initials and shield number. He handed the book back to Marino.

"What d'ya got?" he asked again.

Marino cleared his throat. "I'm not the guy from the scene. That was Willis. He was off at midnight, so he turned it to us and went home. I just got some notes here. Female Caucasian, Amy Taylor, twenty-six, single, lives at 1860 61st Street. Coming off the subway at 62nd Street about 11 o'clock, 23:00, the station's got no clerk on duty after 9. She goes into one of them—what d'ya call it?—one-way exit-door turnstile things, the ones that'll only let you out, not in. Some guy jumps out of nowhere and grabs her."

At that point, Rizzo walked up. "Hey, Mike, you okay with this for a while? My niece is a nurse here, I'm gonna go say hello, okay?"

Mike glanced at his partner, "Yeah, sure, okay, Joe, go ahead."

McQueen turned back to Marino. "Go on."

Marino dropped his eyes back to his notes. "So this guy pins her in the revolving door and shoves a knife in her face. Tells her he's gonna cut her bad if she don't help him."

"Help him with what?"

Marino shrugged. "Who the fuck knows? Guy's got the knife in one hand and his johnson in the other. He's trying to whack off on her. Never says another word to her, just presses the knife against her throat. Anyway, somehow he drops the weapon and she gets loose, starts to run away. The guy goes after her. She comes out of the station screaming, Willis is on a foot post doing a four-to-midnight, sees her running and screaming, and goes over her way. She takes a fall, faints or something, bangs up her head and swells up her knee and breaks two fingers. They got her upstairs in a room, for observation on account of the head wound."

McQueen thought for a moment. "Did Willis see the guy?"

"No, never saw him."

"Any description from the girl?"

"I don't know, I never even seen her. When I got here she was upstairs."

"Okay, stick around till your sergeant shows up and cuts you loose."

"Can't you, detective?"

"Can't I what?"

"Cut me loose?"

McQueen frowned and pushed a hand through his hair. "I don't know. I think I can. Do me a favor, though, wait for the sarge, okay?"

Marino shook his head and turned his lips downward. "Yeah, sure, a favor. I'll go sniff some ether or something." He walked away, his head still shaking.

McQueen looked around the brightly lit emergency room. He saw Rizzo down a hall, leaning against a wall, talking to a bleached-blond nurse who looked to be about Rizzo's age: fifty. McQueen walked over.

"Hey, Joe, you going to introduce me to your niece?"

Joe turned and looked at McQueen with a puzzled look, then smiled.

"Oh, no, no, turns out she's not working tonight. I'm just making a new friend here, is all."

"Well, we need to go talk to the victim, this Amy Taylor."

Rizzo frowned. "She a dit-soon?"

"A what?" McQueen asked.

Rizzo shook his head. "Is she black?"

"No, cop told me Caucasian. Why?"

"Kid, I know you're new here to Bensonhurst, so I'm gonna be patient. Anybody in this neighborhood named Amy Taylor is either a dit-soon or a yuppie pain-in-the-ass moved here from Boston to be an artist or a dancer or a Broadway star, and she can't afford to live in Park Slope or

Brooklyn Heights or across the river. This here neighbor-
hood is all Italian, kid, everybody—cops, crooks, butchers,
bakers, and candlestick makers. Except for you, of course.
You're the exception. By the way, did I introduce you two?
This here is the morning shift head nurse, Rosalie
Mazzarino. Rosalie, say hello to my boy wonder partner,
Mike Mick-fucking-Queen."

The woman smiled and held out a hand. "Nice to meet
you, Mike. And don't believe a thing this guy tells you.
Making new friends! I've known him since he was your age
and chasing every nurse in the place." She squinted at
McQueen then and slipped a pair of glasses out of her hair
and over her eyes. "How old are you—twelve?"

Mike laughed. "I'm twenty-eight."

She twisted her mouth up and nodded her head in an
approving manner. "And a third grade detective already? I'm
impressed."

Rizzo laughed. "Yeah, so was the mayor. This boy's a genuine hero with the alma mater gals."

"Okay, Joe, very good. Now, can we go see the victim?"

"You know, kid, I got a problem with that. I can tell you
her whole story from right here. She's from Boston, wants to
be a star, and as soon as you lock up the guy raped her, she's
gonna bring a complaint against you 'cause you showed no
respect for the poor shit, a victim of society and all. Why
don't *you* talk to her, I'll go see the doctor and get the rape
kit and the panties, and we'll get out of here."

McQueen shook his head. "Wrong crime, partner. No
rape, some kind of sexual assault or abuse or whatever."

"Go ahead, kid, talk to her. It'll be good experience for
you. Me and Rosalie'll be in one of these linen closets when
you get back. I did tell you she was the *head* nurse, right?"

McQueen walked away with her laughter in his ear. It was going to be a long night. Just like Joe had figured.

He checked the room number twice before entering. It was a small room with barely enough space for the two hospital beds it held. They were separated by a seriously despondent looking curtain. The one nearest the door was empty, the mattress exposed. In the dim lighting, McQueen could see the foot of the second bed. The outline of someone's feet showed through the bedding. A faint and sterile yet vaguely unpleasant odor touched his nostrils. He waited a moment longer for his eyes to adjust to the low light, so soft after the harsh fluorescent glare of the hall. He glanced around for something to knock on to announce his presence. He settled on the footboard of the near bed and rapped gently on the cold metal.

"Hello?" he said softly. "Hello, Ms. Taylor?"

The covered feet stirred. He heard the low rustle of linens. He raised his voice a bit when he spoke again.

"Ms. Taylor? I'm Detective McQueen, police. May I see you for a moment?"

A light switched on, hidden by the curtain but near the head of the bed. McQueen stood and waited.

"Ms. Taylor? Hello?"

The voice was sleepy, possibly sedated. It was a gentle and clear voice, yet it held a tension, an edginess. McQueen imagined he had awoken her and now the memories were flooding through her, the reality of it: yes, it had actually happened, no, it hadn't been a dream. He had seen it a thousand times: the burglarized, the beaten, the raped, robbed, shot, stabbed, pissed on whole lot of them. He had seen it.

"Detective? Did you say 'detective'? Hello? I can't see you."

He stepped further into the room, slowly venturing past the curtain. Slow and steady, don't move fast and remember to speak softly. Get her to relax, don't freak her out.

Her beauty struck him immediately. She was sitting, propped on two pillows, the sheet raised and folded over her breasts. Her arms lay beside her on the bed, palms down, straight out. She appeared to be clinging to the bed, steadying herself against some unseen, not possible force. Her skin was almost translucent, a soft glow emanating from it. Her wide set eyes were like liquid sapphire, and they met and held his own. Her lips were full and rounded and sat perfectly under her straight, narrow nose, her face framed with shoulder-length black hair. She wore no makeup, and an ugly purple-yellow bruise marked her left temple and part of her cheekbone. Yet she was the most beautiful woman McQueen had ever seen.

After almost three years working the richest, most sophisticated square mile in the world, here, now, in this godforsaken corner of Brooklyn, he sees this woman. For a moment, he forgot why he had come.

"Yes? Can I help you?" she asked as he stood in her sight.

He blinked himself back and cleared his throat. He glanced down to the blank page of the notepad in his hand, just to steal an instant more before he had to speak.

"Yes, yes, Ms. Taylor. I'm Detective McQueen, six-two detective squad. I need to see you for a few minutes. If you don't mind."

She frowned, and he saw pain in her eyes. For an instant he thought his heart would break. He shook his head slightly. What the hell? What the hell was this?

"I've already spoken to two or three police officers. I've already told them what happened." Her eyes closed. "I'm very tired. My head hurts." She opened her eyes and they were welled with tears. McQueen used all his willpower not to move to her, to cradle her head, to tell her it was okay, it was all over, he was here now.

"Yeah, yeah, I know that," he said instead. "But my partner and I caught the case. We'll be handling it. I need some information. Just a few minutes. The sooner we get started, the better chance we have of catching this guy."

She seemed to think it over as she held his gaze. When she tried to blink the tears away, they spilled down onto her cheeks. She made no effort to brush them away. "All right," was all she said.

McQueen felt his body relax, and he realized he had been holding himself so tightly that his back and shoulders ached. "May I sit down?" he asked softly.

"Yes, of course."

He slid the too-large-for-the-room chair to the far side of the bed and sat with his back to the windows. He heard rain rattle against the panes and the sound chilled him and made him shiver. He found himself hoping she hadn't noticed.

"I already know pretty much what happened. There's no need to go over it all, really. I just have a few questions. Most of them are formalities, please don't read anything into it. I just need to know certain things. For the reports. And to help us find this guy. Okay?"

She squeezed her eyes closed again and more tears escaped. She nodded yes to him and reopened her eyes. He couldn't look away from them.

"This happened about 11, 11:10?"

"Yes, about."

"You had gotten off the train at the 62nd Street subway station?"

"Yes."

"Alone?"

"Yes."

"What train is that?"

"The N."

"Where were you going?"

"Home."

"Where were you coming from?"

"My art class in Manhattan."

McQueen looked up from his notes. Art class? Rizzo's inane preamble resounded in his mind. He squinted at her and said, "You're not originally from Boston, are you?"

For the first time she smiled slightly, and McQueen found it disproportionately endearing. "No, Connecticut. Do you think I sound like a Bostonian?"

He laughed. "No, no, not at all. Just something somebody said to me. Long story, pay no attention."

She smiled again, and he could see it in her eyes that the facial movement had caused her some pain. "A lot of you Brooklynites think anyone from out of town sounds like they come from Boston."

McQueen sat back in his chair and raised his eyebrows in mock indignation. "'Brooklynite?' You think I sound like a Brooklynite?"

"Sure do."

"Well, Ms. Taylor, just so you know, I live in the city. Not Brooklyn." He kept his voice light, singsong.

"Isn't Brooklyn in the city?"

"Well, yeah, geographically. But the city is Manhattan. I was born on Long Island but I've lived in the city for fifteen years."

"All right, then," she said, with a pitched nod of her head.

McQueen tapped his pen on his notepad and looked at the ugly bruise on her temple. He dropped his gaze to the splinted, bandaged broken fingers of her right hand.

"How are you doing? I know you took a bad fall and had a real bad scare. But how are you doing?"

She seemed to tremble briefly, and he regretted having asked. But she met his gaze with her answer.

"I'll be fine. Everything is superficial, except for the fingers, and they'll heal. I'll be fine."

He nodded to show he believed her and that yes, of course, she was right, she would be fine. He wondered, though, if she really would be.

"Can you describe the man to me?"

"It happened very fast. I mean, it seemed to last for hours, but . . . but . . ."

McQueen leaned forward and spoke more softly so she would have to focus on the sound of his voice in order to hear, focus on hearing the words and not the memory at hand.

"Was he taller than you?"

"Yes."

"How tall are you?"

"Five-eight."

"And him?"

She thought for a moment. "Five-nine or -ten."

"His hair?"

"Black. Long. Very dirty." She looked down at the sheet and nervously picked at a loose thread. "It . . . It . . ."

McQueen leaned in closer, his knees against the side of the bed. He imagined what it would be like to touch her. "It what?" he asked gently.

"It smelled." She looked up sharply with the near panic

of a frightened deer in her eyes. She whispered, "His hair was so dirty, I could smell it."

She started to sob. McQueen sat back in his chair.

He needed to find this man. Badly.

"I want to keep this one."

McQueen started the engine and glanced down at his wristwatch as he spoke to Rizzo. It was 2 in the morning, and his eyes stung with the grit of someone who had been too long awake.

Rizzo shifted in the seat and adjusted his jacket. He settled in and turned to the younger detective.

"You what?" he asked absently.

"I want this one. I want to keep it. We can handle this case, Joe, and I want it."

Rizzo shook his head and frowned. "Doesn't work that way, kid. The morning shift catches and pokes around a little, does a rah-rah for the victim, and then turns the case to the day tour. You know that, that's the way it is. Let's get us back to the house and do the reports and grab a few Zs. We'll pick up enough of our own work next day tour we pull. We don't need to grab something ain't our problem. Okay?"

McQueen stared out of the window into the falling rain on the dark street. He didn't turn his head when he spoke.

"Joe, I'm telling you, I want this case. If you're in, fine. If not, I go to the squad boss tomorrow and ask for the case and a partner to go with it." Now he turned to face the older man and met his eyes. "Up to you, Joe. You tell me."

Rizzo turned away and spoke into the windshield before him. He let his eyes watch McQueen's watery reflection. "Pretty rough for a fuckin' guy with three days under his belt." He sighed and turned slowly before he spoke again.

"One of the cops in the ER told me this broad was a looker. So now I get extra work 'cause you got a hard-on?"

McQueen shook his head. "Joe, it's not like that."

Rizzo smiled. "Mike, you're how old? Twenty-seven, twenty-eight? It's like that, all right, it's always like that."

"Not this time. And not me. It's wrong for you to say that, Joe."

At that, Rizzo laughed aloud. "Mike," he said through a lingering chuckle, "there ain't no wrong. And there ain't no right. There just *is*, that's all."

Now it was McQueen who laughed. "Who told you that, a guru?"

Rizzo fumbled through his jacket pockets and produced a battered and bent Chesterfield. "Sort of," he said as he lit it. "My grandfather told me that. Do you know where I was born?"

McQueen, puzzled by the question, shook his head. "How would I know? Brooklyn?"

"Omaha-fuckin'-Nebraska, that's where. My old man was a lifer in the Air Force stationed out there. Well, when I was nine years old he dropped dead. Me and my mother and big sister came back to Brooklyn to live with my grandparents. My grandfather was a first grade detective working Chinatown back then. The first night we was home, I broke down, crying to him about how wrong it was, my old man dying and all, how it wasn't right and all like that. He got down on his knees and leaned right into my face. I still remember the smell of beer and garlic sauce on his breath. He leaned right in and said, 'Kid, nothing is wrong. And nothing is right. It just is.' I never forgot that. He was dead-on correct about that, I'll tell you."

McQueen drummed his fingers lightly on the wheel and

scanned the mirrors. The street was empty. He pulled the Impala away from the curb and drove back toward the Belt Parkway. After they had entered the westbound lanes, Rizzo spoke again.

"Besides, Mike, this case won't even stay with the squad. Rapes go to sex crimes and they get handled by the broads and the guys with the master's degrees in fundamental and advanced bullshit. Can you imagine the bitch that Betty Friedan and Bella Abzug would pitch if they knew an insensitive prick like me was handling a rape?"

"Joe, Bella Abzug died about twenty years ago."

Rizzo nodded. "Whatever. You get my point."

"And I told you already, this isn't a rape. A guy grabbed her, threatened her with a blade, and was yanking on his own chain while he held her there. No rape. Abuse and assault, tops."

For the first time since they had worked together, McQueen heard a shadow of interest in Rizzo's voice when the older man next spoke.

"Blade? Whackin' off? Did the guy come?"

McQueen glanced over at his partner. "What?" he asked.

"Did the guy bust a nut, or not?"

McQueen squinted through the windshield: Had he thought to ask her that? No. No he hadn't. It simply hadn't occurred to him.

"Is that real important to this, Joe, or are you just making a case for your insensitive-prick status?"

Rizzo laughed out loud and expelled a gray cloud of cigarette smoke in the process. McQueen reached for the power button and cracked his window.

"No, no, kid, really, official request. Did this asshole come?"

"I don't know. I didn't ask her. Why?"

Rizzo laughed again. "Didn't want to embarrass her on the first date, eh, Mike? Understandable, but totally unacceptable detective work."

"Is this going somewhere, Joe?"

Rizzo nodded and smiled. "Yeah, it's going toward granting your rude request that we keep this one. If I can catch a case I can clear up quick, I'll always keep it. See, about four, five years ago we had some schmuck running around the precinct grabbing girls and forcing them into doorways and alleyways. Used a knife. He'd hold them there and beat off till the thing started to look like a stick of chop meat. One victim said she stared at a bank clock across the street the whole time to sort of distract herself from the intimacy of the situation, and she said the guy was hammering himself for twenty-five minutes. But he could never get the job done. Psychological, probably. Sort of a major failure at his crime of choice. Never hurt no one, physically, but one of his victims was only thirteen. She must be popping Prozac by the handful now somewheres. We caught the guy. Not me, but some guys from the squad. Turned out to be a strung-out junkie shitbag we all knew. Thing is, junkies don't usually cross over into the sex stuff. No cash or H in it. I bet this is the same guy. He'd be long out by now. And except for the subway, it's his footprint. We can clear this one, Mike. You and me. I'm gonna make you look like a star, first case. The mayor will be so proud of himself for grabbing that gold shield for you, he'll probably make you the fuckin' commissioner!"

Two days later, McQueen sat at his desk in the cramped detective squad room, gazing once again into the eyes of Amy Taylor. He cleared his voice before he spoke, and noticed the bruise at her temple had subsided a bit and that no attempt to cover it with makeup had been made.

"What I'd like to do is show you some photographs. I'd like you to take a look at some suspects and tell me if one of them is the perpetrator."

Her eyes smiled at him as she spoke. "I've talked to about five police officers in the last few days, and you're the first one to say 'perpetrator.'"

He felt himself flush a little. "Well," he said with a forced laugh, "it's a fairly appropriate word for what we're doing here."

"Yes, it is. It's just unsettling to hear it actually said. Does that make sense?"

He nodded. "I think I know what you mean."

"Good," she said with the pitched nod of her head that he suddenly realized he had been looking forward to seeing again. "I didn't mean it as an insult or anything. Do I look at the mug books now?"

This time McQueen's laugh was genuine. "No, no, that's your words now. We call it a photo array. I'll show you eight photos of men roughly matching the description you gave me. You tell me if one of them is the right one."

"All right, then." She straightened herself in her chair and folded her hands in her lap. She cradled the broken right fingers in the long slender ones of her left hand. The gentleness made McQueen's head swim with—what?—grief?—pity? He didn't know.

When he came around to her side of the desk and spread out the color photos before her, he knew immediately. She looked up at him—and the sapphires swam in tears yet again. She turned back to the photos and lightly touched one.

"Him," was all she said.

* * *

"You know," Rizzo said, chewing on a hamburger as he spoke, "you can never overestimate the stupidity of these assholes."

It was just after 9 on a Thursday night, and the two detectives sat in the Chevrolet and ate their meals. The car stood backed into a slot at the rear of the Burger King's parking lot, nestled in the darkness between circles of glare from two lampposts. Three weeks had passed since the assault on Amy Taylor.

McQueen turned to his partner. "Which assholes we talking about here, Joe?" In the short time he had been working with Rizzo, McQueen had developed a grudging respect for the older man. What Rizzo appeared to lack in enthusiasm, he more than made up for in experience and with an ironic, grizzled sort of street smarts. McQueen had learned much from him and knew he was about to learn more.

"Criminals," Rizzo continued. "Skells in general. This burglary call we just took reminded me of something. Old case I handled seven, eight years ago. Jewelry store got robbed, over on Thirteenth Avenue. Me and my partner, guy named Giacalone, go over there and see the victim. Old Sicilian lived in the neighborhood forever, salt-of-the-earth type. So me and Giacalone, we go all out for this guy. We even called for the fingerprint team, we were right on it. So we look around, talk to the guy, get the description of the perp and the gun used, and we tell the old guy to sit tight and wait for the fingerprint team to show up and we'll be in touch in a couple of days. Well, the old man is so grateful, he walks us out to the car. Just as we're about to pull away, the guy says, 'You know, the guy that robbed me cased the joint first.' Imagine that?— 'cased the joint'—Musta watched a lot of TV, this old guy. So I say to him, 'What d'ya mean, cased the joint?' And he says,

'Yeah, two days ago the same guy came in to get his watch fixed. Left it with me and everything. Even filled out a receipt card with his name and address and phone number. Must have been just casing the place. Well, he sure fooled me.'"

Rizzo chuckled and bit into his burger. "So," he continued through a full mouth, "old Giacalone puts the car back into park and he leans across me and says, 'You still got that receipt slip?' The old guy goes, 'Yeah, but it must be all phony. He was just trying to get a look around.' Well, me and Giacalone go back in and we get the slip. We cancel the print guys and drive out to Canarsie. Guess what? The asshole is home. We grab him and go get a warrant for the apartment. Gun, jewelry, and cash, bing-bang-boom. The guy cops to rob-three and does four-to-seven."

Rizzo smiled broadly at McQueen. "His girlfriend lived in the precinct, and while he was visiting her, he figured he'd get his watch fixed. Then when he sees what a mark the old guy is, he has an inspiration! See? Assholes."

"Yeah, well, it's a good thing," McQueen said. "I haven't run across too many geniuses working this job."

Rizzo laughed and crumpled up the wrappings spread across his lap. "Amen," he said.

They sat in silence, Rizzo smoking, McQueen watching the people and cars moving around the parking lot.

"Hey, Joe," McQueen said after a while. "Your theory about this neighborhood is a little bit off base. For a place supposed to be all Italian, I notice a lot of Asians around. Not to mention the Russians."

Rizzo waved a hand through his cigarette smoke. "Yeah, somebody's got to wait the tables in the Chinese restaurants and drive car service. You still can't throw a rock without hitting a fucking guinea."

The Motorola crackled to life at McQueen's side. It was dispatch directing them to call the Precinct via telephone. McQueen took his cell from his jacket pocket as Rizzo keyed the radio and gave a curt "Ten-four."

McQueen placed the call and the desk put him through to the squad. A detective named Borrelli came on the line. McQueen listened. His eyes narrowed and, taking a pen from his shirt, he scribbled on the back of a newspaper. He hung up the phone and turned to Rizzo.

"We've got him," he said softly.

Rizzo belched loudly. "Got who?"

McQueen leaned forward and started the engine. He switched on the headlights and pulled away. After three weeks in Bensonhurst, he no longer needed directions. He knew where he was going.

"Flain," he said. "Peter Flain."

Rizzo reached back, pulled on his shoulder belt, and buckled up. "Imagine that," he said with a faint grin. "And here we was, just a minute ago, talking about assholes. Imagine that."

McQueen drove hard and quickly toward Eighteenth Avenue. Traffic was light, and he carefully jumped a red signal at Bay Parkway and turned left onto 75th Street. He accelerated to Eighteenth Avenue and turned right.

As he drove, he reflected on the investigation that was now about to unfold.

It had been Rizzo who had gotten it started when he recalled the prior crimes with the same pattern. He had asked around the Precinct and someone remembered the name of the perp. Flain. Peter Flain.

The precinct computer had spit out his last known

address in the Bronx and the parole officer assigned to the junkie ex-con. A call to the officer told them that Flain had been living in the Bronx for some years, serving out his parole without incident. He had been placed in a methadone program and was clean. Then, about three months ago, he disappeared. His parole officer checked around in the Bronx, but Flain had simply vanished. The officer put a violation on Flain's parole and notified the state police, the New York Supreme Court, and NYPD headquarters. And that's where it had ended, as far as he was concerned.

McQueen had printed a color print from the computer and assembled the photo array. Amy Taylor picked Flain's face from it. Flain had returned to the Six-two Precinct.

Then Rizzo had really gone to work. He spent the better part of a four-to-midnight hitting every known junkie haunt in the precinct. He had made it known he wanted Flain. He had made it known that he would not be happy with any bar, poolroom, candy store, or after-hours joint that would harbor Flain and fail to give him up with a phone call to the squad.

And tonight, that call had been made.

McQueen swung the Chevy into the curb, killing the lights as the car rolled to a slow stop. Three storefronts down, just off the corner of 69th Street, the faded fluorescent of the Keyboard Bar shone in the night. He twisted the key to shut off the engine. As he reached for the door handle and was about to pull it open, he felt the firm, tight grasp of Rizzo's large hand on his right shoulder. He turned to face him.

Rizzo's face held no sign of emotion. When he spoke, it was in a low, conversational tone. McQueen had never heard the older man enunciate more clearly. "Kid," Rizzo began, "I know you like this girl. And I know you took her out to dinner last week. Now, we both know you shouldn't even be working this collar since you been seeing the victim socially. I been working with you for three weeks now, and you're a good cop. But this here is the first bit of real shit we had to do. Let me handle it. Don't be stupid. We pinch him and read him the rights and off he goes." Rizzo paused and let his dark brown eyes run over McQueen's face. When they returned to the cold blue of McQueen's own eyes, they bored in.

"Right?" Rizzo asked.

McQueen nodded. "Just one thing, Joe."

Rizzo let his hand slide gently off McQueen's shoulder.

"What?" he asked.

"I'll process it. I'll walk him through central booking. I'll do the paperwork. Just do me one favor."

"What?" Rizzo repeated.

"I don't know any Brooklyn ADAs. I need you to talk to the ADA writing tonight. I want this to go hard. Two top counts, D felonies. Assault two and sexual abuse one. I don't want this prick copping to an A misdemeanor assault or some bullshit E felony. Okay?"

Rizzo smiled, and McQueen became aware of the tension that had been hidden in the older man's face only as he saw it melt away. "Sure, kid," he nodded. "I'll go down there myself and cash in a favor. No problem." He pushed his face in the direction of the bar and said, "Now, let's go get him."

Rizzo walked in first and went directly to the bar. McQueen hung back near the door, his back angled to the bare barroom wall. His eyes adjusted to the dimness of the large room and he scanned the half-dozen drinkers scattered along its length. He noticed two empty barstools with drinks and money and cigarettes spread before them on the worn Formica surface. At least two people were in the place somewhere, but not visible. He glanced over at Joe Rizzo.

Rizzo stood silently, his forearms resting on the bar. The bartender, a man of about sixty, was slowly walking toward him.

"Hello, Andrew," McQueen heard Rizzo say. "How the hell you been?" McQueen watched as the two men, out of earshot of the others, whispered briefly to one another. McQueen noticed the start of nervous stirrings as the drinkers came to realize that something was suddenly different here. He saw a small envelope drop to the floor at the feet of one man.

Rizzo stepped away from the bar and came back to McQueen.

He smiled. "This joint is so crooked, old Andrew over there would give up Jesus Christ Himself to keep me away from here." With a flick of his index finger, Rizzo indicated the men's room at the very rear in the left corner.

"Our boy's in there. Ain't feeling too chipper this evening, according to Andrew. Flain's back on the junk, hard. He's been sucking down Cokes all night. Andrew says he's been in there for twenty minutes."

McQueen looked at the distant door. "Must have nodded off."

Rizzo twisted his lips. "Or he read Andrew like a book and climbed out the fucking window. Lets us go see."

Rizzo started toward the men's room, unbuttoning his coat with his left hand as he walked. McQueen suddenly became aware of the weight of the 9mm Glock automatic belted to his own right hip. His groin broke into a sudden sweat as he realized he couldn't remember having chambered a round before leaving his apartment for work. He unbuttoned his coat and followed his partner.

The men's room was small. A urinal hung on the wall to their left, brimming with dark urine and blackened cigarette butts. A cracked mirror hung above a blue-green stained sink. The metallic rattle of a worn, useless ventilation fan clamored. The stench of disinfectant surrendered to—what?—vomit? Yes, vomit.

The single stall stood against the wall before them. The door was closed. Feet showed beneath it.

McQueen reached for his Glock and watched as Rizzo slipped an ancient-looking Colt revolver from under his coat.

Then Rizzo leaned his weight back, his shoulder brushing against McQueen's chest, and heaved a heavy foot at the stress point of the stall door. He threw his weight behind it, and as the door flew inward, he stepped deftly aside, at the same time gently shoving McQueen the other way. The door crashed against the stall occupant and Rizzo rushed forward, holding the bouncing door back with one hand, pointing the Colt with the other.

Peter Flain sat motionless on the toilet. His pants and underwear lay crumpled around his ankles. His legs were spread wide, pale and varicosed, and capped by bony knees. His head hung forward onto his chest, still. McQueen's eyes fell on the man's greasy black hair. Flain's dirty gray shirt was covered with a brown, foamy, blood-streaked vomit. More blood, dark and thick, ran from his nostrils and pooled in the crook of his chin. His fists were clenched.

Rizzo leaned forward and, carefully avoiding the fluids, lay two fingers across the jugular.

He stood erect and holstered his gun. He turned to McQueen.

"*Morte*," he said. "The prick died on us!"

McQueen looked away from Rizzo and back to Flain. He tried to feel what he felt, but couldn't. "Well," he said, just to hear his own voice.

Rizzo let the door swing closed on the sight of Flain. He turned to McQueen with sudden anger on his face. "You know what this means?" he said.

McQueen watched as the door swung slowly back open. He looked at Flain, but spoke to Rizzo.

"It means he's dead. It's over."

Rizzo shook his head angrily. "No, no, that's not what it fucking means. It means no conviction. No guilty plea. It means, 'Investigation abated by death'! That's what it means."

McQueen shook his head. "So?" he asked. "So what?"

Rizzo frowned and leaned back against the tiled wall. Some of the anger left him. "So what?" he said, now more sad than angry. "I'll tell you 'so what.' Without a conviction or a plea, we don't clear this case. We don't clear this case, we don't get credit for it. We don't clear this case, we did all this shit for nothing. Fucker would have died tonight anyway, with or without us bustin' our asses to find him."

They stood in silence for a moment. Then, suddenly, Rizzo brightened. He turned to McQueen with a sly grin, and when he spoke, he did so in a softer tone.

"Unless," he said, "unless we start to get smart."

In six years on the job, McQueen had been present in other places, at other times, with other cops, when one of them had said, "Unless . . ." with just such a grin. He felt his facial muscles begin to tighten.

"What, Joe? Unless what?"

"Un-less when we got here, came in the john, this guy was still alive. In acute respiratory distress. Pukin' on himself. Scared, real scared 'cause he knew this was the final overdose. And we, well, we tried to help, but we ain't doctors, right? So he knows he's gonna die and he says to us, 'I'm sorry.' And we say, 'What, Pete, sorry about what?' And he says, 'I'm sorry about that girl, that last pretty girl, in the subway. I shouldn'ta done that.' And I say to him, 'Done what, Pete, what'd you do?' And he says, 'I did like I did before, with the others, with the knife.' And then, just like that, he drops dead!"

McQueen wrinkled his forehead. "I'm not following this, Joe. How does that change anything?"

Rizzo leaned closer to McQueen. "It changes everything," he whispered, holding his thumb to his fingers and shaking his hand, palm up, at McQueen's face. "Don't you get it? It's a deathbed confession, rock-solid evidence, even admissible in court. Bang—case closed! And we're the ones who closed it. Don't you see? It's fucking beautiful."

McQueen looked back at the grotesque body of the dead junkie. He felt bile rising in his throat, and he swallowed it down.

He shook his head slowly, his eyes still on the corpse.

"Jesus, Joe," he said, the bile searing at his throat. "Jesus Christ, Joe, that's not right. We can't do that. That's just fucking wrong!"

Rizzo reddened, the anger suddenly coming back to him.

"Kid," he said, "don't make me say you owe me. Don't make me say it. I took this case on for you, remember?"

But it was not the way McQueen remembered it. He looked into the older man's eyes.

"Jesus, Joe," he said.

Rizzo shook his head, "Jesus got nothin' to do with it."

"It's wrong, Joe," McQueen said, even as his ears flushed red with the realization of what they were about to do. "It's just wrong."

Rizzo leaned in close, speaking more softly, directly into McQueen's ear. The sound of people approaching the men's room forced an urgency into his voice. McQueen felt the warmth of Rizzo's breath touching him.

"I tole you this, kid. I already tole you this. There is no right. There is no wrong." He turned and looked down at the hideous corpse. "There just *is*."

EATING ITALIAN

BY LUCIANO GUERRIERO

Red Hook

Buoy bells in Buttermilk Channel gave DeGraw and Mintz lazy company as they started their waterfront stroll at India Wharf off Summit Street. Even as late as 3 in the morning, the constant hum of vehicles entering the Brooklyn Battery Tunnel off the Gowanus Expressway lent the bells a pleasant harmony.

The nightly foot patrols these cops made through the labyrinth of freight containers and warehouses were keeping Wild Willy's crew—Red Hook's Mafia bad boys—from molesting the busiest stretch of freight piers left in the big city. Every year, the derricks at the water's edge offloaded 120,000 containers of cocoa, coffee, salt, pumice, and all sorts of other goods—especially those of the electronic variety— that became catnip to thugs looking to take their taste of things.

There was pressure for DeGraw and Mintz to look the other way, a lot in the way of temptation thrown at them. But they resisted the escalating bribe offers, even arrested some of Wild Willy's tougher customers, and this patch of waterfront got so quiet on the overnight shift that the dynamic duo started hating the isolation, felt cursed by their own success. With nothing much to do, even the night watchmen of the local freight hauling companies left them alone, retreating to some dim office somewhere to play poker.

DeGraw tried to get the duty changed so that at least some of the other overnight cops could split patrol time in the waterfront area, but Mintz followed him in to the brass and argued against it, the son of a bitch.

DeGraw couldn't understand being blocked by a partner who went behind his back. It bugged him. But then, for their two years together, Mintz was always a strange partner. He was a bundle of quirks and nerves and had a bad habit of busting balls just a little too often. Sometimes it made DeGraw question where Mintz's head and heart were.

Ultimately, though, DeGraw decided that Mintz was just a strange guy—one who sometimes played dumb so he could shirk some duty, sure, but one who wouldn't sell you short when it really counted. He believed that for all his faults, Mintz was a decent enough cop, clearly not a gung ho type but a guy who'd stood up during some heavy-duty moments they'd faced together. DeGraw figured he could do worse for a partner.

And maybe Mintz had been right to fight for the waterfront patrol. The piers even began to grow on them when they realized that the duty was cake. In fact, the precinct commander was so happy to reap the glory for their accomplishments that they were given latitude to freelance with no brass looking over their shoulders, a rare privilege for cops in uniform. Long as they got back to Red Hook Park when they were supposed to patrol it, the duty sarge let them do as they pleased. Wasn't the first time what started as a crap assignment turned out to be okay.

They were so isolated as they made their way from India Wharf south across Commercial Wharf and onto Clinton Wharf, tugging on all the locked warehouse doors, looking down all the alleys and between the big metal containers, that they'd taken to eating their lunch on the Clinton pier head near the railroad yard, under one of the big red derricks. If the weather was right, it was actually a pretty peaceful spot, except for the occasional turf war that broke out between armies of river rats.

On a clear night, the partners could see Lady Liberty standing vigil on the Jersey side of upper New York Bay, but on this balmy mid-September night, rain was forecast. Taking lunch, DeGraw and Mintz could hardly see Governor's Island across the Buttermilk because a fog was starting to blanket the water where the upper bay became the East River.

Mintz dropped the last piece of crust from his meatball Parmesan hero and it didn't bob on the undulating black water for even five seconds before some unseen creature snatched it under.

Probably a striped bass, DeGraw figured.

"Prob'ly a striper," Mintz said.

Still trying to drown the breakup of his marriage, DeGraw's lunch consisted of four bottles of tepid beer and eight cigarettes. Draining the last bottle, he flipped the empty into the water and let go a satisfying belch.

After a still moment spent staring at the water, they stood up on the pier, unzipped, and started peeing into the brine— another nightly ritual.

"Actually got plenty of time, you know," Mintz said.

"Might as well finish up early," DeGraw said, "go back and get the park done."

"What's this job do to your mind, Frankie?" Mintz said. "I mean, we're out here foiling the bad guys all the time, we gotta imagine how these skells think, don't we? Gotta do something to the way we think, don't it?"

"Nah, we thought like this to begin with," DeGraw said, peeing on and on. "Some of us, if we don't put on a uniform, we end up doing exactly what the skells do."

"You sayin' I have a criminal mentality?"

"We look at these buildings and containers and we see what the criminals see. God help me, Lou, but if we're not wearin' these uni's, you and me are in there even before Wild Willy's guys, taking shit outa here and fencin' it. I do believe that's true."

"I sold fireworks when I was a kid," Mintz said. "Made myself fat green while the other guys got pinched. Guess I got a talent for puttin' the other guy 'tween me and danger."

"Criminal mentality," DeGraw said. "I boosted cars, sold nickel bags. Then we lied on the police interview, another dishonesty. Face it, pal. Takes one to know one."

"Guess that's true, with, uh . . ." Mintz said, "with that other stuff you do."

DeGraw almost came back at Mintz for making mention of his outside activities. As far as DeGraw knew, Mintz was the only one on the force who was aware that he sold illegal guns, and DeGraw had made it understood that the touchy subject was to be off limits. DeGraw kept it all fairly well hidden, but unnecessary talk could put him in jeopardy. Still, DeGraw thought better of scolding Mintz, because it would have required him to talk about it.

They let go the last drops of pee in silence, shook themselves, and zipped up.

". . . 'Cuz we're two friggin' corrupt sons a bitches . . ." Mintz muttered as they made their usual way out toward Ferris and Wolcott, checking doors and alleys as they went. ". . . And remember, whatever I learned about crime I learned from you, Frank. So if all that's in our bones, why do we play it straight? Why don't we go, you know, like they say in the movies, to the dark side?"

"Don't know about you," DeGraw said, "but I don't wanna get too fat on the ill-gotten gains, 'cuz ya never know when that feast'll be over, and then yer fucked. Keepin' it more or less clean, maybe I don't eat so good but at least I eat in peace."

Then DeGraw stopped short. In the dim diffuse light, the hand on the sidewalk at the head of the alley didn't look real. The yellow skin with black splotches looked like painted latex, but the ragged end of the wrist gave it away; it trailed strands of sinew and a small ooze of blood. Accepting the possibility that the hand was real, DeGraw waved Mintz over and started to go queasy.

Mintz didn't say a word, his mouth agape at the sight of the hand.

"Who's goin' in?" DeGraw whispered, using his chin to point down the alley.

Mintz put a hand to his belly and backed away a step, stammering, "But, but I . . . I can't . . . I . . . I . . ."

DeGraw signaled for Mintz to stand watch as he turned and gazed into the alley's murk. They both drew their 9mm Glock handguns, dangled them at their sides, clicked off the safeties.

Stepping into the alley, DeGraw slid a big Maglite from his belt and clicked it on. He still couldn't glimpse the length of the alley. Not much more than a small mountain of stacked garbage was to be seen from the sidewalk, so he moved to it, peeked around it, and crept forward, all while Mintz stayed put.

When Mintz said, "Careful," DeGraw jumped because he thought Mintz was warning of an attacker. He lost his grip on the flashlight and it clattered to the ground. Stifling his impulse to go back and pummel Mintz, DeGraw stooped to retrieve the Maglite. Light rays glinting off something ten feet hence caught his eye. Then the bulb blew out and the alley fell into blackness again.

Rather than retreat, DeGraw went to where he'd seen the red flash, stooped, and opened his eyes as wide as he could. He noticed wetness on the cement. Squatting, DeGraw could smell the distinct odor of blood. Then he made out objects in the center of the blood puddle. Setting his feet close to it, he hunched over and went down to one knee, feeling blood soak into his pants. Squinting until he knew what he was looking at, he saw a scrotum, and about a foot away from that, a severed penis.

Mintz, agonizing, broke the silence again, "Whatcha got?"

"Fuckin' set of balls and a mutilated thingy," DeGraw said with more calm than his heart commanded.

"Friggin' Christ," Mintz moaned. "Are you *shittin'* me?"

There's an extremely unhappy man in Brooklyn tonight, DeGraw thought as he stood, found the wall with his shoulder, and crept further down the alley, gun out front. He knew he was walking through more blood, soon coming to a severed human arm without a hand, and eventually to a torso that was missing the sex organs, one arm, and its head. He noticed that the head had been propped on a barrel against the opposite wall, eyes open like it was viewing the scene.

His heart trying to pound its way out of his chest, DeGraw wanted to run. But he filled his lungs to the brim and exhaled out loud, forcing himself to do his job, make observations. The victim seemed to be a male Caucasian, late twenties/early thirties, minus the aforementioned body parts.

DeGraw lit a cigarette and then held the lighter in front

of the victim's vaguely familiar face. It was bloody, mouth twisted in what had to be either the victim's final agony or some kind of sick last laugh.

Holding the lighter up, he could see nobody else in the alley, which ended at a solid wall. He scanned up the sides of both buildings and could see no one on a rooftop, so he turned back to the sidewalk, away from the victim and toward Mintz.

Emerging from the alley, gun holstered, DeGraw remained silent because he wanted to make Mintz ask, just to bust nuts a little bit.

"Well?" Mintz said.

"Well what?"

"What'd you find? . . . Jesus Christ, Frank."

"Call it in. Rest of the guy's down there, in pieces."

As Mintz pulled his radio, DeGraw walked over to a puddle, patting at his pockets. "Gimme some gloves, Louie."

DeGraw took one last drag from his cigarette and flicked it away. Then he slipped on the surgical gloves Mintz handed him, lifted a soggy wallet, and flipped it open. Mintz held his Maglite on it, peering over DeGraw's shoulder.

As if DeGraw needed another shock right at that moment, he saw the driver's license photo of a man he was now sure he recognized.

"Hold that call," DeGraw said, and then looked over at Mintz. "Know who we got here? None other than William Montemarano."

"Wild Willy?" Mintz said. "And they left him here? . . . Why, Frank?"

"'Cuz we put him outa business for good, I guess," DeGraw said. "Aw, fuck, and I never knew before this second, but this guy's the scumbag who goes out with my ex."

"Wait, Sandra? How the hell's Sandy go out with a Mafioso like Wild Willy?"

"I don't think she knew he was the same guy. I sure didn't. To me, he's just Bill-some-Italian-guy, Bill the guy who owned a tow truck company. We never ran into him down here anyway, just his crew, so I didn't know what he looked like. Did you?"

"Oh shit, oh shit, oh shit," Mintz said. "She serious about this guy?"

"Fuck," DeGraw said, face going dark as the full extent of the situation dawned on him. "Whole time together, I never laid a hand on my wife she didn't want me to . . ."

"What?" Mintz said, not quite following the train of thought.

"You know, I just spanked her and stuff like that, but . . ."

"Frank, I don't wanna know about . . . Why you talkin' about yer sex life?"

"Was just a game," DeGraw said. "Never, and I mean *never*, did I raise my hand to Sandy in anger."

"Fine. But what's that gotta do with Wild Willy in pieces in the alley here?"

"Once, Lou, one time only, I hit Sandy. Big argument, she was slammin' me with a telephone 'cuz I wouldn't let her make a call to this mutt, this new boyfriend."

"Who turns out to be Wild Willy, but okay, what does you hittin' Sandy . . . ?"

"I wasn't even outa the house yet and she's whorin' herself with this guy. I'm givin' her shit about it, and she's really pummelin' me in the chest. Which is fine, but then she clips me in the face and I just react, on reflex. I cuff her one on the chin and she goes down in a heap like I'd really hauled off, which, you know, I absolutely did not do."

"Okay, got it, stormy freakin' romance," Mintz said. "But . . ."

"I shouldna had those beers at lunch."

"Wait a minute," Mintz said. "Yer makin' turns here . . ."

"I just had four frickin' beers, dunce, and six before we started the shift."

"So what, there's nobody around," Mintz said. "Yer not makin' sense."

"If we call this in, they'll *come* around. They find out I know the victim, they're gonna sit me down for questions, and I don't want no beer on my breath, okay?"

"All right, but we gotta call this in," Mintz said. "We'll get ya some mints when we go back. And yer not drunk anyway, so what da fuck 'er ya talkin' about?"

"Listen," DeGraw said, grabbing Mintz by the arms. "One time I was violent with my wife over the guy, and another time . . . I threatened this guy's life." Mintz's jaw went slack again as DeGraw continued, pointing each word, "He was smackin' her around, so I threatened him in front of half my friggin' neighborhood in Gravesend. They all heard me threaten to cut Wild Willy's balls off if he hit Sandy again in front of the baby."

"Whoa," Mintz said, breathing heavier. "When did this happen?"

"Couple weeks ago, Labor Day. I stopped in to see the baby. So I'm inside, and everybody's outside drinkin', and then he and she start to argue over something, I don't know what, and things fly outa hand. So I go out, and he's manhandlin' her, and all of a sudden I'm handin' the kid off and steppin' in. Big friggin' scene, right in the street."

"And you don't tell me this weeks ago?"

"Fuck you," DeGraw said. "You gossip way too much."

"And I just heard twelve too many details for one night, so shut the fuck up."

DeGraw poked a finger at Mintz's chest. "You and me, we gotta get on the same page here, or this thing's gonna get nasty."

"Oh, it's already nasty," Mintz said, half-laughing with a hysterical little whoop. DeGraw recognized it as Mintz's nervous habit when he felt he was in over his head.

"I need ya, Lou. I ain't sittin' in a cell for somethin' I had nuttina do with."

"Hold on, just hold on and tell me something," Mintz said, mustering his courage, taking a breath and squaring himself in front of DeGraw. "Did you ice this guy? . . . No, no, no, don't tell me, please don't tell me, I don't want to know . . ."

"You fuckin' hump," DeGraw said, grabbing his hat from his head and swiping a meaty paw across his face and through his hair. "I mean, you *really think* . . ."

"It's a proper question," Mintz said, trying to beat back another whoop. "And if you can't handle it comin' from me, how you gonna do when they sit you down?"

DeGraw let his body go slack. He needed Mintz to be as cool as possible, for moral support at the very least, and maybe more than that. "Awright, listen, Mintzy. Everybody knows the world's a little better now that this guy stopped breathin'. Cripes, I'd like to be able to say that I did do this guy. But it just so happens that I did *not* ice this muthuh. And now my footprints are down there in his friggin' *blood*, okay?"

"Oh shit."

"*Oh shit* is right," DeGraw said. "What am I gonna do with all this?"

"Wow, I don't know, Frank. What do ya think?"

"Look, my footprints are down there. You think maybe

you could walk down there too and put your footprints all over? Then we could maybe say you were the one who went down and not me, I stayed out here."

"Geez," Mintz said, trying not to hyperventilate. "You want me to say I'm the one who found him?"

"Now that I think about it," DeGraw said, "there might be a lot of footprints down there, how you gonna step into all the ones that are mine?"

"Exactly."

"And second, I already got his blood on my shoes, in my pants, and who knows where else. When somebody tells a detective how I threatened Willy on Labor Day, I'm an instant suspect. And when they test this uniform for Willy's blood, I am screwed."

"But I can still vouch for ya, Frank," Mintz said. "We were together all night."

"Which makes you a secondary suspect."

"Well, then fuck it, the only thing I can do is read you your rights," Mintz said, whooping as he removed handcuffs from their belt holster. "You are under arrest."

"Just cut it out, all right?" DeGraw said as Mintz laughed. "You know, I hate it when you enjoy my predicaments."

"Somebody's gotta lighten this mood, Frank, 'cuz lemme tell ya, this mood sucks."

DeGraw leaned back on the wall and eyed the bloody hand on the sidewalk, taking out cigarettes. He put one in his mouth, gave Mintz one, then lit them both.

"Awright, face it, yer screwed anyway," Mintz said, fighting for control. "They gonna find out what you said to Wild Willy on Labor Day, so ya gotta figure goin' in they're gonna take a good hard look at you, at least as a formality. Holy shit, yer *fucked*."

"Do me a favor and stop laughin', ya prick."

"Just nerves, Frank. You know I get this way. Don't be mad at me."

"It makes me frickin' nuts, so stop it, okay? What am I gonna do here?"

"What do you mean, *do?*" Mintz said. "We gotta call this in."

"I don't know, is that true?"

Mintz contemplated his meaning for a second. "Whoa, whoa, wait a minute . . ."

DeGraw said, "Where are we?"

Mintz didn't understand the question. "Red Hook."

"Red Hook *waterfront,*" DeGraw said, like he was leading an idiot. "And what are those? Those things right over there, and all over here?"

"Metal drums."

"Some rusted, with holes in 'em. And over there we got cinderblocks."

"Oh no," Mintz said. "Oh God, no, no, no."

"Why not?"

"But, but, but, but . . ."

"But give me one reason."

"How 'bout it's against the *LAW,* goddamnit!" Mintz said.

"We are *cops,*" DeGraw replied. "We're on the right side of the law, my friend."

"But you're not guilty," Mintz whined. "What would you be coverin' up for?"

"Bear with me," DeGraw said. "It's clear this blood is fresh, and we've been together all night. So if I get jammed up for this, you do too, right? So, since you got a stake here, I say the freakin' Mafia dumps so many bodies out there in the Buttermilk you can practically walk across to Governor's Island—and don't tell me I don't know what I'm talking about. So let's just pick up the pieces of Wild Willy, stuff 'em all in a barrel with cinderblocks, walk it out to the pier head there—and finish the frickin' job."

"Jesus," Mintz said, gulping air and whooping again.

DeGraw was speaking in earnest, but kept his tone even. "What would be left to find? Blood? It's gonna rain the rest of the night and tomorrow too. Guaran*teed* there's no blood to notice between these two warehouses when the sun comes up. Then it's a missing-person case at most and chances are it never goes beyond that."

"Interesting theory," Mintz said. "You willin' to stake your career on that?"

"I'm willin' to stake my *freedom* on that, and nobody would hate jail more than me, Louie. And we might as well face another fact while we're at it—this thing *ain't no coincidence*. It's aimed right at *me*."

"Oh sure, like the world revolves around you," Mintz said. "How ya figure?"

"The wallet. They wanted this guy found and identified." Mintz began to pace back and forth while DeGraw held up the warehouse with his back and thought out loud. "I think chances are excellent that somebody, maybe some twisted individual right in Gravesend, who maybe witnessed me threaten this guy with murder and mutilation . . ."

"Not necessarily in that order," Mintz said.

"And maybe that sick individual has one huge case of the hots for Sandy, which could be the key here . . ."

"She is pretty hot, if you don't mind me sayin', Frank."

DeGraw went on, "And maybe he got in his mind that if he conks this Willy guy on the head, cuts him up and puts him exactly where he knew I'd be tonight, he can run with the opportunity I myself inadvertently provided on friggin' Labor Day."

"Wait, you're sayin' all this happens because the guy wants a shot at Sandy?"

"Smart move, ain't it? With means, motive, and opportunity, the heat is right on me. I could go away for a long time off this or maybe even end up on Death Row."

"I apologize for puttin' it this way," Mintz said, "but you yourself said many times in the past coupla years that a guy ain't gotta murder *nobody* to get in Sandy's pants. You call that woman a slut all the time. So who better than you would know that all it takes is a coupla seven-and-sevens and you're in like Flynn."

"I divorced her, didn't I? How do you know she drinks seven-and-sevens?"

"You told me once, a long time ago. Anyway, so okay, so who needs to commit a murder and pin it on you to get a piece of yer ex-wife?"

New emotions began creasing DeGraw's face. "'Tween you an' me—my son don't even look like me. I hate to say it. It kills me. But I can't shake this feeling."

"Stop it, stop it right now," Mintz said. "The kid looks just like you and that's that. If not exactly, then close enough. So put it all right outa yer head."

DeGraw reined in his feelings and pushed on, "All right, I'll give you another motive, Louie. We been doin' too good a job around here, breakin' up Wild Willy's gravy train. Face it, they might even like Wild Willy, but if his corpse means they can get back to the way they were haulin' hot shit outa here, Willy is dead. Or maybe they're pissed off for some unrelated reason and want Willy out of the picture. So off of that alone, partner, maybe some enterprising mob wanna-be sees a chance to take Willy out and pin it on the very cops screwed things up on the waterfront, so he takes a shot."

"Much as I hate to admit it," Mintz said, "*that one* makes a certain sense. With both Willy and us gone, things go back to normal . . . But can we really do this?"

"Come on, partner," DeGraw said, taking another pair of surgical gloves from Mintz's pocket. "Nobody here. All we do is introduce what's left of Mr. Wild Willy to the depths of the East River, where the little fishies will enjoy eating Italian once again. Then we're home free: no murder, no suspects, no change on the Red Hook waterfront."

"God help me," Mintz answered, closing his eyes and trying to force a swallow through a dry throat, "but I just can't do this. It's too risky."

Deflated, DeGraw slumped back against the building. "Okay, man. I understand."

"Look, Frank, I'm sorry, but I just . . ."

"It's okay, partner. I'll handle it . . . how I handle it. Why don't you just call it in."

Mintz lifted the radio and hesitated, fingering the broadcast key without activating the call. "Wait a minute, what am I thinking? We have to do this."

"No we don't," DeGraw said. "I'll handle it."

"No you won't. You're right about what they'll do. They'll investigate you."

"Right," DeGraw said, noticing that Mintz was calmer now.

"And you know, they might not find that you iced ol' Willy, but if they nose around into your activities, they're bound to find out about the boosted guns, don't ya think?"

"That's not for you, that's for me to worry about. How many times do I . . ."

"I'm sorry for bringin' it up, Frank, but you could end up stuck with gun charges off of Wild Willy bein' found dead here, so we *gotta* do what you suggest, right? We gotta dump Willy in the channel. Just promise me, Frank, if this goes wrong, you'll step up and protect me."

"I got yer back from now till the tomb, partner," DeGraw replied, slipping the gloves onto Mintz's hands.

"Faster we're outa here, better I'll feel," Mintz said. "Let's go."

Stomachs in knots, they collected all the parts of Wild Willy—including the Mafioso's wallet—and packed them into a rusted barrel, which they topped off with cinderblocks. Then DeGraw used the side of his Glock to tamp down the metal tabs on the barrel lid until it was secure, and they rolled the barrel to the end of the pier where, without ceremony, they sent the creatures of Buttermilk Channel fresh Italian to eat.

This took longer than they expected. They were late, so they trotted out from the warehouses, heading along Wolcott, making a left on Richards, and sauntering into Red Hook Park.

A sector car was waiting for them.

Nico Dounis, a Greek patrol sergeant everybody called Nicky Donuts, got out of the car when they approached. "Don't nobody answer the radio no more?"

Mintz looked down at his belt and found the radio turned off. "Shit, sarge, I guess I accidentally turned it off."

"You two have a brawl?" Dounis asked.

"No," DeGraw said. "Why?"

"You're all sweaty."

"Don't know what yer talkin' about, sarge," Mintz said. "Not sweaty at all."

"Climbing around the warehouses," DeGraw said.

"Humid out tonight," Mintz added. "Uh, horseplay, you know, boys'll be boys."

DeGraw recognized three too many excuses when he heard them.

Dounis did too. "Okay, what's goin' on?"

DeGraw could see Mintz's mind go into overdrive, a panicky thought making its way toward the lips, so he took Mintz's arm and turned him away, stepping forward himself to answer. "Little argument, that's all. Nothin', really. He don't know a guy's still got feelings for his ex-wife even if they get divorced, so I had to straighten him out."

Dounis studied DeGraw through squinted eyes, but he stifled an urge to pursue it.

"Hey, it's late," Mintz said. "We should walk the park."

"I walked it myself," Dounis said. "It's done."

"But we're not that late, are we, sarge?" Mintz asked, and again DeGraw wanted to pound him into unconsciousness, but resisted the urge.

"Forty-five minutes I'm callin', and I got no word on the radio," Dounis said. "What's that on your knee, Frank?"

They all looked down and saw the purplish-red splotch visible even on DeGraw's navy blue pant leg.

"Oil, I guess," DeGraw said. "I knelt down to tie my shoe."

"I ain't no dope and I don't appreciate bein' treated like one," Dounis said. "Yer late, ya don't answer the radio, yer all disheveled like ya been fightin', ya smell like a frickin' brewery, and ya got blood on yer pants. Don't tell me that's oil, 'cuz I know the difference."

The two patrolmen were stunned. Mintz was ready to speak again but DeGraw spoke first: "Yer absolutely right, sarge. We were negligent. We had a few beers at lunch and lost track of time. Then he insults my ex and I had to straighten him out. Only he don't show proper respect, so we scuffled a little bit. I took a head butt to the nose and bled, after which I knelt in it when I went down to tie my shoe."

DeGraw and Mintz waited a tense second while Dounis processed the new information.

"Over here," Dounis said, walking Mintz about twenty feet away.

Much as he tried, DeGraw couldn't make out what they were talking about.

Dounis then returned to DeGraw while Mintz stayed behind.

"Turn away from Mintz," Dounis said, and DeGraw obeyed. "Exactly where was it you two went at each other?"

"Shit, I don't know," DeGraw answered. "What the hell did we ever do to you?"

"Where was it you bled? I need to know exact."

"I don't know, one of the piers."

"The piers is your whole patrol, asshole. Which one?"

"How'm I s'posed to know? They all look alike. Like Greeks."

"After two years, you know those piers like they was yer own pecker."

"Somewhere around the railroad yard, I'm guessing. Can't be sure, sarge."

"That's not what Mintz said."

"What d'ya want from me? One of us is right and the other forgot. No big deal."

"I gotta do somethin' about this, don't I?" Dounis said.

"Yer bein' a hardass, Nicky Donuts. What's wrong?" DeGraw said. "I never crossed you, not even once."

Dounis turned to Mintz and said, "Don't come over here and don't you two talk to each other." Then Dounis sat in the cruiser and made a call to the precinct while DeGraw and Mintz could only stare at each other, reading worry on each other's faces.

When, within a minute, five police cruisers came tearing to that corner of Red Hook Park, Dounis had DeGraw and Mintz taken into custody.

Unfortunately for DeGraw, the forecast was wrong. It never rained that night. Wild Willy's blood stayed on the pavement and was collected by the crime scene unit.

By noon, DeGraw had spent hours in an interrogation room at the 76th Precinct, where he was interviewed by Catucci and Bourne, two homicide detectives, and Gonzalez, an ADA who'd been summoned from the Brooklyn homicide bureau. Cho and Santos, of Internal Affairs, also watched through the two-way mirror.

To show good faith, DeGraw had waived the "forty-eight-hour rule," which gives a policeman accused of a crime the chance to arrange for representation without having to answer questions. But he had invoked his right to have his Policemen's Benevolent Association representative present, so Ken Stanley sat off in a corner.

Not hearing a radio check from DeGraw and Mintz, Dounis had sent other officers onto the piers to look for them. When they arrived, unnoticed in the thickening fog, they watched DeGraw and Mintz pack Wild Willy into the barrel with the cinderblocks and then roll it into the drink.

What was worse, DeGraw soon found out, was the fact that Mintz had turned on him under the pressure of the questioning and was offering his full cooperation against DeGraw in return for a clean walk—which he was granted. It left DeGraw dumfounded.

"But how?" DeGraw asked. "How can he say I did the friggin' murder? I was with him the whole time, and I swear, we didn't kill the guy, we just dumped him."

"'Cuz you were scared you'd be a suspect," Bourne said, and DeGraw nodded.

"Not a bad story, but not good enough," Gonzalez said. "Mintz told us everything. And they just raised the barrel, so I got a slam-dunk case against you. Do yourself a favor, pal, cop to a plea and I'll cut you the best deal I can."

"Be smart, Frank," Bourne said. "Wait for your lawyer before you cut any deals."

DeGraw hung his head and wondered how it all could have gone so wrong so fast.

At that same moment, Lou Mintz was a free man, cruising the streets of Brooklyn in his brand new Lincoln Navigator while singing off-key to a Dean Martin CD.

He hung a right on Bay Parkway and stopped on the corner of Cropsey Avenue, half-dancing his way into Bensonhurst Park. His feet felt like they were barely denting the grass as he approached two men sitting on a bench. One was an older gentleman named Bonfiglio, although Mintz knew him only as Big Fig.

"Nice new car, huh?" Bonfiglio said. "Pretty flashy."

"That's my new baby," Mintz said. "Ride's like a dream."

Bonfiglio reached into his inner blazer pocket as Mintz sat next to him, then stuffed a bulging envelope into a copy of the New York Post and placed it on the wooden bench slats. Mintz picked it up and held the newspaper open while thumbing through a thick wad of hundred-dollar bills.

"Count it if you want," Bonfiglio said.

Mintz sat back, putting the newspaper down again. "Looks about right."

"Suit y'self, but later, when you do count it," Bonfiglio said, "you'll find more than we bargained for, just to show how appreciative I can be for a job well done."

"'Preciate that," Mintz said, and leaned forward to look at the other man. "Ya get the same appreciation, Nico?"

"More," Nicky Donuts replied. "I got more."

"Why him and not me?" Mintz said to Bonfiglio.

"He set it up," Bonfiglio answered.

"But I did all the work," Mintz said. "And damn good work it was."

"Management always takes less risk and gets a bigger cut," Dounis said. "Ain't you hip to that yet?"

Bonfiglio laughed. "God rest him, but Willy never knew that, and now look."

"Shit, I still gotta testify," Mintz said. "Hardly seems fair that I get less."

"Don't worry, kid," Bonfiglio said. "Cashflow won't be no problem once we're back to business in Red Hook. You'll get everything what's comin' to ya."

"Know what? I believe ya," Mintz said, sashaying back toward his Navigator with the *Post* and envelope clenched under his arm. "Have yerselves a great day, gents."

Five minutes later, Mintz turned off Shore Parkway onto Bay 17th Street, parked in the driveway of a quaint little white clapboard house, and went in through a side door. Without a word, he went upstairs to a bedroom.

Entering, Mintz tossed the *Post* and envelope onto the bed. Sandy turned away from the bureau and folded herself into Mintz's arms.

"Went off without a hitch," Mintz said, nuzzling her neck.

Mintz, the neurotic weasel who'd shy away from a dicey situation and whine about the danger, was now gone. Sandy gasped as this new Mintz balled her hair in his fist, tilted her head back, and took the front of her throat in his teeth. Then he trailed his tongue to her ear and took the lobe between his lips, all while she rubbed up against him.

"I can't get enough of you," she said, and when he moaned, she added, "Shush, the baby's down for a nap."

"I won't wake him up," Mintz whispered, leading her into the baby's room. Watching the ten-month-old sleep, Mintz couldn't help but smile.

"Looks just like his old man," Sandy whispered.

Mintz beamed, patted the kid's foot, and led her out of the room.

In the hall, Mintz kissed her and said, "Dress up nice and call the sitter, I'm takin' us out tonight, special celebration."

"Yeah?" she said. "Where?"

"Carmine's, Italian place in the city," Mintz said. "Food is absolutely to die for."

Back at Bensonhurst Park, Dounis and Bonfiglio were still enjoying the high sun and the salt air that was wafting in off Gravesend Bay.

"The case against DeGraw?" Bonfiglio said.

"As much of a sure thing you can have against a cop," Dounis said.

"Even with just the word of the guys you sent in there?"

"They watched the whole thing," Dounis said. "Their testimony is all we need."

"I don't like the attitude on this Mintz," Bonfiglio said. "The cocky ones like that, they're trouble."

"And spreading money around? This flashy car all of a sudden?" Dounis said. "Fuckin' idiot don't even know he's forcin' us ta be responsible here. And it's too fuckin' bad, I don't care if he did do us a good job last night. He's now officially dangerous."

"Okay, so since we don't need him for the case," Bonfiglio asked, "where's he gonna be tonight?"

"He told me he's eatin' at Carmine's. Upper West Side."

"Shall I let him have his meal first, or make sure they do him on the way in?"

"Mintzy's a good kid," Dounis replied. "Let him eat, drink his wine."

"You old softy," Bonfiglio said, laughing. Dounis didn't laugh.

"When it might be my time," Dounis said, "I hope I get the same consideration."

"Cripes, yer goin' all emotional in your old age," Bonfiglio said.

"Guess I am."

"It's kinda sweet."

"He did good work for us, Fig, helped us get Red Hook back. Give the kid his last meal, I happen to know he loves eatin' Italian."

"Hell, who don't?"

They both nodded and thought of their favorite Italian dishes.

That night at the 76th, DeGraw still hadn't been arraigned or made bail, but he didn't have to stay cooped in a cell. Instead, the detectives gave him the professional courtesy of letting him wait it out in the relative comfort of an interrogation room. They even brought him pizza from Mario's Place down the block, just the way he liked it: piping hot Sicilian slices with extra mozzarella cheese and spicy Italian sausage. Much as it pleased DeGraw's palate, it still left him with indigestion.

After a sweaty hump and a few hours' nap on DeGraw's ex-bed, the babysitter came over and Mintz drove Sandy to Carmine's Restaurant, Broadway between 90th and 91st Streets on the Upper West Side of Manhattan.

The large upper room was crowded and festive, as usual. People flocked to this place that prepared such sumptuous Southern Italian fare and served it in great, heaping platters. Folks didn't just grab a bite at Carmine's place, they ate big and left feeling like they'd participated in an event.

Mintz fingered the wad of hundreds in his pocket and ordered up more bottles of Carmine's best Montepulciano D'Abruzzo to go with the seafood antipasto that was as large and fulfilling as most normal meals. He and Sandy swooned over practically every sip of the red wine in between bites of the calamari, baked clams, baccala, whiting, muscles, bay scallops, and butterfly shrimp, the tangy red sauce sopped up with fresh homemade garlic bread.

A middle-aged gent at the next table couldn't help but notice them. "Excuse me, but it's my first time here and it's great to see you two look like you're enjoying yourselves. That food as good as it looks?"

"Better," Mintz said. "You eatin' alone?"

"Uh, well, blind date," the professorial gent said. "Internet kind of thing. I guess either something went wrong or she got cold feet."

"Tough stuff, buddy," Mintz said. "Might as well go ahead and order. This shit's too good not to eat once yer here."

The gent shrugged and nodded with a sad smile.

"Fuck 'er," Sandy added. "She don't know what she's missin', does she? Might as well enjoy your evenin'."

"I'd invite you to join us," Mintz said, "but this is kind of a special occasion, and, well, you understand."

"Oh, by all means," the tweedy gent said. "Enjoy your meal."

He thanked them with a nod when Mintz had the waiter put a glass of their Montepulciano on his table and then raised the glass in a silent toast.

After that, while the gent ate alone, he took sidelong glances to see Mintz and Sandy happily tucking into entrees of Lasagna Bolognese, Fettuccini Alfredo, penne in olive oil with broccoli, gnocchi, bragiole, veal Parmesan.

The gent was amazed when Mintz and Sandy ordered dessert: espresso, tiramisu, spumoni, and chocolate-covered mini-cannoli. Then they topped it all off with large snifters of Sambuca Romana, a sweet anise-tasting Italian liqueur sipped with three coffee beans floating in it.

They had of course ordered far more food than they'd consumed, and had the leftovers wrapped to take home with them, good Italian food always tasting even better the next day. The containers filled two shopping bags, which Mintz carried in one hand as they rose to take their leave. He turned to say goodnight to the gent, but the guy wasn't at the table and Mintz couldn't remember seeing him go.

The cool night air made their bodies glow with the alcohol and the great food, as Mintz and Sandy sauntered back around the corner toward where the new Navigator was parked. Just when the world seemed like a perfectly lovely place and Sandy hooked her hand around Mintz's arm, the gent stepped out from behind a van, raised the .38 with a silencer attached, and began pumping shots into them.

Head-shot, Sandy was dead before she hit the sidewalk. Unable to grab his off-duty gun and already hit in the chest, all Mintz could do was swing the shopping bags at the gent, who raised his free arm to fend them off. The bags burst open and the containers rained great food all over the sidewalk.

When Mintz also fell dead, the gent plucked a piece of penne from the shoulder of his cashmere overcoat and popped it into his mouth. Then he pocketed the handgun and walked away.

Within seconds, a big black stray mutt happened upon the bodies of Mintz and Sandy and straightaway began to enjoy the best Italian meal he'd ever had, although truth be told, he really didn't care much for the broccoli.

THURSDAY
BY KENJI JASPER
Bedford-Stuyvesant

There're a lot of ways to deal with what "The Stuy" doles out. Some drink. Some get high. Some beat the shit out of the spouse within closest reach. But me, I fuck.

This is not to say that I do not engage in the act of making love. Nor is it to imply that I'm one of those dudes who suffers from that meeting-in-the-ladies'-room catch phrase known as *emotional unavailability*. I just know that when you're bending her legs back as far as they go, aiming a stiff rod toward the uterus while her head indents the drywall, as your sweat lines the valley that runs from between her shoulder blades to the crack of her ass, that it cannot be considered an act of *intimacy*.

They like it because what I have to give isn't as watered down as what they get at home, the sum of what's left after their men's hard days at bullshit 9-to-5s. I don't care if she leaves traces of my semen on her kids' cheeks. I don't care if she picks up another ten pounds from eating Doritos and watching *Divorce Court*. I only ask that she leave before I start caring.

"You got any more of that tea?" Jenna asks.

She's the only one I've ever let stay, because I love her, or at least I used to, until she left me for another dude after she caught me in a three with Sarah and Dahlia, these two bi-broads I'd met at The Five Spot the night of one of my little book things. They were in the mood for dick and I had one, not to mention a dub of weed and a queen-size mattress with fresh sheets.

Jenna didn't live with me but she had keys, the unavoidable side effect of my dislike for feminine whines and complaints. Nothing gets to me more, not even the inevitable loss of privacy that comes with giving someone carte blanche access to your home. One night she started missing me just as I wasn't missing Dahlia's g-spot, with Sarah adding a little tongue to the mix.

I can't even say that I remember their faces, only a fleshy set of buttocks and thick nipples harder than granite. One Cuban, one Jewish, and both light on their feet when Jenna started swinging the antique coat rack.

My friends in other boroughs don't believe me when I tell them stories like this one. They dismiss them as something like the fodder passed off as correspondence in the pages of *Penthouse Letters*. But they don't live in The Stuy. They don't understand that anything out here is possible as long as you believe it is, a crisscross grid of blocks and corners waiting to be remade just the way you want them, as long as you got juice, dough, or even better, both.

I'm a writer, if you haven't figured it out yet. The words are the way I live, except when the freelance checks come late, or sometimes not at all. Then I'm left to the mercy of the streets, and a pile of manuscript I'll probably never sell. But this isn't about writing, this is about money, money on a Thursday, and how I ended up with it. The "what" I needed it for comes six graphs away from this one.

Flakes of jasmine in the metal ball you drop into boiling water. Add exactly three tablespoons of honey and let it steep. This is what makes Jenna happy. She comes to see me whenever her man's away, or when there happens to be a hole in my busy schedule, which is rather often. By the time I get the cup back to the bedroom, she's already clasping the bra behind her lovely back.

"It's gonna take a second for this shit to cool," I say as she takes the cup. Her skin is the color of coal and without a single blemish. Narrow shoulders and torso spread into wide hips and delicious quads that could choke a small animal. I still love her, even though she ain't mine no more.

"I might have to take it with me," she says, tucking the cranberry blouse into jeans of the deepest blue. "I got people in the chair all day."

Of all the women to fall in love with, I had to pick a braider. Twelve-hour days and one Saturday a month off. Her man sees less of her than I do, even though he works at the home where they now live, three blocks over on Marcy and Jefferson.

If you have to know, I stay on Halsey and Bedford, though everyone will say it's Hancock and Nostrand, where the more famous author happens to live. We're both the same age and from the same town, and yet we've never been in the same place at the same time. But perhaps that's a good thing. I read his last book and would be really tempted to hurt his feelings if he happened to ask me for a critique.

"He wants to take me to Brazil next month" she says, after sucking the hot liquid down to half. Her tongue has always been made of fire-retardant foam.

She says this only to make me jealous, knowing that I hate when she goes away, not to mention with him. It is my punishment for that night two years ago. I can have her body for the rest of eternity, but someone else will always hold the title to her soul.

"I'm sure he wants to do a lot of things," I say. "But that kinda trip costs the kinda cake he has to save up for a year for."

She zips her bag and wraps the butter-smooth leather I bought her around the blouse, and then smiles. She knows something that I don't.

"He doesn't have to save anything. He put his tax return in a nine-month CD at seven percent. He's gonna cash it in on Monday." And after that bit of data she departs, down the three flights of stairs to the inner door, followed by the outer, and then to the street.

She still knows the tender spots, especially in the after-glow. Brazil was the only place she'd ever wanted to go that she hadn't made it to yet. I'd sold a big article and used the check to get us advance tickets and a good hotel. I couldn't even get a refund because she backed out too close to the departure date.

And now she is going with Mr. Right, a four-inch one-minute man who a few of my homegirls have sampled over the years, all less than impressed. She is doing it just to spite me. Jenna does everything just to spite me.

She has no intention of going on that trip in those weeks ahead. If that's what she wants, she never would've told me about it. She knows how determined I am. And she knows that even though I write, I am also a man of action when it comes to handling my business. So she also has to know that there's no way in hell I'm going to let her roll anywhere below the equator with that clown. I'll have this sewn up by the end of the day, no problem.

"Twenty-three-hundred, forty-seven, ninety-six," Winston utters, his eyes never leaving the calculator on his computer screen. "You want me to book it now?"

The Bogart Travel Agency is a custom-made 2000-mega-hertz computer system hacked into the DSL substation box at Fulton and Classon. In other words, Bradley siphons all his business and info from the big travel agency up the street. It's nothing personal. They just happen to have what he needs for this season's hustle. Come December he'll be into something else, somewhere else.

I've got about six yards in my stash box over at Carver Bank, which is far from enough. Winston doesn't have a lay-away plan, nor does he accept bad checks. And his price is the best I'll ever see on such short notice.

Winston's almost forty years old and he still lives in the house he was born in, not far from the room he's renting to accomodate his bootleg travel setup. Lewis and Madison used to be a whole lot worse than it is, which just means that you no longer need someone to cover you with a pistol every time you get the mail. He always talks about moving back to Guyana with his grandma, even though she's on oxygen and hasn't left the house for years.

"How long can you hold the fare?" I ask.

"End of the day, max," he replies, his eyes now locked on Judge Hatchett's new hairdo, which means it's after 11 and I need to get moving.

"So that's 5 p.m., right?"

"It's actually 6 in the travel biz."

"Then I'll be here at 5:55."

"White people got ahold of everything now," Shango Alafia tells me between bites of french toast at the Doctor's Cave, this little hole on Marcy where I take a meal every once in a while. Shango's there every day though, mainly to eye Jean, the dreadlocked and beautiful better half of Tim, who prepares all of the meals he loves so much. Shango also happens to be Winston's brother-in-law and third cousin twice removed. But that's an entirely different story.

"I put in the best bid on that pair of brownstones down on Greene. Had the shit locked for like three days, and then eight hours before the cutoff some whiteboy coalition comes in and chops my head off."

"Hey, real estate's a cutthroat business," I say. The frown on his face softens into a smile. He knows something I do not.

"You're right. That's actually why I called you down here."

Shango and I never use land lines, cells, or even e-mail. If he needs to see me, the right corner of the front page of my *Daily News* will be missing. If it's a little piece, I'll find him at the gym over on Kingston. If it's a lot, he's over at Jean's.

Shango's sort of like my agent in this maze of a neighborhood, and has been ever since I moved here five years ago. He helped me out with a certain situation, involving certain people that you don't need to know about, or at least not in the context of this particular tale.

"So what's the deal?" I ask him.

"Reuben's got a problem," he says, dabbing his lips with one of the moist towelettes he carries everywhere he goes.

Reuben Goren owns a nice piece of Fulton Street, mostly storefronts that have been in the family for almost two generations. Needless to say, any problem he has is likely to be an expensive one.

"What kind of problem?"

"Yardies want that corner building he's got on Fulton and Nostrand, you know the one with the optician and the furniture store up top?"

"I see it every time I go to the train," I say. "So what, they've got him under pressure?"

"You could say that. But more importantly, they've got us under contract."

"Under contract to do what?"

"A little FYI."

"FYI?"

"We need to let him know they're not fuckin' around."

"And let me guess, he wants me to come up with a plan."

"Plan and execution."

"For how much?"

"Five."

"That's a little low, isn't it?" I say, knowing that it's more than I need. Greed is the most deadly of all sins.

"It's more than what you need for those Brazil tickets," he says, signaling Jean for coffee just so she can show him her behind while she pours.

"Always ahead of my game, huh?"

"I gotta be to take fifteen percent." My brain calculates options at the speed of light. Then my compass points me north. "I already took my fee out of the number by the way."

"Figured as much," I nod, still pensive. Then it comes to me. "I'm gonna need to see Sam."

Shango smiles again. "I told him you'd be there in thirty minutes."

"You know anybody that needs four .45s with no firing pins?" Sam asks, twenty-three minutes later.

He's a barber by trade. But he picked up a few other skills during the early nineties, when that nappy 'fro trend kept a lot of his usual cake out-of-pocket. On the table before him are four lines of coke and a plate of short ribs. He snorts and chews in twenty-second intervals, using the nostril that isn't outlined with crusted blood.

"I might," I say, the most strategic answer to give.

The rear of Sam's Shears is the local arsenal. You come to him for both offense and defense, for gaining ground and covering your ass. For pistols, rifles, hollow-tips, and even explosives, he's the undisputed motherfuckin' man, and the key element to my equation on this particular Thursday.

"But what I need," I continue, "is something that blows. Compact with high impact."

"What for?"

"It's on a need-to-know basis, my friend," I say with the wave of a finger. "Besides, curious cats end up in the carry-out."

"You make any money from that writing shit?" he asks, just before doing another line, his gray t-shirt now smeared with barbecue sauce and pork grease.

"Sometimes," I say.

"What about the rest of the time?"

"I do this. But look, Sam, I'm kinda on a schedule. Can you get me what I need?"

"Already got it. It's right there under the blanket." I remove the fabric to reveal a half-liter nitro glycerin charge with a twelve-second trigger. He makes them for a third of what seasoned pros might charge. A half-liter is a little much, but it'll have to do.

"Did I hit the nail on the head?" he asks.

"More like a fly with a hammer. But I'll take what I can get."

Sam and I don't deal in cash. Favors are our particular currency. So while such equipment would easily go for five figures on the Stuy market, I'll take it off his hands for no money down, as long as I get him what he wants.

"You know, there's only one cruiser in each precinct with a shotgun?" he asks, as if making small talk. But I know what's next. I'm finally one step ahead of somebody.

"Nabors," I begin. "He's the dayshift patrolman for the Marcy projects. Pump-action Mossberg with a wood-grain slide. Takes a large curry chicken for lunch at 4:55 every day. Corner of Fulton and Nostrand."

"Right across the street from the optician and the furniture store."

"What a coincidence," I grin. "That's what you want?" He nods. For some reason the coke makes him subdued instead of hyper. He doesn't want the gun to sell, but for something more inventive. Perhaps one of his clients would enjoy the irony of killing the officer with his own weapon.

"Yup, that's it."

"I'll send my man by for the hardware," I say on my way out. "And pencil me in for a shape-up tomorrow at 4." Arsenal or not, Sam gives the best cuts in The Stuy.

"I miss jail," Brownie tells me from the beanbag recliner by the window. He did six months in Otisville for intent-to-distribute before they gave him time served for rolling over on some whiteboys, one of whom, Brownie had discovered, was fucking his girl.

He is the clinical definition of a sociopath, a man who has raped and killed, six feet and 295 pounds of evil that just happens to deal the best weed in the neighborhood. Thus, I allow him into my home from time to time, for as long as the high lasts.

"What do you mean, you miss jail?" I ask, pulling on what that remains of the once-ample spliff. He is called Brownie because of his fudge-colored face. His real name can only be found on the lips of his elderly mother or on the rap sheet longer than my bedspread, or duvet, as Jenna describes it.

"A nigga like me needs some discipline," he says. "I realize that now. In there they told me what to be and where to go. Kept me in a cage and made me follow the rules. Out here I just get into shit. Out here I'm a fuse ready to blow."

Sam used to be married to Brownie's older sister, but that was before she divorced him and moved back to Panama. Sam had apparently been tapping some high school girl. But Brownie and Sam are still like brothers. The local arsenal even had a chrome Desert Eagle with a filed serial number waiting for him the minute he got out of the clink.

"You sound like you're itchin' to get knocked," I say, swigging bottled water to wash away the taste of smoke. "What you gonna do? Go out and fuck up on purpose?"

Instead of answering, he climbs to his feet and goes over to one of the windows to look down at the street.

"That's the only thing I hate about the inside," he grins. "You never get windows this big."

"You don't get to leave either. You don't get to see your kids. You don't—"

"Fuck my kids!" he explodes, turning to me. "Neither of them bitches won't even let me see'em no how, unless I got some cash. Besides, it ain't like I'm even close to bein' a good daddy. I'm a street-nigga man. That's the only shit I know."

On any other day there might be a speech for me to offer, something about him not needing to go back to jail to find the happiness he seeks. It would be this existential rant about how what he does isn't wrong, that he only does what God wants him to do. I would say it all with conviction just so he'd have that thirty-dollar bag for me every other Thursday. But

I'm trying to cut down. And besides, I need him to play a part in my plan.

"Can I ask you a question?"

"Shoot," he says.

"If you were gonna get yourself knocked, how would you do it?"

He turns to me with a pensive look, like a child trying to solve a Sajak puzzle.

"I don't know," he says. "I been thinkin' about it though. Why? You got an idea or sumpin'?"

I connect four just as he ends the question.

"I might," I say.

"Where you goin' with all that food?" Miel Rodriguez asks me, her bedroom eyes narrowed to slits outside of the Splash and Suds on the corner of Nostrand and Halsey. I am carrying two large bags of food from Yummy's carry-out, a half-gallon of shrimp fried rice, three small wanton soups, four egg rolls, and a six-pack of grape soda.

Miel would dig me if I was all about the Benjamins, or if I drove an Escalade with twenty-two-inch rims like the one she's seated in, compliments of her man of the moment. But I'm a writer, and she doesn't read. So we only flirt every now and again. I wouldn't mind getting my lips on those D-cups of hers. But intuition tells me that Jenna could outfuck her any day of the week.

Miel is beautiful though, with those dark brown eyes and golden flesh, long Indian hair shiny with oil sheen. The man of the minute is a lucky one, if he can hold on to what he's got.

"I got some people in town," I tell her.

"From where?" she asks.

"Atlanta," I say. "I went to school there."

"Oh," she replies, interested in nothing beyond the five boroughs. Twenty-three years old and she suffers from the worst ailment of them all, *Hoodvision*, that inability to see past the blocks where she was born.

Behind the front seats are two different shopping bags, each topped off with a folded knit sweater. Beneath one is her current man's stash of product, the other, his take for the week, to be dropped off at an undisclosed location at the end of the day. Heroin has been in short supply since the DEA raid on Jefferson a few days ago. Her boy was suspiciously the only one to make it out before the siege.

It's not that I don't know his name. I just choose not to use it. He's an X-factor in the day's proceedings, perhaps a catalyst, perhaps a not-so-innocent bystander. We'll know soon enough.

"How come you never try and talk to me?" she asks, offering a sexy smile, her slight overbite gleaming in the sun-rays from above.

"I'm talking to you right now."

"That's not what I mean," she says.

"What about your man?" I ask.

"His days are numbered," she says.

"What's he doing in the laundromat anyway?"

"Droppin' off his clothes. We gotta come back and pick-'em up at 5."

I glance at the bags in the rear again and know that Miel is carrying. There's no other way this guy would leave her alone in the ride for this long. I see him starting out of the building and know it's my cue.

"Well, lemme get this food, home girl. I'll see you around." I start away, knowing she'll do anything to have the last word.

"You didn't answer my question," she says, just as her boy hits the sidewalk."

"I know," I yell back, picking up the pace. It's almost 3:00. I have to move quickly.

The Le Starving Artist Café has barely been built, but there are already rats living in the basement. Not the disease-carrying rodents that infest the city, but four motherfuckers who I have a score to settle with. They are two sets of brothers, Trevor and Neville of Gates Avenue by way of St. Kitts, and Steve and Stacy of Harlem by way of grandparents that moved there from the Carolinas in the 1940s.

Weeks ago they took a stab at looting my crib while I was away at a speaking gig. They jimmied the front doors and came right up the stairs to the cheap wood my landlord assumed would keep out thieves. He was wrong. They made off with some DVDs and my 100-disc changer, ignoring the original Basquiat and twin lamps from Tiffany's.

Tesa Forsythe saw them from across the street and told me about it. Now the time has come to make things right.

They live in the basement beneath this café. Blankets and space heaters have kept them alive since the autumn chill began. Various hustles keep them fed and functioning. But what's money worth when there's no product close by? And the prices in Crown Heights are already through the roof.

"Good lookin' out," Stacy yells, draped in the same Pittsburgh jersey he's been wearing since Monday. They're all short on costumes since most of the dough vanishes into the good veins they have left.

Food won't make their jonesing any easier. But it'll give them more energy, which they'll be needing shortly. They immediately tear into what I've offered.

"Anything I can do for my peoples," I say. The "peoples" part is not fully untrue since we all used to play ball together in the summer, before they started sniffing and shooting, before the Internet crash that killed their entrepreneurial dreams. But that's another story. Seems like everybody in The Stuy has a story.

"Besides, I know y'all sufferin' right now."

"What you talkin' about!" Trevor demands, pulling a sleeve down over the arm he punctures most often.

"It ain't like he don't know," Neville argues between mouthfuls of shrimp fried rice. "The man looks like he got somethin' to say."

"Only if you want to hear me," I reply, watching them tear into the food.

"We want to hear you," Steve assures me as he slurps his soup. The warm liquid returns the yellow to his fair skin.

"You need powder and I need money," I say. "Somebody's got both less than a block from here."

"Who?" Trevor demands.

"I can't say. But I can say what he drives. '03 Escalade. Twenty-two-inch rims. Two shopping bags in the backseat. He's picking up his laundry at 5. Just him and his girl."

"How do you know?" Neville asks.

"I know the girl," I say. "And she says this dude's days are numbered, if you know what I mean."

They all look at each other, some trembling with the shakes, others shivering from the chills. Like most addicts, they don't think things through. They just react, moths drawn to the proverbial flame.

"But we ain't got no heat," Stacy laments. "I mean, we can't just run up on the car with nothin'. You know he's gonna be strapped."

272 // Brooklyn Noir

"Yeah, and ain't no way to get four gats in a hour and a half."

I clear my throat. "I might be able to help you there."

It is a quarter to 5 when I get the urge for something to drink. It happens every once in a while during *Texas Justice*, and today is no different. But for some reason I'm also in the mood for yoga. So I grab the carrying case for my mat on the way out the door, but forget the mat itself.

Both sides of Nostrand are packed with beings headed in every rush-houred direction. From their trains to their homes, from those homes to stores for the ingredients to make meals in time for the best that TV has to offer. Kids of all ages journey from one block to the next to bond with friends and more-than-friends alike.

I see patrolman Nabors enter the Golden Krust carry-out at the corner. I see Miel Rodriguez and her man pull up to the laundromat between Halsey and Macon. I see a gypsy cab slow to a halt in front of Reuben Goren's precious storefront. Then it all unfolds.

Brownie emerges from the cab's rear with a half-liter nitro glycerin charge. He kicks a hole in one of the storefront windows and tosses it in. The boom all but deafens everyone in a four-block radius and coats the entire street in shattered glass. The blast knocks Brownie to the ground, but he gets up quickly and begins to run down Fulton Street and into patrolman Nabors's field of vision, knocking over a grandma and a pack of teenage moms with an endless supply of strollered kids.

Officer Nabors IDs the perpetrator and calls for backup, dropping his large container of curry chicken to the ground as he begins to chase the man on foot. Fulton Street, or at least the people on it who are not still climbing up from the explosion, cheer both men on as the chase moves westward.

I then turn around to see four armed men surrounding the Escalade that's just pulled up in front of the laundromat, their .45 pistols trained on the driver and passenger. Moments later they are chased off by the loaded weapons of those inside of the vehicle.

The thieves are shocked to find that the pistols they'd gotten on loan from a man called Sam were without firing pins. They should've known better though, especially since the quartet stiffed the very same man for a pair of Glocks the previous summer, having sprayed him with mace before making a run for it with the merchandise. Addicts don't think. They just react.

Backup units arrive to aid Nabors, and some splinter off to chase the armed men fleeing from the laundromat. But none of the blue boys notice that the driver's-side window on Nabors's squad car is down. Nor do they see the young writer reach through the opening to commandeer the Mossberg shotgun in the holster next to the shifter. The writer slides the weapon into a nylon sleeve normally used for his yoga mat and slings it over his shoulder before disappearing into the local Bravo supermarket for a bottle of Snapple Peach Iced Tea. People see him, but they are not the kind to snitch to the authorities.

Brownie is tackled, clubbed, stomped, kicked, and then arrested by several white officers who don't have the brains to make it in any other profession. Trevor and Steve take one for the team as they too are apprehended by officers with few other career options.

Twenty minutes later the fire department is taming the

blaze. Three men are on their way to Brooklyn central booking and the young writer is on his way back down Nostrand to his residence, having never earned as much as a glance from the authorities during the entire mêlée.

Sam has his Mossberg by 5:35 p.m. Shango has my money fifteen minutes later. Reuben Goren has a concussion and a cake of shit in his pants. And by five to the hour, Winston will be handing me my tickets.

I am smiling on the inside as I turn onto Madison, anticipating the surprise I'll find on Jenna's dark and lovely face. It's the last house on the left at the end of the block. She lives with a thirty-eight-year-old man who still rents. Tsk tsk.

But then I notice the taxicab in front of the rented residence they share, the place she moved into to remind me of my past transgressions. Perhaps he's heading into the city to buy some testicles, or maybe a rug for that hairline that keeps going back. Then I see that he's carrying bags. And she's right behind him, holding what appears to be a pair of plane tickets.

That's when I know that the trip to Brazil begins today. The whole "next month" thing was a screen of smoke to throw me off. She knows me so well. She still knows how to make me suffer.

Another rock rolled up that long steep hill, another show of cunning and strength, before I stumble and fall, bouncing all the way back to the beginning. Jenna and I are the only loop I can't escape, the only checkmate that always evades me. She is like the sound Coltrane chased in his dreams, never to be had, never to be held, never to be won, in a season of games that lasts forever.

ONE MORE FOR THE ROAD

BY ROBERT KNIGHTLY

Greenpoint

Officer David Lodge stumbles when he attempts to enter the blue and white patrol car triple-parked in front of the 94th Precinct, dropping first to one knee, then to the seat of his pants. His nightstick, which he forgot to remove from the ring attached to his belt, is the most immediate cause of his fall. When it jammed between the door and the frame, Lodge had one leg in the vehicle with the other just coming up. From that point, there was nowhere to go but down.

Lodge ignores the guffaws of his colleagues, the eleven other cops of the midnight-to-eight tour, the adrenalin pumping as they mount up to ride out to patrol their assigned sectors. For a moment, as he struggles to gather himself, he stares at a full moon hanging over Meserole Avenue. He wonders if the moon's bloated appearance is due to the brown haze and drenching humidity trapped in the atmosphere. Or if it's just that his eyes won't focus because he passed the hours prior to his tour at the local cop bar, the B & G, just a few doors down from the precinct. Lodge has reached that stage of inebriation characterized by powerful emotions and he stares at the moon as if prepared to cradle it in his arms, to embrace a truth he is certain it embodies.

"Yo, spaceman, you comin' or what?"

The voice belongs to Lodge's partner, Dante Russo.

Lodge works his way to his feet, then yanks his nightstick free before getting into the car. He is about to address his partner, to offer a halfhearted apology, when the radio crackles to life.

"*Nine-four George, K?*"

Russo fires up the engine, shifts into gear, and pulls away. "That's us, Dave," he reminds his partner.

Lodge brings the microphone to his mouth. "Nine-four George, Central."

"*George, we have a 10-54 sick at one-three-seven South 4th Street. See the man. A woman unconscious in the hallway.*"

"That's in Boy's sector, Central."

"*Nine-four Boy is on another job, K.*"

"Ten-four, Central."

Russo proceeds down Metropolitan Avenue at trolling speed, passing beneath the Brooklyn-Queens Expressway, before turning onto Morgan Avenue. The job on South 4th Street is now far behind them.

"Where we goin', Dante?" Lodge adjusts the louvers on the air-conditioning vents, directing the flow to his crotch. "The job's in the other direction."

"We're goin' where we always go."

"Acme Cake? You serious?"

Lodge steals a glance at his partner when his questions go unanswered. Dante's thin nose is in the air, his jaw thrust forward, his lips pinched into a thin, disapproving line.

Not for the first time, Lodge feels an urge to drive his fist into that chin, to flatten that nose, to bloody that mouth. Instead, he settles his weight against the backrest and faces the truth. Without Dante Russo, David Lodge wouldn't make it through his tours, not since he started having blackouts. Nobody else will work with him, he knows. Shitkicker is what they call him. As in, *You hear what the shitkicker did last night?*

"What about the job?" he finally says. "What do I tell Central if they wanna know where we are?"

Russo sighs, another irritating habit. "C'mon, Dave, wise up. We both know it's gonna be some junkie so overdosed her buddies dumped her in the lobby like yesterday's garbage. Now maybe you wanna go mouth-to-mouth, suck up that good HIV spit, but me, I'm gonna let the paramedics worry about catchin' a dreaded disease. They got a better health plan."

When Lodge and Russo finally roll up on the scene twenty minutes later, two Fire Department paramedics are loading a gurney into an ambulance. A woman strapped to the gurney attempts to sit up, despite the restraints.

"You see what I'm sayin'?" Dante Russo washes down the last of his frosted donut with the last of his coffee. "Things worked out all right. No harm, no foul."

Three hours later, Russo breaks a long silence with an appreciative whistle. "Well, lookee here, just the man I want to see."

Lodge brings a soda bottle to his mouth and takes a quick sip. The one-to-one mix of 7-UP and vodka lifts his spirits. He is on the verge of a blackout now, and predictably reckless.

"What's up?"

"The Beemer." Russo jerks his chin at a white BMW trimmed with gold chrome, stopped for the light at the intersection of Metropolitan and Kingsland Avenues.

"What about it?"

"That's our boy."

"What boy?"

Russo pauses long enough to make his annoyance clear. "That there car belongs to Mr. Clarence Spott."

"Who?"

"Spott's picture is hangin' in the muster room. He's one of the bad guys." Dante's mouth expands into a humorless smile. "Whatta ya say we bust his balls a little?"

"Fine by me."

When Russo momentarily lights up the roof rack and the BMW pulls to the curb, both cops immediately leave their car. They are on Metropolitan Avenue, a main commercial street in the northside section of Greenpoint. The small retail stores lining both sides of the avenue are long closed, their gates down and padlocked, but several men stand in front of an after-hours club across the street. David Lodge stares at the men till they turn away, then he joins Russo who stands a few feet from the BMW's open window. Lodge knows he should approach the vehicle from the passenger side, that his job here is to cover his partner on the driver's side. But David Lodge has never been a by-the-book officer, far from it, and knowing his partner won't object, he settles down to enjoy the show.

"Why you stoppin' me, man?" Clarence Spott's full mouth is twisted into a pained grimace. "I ain't done nothin'."

"Step outa the car," Russo orders. "And that's *officer*, not *man*."

"I ain't goin' no place till I find out why you stopped me. This here is racial profilin'. It's unconstitutional."

Russo slaps his nightstick against the palm of his hand. "Clarence, you don't come out, and I mean right this fuckin' minute, I'm gonna crack your windshield."

The door opens and Spott emerges. A short, heavily mus-cled black man, his expression—eyes wide, brows raised, big mouth already moving—reeks of outrage. Lodge can smell the stink from where he stands. And it's not as if Spott, who keeps his hands in view at all times, isn't familiar with the rules of the game. There's just something in him that doesn't know when to shut up.

"Ah'm still axin' the same question. Why you pull me over when I'm drivin' down a public street, mindin' my own damn business?"

Russo ignores the inquiry. "I want you to put your hands on top of the vehicle and spread your legs. I want you to do it right now."

Spott finally crosses the line, as Lodge knew he would, by adding the word *pig* to his next sentence. Lodge slaps him in the face, a mild reprimand from Lodge's point of view, but Spott sees it differently. His eyes close for a moment as he draws a long breath through his nose. Then he uncoils, quick as a snake, and drives his fist into the left side of David Lodge's face.

Taken by surprise, Lodge staggers backward, leaving Spott to Dante Russo, who assumes a two-handed grip on his nightstick before cracking it into Spott's unprotected shins. When Spott drops to his knees on the pavement, Russo slides the nightstick beneath his throat and pulls back, choking off a howl of pain.

"How you wanna do this, Clarence? Easy or hard?"

As Spott cannot speak, he indicates compliance by going limp and crossing his hands behind his back.

Russo eases up slightly, then pushes Spott forward onto his chest. "You all right?" he asks his partner.

"Never better."

David Lodge brings his hand to the blood running from a deep cut along his cheekbone. Suddenly, he feels sharp, even purposeful. As he watches his partner cuff and search the prisoner before loading him into the backseat, he thinks, *Okay, this is where it gets good.* His hand goes almost of itself to the soda bottle stuffed beneath the seat when he enters the vehicle. He barely tastes the vodka as it slides down his throat.

"You got any particular place in mind?" his partner asks as he shifts the patrol car into gear.

"Not as long as it's private. One thing I hate, it's bein' interrupted when I'm on a roll."

Lieutenant Justin Whitlock sets the precinct log aside when David Lodge and Dante Russo lead Clarence Spott into the nine-four. Both sides of Spott's face are bruised and he leans to the left with his arm pressed to his ribs. His right eye, already crusting, is swollen shut.

Whitlock is seated at a desk behind a wooden railing that runs across the nine-four's reception area. He glances from the prisoner to Russo, then notices the blood on David Lodge's face and Lodge's blood-soaked collar.

"That your blood, Lodge?"

"Yeah. The mutt caught me a good one and we hadda subdue him."

Whitlock nods twice. The injury is something he can work with.

"I want you to go over to the emergency room at Wyckoff Heights and have that wound sewn up. Count the stitches and make sure you obtain a copy of the medical report. Better yet, insist that a micro-surgeon do the job. Tell 'em you don't wanna spoil your good looks."

"What about the paperwork on the arrest, loo? Shouldn't I get started?"

"No, secure the prisoner, then get your ass over to Wyckoff. Your partner will handle the paperwork." Whitlock's expression softens as he turns to Russo. "How 'bout you, Dante? You hurt?"

Russo flicks out a left jab. "Not me, loo, I'm too quick."

Whitlock glances at the prisoner. "I see." When Russo fails to respond, he continues. "Did the mutt use a weapon?"

"Yeah, loo, that ring. That's what cut Dave's cheek." Russo lifts Spott's right hand to display a pinkie ring with a single large diamond at its center. "You know what woulda happened if Dave had gotten hit in the eye?"

"He'd be out on the street with a cane." Whitlock's smile broadens. He and Russo are on the same track. "Charge the hump with aggravated assault on a police officer. That should keep the asshole busy. And make sure you take that ring. That ring is evidence."

Spott finally speaks up. "I wanna call my lawyer," he mumbles through swollen lips.

"What'd he say?" Whitlock asks.

"I think he said something about your mother, lieutenant," Russo declares. "And it wasn't complimentary."

Russo leads Spott through a gate in the railing, then shoves him toward the cells at the rear of the building. "Hi ho, hi ho," he sings, "it's off to jail we go."

Smiling at his partner's cop humor, David Lodge trails behind.

Five minutes later, Dante Russo emerges to announce, "The prisoner is secure and Officer Lodge is off to the hospital."

"You think he's sober enough to find his way?"

Russo starts to defend his partner, then suddenly changes tack with a shrug of his shoulders. "Dave's out of control," he admits. "If I wasn't there tonight, who knows what would've happened. I mean, I been tryin' to straighten the guy out, but he just won't listen."

"I coulda told you that when you took him on as your partner."

"What was I supposed to do? When I was told that nobody wanted to work with him? I'm the PBA delegate, remember? Helping cops in trouble is part of my job."

From David Lodge, the conversation drifts for a bit, finally settling on the precinct commander, Captain Joe Hagerty. Crime is up in the precinct for the second straight year and Hagerty is on the way out. Though his replacement has yet to be named, the veterans fear a wholesale shake-up. Dante Russo, of course, at age twenty-five, is far from a veteran. But he's definitely a rising star within the cop union, the Patrolman's Benevolent Association, a rising star with serious connections. Dante's uncle is the trustee for Brooklyn North and sits on the PBA's Board of Directors.

They are still at it thirty minutes later when Officers Daryl Johnson and Hector Arias waltz an adolescent prisoner into the building. Dwarfed by the two cops, the boy is weeping.

"He done the crime," Arias observes, "but he don't wanna do the time."

"Found him comin' out a window of the Sung Ri warehouse on Gratton Street," Daryl Johnson adds. "He had this TV in his arms, the thing was bigger than he was." Johnson gives his prisoner an affectionate cuff on the back of the head. "What were ya gonna do, jerk, carry it all the way back to the projects?"

"Put him in a cell," Whitlock says, "and notify the detectives. They'll wanna talk to him in the morning."

"Ten-four, loo."

Within seconds, Daryl Johnson returns. Johnson is a short, overweight black man long renowned for his deadpan expression. This time, however, his heavy jowls are lifted by an extension of his lips unrelated to a smile. "That mope locked up back there? I mean, it's none of my business, but who does he belong to?"

"Me," Russo responds. "Why?"

"Because he's dead is why. Because somebody caved in his fucking skull."

The evidence implicating David Lodge in the death of Clarence Spott is compelling, as Ted Savio explains in the course of a fateful meeting on Rikers Island several months later. Ted Savio is Lodge's attorney, provided *gratis* by the PBA.

Although Savio's advice is perfectly reasonable, Lodge is nevertheless reluctant to accept it. Lodge has been ninety days without a drink and the ordeal of cold turkey withdrawal has produced in him a nearly feral sense of caution. Alone in his cell day after day, he has become as untrusting as an animal caught in a snare. At times, especially at night, the urge to escape the inescapable pushes him to the brink of uncontrolled panic. At other times, he drops into a black hole of despair that leaves him barely able to respond to the demands of his keepers.

"You gotta face the facts here, Dave," Savio patiently explains, "which, I note, are lined up against you. You can't even account for your movements."

"I had a blackout. It wasn't the first time."

"You say that like you maybe lost your concentration for a minute. Meanwhile, they found you passed out in the basement. Holding a bottle in your hands."

"I knew that's where it was kept," Lodge admits. "But just because I was drunk doesn't mean I killed Spott."

"You had the victim's blood on your uniform and your blood was found on the victim."

"That could've happened when we subdued the mutt."

"We?"

"Me and my partner."

"Dave, your partner didn't have a drop of blood on him." Savio makes an unsuccessful attempt at eye contact with his client, then continues. "What you need to do here is see the big picture. Dante Russo told Lieutenant Whitlock that he had to pull you off Clarence Spott. He said this before the body was found, he repeated it to a Grand Jury, he'll testify to it in open court. That's enough to bury you all by itself, even without Officer Anthony Szarek's testimony.

"The Broom," Lodge moans. "I'm being done in by the fucking Broom."

"The Broom?"

"Szarek, he's a couple years short of a thirty-year pension and the job's carrying him. He spends most of his tour sweeping the precinct. That bottle they found me with? That was his."

"Well, Broom or not, Szarek's gonna say that he was present when you and Russo brought Spott to the holding cells, that he heard Russo tell you to go to the hospital, that he watched Russo walk away . . ."

"Stop sayin' his name." Lodge raises a fist to his shoulder as if about to deliver a punch. "Fucking Dante Russo. If I could just get to him, just for a minute."

"What'd you think? That you and your partner would go down with the ship together? Maybe holding hands? Well, Dave, it's time for you to start using your head."

Lodge draws a deep breath, then glances around the room. Gray concrete floor, green cinder-block walls, a table bolted to the floor, plastic chairs on metal legs. And that's it. The room where he confers with his attorney is as barren as his cell, as barren as the message his attorney delivers.

"Face the facts, Dave. Take the plea. It's not gonna get any better and it could be withdrawn."

"Man-one?"

"That's right, first-degree manslaughter. You take the deal, you'll be out in seven years. On the other hand, you go to trial, find yourself convicted of second-degree murder, you could be lookin' at twenty-five to life. Right now you're thirty-seven years old. You can do the seven years and still have a reason to live when you're released."

Though Lodge believes his lawyer, he still can't bring himself to accept Savio's counsel. At times over the past months, he's literally banged his head against the wall in an effort to jog his memory. Drunk or sober, he feels no guilt about the parts he can vaguely recall. Yeah, he tuned Spott up. He must have because he remembers Russo driving to a heavily industrial section of Greenpoint, north of Flushing Avenue, remembers turning onto Bogart Street where it dead-ends against the railroad tracks, remembers yanking Spott out of the backseat. Spott had resisted despite the cuffs.

But Spott deserved his punishment. He'd committed a crime familiar to every member of every police force in the world: Contempt of Cop. You didn't run from cops, you didn't disrespect them with your big mouth, and you never, under any circumstances, hit them. If you did, you paid a price.

That was it, though, the full extent as far as Lodge was concerned. To the best of his knowledge, he'd never beaten a prisoner with any weapon but his hands. Never.

"What if I'm innocent?" he finally asks his lawyer.

"What if there's a million black people residing in Brooklyn who already think you're guilty?"

One week later, suspended Police Officer David Lodge appears before Justice Harold Roth in Part 70 of the Criminal Term of Brooklyn Supreme Court. Lodge is the last piece of business on Roth's calendar late this Friday afternoon. It's a cameo shot, posed in front of the raised dais where Roth sits—Lodge, his lawyer Savio, and the deputy chief of the District Attorney's Homicide Bureau—nobody is in the audience in the cavernous courtroom.

Justice Roth is not one to smile unduly or waste words. "Well, counsellor?"

"Yes, your honor," Savio marshalls his words. "My client has authorized me to withdraw his previously entered plea of not guilty and now offers to plead guilty to manslaughter in the first degree, a class-C violent felony, under the first count of the indictment, in satisfaction of the entire indictment." Savio stops then, but does not look at Lodge, who is three feet to his right, standing ram-rod straight, staring fixedly at the judge. Lodge heard not a word Savio said.

"Is that what you want to do, Mr. Lodge?" Roth asks, not unkindly.

Mister Lodge. The words rock him like a blow to the body. Yet he remains transfixed, mute.

A full minute has passed. Roth has had enough. "Come up."

The lawyers hasten up to the bench, huddling with Roth at the sidebar. Savio earnestly explains that his client is unable to admit guilt because he was in the throes of an alcoholic blackout when he allegedly bludgeoned the victim, and so has no memory of the event. After several minutes of back-and-forth, Roth ends the debate.

"He can have an *Alford-Serrano*. Step back."

At Lodge's side, Savio explains their good fortune. In an *Alford-Serrano* plea—normally reserved for the insane—Roth will simply ask Lodge if he is pleading guilty because Lodge believes that the evidence is such that he will be found guilty at trial. Savio whispers urgently in Lodge's ear, an Iago to his Othello.

Suddenly, David Lodge's body goes slack, his gaze falters. Lodge has an epiphany. He sees the faces of all the skells he'd ever arrested who'd whined innocent, and for the only time in his life he's flooded with a compassion, till the fear takes hold—the fear of a small child upon awaking alone in the dark in an empty house.

PART IV

Backwater Brooklyn

TRIPLE HARRISON

BY MAGGIE ESTEP
East New York

She was wearing her t-shirt but she'd shed her jeans and her bleach-stained panties. She had me pinned down by the shoulders and her long dirty hair was tickling my cheeks as she hovered over me. I kept trying to look into her eyes but she had her face turned away. Even though her body was doing things to mine, she didn't want me seeing what her eyes thought about it.

"Stella." I said her name but she wouldn't look at me. She took one hand off my shoulder and started raking her fingernails down my chest a little too violently.

"Hey, that hurts, girl," I warned, trying to grab at her hand.

"What?" she asked.

"You're hurting me," I repeated.

Her eyes suddenly got smaller, her mouth shrank like a flower losing life, and she slapped me.

"Hey! Shit, stop that, Stella," I protested, shocked. I didn't know much about the girl but what I'd seen had been distinctly reserved and nonviolent.

"What's the matter?" I asked her.

She slapped me again. I tried to grab her hands but she made fists and pummeled my chest.

"You fuck!" she screamed.

I was pretty baffled. I'd been seeing Stella for a couple of months. She never said much, but up until now, she'd seemed to like me just fine. She would turn up on my doorstep late at night, peel off her clothes, and get in my bed. I'd bought her flowers once and taken her out to dinner twice. I'd never said anything but nice things to her and I didn't think I'd done anything to incur her fists.

"What's the matter, Stella?" I asked again, finally getting hold of her wrists and flipping her under me.

"Get offa me, Triple," she spat, wiggling like an electrified snake.

I released her wrists and slid my body off hers. I lay there, panting a little from the effort of the struggle.

I watched Stella scramble to her feet, then pick her panties and jeans off the floor. She yanked her clothes on. She was so angry she put her pants on backwards.

"I don't get it, what'd I do, Stella?" I asked her, as she furiously took her pants back off then put them on the right way. She ignored me.

I was really starting to like Stella. Maybe that's what got her mad.

She zipped her pants, slipped her feet into her cheap sneakers, then went to the door and walked out, slamming it behind her.

"What the fuck?" I said aloud. There was no one to hear me though. My dog had died of old age and the stray cat I'd taken in had gotten tired of me and moved on. It was just me and the peeling walls of the tiny wood-frame house. And all of a sudden that didn't feel like much at all.

Ever since Stella had come along, I hadn't dwelled on any of it. On being broke and close to forty and living in a condemned house that was so far gone no one bothered to come kick me out of it. But now, for mysterious reasons, Stella probably wouldn't be back and there wasn't much to distract me from my condition. I only had one thing left that gave me any hope, and that was my horse. As it happened, it was just about time to go feed her, so I put on my clothes and went out, heading for the barn a hundred yards down from the house. I don't suppose too many Brooklynites have horses, period, never mind keep them a hundred yards from the house. But real estate isn't exactly at a premium here at the ass-end of Dumont Avenue, where Brooklyn meets up with the edge of Queens.

It was close to dawn now and the newborn sun was throwing itself over the bumpy road. Two dogs were lying on a heap of garbage ten yards down from my house. One of them, some kind of shepherd mix, looked up at me. He showed a few teeth but left it at that.

Our little neighborhood is technically called Lindenwood but most people call it The Hole. A canyon in a cul-de-sac at the edge of East New York. It had been farmland in the not-so-distant past, then, as projects sprung up around it, it became a dumping ground. A few old-timers held on, maintaining their little frame houses, keeping chickens and goats in their yards. I don't know who the first person to keep a horse here was, but it caught on. Within five years, about a dozen different ramshackle stables were built using old truck trailers and garden sheds. Each stable had its own little yard, some with paddocks in the back, all of it spread over less than five acres. Now, about forty horses live in The Hole, including my mare, Kiss the Culprit. I brought her here six months ago. It's not exactly pastoral but we make due.

I reached the big steel gate enclosing the stable yard, unlocked it, and pushed it open. The little area looked like it usually did. A patch of dirt with a few nubs of grass fighting for life in front of the green truck trailer that had been converted to horse stalls. Beth, the goat, butted me with her head. The six horses started kicking at their stall doors, clamoring for breakfast, their ruckus waking up the horses in the surrounding barns so that, within a few minutes, the entire area was sounding like a bucolic barnyard in rural Maryland and, in spite of my troubles, I suddenly felt good all over. Particularly as I took my first look of the day at Kiss the Culprit. She had her head hanging over her stall door and was looking at me expectantly. She looked especially good that morning in spite of the fact that, by most standards, she's not considered a perfect specimen of the Thoroughbred breed. She's small with an upside-down neck and a head too big for the rest of her. She's slightly pigeon-toed and, back in her racing days, she'd run with a funny gait that only I thought resembled the great Seabiscuit's.

"Hey, girl," I said, putting one hand on her muzzle and leaning in close to catch a whiff of her warm creature smell. She wanted breakfast though, not cuddling. She pinned her ears and tried to bite me.

"All right, then," I laughed, and walked off to the little feed room.

I fed all six horses even though only Culprit is mine. I keep her here free but I have to look after other people's horses in exchange. Which suits me fine. The only job I have right now is working as a lifeguard at a pool in Downtown Brooklyn. No way I could afford to pay board for my mare.

As the horses ate their grain, I started raking the stable yard's nubby dirt, trying to make the place look presentable despite the fact that there were ominous puddles in front of the stalls and the lone flower box near the tack room had a propensity for killing anything we planted in it. This week it was working on terminating some hapless petunias.

I was raking pretty violently, trying to keep Stella out of my mind. The way her black hair fell in her face. The way her ass had hung out of her crappy cutoffs that first night I'd met her at the bar. I started focusing harder on the rake I was using and how it was falling apart. I envisioned a trip to the Home Depot out at Coney Island to get a new one. I imagined the brightly lit aisles full of useful items. Then I imagined Stella in there with me. I stopped raking.

I was standing there half-paralyzed by my thoughts when the front gate rattled and Dwight Ross suddenly appeared in the stable yard.

I wasn't glad to see him and the feeling was obviously mutual.

"Triple Harrison, I want my fucking horse back," Ross said.

Dwight Ross had always been on the thin side, but now he looked like a whisper would knock him down. His red hair needed cutting and, as he came close, I could see that his navy blue suit had pea-sized pills all over it.

"You stole my mare," Dwight hissed, coming to stand two inches away from me. "Don't fuck with me, Triple, took me six months to find you and I'm not leaving without my horse."

"She's mine now," I said, trying to seem calm even though I was anything but. I pulled air into my lungs, trying to make myself huge. Dwight backed up a little and started looking around at the horse stalls. He located Culprit's and started unlatching it.

"Don't go in there, Ross," I said. "Don't touch that horse." I felt myself getting hysterical.

"You want to take this to the law?" Dwight asked, as he got the latch undone and went to stand next to my mare.

"I don't think you do," I warned. Six months earlier, I'd been working as a groom, looking after Dwight Ross's string of horses at Aqueduct Racetrack. One day about a month into my tenure there, I caught Dwight trying to inject E. coli into Kiss the Culprit's knee. Of course, I hadn't realized what was in the syringe at the time, but I could tell by the way Dwight jumped when I walked in that the massive syringe did not belong in Culprit's knee. I'd already been suspicious about some of the stuff he was doing to his horses, though it wasn't till that moment that I fully realized he was one evil motherfucker. He was trying to kill the mare to collect the insurance and split the proceeds with the owner.

I happened to have a pitchfork in my hand and I didn't hesitate to use it. I pinned Ross to the wall and made him hand the syringe over and get out. He issued a few choice threats as he backed out of the stall. I figured it wouldn't take long for him to make good on the threats, but for that moment, he had hightailed it away from the barn. I had skipped bail on a beef in Florida two years earlier so I wasn't in a position to go to the authorities. I couldn't stand the idea of leaving the horse there unprotected though, so I decided to take her. I went into Dwight's office and forged the paperwork, then I loaded the mare into Dwight's horse trailer. She walked into the trailer without fussing. It seemed to me she knew I was saving her. As I passed through security and drove the trailer away from the Aqueduct backside, I kept expecting to hit a snag and get caught. But I made it. I stashed Culprit at a little stable near Prospect Park while I figured out what to do. I was now unemployed and broke with a horse to take care of. I figured I'd make do though.

All my life I'd been taking care of things, stray cats and dogs and crazy women.

After a week, I got the lifeguard job—swimming was the only thing I was good at apart from taking care of horses—and, not long after I'd made arrangements for keeping Culprit at The Hole, I'd moved into one of the abandoned houses just down the road. I hooked into the electric at one of the stables, and ran a hose in from the yard for water. Culprit and I had settled into a nice daily routine and we'd both been doing just fine. Until now.

Dwight Ross was still standing in my mare's stall.

"Come on, Ross," I said in a quiet voice, "get out of there. Now."

At that he smiled. I didn't see what was funny though.

"I had the crazy idea you'd be reasonable about this," Dwight said, leveling a gun I didn't know he had at me.

"That was a crazy idea, all right," I told him. I could see worry in his eyes even though he was the one with a gun.

"I'm taking my mare back and I will hurt you if I have to," he said in a shrill voice. He stepped out of the stall to reach for Culprit's halter.

I didn't think. Just grabbed for something. Turned out to be a shovel. Ross had his back to me. He heard me move but not in time. I slammed the business end of the shovel into the side of his head. He went down face first. Culprit spooked and her eyes got huge.

I walked over and put my palm over the end of my mare's nose and brought her big head against my chest.

"It's okay," I told the horse as I scratched her muzzle.

I looked down at Ross. He wasn't moving. I pushed on his shoulder, trying to turn him over. His body felt funny. His eyes and mouth were open. There was blood matted into his red hair. I realized he wasn't just unconscious.

I started feeling dizzy and I couldn't get myself to move. Culprit was looking at me with curiosity, her ears pricked forward.

"What do I do now, girl?" I asked. She just kept looking at me though.

It was getting close to 7 a.m. Pretty soon, people would be arriving at the other barns.

I left Dwight's body in the stall but led my mare out and tied her up in the yard. I didn't want her looking at the body.

I walked back to my house to get the car keys. My stomach was doing backflips. I went inside and it smelled a little like Stella. That didn't help any.

I got my keys and went back outside. My '86 Chevy Caprice Classic had once been blue but now it was just dirt-colored. It still ran though. The engine coughed to life and I drove to the front of the stable yard. I opened the big metal gates wide enough to get the car in, nosing it ahead slowly so as not to alarm Culprit. She stared at the car but she didn't spook.

I dragged Dwight's body out of the stall, pulling it by the feet. The head bounced along the dirt making a funny sound that made me sick.

I had to shuffle the shit in my trunk around. There were some empty feedbags, a small cooler, a horseshoe, and a pair of Stella's panties. I made room, then hoisted the body in. Dwight Ross was much heavier in death than he'd ever been in life. I had to bunch him into a fetal position to get him to fit. I put the empty feedbags over his body, then closed the trunk. My heart was beating too fast.

I went and put Culprit back into her stall. I stood for a

few minutes leaning my head against her muscular neck, getting strength. My mare just stood there, seeming to understand.

I made sure all the horses had enough water before getting in the car, driving it out, and locking the stable gates behind me.

The minute I pulled out onto Linden Boulevard, I found that I needed a cigarette. I hadn't had one in four years. I drove a few blocks through thickening morning traffic. The sun was up high now, a glowing yellow ball in a faultless blue sky. The brightness made me need that cigarette even more.

I pulled off the road when I came to a little grocery store. Nosed the Chevy near the front door of the place and ran in. Asked for a pack of Newports. I was dying for a smoke but I didn't want a brand I actually liked. I paid the thin old man at the counter and took the wrapping off the pack.

"No smoking in here," the old man said. I nodded, pulled one cigarette from the pack, and stepped outside to light it. I figured I would smoke it there so as not to stink up the car. But my car wasn't there. I looked left and right and ahead, to the thick traffic of Linden Boulevard. My car was gone.

I went back into the store.

"Yeah?" the old man said, cocking his chin at me.

"You seen my car?"

"What?" He sounded angry.

"My car, it was right there," I said, motioning to the store's tiny parking lot.

The old man just looked at me like I was a fool.

I went back out. Looked around some more. I felt my body getting heavier. I couldn't stand up anymore. I sunk down to the lip of the sidewalk and held my head between my hands. Eventually, I lit the cigarette. It scorched my lungs and felt nice. A car pulled into the tiny lot and went right where my Caprice had been. Two teenaged girls got out. They both had oil in their black hair and the sun made it shine.

I smoked.

I'd had a lot of problems in my thirty-nine years of life, but never this many. I lit a second cigarette. I coughed a little but kept smoking anyway. The girls emerged from the store, both clutching bottles of Yoo-hoo. Seemed to me Yoo-hoo would be unpleasant at 7:30 in the morning.

Eventually, the thin old man came out of his store and told me to leave. I guess for the price of a pack of smokes, I was entitled to twenty-some minutes on his sidewalk, but no more. I got up and walked.

The air was getting warmer and the sun looked too big looming above Linden Boulevard. I imagined the giant orb swelling so much it got too heavy for the sky and came plummeting down, plunging the world into darkness.

As I walked the few blocks back to The Hole, I kept glancing over at the cars that passed by on the busy avenue. None of them were mine.

When I got to Dumont Avenue, I stood there for a minute, at the periphery of The Hole, looking at the newly constructed houses that had recently sprung up all along the edge of the little canyon. Square cement boxes that already looked depressed, even though they were brand new and hadn't killed anybody's dreams yet.

I walked on down the dip where paved road gave way to dirt. The barns were humming with activity now. Feed was being dispensed, stalls were being mucked. These were comforting, normal sounds, but I didn't feel comforted.

I went into Culprit's stall and started currying her. Taking extra care with every aspect of the grooming procedure, knowing maybe this was the last time.

Two weeks passed. There was fear in me but I didn't cultivate it. All I kept thinking was how I hadn't meant to kill the guy. I'd never killed anything in my life. Not even a goddamned bug.

Now that I had no car, I had to take the bus to work. It was a long ride but I used the time to read some horsemanship books I'd picked up. I studied these books, and every afternoon, when I got off my shift at the pool, I'd take the bus back to East New York, take my mare out, and work with her in the tiny paddock behind the barn. I wasn't even riding her much, mostly just worked her on a lunge line, getting her used to my voice commands. There were pure moments when it was just me and my horse and we saw into each other. Then worry would creep in and sully the joy.

One afternoon, I was in the paddock with Culprit, working on some things. I called out "Canter," saying it slow and drawn out. I said it a few times, and then she threw her head around a little, protesting awhile before finally transitioning into the canter. Something red caught my eye and I looked over my shoulder and saw Stella sitting on a barrel outside the paddock. She was wearing a red sweatshirt and she'd cut bangs in her hair. I told Culprit to halt. My mare looked surprised and then obliged and came to a standstill.

"What's up?" Stella said like it was nothing at all.

"Hi Stella," I said in the same way, even though I'd never expected to see her again.

She watched as I finished up with Culprit then put the mare back in her stall. As I took care of barn chores, Stella sat on a trunk and didn't say much. I didn't ask.

When I'd finished feeding and watering the horses, Stella followed me back to the house.

"Where's your car?" she asked as we walked up the two crooked steps to my porch.

"Stolen," I said.

"You reported it?"

"What for?" I shrugged, not wanting to share the details with her.

"They turn up," she said. "I had one stolen before. Cops found it two months later. You gotta report it."

"Nah," I said, not knowing why she cared about the damned car. She kept on about it too. Asking how I was getting to work and whatnot. She'd never asked so many questions before, about anything. Maybe she was turning over a new leaf.

I was hungry but I'd run out of food, so instead of eating, Stella and I went to bed.

I had some questions for her, but they'd keep.

I put my hands on her hips. She was wearing cutoffs even though it was chilly out. She looked up at me but there was nothing to read in her eyes. She wore a small smile but even that wasn't saying much. I moved my left hand from her hip and up under her t-shirt, tracing her nipple with my fingertip. I lifted the shirt up and bit a line from between her breasts down to her shorts. She wiggled a little, responding, coiling, ready. I peeled her shorts down over her ass. She wasn't wearing panties. She turned around then, showing me her pale and pretty ass. I bent her over the bed and entered her. There was some violence in it.

Stella and I had gone at it twice already and had both passed out on the floor, exhausted. I'm not sure how long I'd been sleeping when she woke me by putting her mouth on me. Then we were making love again. After a few minutes, I pulled back from her and cupped her dark head in my hands.

"Where've you been, Stella?" I asked softly.

"I was mad," she said.

"At what?"

"At you, Triple."

"You wanna tell me why so I don't do it again?"

"Not really," she said with a small shrug. Her shoulders were narrow. They looked cute shrugging.

Okay. I picked her up and carried her into the kitchen. Propped her ass up against the sink and fucked her there. I'd never fucked anyone against a sink before. It got Stella pretty worked up. Her black eyes showed fire. Something close to passion. And, at the same time, she was nicer than usual. Almost tender.

In the morning, she didn't leave. Was still lying in my bed as I got dressed. I felt a little conflicted about it. Half of me wanted her to stay as long as she pleased, but the other half didn't want to go through the changes when she left me for good.

"I gotta go to work soon," I told her.

"Okay," she said.

"Don't you?"

"What?"

"Have to go to work?"

"I got fired," she said casually.

She'd been working at a convenience store over in Howard Beach. I couldn't really imagine how anyone could get fired from that kind of job.

"What happened?" I asked her.

"I got mad," she said, leaving it at that.

"And now you're moving in with me?" I asked.

"If that's all right," she answered, looking at me, not showing anything.

"I guess it is," I said.

I'd had a few women move in with me before. For various reasons having little to do with love or affection. One to get away from a rough husband. Another to be closer to work. I hadn't had one move in out of poverty though. Always room for a first.

I told my new roommate I was heading out to the barn.

"Okay," she said.

I put my clothes and boots on and went out. Fed the horses and mucked their stalls. The sun rose up from its hiding place and another bright day came on like a curse.

I walked back to the house to get some money out of my drawer before heading in to work. I did this in plain view of Stella. If she wanted to hit my little stash then so be it. As I stuffed a twenty in my pocket, Stella actually got up off the bed and kissed me goodbye like an old wife.

I walked to the bus stop.

I sat lording over the pool, reading my horse books. Once in a while Stella would come into my mind, but I didn't let her stay there. Thinking about her too hard might make her vanish.

At the end of my shift, I got the bus back to The Hole. I wanted to spend a good hour working with Culprit. I went into the house first to see if Stella was still there. She was lying on the floor, wearing a pair of baggy gym shorts, reading a tractor manual that for some reason I'd held onto from my days working on a horse farm in Maryland.

She glanced up and smiled. She looked so sweet and good. I got a hard-on and had to do something about it.

We were rolling around against the filthy carpet when I heard the car and saw the flash of cherry lights against the window.

"What's that?" Stella asked.

"Police," I said. I'd been expecting it so long it was almost a relief.

"What do they want?" Stella asked, standing up.

"No idea," I said.

A few heartbeats later they were knocking on the door. I put my pants on, gave Stella a minute to go in the other room, then opened the door.

One cop was white, the other black. They were both wide but built low to the ground. They looked like shrubbery.

"Yes?" I said.

"Triple Harrison?" the black one said.

"Yes?"

"'86 Chevy Caprice Classic? Blue?" the white one asked.

"Yeah, it was stolen," I said. My insides felt funny.

"Right, we got the report," the white one again.

What report? I wondered.

"Vehicle was abandoned in the Rockaways. It's at the tow facility near JFK. You'll have to deal with it," the black cop said.

"Oh," I replied, waiting for the other shoe to drop. It didn't.

The black cop had me sign some papers and wished me a nice day. I stood in my doorway, watching them get back in the patrol car. Mrs. Nagle from next door had her head sticking out of her house.

"They found my car!" I shouted over to Mrs. Nagle. She cocked her head but said nothing. She was mostly senile.

"Your car turned up?" Stella asked as I closed the door. She hadn't found a reason to put her clothes back on.

"Yeah, my car," I said, frowning.

"I reported it stolen," she said proudly. "I went and filled out the forms while you were at work. They found it fast." She smiled, showing teeth.

"Oh," I said, deciding not to tell her this might lead to my being locked up for life.

"Let's go get it," Stella suggested, her face lighting up like we were planning a trip to Disneyworld.

"In a minute," I said. "I got some business with you first." I pressed my body against hers, ran my hands down her sides, then tucked them under the slopes of her ass cheeks.

A half hour later I told her I was going to get the bus over to the tow place. She wanted to come but I told her no, without offering an explanation. She pouted a little. She'd never done that before.

I went and gave the horses an early supper. Figured I'd use my one phone call to tell Cornelius, the cowboy who owned the stable, that he'd have to feed and muck in the morning.

I walked up the slope of 78th Street and out to North Conduit Avenue to head to the bus stop.

The sky was still violently blue.

The people at the tow facility didn't do anything quickly. There was a lumpy white woman who was mad to be alive. By the time she'd gone through all my paperwork and I'd been taken to my car, night was coming on like a headache. My skin felt cold even though it was hot out.

I got into my car and saw that all the trash was gone. I'd had empty soda cans and candy wrappers in there and they were no more. There was one big muddy boot print near the gas pedal.

I pulled the car out onto the road. Expecting some kind of ambush. Dozens of cops, maybe even the feds. Nothing happened. I drove two miles, then finally, when it seemed certain no one was following me, I pulled off onto a side street not far from Aqueduct. It was a narrow road choked with vinyl houses. American flags stood guard over flatline lives. Some kids were throwing a ball at each other. I drove a ways, till the residential area surrendered to a strip mall. Went around the back of the shops and parked the car. Got out and unlocked the trunk. There was nothing there. Not only was Dwight's body gone, but so was all my crap. The empty feedbags, the horseshoe, the cooler, and the panties. I closed the trunk, got back in the car, and drove. I decided to head on over to the upscale stables off the Belt Parkway. Whenever I felt rich, I went there to buy nice alfalfa hay for Culprit.

For once, I had plenty of room in the trunk.

FADE TO . . . BROOKLYN

BY KEN BRUEN
Galway, Ireland

*O*nly the Dead Know Brooklyn.
  Man, isn't that a hell of a title. I love that. Pity it's been used, it's a novel by Thomas Boyle. I read it years ago when the idea of moving to Brooklyn began to seriously appeal. Don't get me wrong, I'm going, got a Gladstone bag packed. Just the essentials, a few nice *shoirts*. See, I'm learning Brooklynese, and it's not as easy a language as the movies would lead you to believe. I've had this notion for so long now, it's "an *idée fixe*." Like that touch of French? I'm no dumbass, I've learned stuff, not all of it kosher. I don't have a whole lot of the frog lingo, so I've got to like, spare it. Trot it out when the special occasion warrants. Say you want to impress a broad, you hit her with a flower and some shit in French, she's already got her knickers off. Okay, that's a bit crude but you get the drift.

  I'm hiding out in an apartment in Salthill. Yeah, yeah, you're thinking . . . but isn't that, like, in Galway, Ireland? I like a challenge.

  Phew-oh, I got me one right here. If only I hadn't shot that Polack, but he got right in my face, you hear what I'm saying? So he wasn't Polish, but I want to accustom myself to speaking American and if I don't practice, I'm going to be in some Italian joint and sounding Mick. How the hell can you ask for linguini, fried calamari, cut spaghetti alla chitarra, ravioli, scallops with a heavy sauce, and my absolute favorite in terms of pronunciation, fresh gnocchi, in any accent other than Brooklyn? It wouldn't fly. The apartment is real fine, huge window looking out over Galway Bay, a storm is coming in from the east, and the waves are lashing over the prom. I love that ferocity, makes me yearn, makes me feel like I'm a player. I don't know how long this place is safe, Sean is due to call and put the heart crossways in me. I have the cell close by. We call them *mobiles*—doesn't, if you'll pardon the pun, have the same ring. And the Sig Sauer, nine mil, holds fifteen rounds. I jacked a fresh one in there first thing this morning and racked the slide, sounds like reassurance. I'm cranked, ready to rock 'n' roll. Sean is a header, a real headbanger. He's from South Armagh, they grow up shooting at helicopters, bandit country, and those fuckers are afraid of nothing. I mean, if you have the British Army kicking in your door at 4 in the morning and calling you a Fenian bastard, you grow up fast and you grow up fierce.

I was doing a stretch in Portlaoise, where they keep the Republican guys. They are seriously chilled. Even the wardens give them space. And, of course, most of the wardens, they have Republican sympathies. I got to hang with them as I had a rep for armed robbery, not a very impressive rep or I wouldn't have been doing bird. Sean and I got tight and after release, he came to Galway for a break and he's been here two years. He is one crazy gumba. We had a sweetheart deal, no big design—like they say in twelve-step programs, we kept it simple. Post offices, that's what we hit. Not the major ones but the small outfits on the outskirts of towns. Forget banks, they've got CCTV and worse, the army does guard detail. Who needs that heat?

Like this.

We'd drive to a village, put on the balaclavas, get the shooters out, and go in loud and lethal, shouting, "Get the fuck down, this is a robbery, give us the fucking money!"

I let Sean do the shouting, as his Northern accent sent its own message. We'd be out of there in three minutes, tops. We never hit the payload, just nice, respectable, tidy sums, but you do enough of them, it begins to mount. We didn't flash the proceeds, kept a low profile. I was saving for Brooklyn, my new life, and Sean, well, he had commitments up north. I'd figured on another five jobs, I was outa there. Had my new ID secured, the money deposited in an English bank, and was working on my American.

Sean didn't get it, would say, "I don't get it."

He meant my whole American love affair. Especially Brooklyn. We'd been downing creamy pints one night, followed by shots of Bushmills, feeling mellow, and I told him of my grand design. We were in Oranmore, a small village outside Galway, lovely old pub, log fire and traditional music from a band in the corner, bodhrans, accordions, tin whistles, spoons and they were doing a set of jigs and reels that would put fire in the belly of a corpse. I'd a nice buzz building, we'd done a job three days before and it netted a solid result. I sank half my pint, wiped the froth off my lip, and said, "Ah, man, Fulton Ferry District, the Brooklyn Bridge, Prospect Park, Cobble Hill, Park Slope, Bed-Stuy, Bensonhurst, Bay Ridge, Coney Island."

These names were like a mantra to me, prayers I never tired of uttering, and I got carried away, let the sheer exuberance show. Big mistake, never let your wants out, especially to a Northerner, those mothers thrive on knowing where you're at. I should have heeded the signs—he'd gone quiet, and a quiet psycho is a fearsome animal. On I went like a dizzy teenager, saying, "I figure I'll get me a place on Atlantic Avenue and you know, blend."

I was flying, seeing the dream, high on it, and he leaned over, said in a whisper, "I never heard such bollixs in me life."

Like slapping me in the tush, cold water in my face. I knew he was heavy, meaning he was carrying, probably a Browning, his gun of choice, and that occurred to me as I registered the mania in his eyes. 'Course, Sean was always packing—when you were as paranoid as him, it came with the territory. He'd always said, "I ain't doing no more time, the cunts will have to take me down."

I believed him.

The band were doing that beautiful piece, "O'Carolan's Lament" . . . the saddest music I know, and it seemed appropriate as he rubbished my dream, when he said, "Cop on, see that band over there, that's your heritage, not some Yank bullshit. You can't turn your back on your birthright. I'd see you dead first, and hey, what's with this fucking Yank accent you trot out sometimes?"

I knew I'd probably have to kill the cocksucker, and the way I was feeling, it would be a goddamm pleasure.

Clip
Whack
Pop
Burn

All the great terms the Americans have for putting your lights out.

Sean ordered a fresh batch of drinks, pints and chasers, and the barman, bringing them over, said, "A grand night for it."

I thought, little do you know.

Sean, raising his glass, clinked mine, said, "Forget that nonsense, we have a lot of work to do. There's going to be an escalation in our operation."

I touched his glass, walloped in the Bush, felt it burn my stomach, and wanted to say, "*Boilermakers, that's what they call it. You get your shot, sink the glass in the beer, and put a Lucky in your mouth, crank it with a Zippo, one that has the logo, 'First Airborne.'*"

What I said was, "God bless the work."

And got the look from him, supposed to strike fear in my gut. He asked, "You fucking with me, son?"

Son . . . the condescending prick, I was five years older, more probably. I raised my hands, palms out, said, "Would I do that? I mean, come on."

Sean had the appearance of a starved greyhound, all sinewy and furtive. He didn't take drugs, as the Organization frowned on it, but man, he was wired, fueled on a mix of hatred and ferocity. He belonged to the darkness and had lived there so long, he didn't even know light existed any-more. He was the personification of the maxim, *retaliate first*, always on the alert. His eyes bored into mine and he said, "Just you remember that."

Then he was up, asking the band for a request. I was pretty sure I could take him, as long as his back was turned and preferably if he was asleep. You don't ever want the likes of those to know you're coming. They live with the expecta-tion of somebody coming every day, so I'd act the dumb fuck he was treating me as. The band launched into "The Men Behind the Wire." Sean came back, a shit-eating grin in place, and as the opening lines began, *"Armored cars and tanks and guns . . ."* he joined with, *"Came to take away our sons . . ."* Leaned over, punched my shoulder, said, "Come on, join me."

I did, sounding almost like I meant it.

* * *

Maybe he's found out by now dat he'll neveh live long enough to know duh whole of Brooklyn. It'd take a life- time to know Brooklyn t'roo an' t'roo. An' even den, yuh wouldn't know it at all.

Thomas Wolfe said that in "Only the Dead Know Brooklyn." I'd never been out of Ireland but I was getting to know Brooklyn. I had a pretty good notion of it. In my bedroom there is a street map, place names heavily underlined in red. I've pored over it a hundred times, and with absolute joy. Using my finger, I'd take a few steps to the corner of Fulton and Flatbush, check the border between Downtown and Fort Greene, I'd glance at Brooklyn's tallest building, the Williamsburg Savings Bank, smile at the idea of taking it down, but I'd be a citizen then, running a small pastry shop, specializing in *babka*, the polish cake. I learnt that from *Seinfeld*. Then maybe stroll on Nassau Street to McCarren Park, heading for the south end to the Russian Church of the Transfiguration, light a candle for the poor fucks whose money I stole.

As well as the books on Brooklyn, I managed to collect over a long period the movies. Got 'em all I think.

Whistling in Brooklyn.
It Happened in Brooklyn
The Lords of Flatbush
Sophie's Choice
Moscow on the Hudson

Waited ages for the top two to come on TV, I mean those were made in 1944 and 1942.

Saturday Night Fever? . . . Bay Ridge, am I right or am I right? *Last Exit to Brooklyn,* book and movie, *yeah, got 'em.* Red Hook, a fairly barren place is . . . lemme see, give me a second here . . . Ah, that's easy, *On the Waterfront.*

Writers too, I've done my work.

Boerum Hill? Washington Irving and James Fenimore Cooper lived there. I'm on a roll here, ask me another. Who's buried in Greenwood Cemetery? Too easy, Mae West and Horace Greeley.

When I was in the joint, other guys did weights, did dope, did each other. Me, I read and reread, became a fixture in the library. I didn't get any grief from the other cons. Sean had my back, better than a Rottweiler. What happened was, he'd got in a beef with the guy running the cigarette gig, the most lucrative deal in the place. I heard the guy was carrying a shiv, fixing to gut Sean in the yard. I tipped off Sean only as this guy had come at me in my early days. He was trailer trash, a real bottom-feeder—if it wasn't for the cigs, he'd have been bottom of the food chain. Mainly I didn't like him, he was a nasty fuck, always whining, bitching, and moaning, bellyaching over some crap or other. I hate shivs, they're the weapon of the sneak who hasn't the *cojones* to front it. Sean hadn't said a whole lot when I told him. He nodded, said, "Okay."

Effusive, yeah?

The shiv guy took a dive from the third tier, broke his back, and the cigarette cartel passed to Sean's crew. From then on, he walked point for me.

Back in the eighties, a song, "Fade to Gray," blasted from every radio—it launched the movement, "New Romantics," and guys got to wear eyeliner and shit. You knew they always wanted to, but now they could call it art.

Gobshites.

But I liked the song, seemed to sum up my life, those days, everything down the crapper, a life of drab existence as gray as the granite on the bleak, blasted landscape of Connamara. That's when I met Maria.

Lemme tell you straight up, I'm no oil painting. My mother told me, "Get a personality 'cos you're fairly ugly."

I think she figured the "fairly" softened the blow.

It didn't.

Nor was I what you'd call a people's person. I didn't have a whole lot of them social skills.

I was at a dance in Seapoint, the massive ballroom perched on the corner of the promenade, the Atlantic hurling at it with intent. Now, it's a bingo hall. That night, a showband, eight guys in red blazers, bad hairpieces, with three bugles, drums, trombone, and a whole lot of neck, were massacring "Satisfaction." They obviously hated the Stones. Those days, there was a sadistic practice known as "ladies' choice."

Jesus.

Pure hell. The guys used it to nip outside and get fortified with shots of Jameson. I was about to join them when I heard, "Would you like to dance?"

A pretty face, gorgeous smile, and I looked behind me to see whom she meant. This girl gave a lovely laugh, said, "I mean you."

Hands down, that is the best second of my life. I haven't had a whole line of them, but it's the pinnacle, the moment when God relented, decided, *"Cut the sucker a little slack."*

'Course, like all divine gifts, he only meant to fuck with

me later. That's okay, I've lived that moment a thousand times. And yeah, you guessed it, she was American . . . from Brooklyn. I loved her accent, her spirit; hell, I loved *her*. Miracle two, she didn't bolt after the dance, stayed for the next one, "Fade to Gray." A slow number, I got to hold her, I was dizzy.

Walked her back to her hotel. I stood with her, trying to prolong the feeling, and she said, "You're kinda cute."

Put it on my headstone, it's all that counts. She kissed me briefly on the mouth and agreed to meet me at 7 the next evening.

She didn't show.

At 10:30, I went into the hotel, heard she checked out that morning. The clerk, a guy I went to school with, told me her surname, Toscini, that she was traveling with her mother. I palmed him a few notes and he let me see the register—the only address was Fulton Street, Brooklyn, New York.

I wrote letter after letter, all came back with, *"Return to sender, address unknown."* Like that dire song.

I began to learn about Brooklyn. I'd find her. Her not showing or leaving a note, it was some awful misunderstanding. Her mother had suddenly decided they were leaving and Maria had no way to contact me. Yeah, had to be that. I made it so. Got to where I could see her pleading, crying with her mother, and being literally dragged away. Yes, like that, I *know*.

Mornings, like a vet, I'd come screaming, sweating outa sleep, going, "Maria, hon, I'm on my way!"

Shit like that, get you killed in prison. They're not real understanding about screamers, though there's plenty of it.

No more than any other guilt-ridden Catholic Irish guy, I'm not superstitious. But I tell you, the omens, they're . . . like . . . there. You just gotta be open to them.

Listen to this: A while ago, there was a horse running at the Curragh. I'm not a gambler but read the sports pages, read them first to show I'm not gay. At 15/1, there was one, Coney Island Red. How could I not? Put a bundle on him, on the nose.

He lost.

See the omen? Maria wouldn't want me gambling, lest I blow the kid's college fund. Over the years, if I was asked about girlfriends, I'd say my girl was nursing in America, and came to believe it. She was caring and ideal for that. 'Course, when the kids arrive, she'll have to give up her career—I wouldn't want my wife working, it's the man's place to do the graft—know they'll appreciate those old values in Brooklyn.

Sean came to see me about the new plan. He was wearing one of those long coats favored by shoplifters or rock stars. The collar turned up to give him some edge. I made coffee and he said, "Nice place you got here." I sat opposite him and he launched: "We're going to do the main post office."

I didn't like the sound of that, said, "Don't like the sound of that."

He gave the grin, no relation to warmth or humor, said, "It's not about what you like or don't like, money is needed and a lot of it. This Thursday, there is going to be a massive sum there, something to do with the payment of pensions and the bonus due for Social Benefit. It's rare for them to handle such a large amount so we have to act now."

I went along with it, there wasn't a whole lot of choice, he wasn't asking me, he was delivering orders.

We went in hard and it was playing out as usual, when I took my eye off the crowd, distracted for one second, and that's when the guy came at me, grabbed my gun, and it went off, taking half his face. Then we were out of there, running like demented things, got in the stolen car, then changed vehicles at Tuam and drove back into town, the exact opposite of what would be anticipated. Sean was breathing hard, said, "You fucked up."

"Hey, he came at me, it was an accident."

He gritted his teeth, a raw sound like a nail on glass, said, "This is going south."

He was right. The dead man was a cop, in plain clothes, and the heat was on. Sean called me that evening, went, "You wasted a fucking policeman, there's going to be serious repercussions. I've a meet with my superiors and I'll let you know what's going to happen."

He slammed down the phone. So I waited, checking my travel arrangements. I'd fly from Shannon to New York, and hell, splurge a little, grab a cab all the way to Brighton Beach, because I liked the sound of it. Then I'd find Maria.

I'd already packed and was trying to decide what movies to bring, when Sean called. "It's bad."

"Tell me."

"We can't have a cop-killer on our hands, the pressure is enormous."

I took a deep breath, said, "You've given me up."

For the first time, he sounded nervous, then, "I'm giving you a chance, I wasn't even supposed to call you."

"You're all heart, Sean. So what's the bottom line?"

Deep breath, then, "They're sending two guys to pick you up, they'll be there in twenty minutes, so get the fuck out and run like hell."

Curious, I asked, "And these guys, they're not bringing me to the authorities, are they?"

"You're wasting time, get moving."

Click.

I've poured a Bush, opened a beer, and am going to have a boilermaker. The Sig is in my lap and I have that song playing, here comes my favorite riff: "*Fade . . .*"

DUMPED

NICOLE BLACKMAN

Fort Greene

I met her at this party on Clinton Street. When I'd see her around the neighborhood I'd just stare at her, like she was unreal. I saw her in the deli, talking on her cellphone, so I followed her around the store just to listen to her talk. She just seemed, I don't know, special, you know? I guess I had a crush on her. One night we both end up at this party, we started talking and I was just blown away. We talked about everything and I kept bringing her drinks just to have something to do. She was smiling and laughing like she thought I was funny, and I think I'm doing really good here, so I'm not going home any time soon. We stayed really late and the sun was coming up and a couple of people were passed out on the couch, so we just crashed on the floor with some blankets and stuff. I'm lying there with my hand on her thinking maybe I've got a shot. I didn't think it would *become* anything, I thought she was messing with me, you know?"

Brian just listened as Sean spoke. The light cast stark, flickering shadows on his face as the cargo van rocked slightly. They'd been on the road for a few hours or more and they still had no idea where they were going.

"Anyway, so she comes over the next night, and then she wants to see me three, four nights a week, and I didn't know how to handle it, or, like, handle *her*, you know? I guess I was just . . . afraid of her. I mean, why was she dating *me*? It's like you dream about something for so long . . . a girl, a car, a new job, whatever. Then if you get it, you still don't think you deserve it. It's a mistake, or someone's playing a trick on you like that movie *Carrie* when they dump pig's blood on her head and it's all a joke.

"She just . . . wasn't like anyone I'd ever dated before. The girls I usually dated worked at indie labels or were somebody's assistant or read manuscripts and fucking hated their jobs, and we'd go out for pizza and see some special effects movie where stuff blew up, you know? We'd get drunk and they'd wake up at my place, hung over and ugly, and maybe we'd see each other again, maybe we wouldn't. I had a system and she didn't fit the system. At all."

Sean sighed, silenced for a moment by the memory of her. He seemed to forget he was sitting in the back of a van, his wrists and ankles bound in gaff tape, arms tied behind him to the van's wall bars, with two other guys he didn't know.

"I mean, I do ad sales and I do okay, but she made a lot more money than me, you know? I didn't know where to take her. We'd go out to dinner and she'd order stuff I couldn't *pronounce,* much less pay for. Dating her was like dating a movie—she'd show up at my place in a black town car, wearing a trench coat with nothing but black lace panties underneath, and dare me to fuck her in the car. I mean, she wanted to go down on me in a taxi as we were going across the Brooklyn Bridge, like she thought it would be a huge turn-on, and I . . . I just couldn't do it."

"A woman wants to blow you in the back of a cab and you *flinch?*" Brian spat.

"I know, I know, but the only thing I could think of was, what if the driver saw? What if other people saw?"

"Who the fuck cares?" Brian really didn't like him now.

Besides, he was short, and short guys were usually weird, like they needed to compensate.

"I cared! It was . . . I guess I just chickened out." Sean was flustered now. "Come on, she knew all kinds of stuff, everywhere we went she had a story about something cool that happened there, and she'd run into people she knew wherever we went. On Sundays I'd wake up and she'd be sitting on my couch reading the *New York Times Magazine.* I didn't know girls like that. Then there's the morning I wake up and she's laughing her ass off."

"About what?"

"She looked at my bookshelf, and she saw a whole row of paperbacks on the shelf facing backwards so you couldn't read the titles. So she started turning them around and burst out laughing."

"What were they, porn?" Brian snorted.

"Nah. Worse," Sean muttered to the floor, glum.

"What's worse than porn?"

"*Star Trek* novels."

"Dude . . ." Brian exhaled a long, pitying sigh.

"I know, I know. Whatever. I *like* them," he pleaded.

"So why'd you turn them around on your shelf then?" Brian leaned as far forward as he could.

"Because it's *embarrassing.* I didn't want people to know that's what I read. Anyway, I knew it wasn't going to last. At first, it was like Christmas every day. I mean, I'd had my eye on her for months, and I'd have fantasies about her when I'd jack off in the shower. The first time I fucked her in that shower I nearly passed out. Come on, she's beautiful, she's smart, she's up for anything, and she wants to be with *me* all the time. I'm thinking, you're kidding, right? After a week or two, I was like, how do I do this? I don't know how to order off a menu with her, much less make conversation, she's going to get bored of me fast. I knew that! Shit, even my friends were like, 'She's so out of your league, enjoy it while it lasts, pal.' So I did what any guy would do to keep a woman hooked on him."

"What, spent all your money on her?" Brian rolled his eyes and leaned against the van wall. They'd spent a long time trying to figure out what they had in common—he couldn't believe it was a woman.

"Uh uh, I went down on her every chance I had. I knew her pussy better than her *gynecologist*." Sean grinned, sitting back. "I'd look up at her and there would be nail polish streaks on the wall over the headboard. Fucking *streaks* on the *wall*. I'd work on her for like twenty minutes and she'd come so hard she'd push my head away and just twitch like she was electrocuted . . ."

Brian thought he saw him wink. God, this guy was such a tool. He wished the blond guy passed out in the corner would wake the fuck up.

". . . Then I'd start all over again. I'd make her come three or four times and she'd be pulling me to her, begging me to fuck her. Now she needed me for something, now I had something she wanted really bad . . ."

Brian chuckled softly and smirked at Sean, knowing he couldn't possibly have anything she wanted. Brian slid his feet as far forward as he could to stretch his legs. He tried to figure out how long they'd been in this van. They had to have been sitting here talking for two hours, another hour or two on top of that when they were passed out. So, three . . . four hours, maybe? When he tried to rub his wrists together he realized his watch was gone. They took his fucking watch.

Fuck. Fuck. Fuck.

". . . Sure, I'd fuck her occasionally," Sean said, carried away by the memory. He could smell her now, feel the curve of her waist. "Really slow, so she'd be moaning for it. I'd get her really worked up and then sometimes I wouldn't finish her off. It was like a control thing, totally passive aggressive, you know?"

Brian was bored. This kid was such a fucking amateur. "Cut to the chase."

Sean had thought about it a lot, he just never said it out loud.

"After two or three months, we went out to dinner and I had it all planned out. It was going to be farewell sex, like a last meal before an execution, you know? In the morning, I just bit the bullet and as soon as she woke up, I told her we needed to talk, and she wrapped herself around me in bed. She got nervous like animals do when they know they're going to be killed, you know? The worst part was she held my hand while I told her all this, like she thought I couldn't be cruel to her if she was holding my hand."

They sat in silence in the windowless van, listening to the sounds of cars and trucks on the highway.

"I told her that I wasn't interested anymore, it was me and not her, this isn't what I wanted, you know, standard dump speech. But I kind of twisted it a little and said I didn't like how she was always doing stuff for me, buying me things and taking me places like she just thought she was just being nice when it was actually a control thing of hers."

"Nice touch. How'd she take it?"

"She just curled up in a ball and cried for an hour. I was in the other room watching TV when she suddenly comes out with her stuff in a bag. She'd called a car service and didn't even look at me, she just grabbed her shit and left. I mean, I felt awful, it was a shit thing to do, but I'd rather have her angry at me than drag everything out."

The silence hung in the air, cold and thick.

"You want to know the truth?" Brian said gently.

Sean nodded, hesitant.

"You were a pity fuck," he spat.

Sean's face hardened.

"She told me about you," Brian continued. "She laughed that you were Transitional Guy, like you were a comic book character, except you didn't know how it was supposed to end. *She* was supposed to end it, not you. So, yeah, it fucked her up and she had serious damage, but what can I tell you? That's my thing, so I moved in."

"What do you mean?" Sean said, chilled.

Brian sized him up carefully, to see if he was worth telling. "I bartend over at the Alibi by the park. This was, like, three years ago. September . . . a couple months after you dumped her. She came in one night with two or three other girls and I just zeroed in on her, 'cause she looked like she hadn't been out in a while. You could tell that her friends took her out to cheer her up, so I kept making eye contact with her when I was at the other end of the bar. I gave her some quarters for the jukebox, asked her to go pick out some Tom Waits, kept her glass filled. Lot of attention, just kept looking at her and then looking away like she caught me. I'm good, right? By the end of the night, her friends are gone, the bar's empty, and it's just the two of us talking.

"She's smiling and playing with her hair, looking up at me, stroking her collarbone and fiddling with her necklace, leaning forward on the bar, it's all body language. You know the thing about showing their palm, right?"

Sean shook his head, his light brown hair falling in his

eyes, making him look even younger. This was a master class, and he tried to keep up. He couldn't believe guys like this actually existed and this was what he was up against.

"When a woman shows you the palm of her hand, she's open," Brian explained patiently. "It's a major sign. It means she's vulnerable and she'll probably show you something else, know what I mean? So anyway, I've got her, I've totally got this chick. It's classic . . . *classic*. Everyone has one thing they're born knowing how to do, right? This is it. This is what I do better than anyone else."

Brian tried to move his arms.

"Fuck, my arm's asleep. Anyway, I know what to talk about: stories about my family, what kinda pets I've had, how much I like to travel, where I've been and where I want to go next. Always say Morocco or Thailand, by the way, just trust me. It gives her a way to size me up, decide if I'm a quality guy, right? And she's just *glowing* across the bar at me. She even says I'm not like the other guys and, you know, I do the blushing thing. You know the blushing thing, right?"

Sean shook his head, confused.

"You have to do it like this," Brian confided, as he leaned forward a bit on the box and looked down at the floor of the van. "When she gives you a compliment or you 'confess' something, you look down like you're a little embarrassed or trying to hide a smile. Then you keep your face down and look up with only your eyes, like this."

He demonstrated, his eyes peeking up shyly through his lashes. "Slays them every time, I'm telling you."

Brian's expression morphed seamlessly from innocent and charming to cold and hard again, and then he grinned as he leaned back against the van wall. With his black hair and sharp eyes he looked even colder. "The best part was she thought *she* was the one pursuing *me,* because I was acting like I had a serious crush, like it was love at first sight and this had never happened to me before.

"We talk about artists we like, so l ask for her number like I'm real shy, say there's this Bill Viola show she might like to see. She's actually blushing, like she's already thinking of how to tell our grandkids how we met. I just knew it."

Brian was smug. "I've never hooked a woman so easy, so fast. *Never.*"

"So what did you do?"

"I didn't even touch her that night, total gentleman. Called her the next day, said I couldn't wait to talk to her, that I'd been thinking about her all day, and she's totally charmed, right? So we made plans to see the gallery in the afternoon and I kind of kept it rolling to dinner and finally back to my place to hang out. We started talking about ecstasy and how she hadn't done it in so long, so I said I had some at my place and we could share it, right?

"She was so wrapped up in the moment," Brian snorted, "thinking I was so easy to talk to, that we had so much in common . . . Fuck, I could have gotten her to do anything . . . I probably could have gotten her to shoot *heroin.* I mean, my place is kind of a dump and she's going on about how amazing the view is and how cool the paintings are and whatever. She's totally delusional at this point, she thinks it's karma, like we've really connected.

"So we have sex and she says it's spiritual and amazing, you know, but it's just E-love. Sex on ecstasy just fucking *bonds* you, except she's never had sex on E before so it's new to her and she thinks this is chemistry. Yeah, it's chemistry, it's fucking *lab* chemistry. So now we're rolling and I love this part, this is where the head-fuck gets *deep.*

"Then it just became a question of how little could I do and still have her want me? It became a game and I stretched it out for *months*. Little by little I pulled away, real small stuff like I stopped kissing her, wouldn't hold her after sex, never went down on her. No foreplay, no talking, it was just fuck her and go to sleep, like when I'm done, *we're* done. I wouldn't even kiss her when she'd cry. I'd roll over with my back to her, and I swear I'd just be lying there, grinning in the dark. She'd sob for a while then finally she'd go to sleep. The next morning I wouldn't say a thing, act like nothing happened. I know, cold, right? But you know what?"

"What?" Sean asked nervously. This is who she ended up with after him?

"She'd call me that night, want to come over, act like nothing *ever happened*," Brian said, incredulously. "And I'd always blow her off, wouldn't call her back for like a week! I'd wait for the voicemail to pile up and she'd get panicky, thinking it was something *she'd* done. I'd be out with the guys and we'd brag about who has the craziest phone messages from a woman, who can string some bitch along the longest, right? And there was no question, I won. I was the king of this, I had proof right here. I'd save the messages and play like a dozen of them to everybody, and they'd start with her all sweet. 'Hi, it's me,' became annoyed, like, 'Hey, where have you been?' and then she'd get concerned, 'Are you okay?' and finally, after a week, it's, 'I'm sorry you're so upset at me, I miss you, please forgive me.' She didn't even know what she'd done to make me disappear but she was already begging me to take her back! The next time I'd see her, and I'd always wait like at least a week or two, she'd apologize to *me* for being such a basket case, and promise it'd never happen again!"

"Jesus . . ."

"I know! Totally fucked up, right?" He was on a roll now, and his dark eyes flashed. "But here's the thing: If a woman thinks she's worthless, if she's been dumped by enough guys and her self-esteem is that low, she'll excuse *anything* to keep you. I was so under her skin, she was dependent on me like a drug, she was hooked just like a junkie and she'd put up with whatever she had to."

Brian was grinning hard now. He'd never had an office job, never made serious money, kept getting fired, and had the shittiest credit of anyone he knew, but in this one sport, he was a champion. "Here's the secret, and I know it's so fucking wrong, but the worse you treat them, the more they want you. It's totally fucked up, but the sooner you understand that, the better off you'll be. I'm telling you."

Sean was quiet and let Brian's story sink in. He was colder now, inside and out. The van hadn't stopped once and they still had no idea where they were going or why. The back of his head was throbbing from where he had pounded his head into the van wall to try and get someone's attention. He looked over to his left and saw the blond guy's eyes were still closed, though he wasn't slumped over anymore.

"Hey, look at him," Sean whispered to Brian. "Is he awake yet?"

"Hey, buddy! You awake?" Brian barked.

Blond guy's eyes opened, suspiciously, like he'd been awake and listening to them for a long time.

"Yeah, Brian," he sneered. "I'm awake."

"How do you know my name?" Brian accused.

"You and your pal, Sean, have been using up all the fucking oxygen in this van for the last hour or two, that's how, genius."

"So who are you, asshole?"

"The name isn't Asshole, it's Frank."

"Do you know why we're here?" Sean said flatly, now a good cop to Brian's bad cop.

"We must all have something in common, right?" Frank smiled. "I'll save you two some time: I'm a trader for Pettigrew Dean and I live on the Upper East Side in the city. I'm forty-one, single, I don't gamble, I don't owe anybody money, I don't deal with the mob, I don't have a criminal record, I don't go to the Alibi, although I own some property in Fort Greene and Park Slope, and I *don't* read *Star Trek* novels . . ."

Frank was kind of enjoying this.

". . . And, oh yeah. I know her too."

The air in the van went ice cold as Sean's eyes shot quickly to Brian, then back to Frank. This was seriously fucked up now.

"I heard all about you guys." Frank narrowed his eyes at Sean. "The time she brought a glass of fresh orange juice and a clean towel to you as you were stepping out of the shower and you just walked right by her. That fucking *slayed* her. She never forgot it."

Sean crumbled at the memory; he'd never told anyone about that. He felt nauseous.

Frank turned to Brian. "And you? Yeah, she told me all about you and how you twisted her inside out like a game. How cold you were, how you used her for fun and then fucked her over. She didn't see anyone for almost a *year* after that, she just holed up in her apartment and didn't go out. Did you know that?"

"No, I didn't know that," Brian admitted quietly, as the bravado slid off his face like he'd been caught by his mother. He leaned back, away from the light of the van's harsh bare bulb. It never occurred to him that there would be real damage. Everybody played hard, it was part of the game.

"Yeah, guess not," Frank said coolly, his pale hair and pale eyes seeming to soak up the light. "Did you know she was on *six* different anti-depressants that year? Did you know she started having a hard time leaving her apartment? Did you know she thought everything was her fault, that she was a terrible person? She thought there had to be something wrong with her for everyone to keep treating her like this, right? By the time I met her, she was so fucking fragile, I thought I'd break her if I held her hand."

Frank was furious now.

"How did you meet her?" Sean asked quietly, staring at the floor. Was that blood?

"At a dinner party." Frank's voice quieted at the memory. "We were sitting next to each other and she was just starting to go out again, but she was so gun shy, she was really having trouble talking to me. It took an hour to even drag a conversation out of her. She couldn't function at all, so I asked her about what she did, and then we talked about movies, cool flea markets, what we were reading, all kinds of stuff.

"I liked her," Frank recalled, moving his head from side to side. His neck was cramped from leaning over for hours. "She seemed sweet and, I don't know, *textured* in some way. She wasn't glossy at all and I could tell by the way she hunched her shoulders and shuffled when she walked that something bad happened to her, she'd been thrown away. She seemed really hurt and tired when she finally told me about it all. It made me furious, and sad, like, how dare they? How dare . . . you?"

Frank seemed larger now, and Sean and Brian had lost their swagger, shamed.

"So I kissed her hand goodnight, really gently, and I gave her my phone number so *she* could decide if she wanted to talk to me. I left it up to her, we'd talk when she was ready. I wasn't going to press her. It was two or three weeks before she called me, and she was so nervous that I knew she'd been practicing what she was going to say. I've gotta tell you, it was so sweet it tore my heart out. She said she had to find a bedside table and did I want to go scout some places on Washington Street? Saturday afternoon, easy enough, no pressure, so I said, yeah, sure. I got there and she was dressed up more than usual, like she'd really thought about what she was going to wear. She had this flared black-and-white tweed skirt and black shoes with a strap across them, like showgirls wear, with this burgundy coat that had a fur collar, and this dark red lipstick sort of smudged like it was an accident. She looked like an old-fashioned movie star on her day off. Adorable, totally adorable.

"We started dating and I spent a lot of time with her. She was real cautious and warned me to go slow with her, that she needed time to work some things out and could I deal with that? I said, sure, she was worth it. So we started talking every day, then we were traveling together, like she'd come out to my place in the Hamptons for the weekend and she'd stay over at my apartment a few nights a week. We were going to the opening of a new club, Plush, you know that one? I took her shopping for a dress, and I guess that freaked her out because she wasn't used to being treated well. Do you believe no guy had even sent her *flowers?* I mean, fuck."

Sean looked at Frank and Brian across from him. He wondered who was thrown in the van first.

"So I took her on as kind of a personal project. Get her out, get her to take some classes . . . We started to take trips together, she got more social, and I started seeing a real difference in her. We'd go to art openings, I took her to some dinner parties, and I'm thinking she could be a good corporate wife, like do charity work during the day and take care of the house stuff. Plan the vacations and take care of the kids—I mean, I've got to start thinking about that because I'm not going anywhere without the wife and family thing . . . Company's not going to promote someone who doesn't fit the picture. Clients don't trust a guy handling their money who's not like them. Like, if you're forty-five and still running around? Forget it. Doesn't matter how good you are.

"Now it's been a few months and I'm thinking she might be the one. So I start training her like they trained me at PD—I start teaching her about my job, how to make chitchat at a charity event, negotiate with antiques dealers . . . had to get her out of that place in Fort Greene. I'm thinking if it works out, I just might marry her, but we never talked about it.

"Anyway, we're out at a club for some party and we end up barhopping all over town with friends. It's really late and she says she wants to go to this one bar by her place, some shithole on Myrtle Avenue, so we end up there and she's drunk, *really* drunk. She's wearing this little foufy lavender dress and the place is pretty crowded, it's hot, she's almost cross-eyed she's so plowed. She wants to dance, and I'm like, forget it, but she drags me downstairs to the basement, it's like this private VIP room, real dark, no bouncers, couple of guys in suits getting smashed at a table, two or three people smoking, whatever. She starts dancing with whoever, but she keeps looking back at me to see if I'm watching her, like it's a private show for me, like it'll turn me on or something."

Frank's legs were pressed tightly against each other, as

though he needed to push against something, but he could only push against himself.

"She doesn't get the response she wants from me, like she's trying to punish me, get me jealous, see how much I really care about her. So she gets on a table to dance and she can barely stand up, and everybody's looking at her. Her hair's all over the place, and her makeup's smeared and she's glistening like she's sweating to death or her body is trying to push all that fucking booze out, and I look at her. I just look at her, horrified. *This is who she is.* No matter how much I try to do for her, how much I try to teach her, she'll never be what I need. She's not marriage material, she's a fucking *mess*, and now she's looking uglier and uglier. I kissed *that?* I thought I could love *that?* And I start getting pissed off, she wasted *my* time, I tried to *save* her and this is how she humiliates me?

"Now, I'm not that buzzed, and when I see this going on, I sober up real quick. She's dancing with any guy in the room and rubbing up against them, rubbing her ass against their crotch like she's a fucking stripper and she wants me to watch. She wants me to *watch* her. She hasn't had sex with me because she says she needs 'time,' and I'm fine with that. For fuck's sake, I'm patient as hell because I think she's worth it—and she ends up rubbing her pussy up against some drunk guy in a bar?"

Frank's eyes were blazing now.

"The place empties out and it's just us and these four guys in suits, and they're out celebrating a birthday or big promotion or something, and they are nasty drunk. They all take turns dancing with her—well, it's more like dragging her at this point, she's so dizzy. She keeps looking around like this isn't fun anymore, and she's trying to find me so I can save her, but I'm just sitting in this one shadowy corner and she doesn't see me. The other guys don't know we came in together, and they can't see me either, so they think it's just them and her. Like, time for a private show, okay?

"Then she falls over backwards on a cocktail table, knocking all the glasses on the floor, and she's yelling, 'Frank! Frank!' but she's slurring so bad they think she's yelling, 'Fuck! Fuck!' And one guy says, 'Whatever the lady wants, right?' and they all start laughing as they unzip their pants. Now she's screaming and crying and trying to push them off, and they turn her over so she's face down on the cocktail table, and the ashtray flips over and a glass breaks on the floor, and one by one they all fuck her. They fuck her till she throws up. She's covered in come and sweat and vomit and she's moaning, her eyes are rolling in her head. Her dress is shredded and her panties are twisted around one leg like they just got ripped off the other, and there's blood on her leg . . ."

Horrified, Brian and Sean couldn't take their eyes off Frank as he spoke, but they didn't see him. All they saw was their own picture of her, helpless and screaming on a table, like a still photo from their own personal film.

". . . And all I can think is: You fucking whore. I mean, we never even slept together! When she said she needed 'time' to work some things out, I was fine with that, but hey, give it away to some guys you meet in a bar? Go ahead! I've gotta tell you, though, when I saw her face all blurry and mashed on that table, slumped over like a rag doll, I thought, 'Well, guess you worked it out, huh?'

"After they all left, I dragged her out of there to her apartment and she was moaning and crying the whole way. It was around 5 a.m., and I left her in front of her apartment. I was done with her. Done. This was the fourth time I had to teach some woman a lesson and I was sick of it. After everything I do for them and they . . . Why can't they just . . . Yeah, I dumped her. I fucking dumped her on the *sidewalk*."

Frank sat back, satisfied. Sean and Brian stared at each other with their mouths slightly open, knowing their rankings had changed.

For a long time, they sat in silence in the windowless van. No one knew what to say. Close enough to talk but not to help each other. Sean wondered why they weren't gagged too? Why would someone want them talking to each other? What were they supposed to figure out?

As the van slowed and finally stopped, they looked at one another anxiously, listening to the sound of water in the background. Ocean? Lake? River? They couldn't tell. Then the clang of equipment, metal and heavy.

"I know why we're here," Sean gasped, his voice crumbled like soft charcoal. He was always the last to figure everything out.

"It's our turn to get dumped."

SLIPPING INTO DARKNESS

BY C.J. SULLIVAN

Bushwick

It wasn't supposed to happen like this—not here. What was she doing on this filthy block back in Bushwick? This was not how it was supposed to play out.

She shook her head as she thought about her parents' warnings. She had been taught—over and over—to stay away from ghetto gangsters, those who lived to pull down their own kind who try to get ahead. She had been raised to be a striver and an achiever—a woman who would reach and attain the American Dream, and bring pride to her Puerto Rican ancestors and family name.

Rosa Lima silently cursed herself as she made her way up Knickerbocker Avenue. At the corner of Himrod Street a bone-chilling winter wind ripped through her suede coat. She shivered as she thought of her parents. They had been right. Every last frightful thing they ever told her had come true. The longer she lived the smarter they became. But since she was little, Rosa always had to test limits. She took nothing on face value. Now it was *all* right in her face.

A few months ago everything was going so well. Maybe too well. And she let her guard down and let him into her life. It felt right. He was smooth and handsome—looked and styled himself after the actor Benjamin Bratt. She liked that he was a Latino on the fast track to a better life. As her mother would say, "He cleaned up well." And she liked his recent pedigree. He went to NYU, was pulling down good grades and talked a good game.

Now she saw just how blind she had been to who he really was. The warning signs were all there. She just hadn't seen them. Or didn't want to. It was like she saw only his shadow. She knew he was rough around the edges and had a temper. When she rode around Brooklyn with him in his leased Acura he was always getting into arguments with other drivers. She'd seen the sawed-off baseball bat under his seat, but he'd never attacked anyone—at least while she was around. She wrote it off to his Latino temper. More telling—and how she ignored this was still a mystery—was that he was always getting called on his cellphone and whispering to whomever was on the other end. Then he had to rush off and end their dates because, "I got some business I gotta go to take care of."

But she found it easy to go light on him. Rosa felt bad for him because she realized he was up against being born and raised on the rough streets of Bushwick, and the ghetto was stronger than any emotion Rosa could muster. The darkness of these streets couldn't be cracked by sunlight or love. But Rosa believed that she would get him out of this and they could start a new life.

Now the whole script was flipped. She was being pulled into his world. A world her parents had invested a lifetime of savings to keep her out of.

His left arm was hanging around her shoulders and he was getting heavier. She took a deep breath and hoisted him up. He gasped and said, "Rosa, Rosa, easy, please. It hurts but keep moving. Just don't stop."

"I got you. Don't worry."

She held him tight as she waited for the light to change.

An old woman in a worn cloth coat stood on the curb staring at them. The woman took a hesitant step away and said, "Child, that man he is bleeding. Bleeding bad."

Rosa wanted to scream and run. She said, "Yes, I know . . . I know. He had an accident at work. We're going to the doctor."

"You should call an ambulance."

"The doctor is on the next block. We're fine, thank you."

The woman walked away shaking her head. Rosa crossed the street as two Latino youths walked by leering at her. One kid looked her up and down, licked his lips, and then kissed at her. The other one laughed and said, "Yo, mami, you got some fine high-water booty. Drop that dope and come with me."

Rosa shot them a dirty look and hissed, "Punks. Get out of here, you little *maricons.*"

The kids kissed at her and walked away laughing as they bopped into a pizzeria. Rosa kept moving. She let out a long sigh and realized he was getting heavier and she didn't know if she could drag him the whole way. She wanted to stop for a moment and lean against a car. Get her breath and strength back.

"Rosa, come on. Keep going. Don't stop! I'm bleeding, dammit. It hurts. It's burning my gut. Oh, man, it hurts. Oh, it hurts so bad. Damn. I'ma get that punk-ass Chino. He dead. He a dead man!"

Rosa put her head down and pushed on. She turned to look behind and saw drops of blood in the dirty slush and snow on the avenue.

"Carlos, listen baby," she said, "you're bleeding bad. Real bad. That wound could kill you. You have to get a doctor to take care of it. We should go to Wycoff Hospital. It's just around the corner."

Carlos hissed, "Dammit, woman! Listen to me. Just get me to Mama's! No hospital. What do you think, they just going to stitch me up and not call the cops? Mama will take care of it. She always does. Come on, hold my weight and let's step."

Rosa and Carlos hobbled down the street as shoppers passed by, staring at the attractive girl holding onto a grimacing young man with a hand to his stomach, thick blood dripping through his fingers.

Rosa had been raised in Bay Ridge, the only child of an accountant father and a mother who worked as an administrator for the Parks Department. Her parents had saved for many years to leave Bushwick and buy a two-story brick on Colonial Road near the water at 91st Street. They always joked with Rosa that they were "cash poor and house rich."

Rosa loved running through the sprawling home but she'd been lonely in Bay Ridge. She was the only Puerto Rican child on her block, and the other kids—and most of the parents—shunned her. She was teased constantly. As she walked home from school, a clique of older girls on her block would chant, "Mira, mira, on the wall, is Rosa the biggest spic of all?"

She would pass them and not even blink. Kept her eyes straight and acted like she didn't hear a thing. Her mother told her that they were nothing more than a pack of barking dogs.

"Would you get mad at a dog in a yard behind a fence yapping at you? You ignore it and walk away. Treat them the same way."

Rosa's mantra as a child was, "Sticks and stones can break my bones but names can never harm me." But that only worked until she reached her room, where she would fall on her bed and scream into her pillow. She knew her mother didn't want to hear it. She was on her own as most children are. Adults forget to ease the pain of youth. Wiping her eyes, she would look up at her wall at her favorite poster of Lou Diamond Phillips posing as Richie Valens for his role in *La Bamba*. She would stare into his face for hours until she would hear him sing softly, "Oh, Rosa."

Rosa's parents dealt with her lack of friends and empty social life by enrolling her into scores of after-school activities. At one time or another, Rosa had studied karate, gymnastics, soccer, trumpet, French, modern dance, ballet, and chess. None of these stuck except for dance. That she loved. As she got older Rosa excelled at school. Her parents took out loans to pay for a private all-girls school in Downtown Brooklyn. Her teachers were pleasantly surprised that a Latina could be so smart and dedicated to her studies. Because of this, the principal saw to it that the white kids left her alone.

She blossomed as a teenager and was thought to be the prettiest girl in her school. The older girls who once taunted her on her block had moved on. Now the white kids in Bay Ridge wanted to hang out with her. She was becoming cool and her ethnicity was no longer an issue. She was one of the most popular girls at her school.

In her junior year she aced her SATs, and as senior she was given a full scholarship to NYU to study Political Science. Her career goal was to work at the UN. As a freshman in college Rosa pulled down a 4.0 index, but she did find some time for socializing. She dated a few boys at school— she lost her virginity to an Irish boy from Bay Ridge whose older sister had once taunted her. To Rosa it seemed that all the boys at NYU wanted was a hot Spanish chick who would put out for them. Rosa wanted more than that. She wanted to fall in love. Crazy love like when she was a kid and had that crush on Lou Diamond Phillips. She knew that someday somewhere she would find that. She had to. It was what she had always dreamed of.

Rosa grew tired of the dating scene in college and decided to just concentrate on her degree. And then it hit her. Like a thunderbolt she knew that the promise of love might have walked into her life, and his name was Carlos.

They met in Loeb cafeteria. Rosa was sitting by herself munching on a tuna sandwich when this handsome man sat down next to her and started a conversation. He told her his name was Carlos Hernandez and they bonded right away over their Brooklyn and Puerto Rican roots. Rosa liked that Carlos was a self-assured junior going for a degree in Business. After her last class that day he took her out to Lusardi's Restaurant—an upscale Italian joint on the Upper East Side. The owner treated him like an old friend and set them up with the best seat in the house. Carlos ordered the food and wine like a veteran.

After dinner they went down to the Roosevelt Island tram, and as the car inched over the East River, Carlos took her hand and gently kissed her. She felt her body jolt. They walked around Roosevelt Island and watched a group of men fish for striped bass. They stood on the promenade and watched the New York skyline as Carlos told her how he was going to knock the city dead. Rosa hung on every word and told him about how lonely she had been. He looked into her eyes and told her he knew all about loneliness, he had felt it his whole life.

The next week Carlos took her home to meet his parents

in Bushwick. While his mama and papa were sweet, they lived on a dark and dangerous block and were first-generation to New York. Mama stayed home and kept their railroad apartment and Papa was the super of the building. Papa wore t-shirts and khaki jeans and grunted and nodded. Mama was a short, chubby woman who always wore house-dresses. She had a pleasant face but had what Rosa's mother would say was "the look of a peasant."

They were poor and Carlos was their only child, not because of any birth-control choice but because of poverty. That made Carlos even more attractive to Rosa. He was the one. He was raising himself out of the ghetto and would take the strength he had to be a success in business. Rosa thought that no one could stop Carlos but Carlos. On that she was right.

She fell hard for him and he seemed to love her right back. He took her to every hot nightclub in the city and everyone seemed to know him and like him. He was always walking off meeting people and telling her he had to do a lit-tle business. Carlos told her he did computer-hacking for cash and some of the folks he worked for were a little seedy, so she would be better off not getting to know them.

Then today it all came down on her. After Rosa's morning International Law class, Carlos met her in the hallway and told her to come with her. Said he had a little deal he had to make and then they would go over to Mama's for lunch. They walked up Broadway to 14th Street and huddled to keep warm from the bitter winter chill. They took the L train to Bushwick and then walked down Knickerbocker Avenue. Carlos told her he had to pick up some serious money from an up-and-coming Latino rap star who Carlos had developed a website for. Carlos had Rosa wait outside Rico's Bodega as he walked across the street to talk with two young Latino men.

Rosa saw that Carlos was getting angry at the men and then—as if Rosa was watching this in a dream—Carlos pulled out a gun. A gun? A gun! Why would a computer programmer need a gun? One man ducked and rolled on the sidewalk and then she heard a shot and Carlos fell to the ground. Carlos landed under a car as Rosa ran across the street screaming. A gypsy cab screeched to a stop, just missing her. As she reached the sidewalk she saw Carlos weakly stand and let off a round at one of the men running away. The man fell to the ground as the other man shot back. Carlos grabbed Rosa and threw her down to the ground.

As she pushed herself up from the cement, it went quiet. Carlos stood and grabbed her, saying, "Get me to Mama's house."

"Carlos, Carlos, what happened?"

Three schoolkids stood on the corner staring at her and Carlos as they staggered up the block.

"I'm hit. Damn, he shot me," Carlos moaned.

"What was that?" Rosa was crying. "Why do you have a gun? Why were you shooting at that man?"

"Because he was going to shoot me, Rosa. This here is Bushwick, not Bay Ridge."

"Why would he shoot you over a website?"

Carlos laughed as a clot of blood spilled out of his mouth, "Website. Oh, baby, I don't do websites. I deal. You know, drugs. Perico and chiva, like that. It pays for college."

"You deal coke and heroin?"

"I do. And now ain't the time to judge me. Do that later. I got to get to Mama's. Get me there. Help me."

"Carlos, you're shot! We got to get you to an emergency room."

"Shut up and take me to Mama's."

How could she not have seen it coming? Everyone was giving him cash. He was always getting calls on his cellphone and having to grab cabs to take care of business. How could she be so stupid? Who needs a website at 2:30 in the morning?

As Rosa turned onto Harmon Street—Mama's house was now 200 feet away—she realized she had believed Carlos because she wanted to. She wanted to believe he wanted out of the ghetto even though he kept going back to it.

"Hold on, Rosa. We're almost there."

Rosa reached the front stoop and rang Mama's bell. Carlos's eyes were closed and his breathing was shallow. Mama opened the door and looked at her son.

"*Díos mío! Mi hijo, mi bebe!*"

"Mama, he got shot."

"Inside. *Avanza!*"

Mama grabbed Carlos's other arm and the women led him down the hallway.

"See, it was meant to be that we live on the ground floor," Mama said as she kicked the door open and then yelled, "Papa! Carlos has a *balazo*. Put all the towels down on the couch. Cover it. Your *hijo* is hurt."

Papa walked up the narrow hallway and ignored Mama and Rosa. He gave his son a sour look and grabbed a stack of towels from a hall cabinet and piled them on the couch in the front room. Mama and Rosa gently let Carlos down, and he slumped on the couch.

"*Mal hijo!*" Papa hissed as he looked at his son.

"Go! Get out!" Mama yelled at him.

Papa scowled at her and turned and walked quickly down the hallway. He slammed the door as he left.

"Papa's *flojo* . . . You know, a weak man. Carlos takes after his mama. Strong. *Fuerte*. Like steel."

"What do we do now?" Rosa asked.

Carlos moved and pulled out his gun from his pants and groaned, "Mama, Mama, get rid of this."

Mama nudged Rosa and said, "Grab the *pistola* and bring it to the kitchen."

Mama waddled down the hallway and Rosa followed her, holding the gun like it was a wild animal. Mama held out a plastic bag and Rosa dropped it in.

"Rosa, we have to stop the bleeding. Go and hold the towels to his wound till I get out there."

"Mama, we need to get him to a hospital."

"Hospital? That is where people go to die. My *bebe* no die. Not today. I know his death day. I saw it in a dream when he was two. He stays here and we take care of him. Stop the *sangre*. His blood has to clot. He'll be fine. Be a good *novia* and help him."

Rosa watched Mama place the gun in a drawer and then reach into one of the pockets of her red house dress and pull out two small strips of tinfoil.

"Rosa, go. Carlos has a *herida de bala*. Stop the bleeding. *Avanza.*"

Rosa turned and ran down the hallway. In the living room she saw that Carlos was leaning back on the couch holding his stomach. She moved his hand and put a towel on the wound and pressed.

Carlos grimaced and turned his head. Rosa held the towel and then pulled it off when it became full of blood. She put it on the floor and picked up a clean one. She jumped when Mama silently touched her shoulder.

"Let me look."

For a little old woman, Mama was strong. She gently moved Carlos forward and looked at his back.

"This might not be so bad. The *bala* went right through him. First we take away his pain. Here, Carlos, sniff." Mama patted Carlos on the face as she held a line of white powder on her thumb.

"What's that?" Rosa asked as Carlos took a long snort.

"Chiva . . . for the pain. Here, *bebe*, take another."

"Heroin? You're giving him heroin?"

"Rosa, you know what you read in your school books. Chiva is the best thing for pain and this *chico* is going to have pain when I clean this wound."

Carlos leaned back on the couch and looked like he was sleeping. Mama took out some more white powder, lifted the towel, and poured it on Carlos's stomach, inside the small hole where the bullet had entered.

"Now this, Rosa, is perico, which will freeze the nerves."

Rosa watched with her mouth open.

"Now hold him by the shoulder."

Rosa moved behind the couch and held onto Carlos.

"Tighter. Strong. He's going to jump like a fish on a line."

Rosa grabbed Carlos's shoulder as Mama poured peroxide into the wound. Carlos's body jolted and he screamed. He collapsed back on the couch.

"Just sit with him," Mama said as she went into the kitchen. She came back in a moment stirring a glass of cloudy water.

"Now we use this dropper and put penicillin down his throat for infection. Hold his head back and open his mouth."

Rosa tilted his head back, and Mama squirted the mixture from the dropper into his mouth.

"Now sit him up and hold the towel. The blood is slowing down. He'll be fine and so will you."

Rosa looked down at the wound and saw that the bleeding had slowed to a trickle. She sat down on the couch and gently held the towel as Mama went into the kitchen.

Rosa sat up on the couch, afraid. The room was dark. Had she slept? She blinked and saw Carlos leaning against her, breathing slowly. She heard a tapping on glass and saw the silhouette of a man trying to look into the window. The shadow moved, and then silence. She just sat there not moving—hardly breathing—when someone banged on the front door. In the hallway she could see Mama opening the door and say, "*Sí?*"

Then Mama flew back against the wall as a young Latino man stormed into the apartment, yelling, "Where's that *cobarde* Carlos?"

The man looked down the hallway and came at her. She saw he had a gun, and Rosa closed her eyes. This is what Carlos has given me. A cheap, stupid death in a ghetto apartment. Rosa jumped as a shot rang out. She heard a moan, and then another shot. She opened her eyes and saw Mama standing over the body of the man. Mama held a black revolver in her hand.

"There, that's for you! You come into my house to kill *mi bebe*. You *pendejo*. Cheap-ass *bandido* . . ." Mama kicked the man, then smiled at Rosa. "How's Carlos?"

"Is he dead?"

"Him, yeah. Come help me drag him into the *bañera*."

"Why are you taking him to the bathtub?"

"Why you think? Think I want to clean him up? We got to get rid of this body. Come on."

Mama grabbed the man's feet and Rosa stood up. She stared at Mama. Mama dropped the feet and walked over and slapped Rosa in the face.

Mama yelled, "You do as I say! You hear me? You brought this here, and you will help me. Now!"

Rosa bent down robotically and took the man by his boots as Mama grabbed the arms. They dragged him down the hall, leaving a trail of blood on the linoleum. Rosa looked down into the dead face and saw he'd been no more than a boy—maybe eighteen. Why was he dead? What was she doing here?

"In here." Mama motioned to the bathroom door. Rosa kicked it open, and with great effort she and Mama lifted the man into the tub and dropped him.

Mama smacked her hands and said, "Got to get rid of this body."

Rosa wanted to scream and run, but she just said, "No."

"Go and get Papa. He's down in the bodega playing dominos. Tell him we need to turn up the furnace all the way. We have something to burn."

Rosa didn't move and just stared at Mama.

"Rosa, go. Now! *Avanza!* And come back. Don't think of going to the cops, because you touched the gun. Your fingerprints are all over that gun. You're one of us now. I hope *mi hijo* picked a good one."

Mama reached into a hall closet and smiled when she turned. "What, you want to watch?" She had a small axe in her hand. She motioned with the hatchet for Rosa to get going. Rosa dully nodded, put on her coat, and opened the door. She moved out of the apartment and floated down the hallway. She opened the lobby door and stepped out into the cold night air and stood on the stoop staring out at the Bushwick street. A gypsy cab cruised by and the driver stared at Rosa. She turned away and saw a shadow move in the alley across the street.

Rosa let out a long sigh and walked down the block, feeling like her body and soul were dying. She would never get out of this neighborhood.

LADIES' MAN

BY CHRIS NILES

Brighton Beach

She was lush like an old-time movie star in black patent-leather shoes, fishnet stockings, and a fur coat. Her hair had been blonded, rolled, sprayed, and teased so that it stiffly circled her face like a halo on a medieval Madonna. She had Angelina Jolie lips and her heavy-lidded eyes were shaded aqua and rimmed with kohl. Crimson-dipped nails grasped fake Louis Vuitton. She didn't look anything like Ana, but that didn't stop me staring.

The rhythm of the train tempted her to doze. Her head dipped. She woke, glanced around, trying not to look anxious, yet tightening her grip on her bag. Falling asleep on the subway. Not a good idea. It was late. The car was filled with a typical assortment of booze- and drug-fueled crazies, myself included. I'd spent the previous few hours with a couple a friends of the family—Eric Ambler and Comrade Stolichnaya.

Brighton Beach, end of the line. She got out. I did too. I stumbled down the steep steps, my eyes blurry from the booze, but my ears sharply focused on the *clip-clip* of her stilettos

She walked west on Brighton Beach Avenue, long strides. It was cold, few people around. I stuffed my hands in my pockets, fingers searching for the Marlboro I knew was lurking somewhere. My head was fuzzy, the cold seemed to be making me drunker. I lit the cigarette and kept pace.

I liked Brighton Beach, it reminded me of my old life. I liked the stores selling canned fish, the babushkas hawking homemade trinkets on the sidewalk, the signs in Russian, the shabby exuberance. After years of exile, the extravagance of Manhattan made me feel ill. Out near the sea, where the choices seemed simpler, I could think again.

She turned left onto a side street lined with nondescript brick apartment buildings. *Clip-clip*. My cigarette was ashes and the promise of cancer by the time we reached the board-walk. I tossed the butt, dodged dogshit. It was spring, but a vindictive wind taunted my exposed skin. I turned up my collar and wondered what shape she was under that big fur coat, what her voice sounded like, what she whispered when having sex.

We passed the handball courts. For an instant my attention was diverted by an old guy in a t-shirt sprinting along the boardwalk. In as long as it took me to think, *Don't these people ever feel the cold?* the woman had gone. I spun around, looking, listening. She was nowhere.

Shrugging, I headed to Ruby's for a drink before my shift began.

People don't tell you this about New York: The reason some never leave is because you can burn up on re-entry. It was almost that way with me. I had tried to make my fortune, or at least my name, as a foreign correspondent, and had failed. Eastern Europe worked for a while and then it didn't, so I headed to Southeast Asia for some professional relaxation. I could have stayed, I suppose, lolling on a beach in Thailand, but there were too many reminders there of the kind of person that I would become—a fat, feckless ex-pat who couldn't have survived a day in any city of consequence. Eventually there was no choice but to make things hard for myself again. So I came back to New York.

I hit the tail end of the 1990s and found it was a very, very different city from the one I had left almost a decade ago. It was as if real journalism had died and nobody had given it a decent funeral. CEOs were now celebrities and all celebrities were gods. The scary thing was, nobody seemed to have noticed. In some sort of crazy bait and switch, all the vicious, crazy, thrilling, real live New Yorkers had been replaced by a bunch of plastic people. The women were a dis-combobulating combination of perky and dull. The men talked about business school as the high point of their exis-tence. All of them believed that every so-called obstacle in their trivial lives could be overcome if only they put in enough hours at the office and hired a personal trainer.

I did not fit. I missed real people. People who know that life's often unfair. That sometimes, through no fault of your own, things just don't work out. So I shunned Manhattan and my old life. I took a job copy-editing, overnights. The pay was crap and the hours were worse. I didn't care.

"Why don't you just fucking go back, man?" Paul Schneider, my companion in hell, asked as he assigned me yet another story about Donald Trump's sex life. "So you hate it here, so leave."

"Can't."

"Yes, you can. You buy a ticket. You get on a plane. Have a crappy meal, drink too much wine, and wake up in Budapest or Bucharest or wherever the fuck you'd rather be. People do it all the time. I'd lend you the money if I had any." Paul was expecting a baby, or at least his wife was, and he was working double shifts so they could afford to move out of their 400-square-foot apartment.

"I'd steal it if you had any. But I can't go back."

The newsroom was quiet. We were both smoking. We'd stuffed a screwdriver in the smoke detectors and bribed Bart, the security guy. Smoking was the only thing that made this bullshit job even close to bearable.

"Why?"

I sighed, pretending to be annoyed at his persistence. "After the Berlin Wall fell, organized crime became the new growth industry in Eastern Europe. I made some trouble. Wrote some stories that made a few gangsters decide I deserved a whole new face."

"So what? Aren't journalists supposed to be fearless?"

"Very funny."

"And what else?"

"Nothing else." I reached for the cigarettes, Paul withdrew them.

"What else?" He held the packet up between two fingers just out of my reach, a practiced move. My lousy pay didn't even come close to covering all my vices. Paul was used to me bumming off him.

"Fuck you."

"Ah, a woman." Paul handed the packet to me after taking one for himself, desperate for a story, anything that would distract him from the numbing hours that stretched before us. "Do tell."

"Ana," I sighed. "Her name was Ana."

"And she broke your heart."

"If you want to put it like that." I struck a match, it snapped in two. I struck another one and the same thing happened. My hands were shaking. Ana could do that to me still, after all these years. Paul took the box from me and deftly lit the match. I started talking to smother my embarrassment.

"She decided one day that she didn't want to see me anymore. I used to pick her up after work—she worked nights—and so I'd sit in this bar in Budapest and wait for her to finish and then walk her home." I shook my head. "And one night she'd reassigned the job. That was it. No explanation, no nothing. I had no idea what I'd done wrong. Still don't. She wouldn't speak to me."

"So no closure."

"No."

"Bummer," Paul said.

"Yeah." Maybe all those yuppies who paid 150 bucks an hour for a shrink were onto something. I hadn't talked to anybody about Ana, I guess I'd been enjoying my own private hell a little too much. But now I felt as if a small burden had lifted. "All the time I was in Hungary it was as if I had an evil cloud hanging over me. Because before Ana, there was Mike McIlvaney."

"He broke up with you too?" Paul stubbed his cigarette out on his shoe and flicked the butt into the bag we used to remove evidence of our illegal habits from the office.

"In a manner of speaking."

They called it the Highway of Death for a very good reason. A two-lane stretch of asphalt between Vienna and Budapest where bunches of flowers, crosses, and stuffed animals bore witness to its incapacity to deal with the enormous daily volume of traffic.

The problem was this: Food and wine were cheap in Budapest and the Viennese were fond of getting into their late-model German automobiles and making a bargain-shopping day of it. Racing the other way for a taste of the West were their less fortunate Eastern European cousins, shaking behind the wheels of their unreliable, two-stroke Trabbants. Most American lawnmowers have more power than the Trabbant, and there were no passing lanes on the Highway of Death. The Austrian drivers, spoiled by superior technology and frustrated at having to sit behind an aerodynamically challenged global-warming machine, took frequent, stupid risks. Trabbie drivers, too, pushed their impotent cars past what they were capable of.

Mike had a Fiat. He, like me, was freelancing, building a name for himself. He had dark hair, a rangy build, and although his parents were American, he'd been raised in Brisbane and had an Australian accent. We'd become friends.

It was a quiet week when we made our decision. The Hungarians had just elected a democratic government and the transition had been fairly smooth. There were rumblings of trouble between Romanians and ethnic Hungarians in Transylvania, and between ethnic Albanians and Serbs in Pristina, but not enough for us to warrant a trip to either place just yet.

"Man cannot live by beer alone, mate," Mike said one night, slightly drunk in a Pest bar. Food in Budapest was good but mostly limited to what the Hungarians could grow—peppers, cherries, tomatoes, meat, bread. "I feel like avocados. Can't remember the last time I had an avocado. Let's go to Vienna."

The next day we set off.

Trouble met us on the way home. Dark had fallen and we'd just crossed the Austrian border when the Fiat choked a couple a times and died. Mike pulled over, popped the hood, took off his seatbelt, and reached into the glove compartment for a flashlight to check it out.

There's not a day that I don't think about what happened next. It was timing that Satan would have been proud of. The nano-second after Mike unbuckled, a Mercedes hit us from behind. It was a heavy car, going fast. I later found out the driver was drunk. The Fiat shunted forward and the impact popped Mike through the windshield, just like that. If he'd had his seat belt on, like me, he'd still be alive.

"Christ," Paul said, sucking deep on a new cigarette when I'd finished.

"Yeah," I said. "Watching someone die, it messes with your head. Between Mike and Ana, I guess I went to pieces."

He studied me, eyes narrowed through smoke. "I guess you did."

This woman had dark hair cut in a bob, dyed ruby red, and glowing olive skin. She was wearing tan pants tucked into knee-length boots and reading a library book in Cyrillic. Someone who'd got on the wrong train asked her for directions and she replied, smiling, in a softly accented voice. I sat across from her from Atlantic Avenue. I caught her eye at Avenue J and smiled. She looked away. I'd been considered good-looking once, but personal grooming wasn't high on my agenda anymore. It was months since I'd had a haircut and I'd become a haphazard shaver.

She got off at Brighton Beach, walked north, and turned left on Coney Island Avenue, clutching her suede coat closely to her even though the evening was mild. She went into a restaurant, ordered two chicken kebabs and a can of Sprite. Food seemed like a good idea for me too, so I had some, although I didn't notice what I ate. She sat silently at her table and didn't look my way, not once. Then she went to the bathroom, where I guess she must've made a phone call or something, because a few minutes later, a guy joined her. She said something to him and he glanced my way and frowned. I could see his pecs flexing under his thin white shirt.

I avoid trouble these days. I called for the check.

"So why don't you start freelancing some articles or something?" Paul asked over our customary breakfast beer at the end of our shift. "You know, get back in the saddle."

"There's nothing to write about."

"That's defeatist crap."

"All right, I can't be bothered." That wasn't quite true. Once, just after I got back and was desperate for cash to make the deposit on my new rental apartment, I had dashed off a travel article about the grand old cafés of Budapest. It didn't require any research, it bored me to write it, but the airline magazine paid promptly and the money was sweet.

Money. For a minute the thought pleased me.

"It'd be better than this crappy shift," Paul said.

"Nah," I said. "It's not my thing," I looked at our glasses, both of which were empty. "Besides, I like the company on this crappy shift. Fancy another?"

"Gotta go, Amanda's having an ultrasound this morning. For some reason she wants me there." Paul stood up, throwing some money on the bar. "You should get some sleep. You look like death."

"Sure." I signaled the bartender for another beer.

The gangster placed his passport, open at the correct page, in front of the immigration officer at John F. Kennedy Airport. The name on the passport wasn't the one his parents had given him, but he thought the photo nicely captured his likeness. "Good afternoon," he said in only slightly accented English.

The officer nodded as he checked the paperwork. "How long will you be staying in New York, sir?"

"Just one week."

"Is this your first visit to America?"

"Yes."

"Do you have friends or relatives here?"

"Some business acquaintances."

"So this is a business trip?"

The gangster smiled. "I hope also to have a little enjoyment in your great city."

He looked like any other guy, he thought, as he checked his reflection in the automatic doors. Any American guy. He wore Levi's, Adidas running shoes, and a t-shirt that said *"Just Do It."* His thick black hair and goatee beard were neatly trimmed. A tiny gold earring in his left ear was a new addition and the lobe was still slightly swollen. He put his hand to touch it, and remembering the piercer's advice, stopped. He didn't want an infection.

There was a line for taxis. He waited patiently, feeling exhilarated despite jetlag. He was in New York! For him, the greatest city in the world.

It wasn't until the yellow cab was speeding toward Manhattan that he unfolded the magazine article that was the reason for his visit. A story about Budapest café society, and, at the bottom, a biographical line that said the author lived in New York City. The gangster believed strongly in fate. Why else would he have chanced upon the year-old copy of an airline magazine while on holiday in the Costa del

Sol? He'd gone into an English pub to escape the heat of mid-day, and seeing a picture of his hometown, had idly turned the pages while waiting for his Guinness to be pulled.

And it was there that he had found him: the shit-fuck guy.

"Got you," the gangster had whispered softly as the bar-man slapped the beer down on the bar and demanded an extortionate amount. For once, the gangster, who was careful with money, having been raised in a household where there wasn't much, was happy to pay. *"Got you,"* he said again, and raised the drink in a toast to the goddess of fortune.

He checked into an anonymous hotel near Times Square and went out in search of a payphone. Times Square was a daz-zling disappointment; he'd expected a smorgasbord of vice, not toy stores and "family" restaurants. He located a phone and called his contact, making a note to ask him, once busi-ness had been conducted, what a *family restaurant* was and how it differed from a regular one.

"Glock 9mm, as ordered," his contact said, sliding the bag across the park bench. "Plus ammo. Price as agreed. U.S. dol-lars, no fucking kopecs or whatever it is you people use."

"We use dollars, same as you," the gangster murmured, handing him the money. He decided this guy probably wasn't the one to ask about restaurants. He didn't seem that friendly.

"And here's the address. Tracked him through the DMV. Everything was like you said. It was a good guess."

The gangster shrugged. "It's what I would have done," he said. "If I was little bit lazy." He took the piece of paper and looked at the address. The words meant nothing to him.

"It's Brighton Beach," his contact said. "Plenty of Russians out there. You'll feel right at home."

"I'm Hungarian," the gangster replied.

A woman passed on rollerblades wearing tight little white shorts. The gangster could see dimples of cellulite in her butt as she pushed herself forward. Her mouth was set in a grim line.

"She looks like the devil is after her," he remarked sadly.

"Nobody in this town's having any fucking fun," his contact said.

He caught a taxi to the apartment, which was on the ground floor of a tired street so close to the sea that he could smell salty air. He let himself in. He didn't plan to kill the shit-fuck guy right away, he wanted to have a little fun first. He was thinking about trashing the place, sending a message, like they did in the movies. Not usually his style, but he felt like being a little expressive for once. This was a special case, after all.

The apartment was a single room. There was no furniture to speak of, just a folded-out futon with a gray sheet screwed up on top of it. A small, old-fashioned television sat unsteadily on a wooden crate. A single poster was tacked to the wall. The gangster recognized it as the original election poster for the Hungarian Democratic Forum. It featured the back of a large, thick-necked Russian military officer. The copy read, in Russian, *"Comrades, it's over!"* The gangster smiled as he remembered simpler days. How happy they had been to get rid of the fucking Russians.

He stepped on tiptoe through the crap on the floor—fast food cartons, empty beer bottles, dirty laundry, newspapers, odd shoes, even a tube of toothpaste. Stacks of crusty dishes filled the sink. The refrigerator door stood ajar and rusty brown liquid leaked onto the linoleum. The smell in the room was stale and thick—a hopeless, exhausted musk of despair. The gangster shuddered in disgust and wiped his hands on his neatly-pressed jeans. It was a waste of time to trash the place, the shit-fuck guy wouldn't even notice.

"You are foreign correspondent?" Lana asked skeptically.

I tried to look mysteriously modest. "Yeah, just got back into town a few days ago, from Bosnia."

"I don't trust journalists."

"Well, you shouldn't trust me, that's for sure." I grinned wolfishly. Her eyes narrowed. Perhaps the lovable-roué routine had worked better when I had a decent haircut and wore a suit. I went to straighten my tie and remembered I wasn't wearing one. "Another drink?" We were sitting in a restaurant a block or two from the beach. The food was Uzbeki, which is to Russians what Mexican is to Americans—cheerfully ethnic, but not too threatening. Arresting pictures of downtown Baku were showing on the television set. The pictures focused on a large building of Soviet design and a wide empty street. The visual tedium was relieved every few minutes by a passing Lada.

"Ever been to Baku?" I put my hand on her knee. It was plump and warm.

"No."

She glanced at me and looked away, staring, so it seemed, at the stuffed animal heads mounted on the wood-paneled walls.

"How long have you lived in the States?"

"Thirteen years."

"Like it?"

"It's okay."

"Got family?"

"Why are you asking me all these questions?"

"Just trying to get to know you."

"What're you doing out here if you're big-time foreign correspondent? Why aren't you at Stork Club or something?"

"I'm not sure the Stork Club is still in business. Anyway, I prefer Brighton Beach. It's got character." I swallowed some vodka, trying to pinpoint the place where the evening had gone south. She had seemed friendly enough when I'd picked her up in a bar an hour or so ago.

"Character," she snorted.

"Is that so wrong?"

"You're liar," she said. "You think I live in the fucking Soviet Union for fifteen years and not learn how to tell?"

"Hey, that's a bit steep," I protested, holding up my hands.

"I met too many men like you." She grabbed her handbag and stood up, spilling the last of her wine. "Fucking Americans. They think every Russian girl is slut. Tell her big story to sleep with her, then gone."

I followed her out of the restaurant.

"Hey," I said, plucking at her sleeve. "I like you. I'm not spinning you a line, honest. I really am a journalist. Don't you want to come back and talk about this?"

She shook my hand off.

"Come on. Don't be like that. Let's grab a coffee and start over. We won't—"

She cut me off, saying something in Russian.

I shook my head. "I don't understand what you're saying."

"She's telling you to get lost. Even you don't need any Russian to understand that."

I recognized the voice. I turned. Istvan Laszlo was standing about ten feet away. Lana glanced at him and then took off. I didn't blame her.

"Mr. McIlvaney."

"Mike McIlvaney is dead," I said evenly.

The gangster smiled. "I'm sure you've told people that, but the truth is, Richard Churcher is dead, Mr. McIlvaney. And you took his name because you thought if you did that, I would never find you."

"I didn't know you were looking."

"Maybe not me specifically, but you knew someone would, sometime." He passed me the article I had written to make my apartment down payment. "A small miracle. Richard Churcher wrote a magazine article about Budapest years after he died in a freak car smash. It's enough to make you believe in God."

I said nothing.

"So I read the story and I have an idea. I have been look-ing for Mike McIlvaney for many years and I can't find him. He's vanished off the earth. But Richard Churcher has risen from the grave. Then I call a guy in America and he explains all about the Social Security number. I found out that Churcher was an American citizen. He was born here. Not too difficult to put it all in place. You get a Social Security number with his name and you live as him. You looked a lit-tle alike. And you grow your hair and a beard and think maybe nobody will notice. Maybe nobody would have . . ." He moved closer and lowered his voice. "Except for this." He folded the article up and slipped it into the back pocket of his jeans. "Too bad for you I like to travel."

"It's not a crime to change your name. What do you want?" My voice shook. I could see the gun tucked into the waistband of his jeans, under a blue jacket, and my life that I'd previously thought of as sub-standard suddenly seemed shining and rare, a precious, precious thing.

"I want to walk," the gangster said. "Let's go to the beach."

Rain threatened and the beach was empty. Seagulls dove and screeched, fighting over a ragged piece of food. The gangster looked out to sea.

"The Duna flooded this year. They found Ana's body buried in a field."

Ana. My chest tightened.

"She had been beaten to death. Cops were able to tell that, even after all this time."

"I'm sorry to hear that."

"I'm sure you are."

"What's this got to do with me?"

"The day she went missing, I felt it in my gut that she was dead." The gangster put his fist to his stomach. "And that you had killed her. You'd beaten her before and threatened her. That's why she no longer wanted you as a client. She was frightened of you."

"Isn't this a little far-fetched?"

"You were hanging around at nights waiting for her to finish work, so I had Peter walk her home. But the night she disappeared Peter got held up and he didn't meet her. And the next day she doesn't turn up for work. I think immediately of you and your threats. I came to your apartment and you had also gone, rather suddenly, the landlord said."

"I got called away on a job. This is stupid, Istvan. I can understand that you're upset at losing one of your working girls, but I didn't kill her. I loved her. I love her still. Look at me, my life's a wreck because of her."

"You were obsessed with her," the gangster said. "Not quite love, something else. Maybe you didn't mean to kill her, but you did it. And your life's wrecked because you can't live with yourself." He pulled the gun casually out of his jeans.

"Please," I said. "Even if what you say is true, this isn't going to bring her back."

"No. But what I'm doing is for the living, not the dead." He raised the Glock and pointed it at my forehead. "You see, I loved her too. I guess you didn't know that."

He gently squeezed the trigger.

I could have run, I suppose. Or tried to fight him. Could have at least made an attempt to do something. But a strange thing happened: When that bullet began its deadly journey, I had a flash of clarity, the first of my whole life. Time slowed, and then slowed some more, and I could see the bullet speeding toward me, right toward my brain. Life is love. That's it, there's no other point, I thought, as I watched the bullet smash into my head. Saw myself fall onto the wet, hard sand. Heard myself think, *Perhaps I'll see her now, and perhaps she'll forgive me.*

A gust of wind carried the sound of the gunshot out into the Atlantic. The seagulls scattered, wings beating. The gangster walked away. He didn't look back. He didn't see the body being claimed by the rising tide.

ABOUT THE CONTRIBUTORS:

Stephen Spevock

PEARL ABRAHAM is the author of the novels *The Romance Reader* and *Giving Up America*. Recent essays have appeared in the *Michigan Quarterly*, the *Forward*, and *Dog Culture: Writers on the Character of Canines*. Abraham teaches in the MFA Writing Program at Sarah Lawrence College. *The Seventh Beggar*, her third novel, will be published in September 2004.

Jimmy Cohrssen

NICOLE BLACKMAN (www.nicoleblackman.com) lives in an undisclosed Brooklyn neighborhood where she prefers eavesdropping on unsuspecting people. She is the creator of the innovative "The Courtesan Tales" performance, and author of the poetry collection *Blood Sugar* (Akashic, 2002). She is currently wanted for questioning in the disappearance of three men in Brooklyn.

Dieter Auner

KEN BRUEN, author of *The Guards* and *The Killing of the Tinkers*, is published around the world. He has been an English teacher in Africa, Japan, Southeast Asia, and South America. He lives in Galway, Ireland.

John Raubenberger

MAGGIE ESTEP has published four books, including *HEX*, the first in a series of "horse noir" crime novels. She has written for the *Village Voice, New York Press,* and Nerve.com, and gives readings of her work throughout the U.S. and Europe on a regular basis. She lives in Brooklyn and likes to hang out at racetracks cheering on longshots. For more information, visit www.maggieestep.com.

NELSON GEORGE is a noted author and filmmaker who has resided in Brooklyn all his forty-six years. His most recent nonfiction work is *Post-Soul Nation* (Viking), and he is the executive producer of two recent TV projects: *The "N" Word* and *Everyday People*, a fictional film made for HBO. For more information visit Nelsongeorge.com.

Wayne Geist

LUCIANO GUERRIERO is the author of one novel, a noir thriller entitled *The Spin,* and has been a resident of Brooklyn or Manhattan for twenty-three years. While writing plays, screenplays, short stories and poetry during that time, he has also acted in or directed sixty-five plays and acted in twenty Hollywood and independent films.

Peter Foley

PETE HAMILL is for many the living embodiment of New York City. In his writing for the *New York Times,* the *New York Daily News,* the *New York Post,* the *New Yorker,* and *Newsday,* he has brought the city to life for millions of readers. He is the author of many bestselling books, including novels *Forever* and *Snow in August,* as well the memoir *A Drinking Life.* He lives in New York City.

Carlton Davis

KENJI JASPER was born and raised in the nation's capital and currently lives in Brooklyn. He is a regular contributor to National Public Radio's *Morning Edition* and has written articles for *Savoy, Essence, VIBE,* the *Village Voice,* the *Charlotte Observer,* and Africana.com. He is the author of three novels, *Dark, Dakota Grand,* and the forthcoming *Seeking Salamanca Mitchell.*

Marcia Wilson

NORMAN KELLEY is the author of the "noir soul" Nina Halligan mystery series, which includes *Black Heat, The Big Mango,* and *A Phat Death.* He is also the author of *Head Negro in Charge Syndrome,* forthcoming from Nation Books, and he edited and contributed to *R&B (Rhythm and Business): The Political Economy of Black Music* (Akashic, 2002). He currently resides in Brooklyn.

Rose Knightly

ROBERT KNIGHTLY is a trial lawyer in the Criminal Defense Division of the Legal Aid Society. In another life, he was a lieutenant in the New York City Police Department. This is his first published fiction, which is a piece of a first novel, *Bodies in Winter.* He was born and raised in Greenpoint, Brooklyn, the locale of the story.

Joanne Manfredo

LOU MANFREDO was born and raised in Brooklyn. He is a former New York City public school teacher and legal investigator. The father of one daughter, Nicole, he currently lives in New Jersey with his wife, Joanne, and their long-haired dachshund. Mr. Manfredo recently completed his first novel.

Victoria Hägglom

ADAM MANSBACH, a resident of Fort Greene, Brooklyn, currently on sabbatical in Berkeley, California, is the author of two novels, *Shackling Water* and the forthcoming *Angry Black White Boy*, and the poetry collection *genius b-boy cynics getting weeded in the garden of delights*. The former editor of the hip hop journal *Elementary*, he serves as an Artistic Consultant to Columbia University's Center for Jazz Studies and is a teacher for Youth Speaks.

Mario Belluomo

TIM MCLOUGHLIN was born and raised in Brooklyn, where he still resides. His debut novel, *Heart of the Old Country* (Akashic, 2001), was a selection of the Barnes & Noble Discover Great New Writers Program and has been optioned for a film. It was also published last year in Great Britain and in Italy, where it won the 2003 Premio Penne award. He is completing his second novel.

Ridley Sperling

ELLEN MILLER is the author of the critically acclaimed bestseller *Like Being Killed*. Her fiction and essays have appeared in many literary magazines and anthologies, most recently *Lost Tribe: Jewish Fiction from the Edge*. She has taught creative writing at New York University, the New School, and the women's unit of a federal prison. She lives in New York City and is at work on her second novel.

Angela Tigarello

THOMAS MORRISSEY is an Army brat who grew up in exotic locations like Okinawa, Heidelberg, and Staten Island. He began writing when, as a child, he found great pleasure playing with his mother's Sears portable typewriter. His first novel, *Faustus Resurrectus*, is on the way.

ARTHUR NERSESIAN is the author of six novels, including *Suicide Casanova, Chinese Takeout, Unlubricated,* and the cult classic bestseller *The Fuck-Up.* The former managing editor of the *Portable Lower East Side,* he currently lives in New York City.

CHRIS NILES was born in New Zealand. In the last fifteen years she has lived in Australia, England, and Hungary. She now lives in Brooklyn and does not intend to move for a very long time. She is also the author of *Hell's Kitchen* (Akashic, 2001), as well as a series of crime mysteries featuring radio reporter Sam Ridley: *Spike It, Run Time,* and *Crossing Live.*

SIDNEY OFFIT is a novelist, author of books for young readers, teacher, member of the board of the PEN American Center, president of the Authors Guild Foundation, and curator of the George Polk Journalism Awards that originate from Long Island University's Brooklyn center. During the mid-fifties he covered the Brooklyn Dodgers, New York Giants, and that other team from New York for *Baseball Magazine.* His most recent book is *Memoir of the Bookie's Son.*

NEAL POLLACK is the author of three books: the cult classic *The Neal Pollack Anthology of American Literature, Beneath the Axis of Evil,* and the rock 'n' roll novel *Never Mind the Pollacks.* A regular contributor to *Vanity Fair, GQ,* and many other magazines, Pollack lives in Austin, Texas.

C.J. SULLIVAN lived in Brooklyn on the Ridgewood/ Bushwick border for seven years and loved the neighborhood. He has worked as a Court Clerk in Brooklyn Supreme since 1994. He has also been a freelance writer for the last ten years. Sullivan has a regular column in the *New York Press* called "The Bronx Stroll." He now lives in Ridgewood, New Jersey with his wife Lisa and his twin daughters, Olivia and Luisa.

Also from AKASHIC BOOKS

HEART OF THE OLD COUNTRY by Tim McLoughlin
A Barnes & Noble Discover Great New Writers selection
217 pages, a trade paperback original, $14.95, ISBN: 1-888451-15-7
"This novel reads like an inspired cross between Richard Price's *Bloodbrothers* and Ross McDonald's *The Chill*."
—*Entertainment Weekly*

"Tim McLoughlin is a master storyteller in the tradition of such great New York City writers as Hubert Selby Jr. and Richard Price. I can't wait for his second book!"
—Kaylie Jones, author of *Speak Now*

HELL'S KITCHEN by Chris Niles
279 pages, a trade paperback original, $15.95, ISBN: 1-888451-21-1
"If the Olympics come to New York, apartment-hunting should be one of the events . . . Nile's fast-paced *Hell's Kitchen* plays with the city's famed high rents and low vacancy rate to put a new spin on the serial-killer novel. Taking aim at contemporary romance, the media, the idle rich, and would-be writers, Niles has written a thriller that's hilarious social satire."
—*Detroit Free Press*

MANHATTAN LOVERBOY by Arthur Nersesian
From the author of the bestselling cult-classic THE FUCK-UP
203 pages, a trade paperback original, $13.95, ISBN: 1-888451-09-2
"*Manhattan Loverboy* is paranoid fantasy and fantastic comedy in the service of social realism, using the methods of L. Frank Baum's *Wizard of Oz* or Kafka's *The Trial* to update the picaresque urban chronicles of Augie March, with a far darker edge . . ."
—*Downtown Magazine*